Circle of Friends

Matthew F. Winn

Other Books by Matthew F. Winn

The Sandman
Bring Me a Dream
Every Picture Tells a Story
Chasing Shadows in the Dark
Stealing Rembrandt
King of Hearts
The Legacy
Shadowman

Coming Soon:

Bokeh
Driven

Available from Artist's Point Press
www.splashofsunset.com

Cover Model: The Lovely Miss Rita Grissom
Cover photography by the author
See more photographic works at www.splashofsunset.com

Printed in the United States of America

To the lovely Miss Rita Grissom

And

To Mom

Chapter One

A white-hot explosion of light brought Kendra Jenkins back from the depths of her dreams, the only solace she had known for what seemed an eternity. In fact, God only knew how long she had been held captive. She had been a prisoner long enough to have almost completely forgotten what freedom was like. What it felt like to take a lungful of crisp morning air. What it felt like to scream just to hear her own voice. Or what it felt like to move so much as even a muscle.

Kendra's eyes adjusted to the intrusive lighting and she slowly became more aware of her bleak surroundings. The same surroundings she had been greeted with morning after morning, or quite possibly it was night after night, for as long as she could remember.

A thick plastic tube forced its way passed her teeth and into her mouth. A familiar, warm sensation quickly began invading her mouth. It was mealtime. She sucked at the gruel, not from a sense of obedience, nor from pangs of hunger, but from a survival standpoint. Kendra was convinced if she did not suck and swallow the oozing mass it would surely drown her. The texture of the iron-enriched substance was not unlike the mucky sludge of decayed leaves and silt found on the bottom of a swampy river. She forced herself to swallow the repulsive goo, gagging to get it to go down.

The young woman struggled to focus her eyes and tried to clear her head of the fog which had taken up permanent residence in her brain. For the life of her she could not recollect where she was or how she had come to be in this place, wherever the hell this place was. Her vision was blurry around the edges like looking through a kaleidoscope filled with cotton balls. Everything within her line of sight was a milky white hue with mysterious shrouds cast upon anything solid. Her chest began to pound with excitement and fear, and she could taste the tinny taste of bile rising up in her throat as it had done for days on end. She tried to raise her hand and wipe her eyes, but she couldn't move. Panicked, Kendra wriggled from side to side against her restraints.

The girl screamed, but the sound was muffled, as if it had come from within the recesses of her own mind. The more her eyes focused, the more the milky white shroud seemed to penetrate them. Her eyes began to sting terribly. Kendra blinked to try and ease the dry grittiness, but her eyelids wouldn't close.

The girl could feel herself hyperventilating and tried to take slow, deliberate sips of air. *It must be a dream.* That was a statement she made to herself every time she was rudely awakened by the intrusive lights, which seemed to happen day after day for an eternity. Kendra had lost count of the days after the first several months.

As the mental fog lifted even more, Kendra's memories flooded back to her, albeit still void of any recollection of time. Tears streamed down her cheeks. Memories of her baby sister's cherubic face smiled back at her as warm and inviting as a mug of hot cocoa in the wintertime. Her little pink tongue danced across her pudgy lips as she giggled with glee over her big sister's loving attention. Kendra could smell her mother's Obsession and her father's Brut. A brand of cologne he always wore because his daughter had given it to him. Neither one of them really cared for the scent, but it was all she had been able to afford when she was five years old and over time it evolved into a traditional birthday gift. Kendra was sure her daddy would wash it off and put on something a little more elegant and expensive once he had gotten to his office. But she was quite mistaken. Her father wore Brut every day, all day. He had even begun reapplying it several times throughout the day since her disappearance a year earlier.

Like a creeping itch that you just cannot seem to find the right place to scratch, pain slowly clawed its way up her face. At first it felt like a radiant glow, somewhat comfortable and not at all frightening. But then it burrowed deeper and deeper into her skin, down into the meat of her lips, cheeks, and forehead. There seemed to be a concentrated center of heat directly in the middle of her face. The tip of her nose felt as though it were on fire. She struggled to move her head from side to side to escape the relentless, fiery hot pain.

Growing in intensity the heat became unbearable and inescapable. Random thoughts bounced around in her head, one thought blending into the next before she had a chance to focus on what it was she was thinking about. She felt as though the pain were driving her to the brink of insanity. Opening her eyes to try and understand what was happening to her, Kendra immediately clamped them closed and found herself thanking this monster for gifting her this small morsel of kindness by removing the clamps that had been holding her eyes open. Her eyeballs felt dry and gritty as though the soft tissue itself were cracking like the paint of an antique portrait.

She curled her toes and squeezed her hands closed into tight fists, digging her fingernails into her palms until the already tender flesh bled. Tiny streams of warm, sticky blood trickled between her fingers. The dull throbbing pain of her hands was no match for the relentless pain invading her face.

An indeterminate amount of time later the agonizing heat began to slowly subside, although the intense pain took much, much longer to dissipate. Every nerve in her face twitched and throbbed. Goosebumps spread across her cooling skin like a wildfire sweeping up a canyon. Although her eyes were closed, she sensed she was bathed in a bright, white light. She desperately wanted to open her eyes and look around, but she remembered the pain from her last attempt and settled for the unknown. Exhausted from fighting the months of agonizing pain her mind whimpered, she was much too tired to cry.

All at once Kendra's world was plunged back into darkness. It took her several minutes to gather the nerve to open her eyes and then several more for them to adjust to the abrupt change in lighting. Slowly, like a reverse fade to black movie screen, her world came sharply into view. She grasped at the harshness of her newly given sight and the information it provided her. She wanted the lights back. She wanted to be plunged back into the darkness of not knowing. She was suddenly faced with her reality and it scared the hell out of her.

Kendra glanced around her tiny world, now illuminated in a different light than she had grown accustomed to. She could now see her tomb, some sort of rectangular container. A see-through box constructed from clear plastic or Plexiglas. She watched the feeder tube as it retracted away from her mouth and disappeared obscenely into a hole in the Plexiglas about an inch in diameter. Now that she could see the gruel dripping from the tube, she could smell it for what she believed was the first time. Her stomach lurched at the malodorous air invading her chamber. It smelled strongly of liver and stale bread.

Kendra heard a familiar sound surrounding her and strained to focus her eyes at her feet. A wounded, animalistic cry escaped her lips when she caught a glimpse of her shriveled, drooping breasts and sunken in stomach. Her leathery skin reminded her of a flattened football. This was not her body. As soon as she saw the water beginning to ooze up from the floor and start covering her toes, she understood what the sound had been all those passing months, or years. She watched the rising water, entranced, fascinated by its fluidity as it crept up her metamorphosed body. Inch by inch the water, while invasive still quite comfortably warm, slithered up her legs. As the water lapped and tickled her buttocks she began to panic. When would it stop? Would it even stop at all? Was she going to drown in this chamber of horrors? Who was doing this to her?

But the water stopped as soon as it reached her waist. Then Kendra felt something familiar moving inside her and realized what she was supposed to do. It had been so long since she had consciously evacuated herself that she had almost forgotten how. However, neither her instincts nor her muscles had forgotten the daily chore. Her bowels let loose, followed quickly by her bladder. She felt a strange sense of relief wash over her. And then there was another familiar sound. The water tickled as it receded down the sides of her body. A familiar sucking sound announced the chamber had emptied itself. A loud clang startled her and then the sound of water flooding into the chamber was all she heard once more. And once more it submerged her for cleansing and once more it drained away.

Goosebumps erupted over the surface of her skin and she shuddered uncontrollably. As if in considerate response to her chill, a warm, gentle breath of air surrounded her body. She could feel the water evaporating from her skin and the chill subsided.

Out of the corner of her eye, Kendra caught a butterfly's shadow of movement flutter across her scope of vision. She tried to rotate her head to follow the vision, but her range of motion was severely limited. Because of her restraints she could only turn her head about an inch to either side. She strained her eyes until she was able to focus on a shadow just off to her left. Kendra was taken aback. It was another Plexiglas chamber just like hers. As quickly as her restraints would allow, she pivoted her head to the right and strained her eyes once more. Prisms of reflected light danced in front of her eyes. There was a chamber to her right as well.

Kendra turned her attention back to the left and began to scan the chamber up and down. Although the details were sketchy at best, she could make out what she believed to be another human to the left of her. As she scanned up the legs and past the pelvic region, she noticed the gentle slope of a woman's breast begin to lift and rise away from her breastbone. The woman's skin was lighter than her own. Much lighter. She pivoted her head to the right and scanned that chamber up and down, quickly deducing there was yet another woman held captive in that chamber as well. This woman's skin was also lighter than her own, but darker than the girl's to the left of her. Kendra tried to bring their faces into focus but there was a rack of bright white lights burning just above the chambers, obscuring their forms from the neck up.

Kendra focused her eyes forward again and scanned the room outside her chamber slowly. A ring of white lights surrounded the perimeter. In fact, the only area not lit up like the North Pole at Christmas was right directly in front of her. How many others were there? She knew of two at least. Was this some alien spacecraft picking up specimens from across the universe? The young woman's brain was aflame with questions. And then an enlightening one struck terror in her heart. Why was she suddenly able to think clearly? Why, after all this time, was she able to see her surroundings? She suppressed a feeling of relief the moment it tried to edge its way into her brain. Although she genuinely wanted to believe the contrary, she was certain these changes didn't mean her captors had any inclination of setting her free.

Her mind flooded with memories and she began to weep. She remembered her life, which seemed eons ago, a life where she was a budding princess on her way to becoming a queen. Everybody loved her. The media. Her fans. It was then Kendra recalled her past life in all its glory. She flicked her head to the left and began scanning the poor creature trapped next to her once again. She struggled to see the detail in the girl's face but found it useless. She blinked rapidly, trying to lubricate her dry, stinging eyes, but nothing happened, her eyelids would not move. She flipped memories through her brain like cards in a Rolodex, searching for something, anything to give her a clue as to what was happening to her.

She remembered being an actress, but was that only in her dreams? She remembered having perfectly round, firm breasts and delicate chocolate skin with not a blemish to be seen. But now, when she looked down at herself, she saw the body of an old woman, one who hadn't bothered to take care of herself. Her once voluptuous breasts now looked like a failed experiment to make kiwi fruit raisins.

Teary eyed and trapped in a cage with her reveries, Kendra looked to the girl on her left again. She seemed tall, lithe, and well built. Her skin tone clouded by the Plexiglas coffin, but she could tell the girl was white and probably a redhead. A sprig of color captured Kendra's scrupulous eye. The girl had a tattoo on her right thigh of a dolphin leaping from a small wave. If Kendra's memories were right, there was another one, exactly the same, on the girl's other thigh. She knew the girl. They had worked together. They had even had lunch together the day Kendra's memories of a normal life stopped.

The girl's name was on the very tip of Kendra's brain, along with a slew of memories she wished she could now forget. There was no longer any question this was not some long, unending nightmare. Nor was her predicament a result of some alien abduction. No, her situation was much more horrific than that.

The lights came on again above Kendra's plastic sarcophagus, plunging the poor girl back into blindness with their brightness. She struggled with the contrasts between the darkness of the room beyond her tomb and the lights bathing her in an almost angelic glow. She saw movement in front of her, but it was slight and indiscernible. A flick here. A shadow there. And there was sound. A strange sort of squeaking, but it was muffled and dull. Kendra tried to concentrate hard on the motion in front of her but was confused by the lack of details. The slurry of movement continued for several minutes and then as suddenly as it had started, it stopped.

There was a startling pop to the lights, and they went out. She was in the dark and alone once again. Not completely alone, she had her cellmates beside her, but they were hardly any comfort.

Once her eyes had adjusted to her surroundings, she saw what the movement had been. There was something drawn in black on the front of her Plexiglas chamber. A rectangle filled with dozens of squares, each with two fresh, large red slashes running diagonally from top to bottom. She studied it for a few minutes when it finally dawned on her it was a calendar with the word December reading backwards in big block letters in the header. It was obviously New Year's Eve   because there was a big red X slashed through the last day's box. The red slashes induced a shiver of fear that ran through her with the force of a hurricane. The countdown was finally over, but a countdown to what? Her pain and delirium allowed only brief moments of conscious fear to overwhelm her. In one of those moments she found herself dreading the turn of the next page in her life.

*   *   *

Detective Vito Lorenz sat on the toilet cursing the world. Currently he was wallowing knee deep in regret from eating too much of his sister's Chile's Rellenos and homemade black bean salsa. But on the bright side, at least his bowels were working fine this morning, a deviation from the norm. He gave a slight belch and his mouth was immediately coated with the lingering flavor of spicy sausage, jalapeno peppers and cumin. He swallowed hard and hoped the next one didn't bring up anything worse than gas.

Puffs of steam from the shower began filling up the bathroom slowly like an eerie fog chewing its way across a cemetery lawn. Vito half expected some Hollywood creation to come bounding through the fog and rip his head off but was comforted by the knowledge the monster would never be able to brave the smell saturating every square inch of the tiny cubicle. He gave himself a courtesy flush and prayed the next round wasn't quite as fiery.

A rattling on the counter startled him back to reality. He picked up his Motorola pager, a dinosaur he refused to retire in this age of cell phones and wiped off the miniature view window. It was the department again. He felt like flushing the annoying beast along with his sister's retribution. Vito was constantly apologizing for beating and picking on her when they were kids and she was constantly getting even by slipping more jalapenos and cumin into his food. He wondered if he would ever learn to quit eating at her place. He would, right about the time he would learn to cook for himself, which was never. He was already damned near fifty and couldn't even boil water without written instructions and fire department back up.

"Lorenz," he half-grunted into the mouthpiece of his cell phone.

He had ignored his cell phone as long as he dared. It had been going off every five minutes since six am and it was more than half past that now.

"Rise and shine sunshine," a familiar voice chimed.

"What do you want, Davenport?" he lashed out at the dispatcher.

"Don't get pissy with me, honey," she responded, snapping her fingers and taking on an air of attitude and even though the detective couldn't see her, he could still visualize her every movement.

"I'm not getting pissy, I hurt, all right. Christ, you know I don't function at this hour."

"Well you had better start to function. Lieutenant Stoddard wants to see you and Haskell at County General ASAP."

"What for?"

"Don't know sugar, but she said it was hot. You better pick her up something sweet to take her edge off, you know she doesn't like mornings too well either. Especially since she's been at the hospital since four," the dispatcher's voice taunted him.

"What in the hell took you so long to call me?" Lorenz screamed over the shower, which wasn't turning out to be quite as therapeutic as he had hoped.

"I've been trying since quarter after four. Damn, boy, she's pissed," the dispatcher laughed.

Lorenz could almost see her jiggling as she laughed. Lucy Davenport was a big woman, big and jiggly.

"Call Lieutenant Stoddard back and tell her something, I was out of town or at my sister's, just something to get me off the top of her shit list."

"Top? Honey, you're not only on the top, you're the only one on it right now. But, I'll see what I can do," she replied, but not before he had to suffer through another round of her acerbic laughter.

Vito turned off the water and stepped out of the shower. He wiped his hand across the mirror and peered at his steamy reflection. Even the fog couldn't hide his body's deterioration. He wiped the mirror once more and combed his hair. The patches of gray on the sides made him look like Grampa Munster. Vito reached into the drawer and pulled out an abused tube of Alberto VO5, squirted a dab in his palm and ruffled it through his hair. Using his fingers as a comb, he ran both hands through his hair. Even though his head look like the loser in a fight between a wolverine and a feather duster it showed less gray, so he left it the way it was.

After making his way to his closet the only shirt Vito could find clean was a Raiders T-shirt back when they won their last AFC championship. He couldn't remember if they were the Oakland Raiders or the L.A. Raiders then and the writing was so faded reading it was out of the question. Several sniff checks later and he settled for a pale blue shirt at least two sizes too small. He rolled up the sleeves before digging his jacket out from beneath his blankets and throwing it on. He ironed out the wrinkles with the palms of his hands and called himself fit for the street.

In the darkest hour of dawn Vito stepped out onto his porch. The world was deathly quiet, having just gone to bed after a long night of ringing in the New Year. Christmas lights blinked in the windows of nearly every house up and down the slumbering street. His porch was dark and gloomy, the bulbs and holiday cheer had burned out many seasons ago.

Vito struggled to keep four Styrofoam cups of steaming liquid life balanced while driving through early morning traffic. He hoped the crullers and danish were fresh enough to appease his boss. Normally he would have just settled for a Bavarian crème long john for himself and a cinnamon powdered doughnut for his new partner, but he thought he had better take Davenport's warnings to heart. He laughed aloud as he recalled watching his partner trying to eat his doughnut without getting powdered sugar all over himself. The man probably didn't even like powdered sugar doughnuts, but because he was still fresh and trying to make a good impression, he ate them without complaint. Vito wondered what Haskell's reaction would be once he found out his senior partner had been jerking his chain all along.

One cup of coffee became a casualty as Vito came to a jerking stop in front of his partner's house. He had learned a long time ago to buy one more cup than he needed due to such mishaps. His partner's front lawn was immaculately groomed and the landscaping professionally done, a far cry from the digs Lorenz called home. Irritated, he gave the horn three short blasts before realizing Haskell was already coming down the walkway. The man was the epitome of everything Vito had grown to hate, not so much out of spite rather than jealousy. He was tall, athletic, smart and boyishly good-looking. Not to mention, quite capable of dressing himself in the morning without his mother's help.

Vito had been partnered with the man less than six months and had yet to make up his mind whether or not he liked him. Haskell was too quiet and stiff-lipped for his tastes, not to mention he was better than ten years Vito's junior. But then again, the man didn't constantly fill his head with mindless drivel either. And as far as Lorenz could tell, the man had some intelligence, which was more than he could say for his last partner.

Greg Sizemore's face flashed through the detective's mind. It was the last time they had seen each other. It was the day Sizemore had been indicted on suspicion of trafficking, extortion and murder. Vito felt a wave of cold chills run over him and gave a sigh of relief. He was damned lucky he had been able to distance himself enough from the man to have been exonerated of all charges without having to testify. There was only one thing worse than a bad cop and that was a cop who turned on his partner. The last good thing Sizemore had ever done with his life was to make sure that Lorenz didn't go down with him. He dotted his fingers across his chest and forehead and kissed his fingers in remembrance. He made a mental note to visit Mary Sizemore. He hadn't seen her since the funeral.

Haskell interrupted Vito's daydream by opening the car door. He bent to pick up the dead soldier off the floor and put the empty cup back into the carrier. He sat down and put the cup carrier and bag of doughnuts on his lap.

"There's one in the bag for you, but not the fancy one, that one's for Stoddard," Vito said, nodding toward the bag on the man's lap.

"Thanks," he replied, cautiously unfolding the top of the white paper sack and peering inside as if expecting some mutated beast to jump out of the bag and rip open his jugular.

Vito almost broke out into laughter when the man's face scrunched up immediately upon spying the powdered sugar doughnut and of course, no napkins. Haskell commenced going about his morning routine of balancing hot coffee while trying to negotiate with an unruly pastry.

"Any clue what this is about?" Vito asked.

"None. I just got a call from Davenport telling me you were on your way. What's up?" Haskell asked, losing the battle with the doughnut and wiping little brown and white flecks off his black tie.

"I don't have a clue either. All I know is Stoddard is at the hospital and has been since four am."

"I wondered about the pastry, but I just thought you were sweet on her," Haskell smirked.

Stoddard and Lorenz got along together as well as Punch and Judy. Haskell was certain there was some sort of history between the two of them but wasn't too clear if it was a good thing that had gone bad or a bad thing that just kept getting worse.

Gregg Haskell was a quiet man, but when he did speak it was usually a one liner good for a laugh. It was his sense of humor alone that had kept Lorenz from being a complete ass to his new partner. He might be quiet, uptight, stuffy, and a little too pretty, but damn it, at least he knew how to laugh. Lorenz suppressed a patented *fuck you* and concentrated on his driving.

"Aw, Christ, did you eat at your sister's again?" Haskell asked, rapidly rolling down the window and thrusting his head out into the somewhat fresh air. The smog outside was much easier to live with than the smog inside of the car.

Vito just laughed and tried to contain his embarrassment, which was minimal at best.

"What was it this time?"

"Chiles Rellenos."

"When are you going to tell that girl your lineage is Italian, not Mexican?"

"There's actually some Mexican in our blood, we're just not certain where," he laughed and thought of rolling down his window for some fresh air of his own.

"Well, I know what part of you isn't Mexican," Gregg said, disgustedly fanning the vile air away from his face.

"I could always go on a steamed broccoli diet."

"You do and I'll shoot you. Man, I should get hazardous duty pay for this shit," he said, jamming his head out of the window once more.

Vito pulled his decades old Plymouth Reliant into the emergency room parking lot and both men made their way into the hospital. He had made certain to take custody of the coffee and cruller away from Haskell so he would get the credit. As they walked through the sliding glass doors, Gregg tried in vain to wipe the remnants of his doughnut from the front of his tie and suit jacket. They spied their lieutenant and made a beeline toward the scowling woman.

"Lorenz, when are you going to grow up?" She raised her voice and glanced at his partner. "And wipe that innocent look off your face, you know exactly what I am talking about. And Haskell, next time this man buys you one of those damned powdered doughnuts make sure you accidentally drop it in his lap. Wait, on second thought, he might enjoy wiping that off too much," she quipped dryly.

"Good morning to you too, Lieutenant," Lorenz said.

"I don't have time to argue with you about anything this morning, Vito, so just give the damned sarcasm a rest."

"Yes, ma'am," he replied, knowing all too well when to back off with his jabs.

"What have you got?" Haskell interjected, trying to get their discussion back to business.

"What we've got is not pretty. Follow me," she said, turning and walking down the long, highly polished corridor.

Both men couldn't help themselves, their animal instincts took control of their better judgment and they studied her as she sashayed in front of them. Subconsciously they hung back a half step, a move that didn't go unnoticed. Karen Stoddard knew she came in a mighty fine package and didn't mind being admired once in a while. Lord knows her husband sure as hell didn't notice anymore. She let her award-winning smile slip away and brought her persona back to that of a hard-assed police lieutenant.

The detectives followed their boss passed the nurse's station where several of the women shot empathetic glances that unnerved Lorenz. He knew when something was bad enough to visibly shake up nurses the situation was usually not very good and usually it involved children. They passed through a set of swinging double doors into the ICU and were immediately led into a scrub room by the charge nurse. Silently the three of them scrubbed up, their insides churning. The detectives because although they were unaware of the details, knew the situation must be terrible if they were disinfecting themselves before being allowed in the victim's room and Stoddard because she had already seen first-hand the carnage hidden behind the wispy white veils in room 407.

"Lieutenant, why are we here, we're homicide?" Haskell asked with an apprehensive tremble in his voice.

"Because Lorenz is the best detective I've got, and you just happen to be his partner. And Lorenz, don't let that last comment go to your head. You might be my best detective, but you're still a slob."

"Thanks for the compliment, can't wait to see my eval," he droned in monotone.

Haskell snickered.

"You don't want to end up on my shit list too, do you?" Stoddard turned on the young detective like a school of piranha on a wounded capybara.

He just shook his head, unable to respond. Haskell was about as blonde as a person could be without the hair color being considered white. With his fair hair came a fair complexion and it was apparent to everyone the lieutenant had embarrassed him. He could feel the heat radiating from his cheeks like they were sunburned. The confrontation caused him to retract back into his shell, secretly vowing to never again speak in the woman's presence. Detective Lorenz fought the urge to come to his partner's defense knowing it would accomplish nothing but putting the young man a few notches higher on the bitch's whipping post.

In her thoughts Karen Stoddard cursed her cheating, lying husband. The bastard had gotten to her again. She made a mental note to apologize to Haskell, later, when Lorenz was out of earshot of course. She knew she had had no right to lash out at the detective the way she had.

And damn it, Lorenz, can't you do that outside?" she asked, her face contorting in disgust.

"I did," he replied weakly, trying desperately to suppress a growing smirk. In fact, he had inched closer to her before letting her feel the brunt of his power.

"And teach your sister to cook lasagna or something."

"Are we going in?" Lorenz asked cautiously.

"Yes, I just needed to gather my thoughts," she responded and pushed the door open gently.

The room reeked of antiseptics, medicines and something else Vito couldn't quite put his finger on, at least not until he caught a glimpse of the patient lying in the hospital bed. He heard an audible gasp escape from Haskell and his own stomach whirled like a carousel on all-you-can-ride-for-free day. The smell of cooked flesh permeated the air. Quickly he reached into his pocket and took out a container of Vick's VapoRub mentholated ointment and dabbed two fingers under each nostril. He handed the royal blue jar to his partner who wordlessly thanked him and followed his lead. The label on the jar was tattered and illegible and most of the paint had been worn of the jar's lid. Normally the Vick's only came out during autopsies and cases where the corpse was well into its decomposition, but this was terrible enough in its own right.

Burnt flesh had a distinctive smell and Lorenz was relieved to say he had only limited experience with the rancorous odor.

After the initial wave of nausea passed due to the stench, the detectives and their lieutenant had to fight off a second wave brought on by what they were seeing. The human shaped lump lying in the hospital bed was horrifying at best. They were unable to discern the person's race or gender due to the blackness of the charred skin. The three of them could do nothing but stare in disbelief.

After several moments Haskell choked, "Lieutenant, can you please explain this?"

"I don't know much. Person or persons unknown brought her in here at about three this morning. A janitor found her propped in a waiting room chair outside the emergency room."

"Who is she?" Haskell asked.

"I don't know. She had no personal effects on her. She was as naked as the day she was born."

"Was this an accident?" Vito asked.

"It was believed to be until the hospital staff found this," she gently pulled the sheet down, exposing the girl's abdomen. There were crimson letters screaming out a message carved into her flesh. "Evangelique Martens will see you February first," screamed the blood-lined lettering.

"What in the hell does that mean?" Vito asked, watching the nurse pull the sheet back up over the girl's exposed breasts.

He made a note of the fact she was only burned from the neck up. Her arms had seemed to be an odd color compared to the rest of her complexion. They were deeper brown, almost black. Vito realized the discoloration was due to bruising.

"I'm afraid I am going to leave that up to you to find out," Stoddard said.

"Pardon me for interrupting," Haskell said, fighting back the flurry of activity in his stomach. "But was her head the only part of her body that was burned?"

"I'm afraid so. There was a little tissue damage at her neckline, but it was only residual heat damage," the doctor interjected as he stepped into the room.

"How old is she? She seems to be around fiftyish and suffering from the effects of severe malnutrition?" Vito asked.

"I'd have to estimate at early twenties," the doctor's voice was somber, yet, Vito could hear the disgusted anger he was trying to mask.

Everyone in the room fell into an unsettling silence, each reflecting upon the girl's tragic situation and mourning her in their own way. Several moments passed before they were able to digest the poor woman's tragic situation enough that their sympathies gave way and allowed their anger to shine through. Vito, of course, was the first.

"What in the hell happened to her, doc?" he asked, spinning to face the man, more as an excuse to turn away from the dying girl than anything else.

"In a nutshell?"

"Yeah, in a nutshell. Give it to me straight so I can understand it in one pass."

"She was slowly cooked," he replied. Instantly he realized he was going to have to explain the situation further just by their disbelieving expressions.

"I guess you better give us the technical version too," Stoddard said, swallowing hard to force back her rising nausea.

"Let's go out in the hall."

"Give me a second," Lorenz said, digging a small digital camera out of his pocket and snapping a few pictures. He gestured for the nurse to pull the sheets back one more time so he could take a few shots of the grim message. Once he was finished, he nodded to her and she pulled the sheet back up and tended to the girl as best she could. Although the nurse's expression was stoic and unemotional the tears in her eyes betrayed a chink in her armor.

The four of them made their way out of the ICU and down to the chapel where they hoped their conversation could be a little more private. White candles flickered flames of undying resolution in the sanctified cubicle. An oaken cross with a carved bronze image of Christ in all his glorious anguish rose elegantly from the surface of a modest kneeler. Its rosewood finish shimmered in the flickering candlelight. The doleful entourage felt a sudden sense of the Almighty wash over them, as if to say He was counting on them to solve this one. Vito didn't like the feeling. What if he failed? Who was this

Evangelique and what if he let her suffer the same fate as the Jane Doe? Vito trembled visibly.

Karen Stoddard saw her detective's reaction and wished she could reach out to him. To comfort him. To touch him and let him know she cared. But there had been too much bad blood between them for her to ever be able to let him know how she truly felt about him. So instead, she overcompensated with hatred. Her shrink had told her it was a classic case. Karen both loved and hated this man at the same time.

"What did you mean by slowly cooked?" Vito asked, turning to face the doctor.

"In most cases when a person is burned this badly the flesh is seared deeply. But in this girl's case, the flesh beneath the epidermis is interlaced with scar tissue, which means her skin has been damaged repeatedly over a prolonged period of time. It is my professional opinion it is not possible for this much damage to have been cause from normal tanning."

"What are you trying to say?" Karen asked with a panic-stricken voice. She knew the answer but didn't want to hear it.

"In short, she was tortured. In my opinion, some sort of very high output ultraviolet lamp was used to burn her repeatedly. Something with more than a five thousand watt output I'd have to say. Not only was she allowed to heal, but she was medically administered to as well. Whoever did this to her went to great pains to keep her alive."

"How long?" The question came out in the form of a low growl, not unlike a guard dog issuing its first warning.

"Excuse me?"

"How long had she been tortured?" Vito asked through his teeth.

"I don't know really, but it would be safe to assume it had been for quite some time. Her arms have a lot of scar tissue built up which looks to me like it was most likely caused by IV's."

"Why the IV's?" Haskell asked, still gagging every so often like a cat trying to work up a stubborn hairball.

"I'd have to say whomever is responsible for this has been administering medication, food and water to her through intravenous procedure."

"Medication, so is there a chance he gave her pain medication?" Stoddard asked.

"Not much. There was nothing to indicate any sense of mercy in her blood work up. No, I'd say her captor was administering antibiotics, vitamins, mild anesthetics, that sort of thing, but as for analgesics or narcotics, there was nothing of that nature. But my tests are only preliminary, I will know more about what went on with her as time goes on," the doctor explained.

"She looks pretty wasted away, how much would you say she weighs?" Haskell asked.

"Sixty, maybe seventy pounds," the doctor replied, fighting back the urge to be sick. He wanted nothing more than for the detectives to leave him alone so he could do the only thing he could do for the girl; comfort her as she died.

"Is she going to make it?"

"Highly doubtful," the doctor sighed. "Now, please, you must excuse me so I can get back to caring for her. And detectives, do me two favors."

"Name them," Vito seethed.

"Find whoever did this to her and don't give them opportunity to do this to anyone else, if you get my meaning. And get me a name of a loved one. Find out who this poor girl is so I can send her into the afterlife at peace and maybe give her family some closure."

The three of them nodded and watched the doctor as he walked out of the chapel. Vito turned and faced the image of Christ and knelt down. He crossed his chest and said a prayer not only for the tortured young woman, but for himself as well. He turned his head back at Lieutenant Stoddard and said, "Thank you."

"For what?"

"For the compliment. You really must think I'm the best you've got if you want me on this case. I just hope I don't let you down."

"I appreciate that, Vito, I really do. And don't worry about letting me down, I know you'll do your best."

He was slightly stunned. This was the first time she had called him by his first name in longer than he could remember.

"I've got to admit something though," she said.

"It's going to be bad, isn't it?" he replied, knowing the tone of her voice all too well.

"Yes, it's bad. I think I know who that girl is. Or at least I think I have an idea."

Both men stared at her waiting for an explanation.

"One month ago today the department received a warning, just like the one carved into the girl's chest, only this was written on a postcard from a train museum in Vancouver. When I saw the note on the postcard, I took it to missing persons and gave it to them for analysis. The only information they were able to come up with was the girl, Kendra Jenkins, had been abducted January first of last year from a movie set in Hollywood. But damn, we had no idea the note was serious, we assumed it was a prank or someone starting to get brave enough to ask for ransom. No ransom had ever been demanded up until we received this note."

"I've got a feeling there's more."

"I had already looked into the case a little while waiting for you and Haskell to show up. I found out Evangelique Martens had been working on the same movie set as Kendra Jenkins. In fact, it turns out the two of them were friends."

"So, this note is not a hoax?"

"I'm afraid not."

"Which means it is quite possible we only have thirty days to find this bastard before we have another cooked young girl on our hands," Vito stated in disgust.

*   *   *

Lorenz, Stoddard and Haskell pored over what little evidence they had, which was very little at best. Lieutenant Stoddard had called the precinct and ordered an interview room cleared out and any and all evidence from the missing person's case involving Kendra Jenkins and Evangelique Martens be placed on the table inside. Everything was perfectly cozy when the detectives arrived, right down to a fresh pot of coffee on the Bunn. Stoddard didn't like throwing her weight around very often but she had no qualms about it at the present time. This case was going to take priority over everything else, including bruised egos. She felt another sea of acid beginning to get ugly in the pit of her stomach. She knew sooner or later she was going to have to present all of this to the Deputy Chief, then to the Chief, and eventually to the press, a task she wasn't relishing in the least.

"Witness statements are pretty vague," Vito broke the silence.

"I can't find anyone who claims to have actually seen either of the two girls taken. There are plenty of references to them being together. Of them being at the set cafeteria together for lunch that day. Of them being on the set together. They were always together," Haskell said.

"What's your point?" Stoddard asked, a little more gruffly than she would have liked.

"My point is this, if they were always together, why was one of the girls kidnapped a month to the very day after the other? And how could someone have abducted one without the other noticing?"

"Okay, so he took Kendra when the two girls were apart, that at least narrows things down."

"But if they were always together?"

"There had to be some time during that day when they were apart. It was New Year's Day, maybe they partied hard the night before? Went home with boyfriends, girlfriends, hell one-night stands for that matter?"

"But why did he wait an entire month to take Evangelique?" Haskell asked.

"Who knows? He's obviously a crazy bastard," Stoddard said with an impatient sigh.

"True, but I think there must be a reason for it. What I am saying is this, Kendra showed up at the hospital exactly one year to the day from when she was abducted and Evangelique is supposedly going to suffer the same fate on February first, which would be exactly one year to the day that she was kidnapped as well. It seems as though our perp took her one month after Kendra Jenkins for no other reason than he wanted to," Haskell observed.

"Well, at least that establishes the fact he has some sort of pattern in his sick, twisted mind," Lorenz stated, trying to be optimistic considering the skimpy evidence.

"Okay, but that still leaves us with not knowing how he was able to take Kendra without Evangelique being there with her. If we could find a time when the two of them were apart then that could narrow things down considerably," Stoddard said. "Which of the witnesses reported her missing?" She asked.

Vito flipped through the files before answering. "None of them. Not the day she disappeared anyway. Someone from the film crew's administrative staff called us after the second day she failed to show up for filming."

"Her parents didn't know?"

"They don't live here in Los Angeles. She's originally from Philadelphia. According to statements from Evangelique, Kendra had only been out here in Los Angeles about a year," Haskell read off the report.

"See if you can find an address or phone number in that file for her parents, Gregg."

"Yes, Ma'am."

"And the only contact the department has had from her kidnapper was this postcard delivered to you a month ago?" Vito asked, holding a postcard with a picture of a museum diorama featuring a train speeding around a mountain trestle one side and the message, *Kendra Jenkins has until New Year's Day!* Written in red felt tip marker on the back.

"I'm afraid to say none. No ransom demands. No threats, hints or allegations. Nothing," Stoddard replied with a sigh.

"Maybe we need to ask her parents about this," Haskell interjected. "I mean, maybe there were demands and they were told not to deal with the police, so they kept quiet about it," he added after seeing the looks on their faces.

"He's got a point," Vito said.

"Yes, I'm afraid he does. This isn't going to be pretty. I must inform the parents of her critical condition and then accuse them of causing it by not coming to the police. Great, just great."

"I can help you if you'd like," Vito said.

"No, don't worry about me. What I really need for you two to do is to find me Evangelique's parents. If the kidnapper is demanding money from them without our knowledge, we need to know this and in a hurry."

"I'll send a hot sheet to DMV and see if we can get an address on them."

"I'll start with the production company, see if they can give me any updated information," Haskell said, the two of them closed the door to the interrogation room on their way out. Both of them could see the pressure written all over their boss's face and knew she needed a few minutes to be alone. Making the phone calls she needed to make was never an easy task and neither detective envied her in the least.

"Lorenz," a detective called from his desk.

"Yeah, what is it Smitty?" He asked the man whose last name was actually Smitty and not a just bastardized version of Smith.

"The hospital just called. The Jenkins girl coded; they couldn't bring her back."

"It's probably just as well," he responded under his breath.

"Thanks Smitty," Haskell added as an afterthought. The man nodded and went back to whatever tragic story he was working on.

Vito sighed as he dropped down into his chair and spun around for the phone. He punched in a series of numbers and waited impatiently while the phone rang and rang in his ear.

"ME's office," a familiar voice chimed in his ear after seventeen rings.

"Running the saw again I see," he said, a little disgusted with having to wait for someone to answer the phone. It was an inconvenience Vito had learned to live with. The county was always understaffed and making cuts and it always seemed the coroner's office and forensics always took the hardest hits.

"Hey, Vito, what's going on?"

"More shit than I care to shake a stick at actually, Morty."

He laughed, "I'll bet. Is there anything in particular I can do for you, or is this a social call?"

"I honestly wish it were a social call, but it's work as usual."

"What have you got?"

"I caught a case today and I need her processed ASAP."

"What's the name?"

"I believe we've listed her as Jenkins, but I don't think you have her yet. She's still at County General."

"I've got her here on my charts. Kendra, correct?"

"Yes, Kendra Jenkins. I would like forensics to go over her with a fine-toothed comb before you start to slice and dice her though, please. Can you hold off until they get finished? And make sure we get a positive ID on this girl, we're only going on assumptions right now."

"Sure, thing, not a problem. I'm up to my elbows in work here anyway, and I mean that literally. I've got a GSW to the chest, the perp used buckshot."

"That's way more information than I needed, Morty, and a lot more than I wanted."

Chapter Two

Evangelique watched in terror as a shadow, which she had already determined to be her captor's hand, drew two slashing red lines across a date on her personal calendar. The other girl was gone now, and had been for twenty days. This was true only if her captor was crossing off the days with any accuracy. The daily visits were bittersweet. On one hand she was being kept apprised of the passing days and finally had some sense of time. But on the other, she knew she only had eleven more days before the big question mark.

Every day she speculated at what had become of her friend, Kendra, and every day her mind created a different outcome, most of them tragic. At times she could barely even remember the girl ever having been entombed with her at all. It all seemed like a distant memory. In fact, Evangelique wouldn't have even considered the reality of Kendra's being next to her had it not been for the vacant Plexiglas chamber on one side of her and an inhabited one on the other. No matter how hard she tried, she couldn't place the girl in the other chamber. All she could make out was that the girl was blonde and was nearly as physically destroyed as she herself was. Scenes from Schindler's List played out in the recesses of her mind, images she threw off with a shudder.

The blinding amber lights which had illuminated the once occupied neighboring chamber had long since been extinguished and Evangelique could no longer find comfort in the glowing heat they had once emitted. She had grown used to the comforting warmth over the passing days and weeks. Now, with the lights no longer burning brightly, her chamber was once again a cold, windless tomb.

Evangelique's stomach gurgled, reminding her it had been days since she had eaten anything. She almost laughed aloud when she realized she was craving the metallic tasting gruel that had been force-fed to her throughout her captivity. In the beginning she had clamped her teeth around the plastic tube so tightly the nutrient enriched paste couldn't even force its way into her mouth. She had bitten down on the tube until her jaws ached so badly that the pain brought tears to her eyes but eventually her muscles failed and the slop easily invaded her gullet. Now, more than anything else, she wanted to feel that invasive slime oozing down her throat and dropping into the hollow snarling pit of her stomach.

The young woman could feel she was weakening. Day by day, little by little, Evangelique could feel herself wasting away. She didn't even have to look down at her pale, cadaver-like skin to know it was no longer the delicate milky white it had once been. Locks of her red hair fell out and tumbled down her slumping shoulders. She could feel the brittle strands lying against her bare breasts. She realized her flaming red hair was gone and she cried or at least she would have had there been enough moisture left in her body for tears.

Evangelique could sense a presence pacing around the perimeter of her chamber. Although the unseen entity chose to remain in the shadows, out of the girl's field of vision, it couldn't control the shadows. That knowledge alone had given the tortured girl a miniscule semblance of comfort. At least the creature couldn't defy the laws of nature, or at least not all of them. She felt the cold drip begin in the IV in her arm and knew it must be feeding time. The iron rich, bitter taste of vitamin B flooded her taste buds forcing her to gag and swallow repeatedly. At least the son of a bitch was keeping her alive. But why?

* * *

"Is that them?" Vito asked his boss.

"Yes, that's her parents," Lieutenant Stoddard replied, glancing sympathetically at a beleaguered looking man and woman leaving the building. The man had a comforting arm around his wife who was near collapse. His soft, gentle face was lined with ragged edges of hatred and anger. They were two of the loneliest people in the world at that very moment.

"At least they loved her. I'm not sure which is worse, sending young girls down to the morgue to be cut up and buried alone, or having to face their parent's pain," Vito sighed.

"How did they respond to your questioning?" Haskell asked.

"It went pretty smoothly actually. Her father is a retired cop from Philly. He knows the routine pretty well and wasn't offended in the least. But he was also adamant about the fact they have never once been contacted by this bastard, not even as much as a postcard," Stoddard explained.

"Damn, that doesn't give us a whole lot to go on. Any ransom demands?" Vito asked.

"None. What about the Martens girl's parents?" Stoddard asked.

"No father that we could find, but her mother is on her way down here from the valley as we speak," Vito replied.

"Have you found any connections between these two?"

"Nothing other than what we already knew. The two of them were working on the same movie together when Kendra disappeared," Haskell said.

"We've already contacted the studio's PR people, who are calling the studio's lawyers, who will be giving us a call when they damned well feel like it I suppose," Vito huffed.

"They had better be damned quick about it or I'll make some calls and cash in some markers," Stoddard barked. She hated dealing with studio moguls who thought they had to answer to no one, not even God.

"I've got the preliminary coroner's report here," Vito said, shaking a faxed piece of paper in his hand.

"Out with it," the lieutenant replied, obviously perturbed.

"Morton Brandt lists the official cause of death as prolonged exposure. I called Morty for myself to get the layman's version. He agrees with the doctor's opinion Kendra Jenkins had been exposed to some type of ultra violet light for a long period of time. He's not too clear on the specifics yet, the exact temperatures or the precise length of time, but he promised to let me know as soon as he learned anything new."

"You mean the sun?"

"More like a sun lamp. The bottom line is this, she was slowly cooked to death."

Both Lieutenant Stoddard and Detective Haskell sucked in a long sip of air and tried to digest this information.

"It gets worse. Morty also said her soft tissue was indeed scarred quite deeply. She had been allowed to heal and then was re-exposed to the light again repeatedly. Morty estimates she endured this over a period of several months at least. He also confirmed the doctor's opinion that great pains had been taken to keep her alive. There were traces antibiotics and anti-inflammatory drugs in her pancreas and liver, but as was suspected earlier, very little traces of painkillers whatsoever. Looks like we've got a real nut case on our hands boss," Vito explained.

"Shit, this is all I need. I'm glad I didn't know any of this when I was breaking the news to her parents. I'll gladly let the doctor carry that burden," she sighed.

"I left instructions with forensics to call me as soon as they know anything about this case," Haskell interjected, his young face already starting to show the haggard lines of a veteran homicide detective.

"Vito, I trust you can handle running this on your own, I'm going to be busy feathering this to the brass and to the press. God forbid the killer makes good on his warning and delivers us another body in seven days. And you have my full support on this. Don't bother coming to me with requests, anything you ask for, you can have," Stoddard said.

"Not a problem boss, I understand completely, and thank you. Hopefully we can get to this Evangelique before this bastard does."

"Just keep me posted, please,"

"Sure thing. And Karen, relax, we'll get this guy," Vito said, turning away from his boss and leaving her to attend to the public relations nightmare, a job he wouldn't have wished on his worst enemy.

*   *   *

To their dismay, the investigation into Evangelique Martens ground away much too slowly. It took the better part of a week just to locate Evangelique's mother and get her into the precinct to break the grisly news to her about her daughter's professed fate. Vito felt himself sinking further and further into a depression he wasn't sure if he would ever be able to pull himself out of. Every time he rolled on a juvenile homicide it took a little piece of him with it. However, this was different. This time he had actually been given a chance, however slight it may be, to save this girl from the executioner's call. But now he was slowly forcing himself to accept the fact he was going to be too late. Much too late. He and Haskell were reduced to merely going through the motions so they would have a better chance of nailing her killer once her body was located.

He studied the green-eyed beauty sitting in the interrogation room, nervously awaiting his arrival. He gathered his composure and stepped into the room, hoping the girl's mother wouldn't see through his façade.

"I'm sorry to have to bother you like this Mrs. Martens, and I certainly don't want to dig up painful memories or give you false hope," Vito voice was laced with sincere warmth and regret.

"No trouble at all detective, and my name is Carla," she offered a delicate hand to him.

"I really don't know how to start this delicately so I am just going to start. Do you know of a Kendra Jenkins?"

"The name seems familiar. Let me think," she paused and looked toward the ceiling.

Vito noticed the woman's haunting green eyes, in fact, he had noticed them the moment he saw her for the very first time on the silver screen more than twenty-five years earlier. He was glad to see Carla Martens, otherwise known as Lolita Larson was still as beautiful as ever. He couldn't help but wonder what had happened to her career. She had made several movies, all of which were his favorites but panned heavily by the critics. In those days it seemed the critics were never big fans of onscreen nudity, unless of course they were behind closed doors and then that was a different story. The last thing Vito remembered seeing her in was some corny, contrite television show that lasted much longer than anyone could have ever guessed. But once the show was canceled, Lolita disappeared from his life forever, or at least until video was invented and he bought all of her movies that had been released on tape, all two of them.

She fluffed her full head of flaming red hair and said. "Now I remember, she worked on a film with Evangelique. In fact, I think they were working on a film together when Kendra disappeared," her words trailed off and face went blank as the recollection slapped her like a wet towel.

"Yes, ma'am. Miss Jenkins was working on the same movie set with your daughter when she disappeared. Your daughter disappeared from the very same set one month later."

"You found Kendra Jenkins, didn't you?" her voice quivered and broke.

"Yes ma'am, I'm sorry to have to tell you this, Kendra died in the hospital a short while ago," he replied, not wanting to divulge any more information about the poor girl's demise than he absolutely needed to.

"Oh my God," she cried out, her lips quivered and tears began to flow freely.

"Like I said, I am very sorry for having to ask you these very difficult questions, but your daughter's name was among the evidence gathered at the scene," he told a white lie, wanting to save her from the bitterness of the truth. Vito fought every urge to tell her he was her biggest fan and that he would do everything within his power to save her little girl from the Big Bad Wolf who prophesied her destruction. Instead, he bit his lip and allowed her to cry.

She sniffled a few times, gathered her composure as best she could and asked. "What do you need from me?"

"Just a few simple answers. I'll try to be as brief as possible."

She gave a frail nod. Vito noticed her green eyes were no longer the sparkling orbs he recalled. Sadness gripped his chest like he had never felt before.

"Did you know Kendra very well at all?"

"We met once or twice, when I came down to the set for visits, but no, we didn't really know each other."

"But her and your daughter were friends, correct?"

"Yes, but they were sort of forced together."

"How do you mean?"

"They were the only young girls involved with the film. Evangelique had called me after her first week on the set and complained about how boring it was and that she had no one to talk to. Kendra was brought onto the set a week or so after Evangelique and the two of them hit it off almost instantly."

"So, they spent a lot of time together?"

"Quite a bit, I think. At least from what Evangelique has told me."

"When did you last speak with your daughter?" The question came out mumbled and hushed.

"Sometime in January last year, I can't recall the exact date. I was in Paris over the holidays. I called her on Christmas Day, New Year's Day and again sometime in late January. I remember she was quite broken up over Kendra's disappearance. She wanted to quit, but I made her tough it out," she began to cry again.

"I got the call from the production company about two weeks later. I just assumed Evangelique had succumbed to the pressures and had simply run off to gather her thoughts for a while. You know how impetuous young girls can be. She's done that sort of thing before, so I wasn't too worried about her, other than the damage she was doing to her career of course. I remember being so angry with her for ruining her career," her trickling tears evolved into heaving sobs.

Vito reached out and put a sympathetic hand on her shoulder and she crumbled into his arms. For the lack of anything better he hugged her tightly while fighting back his own tears.

"You can't blame yourself, it's not your fault," he choked.

She raised her head from his chest and smiled. Haskell knocked on the interview room window and startled both of them. Carla dropped her face into her hands as if embarrassed she had been crying. An old Hollywood habit that was hard to break he assumed.

"That's my partner, he must have something important to tell me," Vito explained the interruption. He stood up from the table and hovered near her.

"Don't let me hold you up, I'll be all right. Just give me a few minutes to compose myself please."

"Certainly. You can stay in here as long as you like. I'll put the occupied sign on the door, so no one bothers you."

"Thank you, Detective, you're really the only one who has shown any sincere interest since Evangelique's disappearance, including myself."

"I'm truly sorry to hear that."

She smiled. "It's not your fault."

"Sometimes this job is just too damned frustrating," he revealed, as if he were talking to an old friend.

"I know the feeling," she reached out and patted his hand. "And Vito, no matter what happens, I won't blame you for anything," her eyes sparkled for just a fraction of a second. Vito couldn't help but wonder if they would continue to sparkle if he allowed her daughter to die at the hands of this maniac.

"Can I call you again if I think of anything else?"

"By all means," she said, waving her hand at him to go to his partner whom had knocked on the window several times.

"What is it?" Vito said, irritated by the interruption.

"I thought you might like to see these," Haskell handed him a large manila envelope.

"What are they?"

"The initial forensics report and an affidavit from the studio's attorney."

"An affidavit? Those rotten bastards couldn't even send someone down here to talk to us?"

"Guess not," he replied, shaking his head in disgust.

"Maybe we need to get someone from Vice to make a few visits to their lots. I'm sure they could find enough drugs on set to make their lives a living hell," Lorenz fumed.

"Read the forensic report first."

Vito pulled out several sheets of paper and began giving them the once over. He continually shook his head as he read line after line of atrocities.

"The message was burned into her abdomen with a surgical laser?"

"I've already got an expert in handwriting analysis working on it just in case it might give us something, but don't hold your breath."

"Why not?"

"The experts I've spoken with all believe he would have probably used a computer-generated program. Something that would have allowed him to simply type the words out on a keyboard and the computer program did the rest. The lettering looks too perfect to have been done by hand."

"Of course, anything else would be too easy. How expensive are one of these surgical lasers? And how big are they?"

"They come in a variety of sizes; some are quite mobile in fact. But they are expensive. Very expensive and not very common."

"That should make this unit easier to trace, correct?"

"Yes, but only once we have the unit itself and the serial numbers. I've already got someone tracking down leads on units purchased over the past two years, but I doubt it will uncover much of anything useful, they're sold all over the world," Gregg sighed.

"Well at least I felt better for a minute or two," Vito grumbled.

"You'll get a kick out of the affidavit too."

"Like hell I will, I'm not fucking reading it," he said, throwing the large manila envelope into a battered trashcan. The spring hinge snapped the mouth of the trashcan closed in protest of Vito's harsh treatment. The lid jolted off the base of the can and came to rest at a cocked angle. The lid remained jammed open in a mock scream of objection, regurgitating the envelope onto the floor.

"What? Why not?"

"Because, we're going down there. Come on," Vito said. He grabbed his jacket off the back of his chair and headed for the exit with Haskell in tow.

*   *   *

Evangelique tried desperately to raise her hands in an effort to defend her face. Her lips felt as though they were on fire. She tried to purse them, bite them, anything to make the fiery hot pain subside. Nevertheless, her efforts were useless. Nothing helped to abate the intense pain.

She opened her eyes as her dream of excruciating pain focused sharply into reality. Her mind was foggy from a drug-induced slumber and she wrestled to gain control of her senses. The only thing she could see was a pinpoint red beam penetrating the darkness. She traced the beam with her teary eyes and became acutely aware of the fact the beam was the source of her pain. Instinctively she turned her head to avoid the beam's assault and immediately felt a searing pain ripping through her cheek. The laser moved back to her lips and continued to burn and chew through her tender flesh.

The beam moved like the carriage on a typewriter, back and forth from left to right. Slowly, effortlessly it gnawed away at her. The acrid smoke of her own burning flesh stung the delicate membranes of her eyes and her nose. The pain was unfathomable. Her toes ached from curling them up against the assault, as they were the only part of her body she could actually move. For her, knowing who was doing this to her was no longer an issue. Neither was the question why.

She retreated into her mind and silently begged them to stop. She prayed to God to make the pain stop. And then she prayed for the angel of death to show her mercy.

She felt the cold, white underbelly of the IV drip snaking up her arm. She breathed a sigh of relief. Surely, they were finally going to administer her pain medication. But it wasn't working. She tried to scream at them and tell them she was still in pain. Then she felt a wave of tingles wash over her scalp and knew what they had done. She had tried methamphetamines at a party once and this was the same feeling. This sadist was feeding her speed to keep her from passing out. Between the flashes of pain she cursed her captor with a fury she had never known.

Evangelique gasped in horror when she felt a piece of her upper lip fall away. Bouncing off her lower lip it slipped and slid all the way down her body like a child's gooey toy thrown against the wall until it made a sick slapping sound when it finally came to rest on the floor of her tomb. Then she winced as a new, even more excruciating pain assaulted her. The laser, having already destroyed the soft tissue of her lip began burning into her gum line. She felt the ultra-sensitive roots of her teeth heating up under the fiery torch of the laser. Her head swam in blackness and pain, but the drugs coursing through her veins refused to let her pass out.

The laser worked its way down her upper lip until there wasn't anything left. But it was still hungry. Famished. Insatiable. Evangelique winced again as the beam cut between the gap between her upper and lower teeth. It cut a painful swath across her tongue before she was able to clench her teeth closed and prevent the attack. The laser continued on its path of destruction and began biting into the tender flesh of her lower lip. Slowly and methodically it worked, slicing, biting, chewing and burning away her face. At some point she felt her body begin to convulse and instinctively fight against the battery. The pinpoint red beam of light faded to gray and then mercifully to black. Her last conscious thought were two red slashes in the last box of her calendar.

*   *   *

"Sir, you can't go in there. Mr. Rademacher is in the middle of an important meeting," a panicked young woman darted her eyes wildly between Vito Lorenz and the door to her boss's office. She made a valiant effort to intercept the lumbering detective with her ninety-five pounds, but Vito barged through the door of the boardroom despite the girl's warnings.

"Gentlemen, this meeting is over," he announced while holding his gold shield in the air for all to see. Most were not impressed. They had seen better Hollywood fakes.

"Might I ask what this rude, unconstitutional intrusion is about?" Rademacher boomed, trying to ruffle his feathers for all to see. He had a captive audience and he was an actor, or at least he fancied himself a thespian.

Oslo Rademacher had an ego much larger than his slight body. He was short and paunchy with jowls large enough to grab by the handfuls. He smelled of stale cigar smoke and expensive cologne, men's but also effeminate. Even as powerful as the cologne was, it was still overpowered by the tobacco.

"Out! Everybody out," Vito corralled the meeting's attendees towards the door to the boardroom where Haskell fed them out into a reception vestibule.

"I'm sorry Mr. Rademacher, they just barged in. There was nothing I could do," the receptionist pleaded as if her job depended on it.

Once the room was empty Vito looked the man in the eye and said as gruffly as he could, "Sit down."

Oslo Rademacher complied without as much as a whimper. Without his audience there was no reason to emote, especially while this detective continued to glare at him with such contempt. He just looked up at the man with question marks in his eyes.

"Look at this," Vito said, shoving a coroner's picture of Kendra Jenkins across the table at him.

Rademacher looked at the picture for several seconds and then glanced back up at Lorenz with the same look of bewilderment.

"You don't recognize her?"

"No," he mouthed, while trying to keep the contents of his stomach a secret. His slick pate glistened in the glow of florescent light.

"She used to work for you. Her name is Kendra Jenkins. And no, that's not Hollywood makeup and special effects she's dead. That's her corpse. And I have less than twenty-four hours to make sure the next picture I show you isn't of Evangelique Martens' corpse."

He gasped and said, "But I still don't understand what any of this has to do with me."

"If anyone from the Los Angeles Police Department, or for that matter any law enforcement agency calls you about information regarding someone who works or worked for you, do not send an affidavit. When I request information from you regarding a missing child, I expect your full cooperation. Do you understand?" He slammed his hands on the table for emphasis. Vito had to force himself to keep from laughing at the terrified expression on Rademacher's face, he swore the man had just shit himself.

The sweating man meekly nodded his head and prayed his bladder would make it through this ordeal.

"Good. Now that the niceties are behind us, I have a few questions and I see you are free for the next hour or so. Do you mind?"

Rademacher contemplated an argument but quickly shook his head and pointed to a chair instead. Vito sat down while Haskell continued his vigil at the door. Over the course of the next half an hour the detective asked all the routine questions and received all the routine answers. The two of them talked back and forth about useless information for the better part of an hour before Vito was ready to summarize all he had learned.

"So, did everyone on the set consider these two inseparable?"

"Pretty much, I think. I mean, they went everywhere together, even the bathroom sometimes," Rademacher replied with a sigh, he was growing weary of the repetitive line of questioning.

"So, if they were inseparable, how did Kendra Jenkins get kidnapped without anyone seeing? Especially not even Evangelique?" he asked, more to hear the question for himself than any other reason.

"I don't have a clue, detective. Isn't that your job to find out?" Oslo let the smart comment slip before he could rein it in.

Vito glared at the Hollywood mogul with more contempt than he had ever had for any one human being in his life.

"I'm sorry, Detective Lorenz, but I am tired of these questions. I'm the boss here," he fanned his arms to indicate the enormity of the studio. "I have neither the time nor the energy to watch after every single actor or project on this lot."

"I understand that, I just thought you might have a little more information you could share with us."

"Well I don't. Hell, I only met Miss Jenkins one time and Miss Martens only twice. I have told you everything I, or any of my staff knows about these two girls. We have been as helpful as humanly possible. I do apologize for the affidavit being sent over to your office, but I assumed doing so would only make your jobs easier," he said, annoyed with the detective's game and quite ready for lunch. He needed a green apple martini now more than ever before.

"If you think of anything else, please contact me at this number," Vito said, standing and reaching across the table to hand the man his card. He knew the interview was over a long time ago. He had sensed the lack of information and knew he wasn't about to learn anything knew from the man. Nevertheless, he felt obliged to screw the man's day up by wasting the better part of it.

"Well, it looks like we're back to square one," Vito sighed as he and Haskell got into the car.

"We sure didn't learn anything from him."

"No, we didn't. I'm afraid we screwed the pooch on this one. That poor girl has got no chance."

"That's not our fault, Vito. We don't have anything to go on. Besides, maybe this is all just some sort of sick game."

"You think this might just be a hoax?"

"Anything is possible," Haskell replied, not believing his own words for a minute. He felt as helpless as his partner did, but he also knew that wallowing in self-pity was the last place the two of them needed to be.

"Want to grab a drink and talk it over? Maybe we can come up with something we're overlooking," Vito asked, looking down at his watch and realizing it was well past quitting time.

"Sounds like a plan to me, I could sure use a cold one right about now."

"I'll call us in," Vito smiled weakly and reached for the hand mike.

*   *   *

Vito looked down at the vibrating pager clipped to his waistband currently interrupting a much-needed escape. It was Stoddard's number, with an emergency warning at the tag end. He guzzled the rest of his coffee and shoved the cup across the bar for a refill, knowing it would probably be his last chance for caffeine for quite some time. With a mouthful of the bitter liquid he made a beeline for the pay phone in the back of the dark bar. Haskell made note of the look on his partner's face, chugged the last of his O'Doul's and followed the disgruntled detective.

"This is Lorenz," he said shortly the moment his lieutenant's voice reverberated on the phone.

"Bad news. Get Haskell and meet me at Glendale Memorial, pronto," she barked and hung up before Vito could respond. Normally he would have been pissed off at her rudeness, but it wasn't incivility he heard in her tone this time, it was frustration.

"Stoddard?" Haskell asked as Vito turned away from the phone.

He nodded and said, "Yeah, come on. I have a terrible feeling it isn't good news she wants to share with us."

The two of them didn't speak a word during the drive to the hospital. Vito maintained a white knuckled grip on the steering wheel while Haskell contemplated a career in basket weaving. They were still several blocks from the emergency room entrance when the first wave of blue lights flickering off the wet pavement came washing over the hood of their car. Both detectives felt their stomachs tighten in anticipation of what was to come. And although they couldn't say for certain what it was they were walking into, their imaginations were working overtime painting a gruesome picture.

Vito pulled within several car lengths of an ambulance that seemed to be the focus of all the attention. The chest-beating sound of a helicopter could be heard approaching in the distance and Vito hoped it was the LAPD corralling the suspect and not a news chopper trying to get in for a closer look. The incessant clicking of cameras could be heard over the roaring din of the night and Vito became aware of what they were facing.

"Is it her?" he asked Stoddard the moment they came face to face on the scene.

She just dropped her head and nodded.

"Is she, dead?" Haskell asked.

She weakly shook her head and said, "Not quite yet, but it looks inevitable."

"Damn it," Vito roared and looked for something to punch, finding only the solid steel side of the ambulance he shoved his hands in his pockets and fought the urge, having learned his lesson many years and many scars ago.

"She was alive when they found her, but she coded within minutes of being admitted into the ER."

"Why all the hoopla around the ambulance?"

"This is where they found her."

Vito and Haskell were clearly at a loss.

"One of the nurses noticed the ambulance parked in the emergency entrance with its lights going. After fifteen minutes or so she came out to investigate what was going on and found Evangelique in the back. She said there was no driver or attendants anywhere to be seen," she explained.

"And I'm guessing it would only be wishful thinking to assume she drove herself here and will be on the road to recovery as we speak," Vito said.

"No, I'm afraid she didn't drive herself, Vito," Stoddard said.

"How much do we know?"

"Not a whole lot yet, the doctors are still working on her. They have resuscitated her several times, but she keeps slipping away from them. I'm afraid they're not going to be able to bring her back to us, not even long enough to get any answers."

"Evening Lorenz, Lieutenant," Robert Morgan's gruff voice greeted them. Robert was a senior crime scene investigator and hated processing scenes involving juveniles as much as the detectives did if not more.

"Bob," Vito nodded.

"What can you tell us?" Stoddard asked.

"Not too much yet. The rig was as clean as a whistle I'm afraid. The only things we found in there so far are things that would normally be there. No stray hairs or fibers. No prints. Nothing," he ran a hand over his balding pate.

Vito found the man's appearance to be humorous to say the least. What little hair the man did have ringed his head like a wreath of laurel, except that it was red. Bright red. In fact, if it were any more orange Morgan would have been a dead ringer for Bozo the Clown, sans white make-up and size one eighty-four and a half shoes of course.

"We're going to need prints from the girl's body once the medical team is finished with her, even if she survives," Vito said.

Morgan nodded as if the order went without saying.

"Anything else?" Stoddard added.

"Another message," he sighed.

"Another name?" Haskell butted in.

Morgan nodded.

"Shit, just what we need, a damned serial killer."

"This girl was cared for just like the other. Kept alive until our man wanted her dead. There was severe bruising to her left arm where an IV had been in place for quite some time. I don't have the actual facts, but I'm guessing she weighs less than one hundred pounds."

"Christ," Haskell gasped.

The four investigators stood silently on the tarmac as a light rain fell from the night sky. It was late winter in Los Angeles and the air was extremely chilly and wet, the kind of wet that grinds little knives into arthritic joints. Tires splashing through puddles as cars cruised passed the hospital out on the boulevard echoed through the darkness. Life went on, oblivious to the horror surrounding it. The crime scene investigation team gathered up what little evidence they had been able to collect from the ambulance and headed inside the emergency room to wait patiently for their turn at Evangelique Martens. It seemed cold and unfeeling, it had to, or it would eat a person alive. Vito knew what that was like. So did Lieutenant Karen Stoddard. Young Gregg Haskell was getting his first taste. It was a hell of a first bite to have to chew and nearly impossible to swallow. A traffic light at the far end of the boulevard had stopped traffic long enough to plunge the four of them into an uncomfortable silence.

The sliding glass doors opened, and the cacophony of the emergency room spilled out onto the tarmac for a brief sliver of time until the doors whooshed closed once more. They all turned to face the young man walking toward them in a knee length lab coat. He was much younger than his face portrayed. He had thick brown hair with red accents that seemed to capture the dazzling brilliance of the flashing emergency beacons. His rugged face seemed haggard and tired. He walked up to the solemn gathering, stuck his hands in the deep white pockets of his coat and thought carefully about what he had to say.

"How is she?" Karen broke the silence.

"I'm sorry, she's gone. We did all we could do," his eyes begged for forgiveness.

"Damn it. Did she say anything?" Vito asked, a lot more heartlessly than he would have liked.

"No, she never regained consciousness."

"I better get in there," Morgan said, leaving the detectives to hear the gruesome story from the doctor. He was going to have to witness the carnage first hand, something he was far from relishing.

"What can you tell us?" Vito asked, purposefully softening his tone.

"I can tell you this poor girl was severely tortured. She has been kept alive for months on end."

"What killed her?"

"A combination of things really. But clinically, I'd have to say she died from hypovolemic shock. Her body just shut down due to the fact she had lost so many fluids. The most sinister part of this is that I don't believe her tormentor wanted her to die. In fact, I think he wanted her to live."

"Why do you say that?" Vito asked.

"There was an extensive effort to keep this woman alive. Her killer had been giving her nutrient enriched fluids. I think he just underestimated how much she needed. There were trace amounts of antibiotics and vitamins in the IV tubing we pulled from her arm."

"Where is the body?"

"She's in the ER. Come on, I'll try to explain her injuries the best I can."

The crime scene investigators were busy meticulously preserving the evidence in the emergency room. The dead girl's hands were covered with evidence bags fastened loosely at her wrists. One of the lab technicians was busy dusting her body for latent prints. Karen Stoddard gasped audibly once she saw the body for the first time. None of them had any clue as to what to expect, and she had certainly not expected to see the gruesome sight on the gurney.

"What in the hell happened to her face?" Vito said, turning away in disgust.

The girl's mouth looked like a plate of freshly ground hamburger with a set of fake Halloween teeth jammed into the center. There were several jagged bloody lines slashing across her face, which was frozen in agony. Thick strands of blood oozed along the corners of her mouth, down her neck and finally pooled up around her earlobes.

"In short, her lips have been burned off," the doctor said, turning away from the corpse as well. She was no longer a patient and looking at her now would only add to the hundreds of emotional scars he already carried with him on a daily basis. It was best for him if he just let this one go.

"How?" Haskell choked.

"It looks to be the work of a surgical laser. The same thing that did this," the doctor said, peeling back the sheet to expose Evangelique's violated torso. Letters were carved in her flesh with the laser to convey another ominous message. *Too late! Rita Sorenson's clock has just started ticking!* Vito, Gregg and Karen stared at the raw, red flesh screaming out its warning. The letters were carved into her skin with pinpoint precision, exactly the same as they were in Kendra Jenkins' case. The edges of the lettering were blackened where the flesh had succumbed to the exposure of the fiery hot laser and the meat inside the blackened outline was painfully pink.

"Do you have any idea how long ago this was carved into her skin?" Karen hissed through her teeth.

"My best guess would have to be no more than a couple of hours before she was delivered at our doorstep. The wounds are still secreting plasma, which indicates they are still quite fresh. The laser cauterized the wounds themselves which kept them from bleeding, but the cauterization doesn't stop the body's lubricating fluids from producing."

"What is wrong with her feet?" Haskell asked, noticing the girl's feet curling upward at the metatarsals.

"They've atrophied."

"What would have caused that?" Stoddard asked.

"Mostly from the lack of use I would suspect," the doctor replied sheepishly.

"Mostly?" Vito questioned.

"I also fear she had held her feet in that position for quite some time in some form of mental battle against the excruciating pain."

All three police officers cringed at the thought. The four of them pondered the findings silently. Not a single one of them could imagine the kind of monster it would take to do these things to these girls.

"I pray to God you know who this Rita Sorenson is," the doctor said, immediately knowing the answer by the looks on the detective's faces.

"Thanks, Doc, please keep is informed of anything else you might find," Karen said.

"I'm afraid I'm done with this poor woman, anything else will be found by your investigators," he turned and walked down the corridor with his head hung down until his chin rested on his breastbone. After several steps he stopped, spun around on his heels and said, "You need to catch this bastard before he does this again," he emphasized the word "need" as if he were going to hold them personally responsible if they didn't, which was exactly the message he wished to convey.

They watched the doctor disappear down the corridor. Vito could feel the bile rising in his stomach and he knew a serious bout of heartburn was on the way. He was quite aware of four very important facts. Lieutenant Stoddard had no clue who Rita Sorenson was. Neither did he, nor did his partner. Nevertheless, one thing was for certain, the killer knew exactly who the ill-fated girl was.

*   *   *

Vito used a sick day, his first in more than five years. Guilt free; he truly was sick. Sick in his gut, sick in his head, but mostly, sick in his heart.

He listened to the preacher serving a heartfelt eulogy that gave Evangelique a personality, a life he never got to know. For that Vito was grateful. She was no longer the tortured shell lying in the morgue. She was real. She was human.

A regaled memory brought a smile to his face. A little girl, all of seven year's old, sneaks downstairs the morning of her eighth birthday to share her birthday cake with the neighbor's dogs. She had a generous nature.

A teenager, on the night of her junior prom, sat with a friend's brother who was terminally ill. The boy had a crush on her and she decided he deserved to be happy. She had a warm heart.

She ran, she jumped, she played. She laughed, she cried, she sang. She did everything a young girl growing into a woman should do. Until some maniac ripped it all away from her. For what? What possible motive could there be for stealing the life away from such a vibrant young woman?

Vito felt his heart shading to black. He tried several times to look at Carla Martens, but he felt guilty. Impotent. Unworthy of her attention.

The preacher finished his eulogy and made an announcement for a luncheon in the church basement, which Vito ignored and mingled amongst the flock. The tears flowed easily for most, but not for some. The detective was far too angry to cry.

"Detective Lorenz, thank you for coming," a harmonious voice sang from behind him.

For a brief second he ignored her. He didn't think he could face her.

"Detective Lorenz?"

"How are you, Miss Martens?" he asked, sporting an obviously forced smile.

"As well as could be expected, I guess. But I still think I am doing far better than you are."

He shrugged.

"Vito, there's no need for you to feel guilty." She reached out and took one of his hands in hers. Her warmth caressed his wounded soul.

"It's in my nature I guess."

"I want to thank you," she smiled.

"Thank me? For what?"

"For caring. It means a lot to me. It would have meant a lot to her. I take it attending funerals isn't something you do on a regular basis."

"No, but I felt it was the least I could do."

Carla Martens led Vito to a small bench away from the burial site. The bench was wrought iron, painted stark white, impeccably maintained. Ornate cherubs with solemn yet happy faces were there in an effort to remind those with wounded souls the world was never quite as bad as it seemed. Their pleasantries had no effect on Vito's hardened heart.

"Will you be open and honest with me?" she asked.

"As much as I possibly can."

"How close are you to finding the man." she took a deep breath and let it out slowly. "To finding the person who did this to my baby?"

Vito ran through the possible answers in his head.

"Please, Vito, the truth."

"I'm afraid to say, we're not very close at all."

She closed her eyes tightly and pointed her face to the sun. A thick bead of tears flowed from the corners of her face. Vito felt gut punched.

"I was afraid of that," she said without moving.

He couldn't talk. The tears were sitting on the back of his tongue with a bag full of screams. Screams that wouldn't stop if they ever got started.

"I'm going to do everything in my power to bring this bastard to justice."

"I don't want him brought to justice, detective, I want him dead. And for that I hate myself."

"Don't," Vito got to his feet. He handed her his card. "Please, if there's anything I can do for you, just call. Anytime."

"I will, Vito, and thank you."

"He tried to smile. "I have to get back, there' s a lot of work to be done."

She nodded and smiled.

On the way back to his car Vito came to the realization death would be much too good for the bastard who was doing this to these girls and their families. He prayed he wouldn't be left alone with the killer, not even for a second.

Chapter Three

Rita's tears had finally stopped flowing. It wasn't that she was no longer fearful or despondent enough to cry, she had simply run out of tears. She stared at the three red X's screaming at her from the face of her Plexiglas tomb and her analytical mind immediately processed nearly ten percent of her time had already been consumed by Father Time. It was as though she were living on a runaway train barreling down an endless track.

Her stomach swam with anxiety as she watched her captor load a redheaded woman onto a gurney and wheel her out of the room. That had been days ago, and the girl had yet to return, just like the cocoa skinned girl before her. And although she argued with her own logic, she knew she was next. But next for what?

There had been a time during her ordeal when Rita had lost all sense of time. She didn't know if each new day was part of a new week or a new month or even a new year, it was just time spent in suspended animation. She choked against the feeding tube's intrusion. Oddly enough, she was looking forward to the day's nutrition, if for no other reason than her captor still wanted her alive.

The pungent aroma of vitamins and iron filled her plastic sarcophagus. Her throat instinctively gulped at the insipid potage. Her eyes rolled back into the back of her head, not unlike a baby bird's as it widened its throat in anticipation of regurgitated earthworms. Rita squirmed against the uncomfortable feeling of her shrunken, tiny belly swelling against the thick, foreign substance being pumped into it.

The sedatives were beginning to wear off and Rita's mind came sharply back into focus. She no longer had that warm, comfortable aura the heavy doses of medication provided. Now, instead of her psyche being curled up beneath an electric blanket, it was thrust into the cold, snowy light of reality. Flecks of memories and experiences dashed at her like snowflakes at a windshield. And although her days were so much similar that they all felt like one enormous span of time, she could still somehow differentiate when the full circle of another day had come about. Her internal clock hadn't completely malfunctioned yet.

Suddenly, she felt a presence in the chamber with her. She could move her head no more than a fraction of an inch in any direction, so she strained her eyes down to where she detected the presence. Two white, shiny objects moved fluidly through the air in front of her stomach. Effortlessly they floated up towards her chest like thick anemone tendrils licking out at baitfish. Fingers. It was then she felt her skin being gently caressed. She wanted to lash out at the pervert. If it weren't bad enough locking her up in this torturous hell, he was going to get his jollies off by feeling her up as well.

Rita recoiled as her nipples were pinched and the skin of her breasts stretched. She could now see her once buxom breasts as they were being pulled away from her body. She felt an incapacitating sadness washing over her. Her once gorgeous, silicone free, body was succumbing to the effects of her hellish capture.

Just as abruptly as the hands had begun, they stopped their exploration of her sagging figure. Rita tasted the telltale medication seeping drop by drop into her IV. Within minutes her head was swimming with confused, drug-induced thought. Once again, her life dissolved back into the blackness of her nightmares.

*   *   *

"Anything from NCIC yet?" Vito asked a couple of detectives in the near desolate squad room as he tossed his coat over the back of his chair.

He received nothing but solemn looks of futility from the night shift detectives and knew there had been no monumental breaks in the case during his restless night.

"Damn, Lorenz, it's only four in the morning," Skip Pendelton commented as Vito's ass hit his chair.

Skip Pendleton was a detective assigned to the night squad mainly because no one could put up with his smart mouth for very long. It wasn't that Skip meant to be an asshole, things just seemed to work out that way. He had an unfortunately unique knack of saying just the wrong thing and at exactly the worst possible moment. Lieutenant Stoddard had transferred him to the night crew in a last-ditch effort to save his job. Skip's pension was a constant source of betting pool amusement amongst the troops.

The most recent faux pas had landed the detective in yet another vat of hot water. He had made some off-color comment about the mayor's butt-ugly wife one night while throwing back a few Jack Blacks and Budweiser's at the local blue-friendly watering hole. It was a damned shame the Captain didn't find the references quite as humorous as the rest of the off-duty officers. But then again, the mayor was married to the captain's sister.

"And you look just peachy," Linda Groves added.

"Funny, I feel like the pits," they all moaned at Vito's weak attempt at humor.

Groves smiled her patented man-killer and Vito felt measures better about life in an instant. Her sparkling blue eyes, petite shape and supermodel complexion were in complete contrast with her choice of careers. Although she would look completely in harmony with the world walking down the catwalk during a spring premier, her heart was miles away from that scene. Linda preferred the smell of gun oil and Luminol to that of expensive colognes and fine wines. Vito found her quite likable but was also quite aware of the fact she was just as dangerous as she was beautiful, so he kept his distance whenever possible. He was quite accustomed to the vicious bite beauty seemed to wear like a badge of honor.

Vito checked the fax machine to make sure it hadn't malfunctioned during the night and all the answers to this riddle were hanging out there in electronic limbo somewhere.

"It's working," Skip said.

"I know it is Skip, but a man has got to have his dreams."

"Yeah, well a man has to sleep in order to have dreams," Groves smiled and winked at Vito. He felt his heart melt like a pint of Hagen Dääs on a dashboard in August. He smiled back weakly and picked up a manila folder with the name Kendra Jenkins printed on it in big block lettering.

Vito fell into a melancholy mood as he read through the dead girl's file. Her entire lifetime had been reduced to a mere couple of pages. Granted, the coroner had yet to add his full input, so the file was incomplete, a fact that didn't cheer him up in the least. He knew poring over the meager information on the two dead girls wasn't going to get him any much further in the investigation. In fact, the case was doomed to stagnate if they couldn't find a connection between Kendra, Evangelique and now Rita. And although Rita Sorenson wasn't technically his concern yet, Vito's gut told him her file would join the others when the sands in the hourglass finally ran out on the ill-fated woman. Unless of course he could be her knight in shining armor and rush in at the last minute to save the day. At the present the only thing Vito felt he was capable of would be to screw things up even worse.

The fax machine came to life, startling Vito and jerking him free from his self-pitying reveries. He eagerly watched the leading edge of the paper as it appeared like magic from the maw of the printer. Slowly it inched its way out of the fax machine, forcing Vito to use every shred of his patience. He wanted to rip the piece of paper from the beast, but he already learned that valuable and embarrassing lesson earlier in his career. He had come to know fax machines were unforgiving beasts with a very warped sense of humor. He waited until the machine jolted to a clunking stop before reaching into the tray for the much sought after prize.

There was no great revelation held within the contents of the fax, only the name Rita Sorenson and the following cold, unfeeling information.

Rita Sorenson - Reported missing from Seattle Washington
February 03, 2015.
D.O.B. July 27, 1994
No known relation.
I.I.C. - Detective Mark Greenburg, Seattle Detective Squad

Vito looked up at the clock, it was still only five am, much too early to be calling the Seattle Police Department. He reread the fax cover and over again as if trying to commit every single drop of ink to memory, allowing it to be absorbed by his probing brain in hopes it would meld with everything else in there and spit out a definitive answer of its own with a resounding 'clunk'. Vito's eyes felt hollow. The kind of hollow that aches. The kind of hollow brought on by sleep deprivation. He had tossed and turned in his bed until three am when he finally relented and deemed sleep was impossible. On the bright side, he now knew there were twenty thousand, three hundred and twenty-two tiny holes in the acoustic ceiling above his bed. He pressed his fingers against his eyeballs to the point where he swore one more iota of pressure would cause the delicate orbs to explode. Still, they felt hollow. He felt hollow.

"Morning Karen," he broke the silence, peeling his fingers apart and glancing up to see his boss standing across his desk.

"How did you know it was me?"

"You forget, I learned from the best. Hercule Poirot, Sam Spade, Sherlock Holmes, and let's not forget, the honorable Charlie Chan," he said in his best smart-assed tone of voice. The fact of the matter was he had smelled her. The unmistakable scent of White Diamonds began to surround him dangerously. He felt something stir inside him. Something he hadn't felt in a long, long time and it scared the hell out of him.

"Please, Vito, no sarcasm this early, huh?"

"Sorry, boss."

"So, have you learned anything new?"

"The Sorenson girl was reported missing a year ago. It fits perfectly with the timeline the killer has given us so far."

"Here in L.A.?"

"No, here's the kicker, the Investigator in Charge is a Seattle detective."

"Seattle?"

"Yep, as in Washington. Rain. Skydome. Space needle. The works."

"I get your point."

"I'll call them as soon as dawn breaks."

"Okay, keep me posted, will you?" she asked, much more sweetly than Vito would have liked. He had heard that tone of voice more times than he cared to admit, and each time he ended up on the raw end of a screwing.

Vito nodded agreement with the lieutenant and watched her sashay down to her office. She was as supple and alluring as she had ever been. Her long blonde hair was pulled up tight, exposing the soft, milky skin of her neck. A small mole marked a spot on her neck that had once been his favorite target to kiss. He tried to concentrate on ugly things in order to control the emotions raging through him. Vito was grateful she was walking away from him and he couldn't see her sparkling, blue eyes and impish smile, they would have proved more than he could handle. He could feel a monster wave surging the coast and he was just too damn old to surf anymore. It wasn't riding the wave that scared him the most it was the crash-landing waiting for him at the end of every ride.

"Morning," Haskell greeted weakly, tossing a Krispy Kreme bag onto the desk and sat down across from his partner.

Vito just nodded an acknowledgment.

"Anything new?"

Vito wordlessly handed his partner the recent fax. It wasn't that he was trying to be rude, Vito just didn't know how to handle this latest torrent of emotions. He didn't like the feeling of helplessness this case was dumping upon him.

An eerie hush enveloped the squad room. The night shift detectives were off somewhere else doing what the nightshift detectives did and the day shift men had yet to begin their slow trickle into the precinct. Haskell and Lorenz studied what little evidence they had been able to gather in the case while Lieutenant Stoddard sat in her glass castle trying to come up with something edible for the press to chew on other than her ass.

"Hey, you went through that profiling course at Quantico, right?" Vito bolted upright in his chair and asked his partner.

"I didn't go through the complete program, but yes, I did take a course or two on profiling," Haskell replied while suppressing a yawn.

Vito fell silent again for several moments. Haskell waited for the next question, but when it was obviously not coming, he once again buried his thoughts into the case files.

"So, what impression do you get about this guy?"

"What guy?" Haskell asked, caught off guard by Lorenz's question.

"The killer."

"I think he's quite brutal."

"But is he crazy?"

"Aren't they all?" Haskell replied. He began again once he saw the perturbed look spreading across Vito's face. "In a manner of speaking, cleverly so."

"Meaning?"

"I mean, he's not just randomly picking these girls and killing them out of some uncontrollable bloodlust. There seems to be a definitive purpose to the killings. So far, we haven't found any semen, nor have there be any signs of penetration or mutilation of a sexual nature. I have to think this individual is not doing this merely to get his rocks off. He's not your garden-variety, sexually motivated serial killer. There's something in this person goes much deeper than that," Haskell theorized.

"Like anger? These girls have angered him in some way? Maybe rejected him at some point?"

"That's possible, but unlikely. No, I see these as more vengeful killings. This is not a perp who lost control during the heat of the moment, rather, I feel he killed them when he wanted to because that's when he wanted them to die. Part of some grand design."

"Which should mean they are all linked in some way or another?"

"One would be able to comfortably draw that conclusion, yes."

"So, his killing of these two girls was more than likely directly motivated by his hatred of them specifically? And he must have hated each one of them equally, but for separate reasons?" Vito was not really asking Haskell for his opinion or his answers, rather than he was using the man as a sounding board.

"That's the conclusion I would draw right now if I were forced to. Also, there must be a reason for this timeline. There is a direct correlation between when he kills his victims and why."

"But that would mean there has got to be a common thread. In Jenkins and Martens we have that thread. But what the hell does Rita Sorenson have to do with all of this?" Vito slammed the file folder shut and rubbed his eyes.

"You could probably call Seattle now," Haskell suggested gingerly.

"I sent a fax back to Seattle asking Detective Greenburg to call me as soon as he got in. I plan to call him if I don't hear anything by seven. I figured I'd at least give the man a chance to feel the sun on his ass before I started in on him," Vito smiled back weakly.

"So, do you guys have a history or something?" Haskell nodded toward the crystal palace. Stoddard's office was a glass encased cubicle situated in the center of the squad room.

Three of the walls were entirely made of glass, the fourth, the one facing a row of windows looking out on the outside world was framed drywall. The only picture in the cubicle was one of Karen and her husband George at the Great Pyramid in Egypt. She had droned on and on for weeks about how wonderful that trip was. That seed planted an image so vivid that now Vito always associated at her with the evil Queen Cleopatra with scepter in hand lording over her subjects.

"What makes you say that?" Vito replied defensively.

"It's in the way you look at each other. It's in your eyes."

"They teach you that in profiling school too?" He snapped and reopened the file folder. He ignored Haskell and began reading again just to keep from thinking about the sore subject.

Haskell chuckled and said, "No, I learned that one on my own. Besides, you guys are pretty obvious about it."

"Is that so?" Vito huffed and refused to look up at the man who was so rudely interrogating him about his personal life.

"I'm sorry, I guess it's none of my business."

"Damned skippy it ain't."

They fell into another lull of silence. Haskell might have pressed the issue a little more, but the squad room was starting to fill up and he decided it best if he respected his partner's privacy. They both looked up at the sound of Karen Stoddard rapping her knuckles against the glass wall of her office. She held her hand up with her thumb cocked to her ear and her pinky against her lips indicating there was a phone call for them.

Vito picked up the phone, pressed a blinking amber button on the face of his phone and barked, "Lorenz."

"Detective Vito Lorenz?" the caller asked.

"Yeah, this is Lorenz."

"Good morning. This is Detective Greenburg out of Seattle. I just received your fax."

"Great. Thanks for getting back with me so quickly."

"What can I do for you detective?"

"What can you tell me about this missing person case of yours involving a Rita Sorenson?"

"Not a whole lot really, but I'll give you what I have."

"I'd appreciate it."

"On February third of last year we took a missing persons report for a Rita Sorenson, date of birth, July, 1994. Blonde hair, blue eyes, medium height. Very attractive. As far as I have been able to tell she has no known relations."

"Who reported her missing?"

"Her agent."

"She's an actress?" Vito asked hopefully. A hundred questions were spinning through his head and he had to force himself to slow down and think about the answers more clearly.

"No, she's a model. When she didn't show up for a shoot on the first of February, her agent got worried about her and called us. We told the agent, Marcus Milbourne, that since Miss Sorenson was of legal age we could not, according to policy, file a missing person's report until she had been missing for at least forty-eight hours," he reported coldly. Vito couldn't help but wonder if he was talking with a robot.

"So, did this Agent Milbourne called back later?" Vito prodded.

"Yes. Miss Sorenson had yet to show up or return any phone calls. We checked out her apartment and found it empty, but lived in. Her clothes were still in the closets. There was food in the refrigerator, some of it outdated, but most was still fairly fresh. Oh, and there was a cat, a very hungry cat."

"Doesn't sound like she had planned on taking a trip."

"Exactly. I have to admit, at first, I thought this was just another case of some prima donna stressing out and disappearing for a while on her own accord. However, once I saw her apartment, the bells and whistles started going off in my head, so I dug a little deeper."

"Find anything interesting?"

"Nothing in particular. She went to work on the twenty-eighth and was fitted for all the outfits she was going to wear during the shoot on the first. The wardrobe girl was the last person to see her. She said she remembered Miss Sorenson being in pretty good spirits and had planned on stopping at the video store before going home to feed her cat and curl up into bed. Might I ask why this case is of interest to the LAPD?"

"We've had two girls show up at a local area hospital after being missing for a year. Both girls died as a result of wounds received during their captivity. The first girl had a message for us carved into her skin."

"My god," he gasped.

"It gets worse. The message was a warning that we only had thirty days to save the second girl."

"And I take it you ran out of time."

"Regretfully yes. But this is where your missing person comes into play. The Sorenson girl's name was burned into our second girl's abdomen with a warning her clock was ticking as well. When I fed Miss Sorenson's name into NCIC, your name and contact information popped up."

"I see. My missing person's report is likely to turn into your homicide in less than a month?"

"The way things are going, I would assume so."

"How can I help?"

"I'm not sure if you can. We feel there must be a connection between these three girls. The two girls had been friends, actresses, working on the same film together. We had been working that thread of connectivity until Miss Sorenson was thrown into the mix. Her name wasn't on the list of people involved with the film we obtained from the production company so we dead-ended on that angle. I was hoping it was just an oversight on their part, but I guess that's not the case."

"Probably not. I didn't find any connections between Rita Sorenson and Los Angeles."

"What about her parents?"

"They were Danish. Both were killed in an auto accident in Denmark when Rita was very young. Her aunt brought her to the United States when she was four."

"Where's the aunt now?"

"She died one month after Miss Sorenson disappeared."

"No other family?"

"None I could uncover," Detective Greenburg replied.

"Damn. What about any friends?"

"Not too many. She kept to herself."

"No boyfriend?"

"Again, none that I could dig up. I wish I could be of more help."

"Yeah, me too."

"So, do you think this is a serial killer?"

"For lack of a better term, yes. But I don't think these are random killings. They seem to be too personal for that. But, maybe I'm wrong."

"I'll send you a copy of all of my notes and case files on Miss Sorenson as soon as I can get them photocopied."

"I'd appreciate that," Vito responded.

"I'll reopen the investigation on this end as well. Maybe I overlooked something the first time."

"I'll send you what information I have on Kendra Jenkins and Evangelique Martens, the two girls we have here," Vito said, feeling slightly better about the positive turn in the case, but only slightly.

"Sounds good. I'll see if there is a connection or any record either of them ever visited Seattle."

"Thank you for your time, Detective Greenburg."

"No trouble at all."

"I'll keep in touch," Vito hung up the phone and headed for the lieutenant's office with Haskell in tow.

"Well?" She met them at her door.

Vito lowered his head and shook it slowly from side to side.

"Damn. Is there anything I should know?"

"Nothing special. The investigator in Seattle is going to reopen the case and hopefully he can help us to come up with a connection between these girls."

"How long do we have?" she asked, glancing back into her office at the calendar hanging on her wall.

"Less than two weeks," Haskell said grimly.

"That's not much. What do you have planned next?" Karen Stoddard asked.

"I think we should go back to the production company and see what Rita Sorenson's name digs up. Maybe someone working on the set will remember her. The problem is since they have been done with shooting the film for better than six months, most of the actors are working on other projects and are most likely to be scattered all around the world."

"The best you can do right now is to talk to the people who work at the studio year-round. Anything I should withhold from the press?"

"Yeah, everything," Vito mouthed facetiously.

"I wish it were that easy, Lorenz, but I have to feed the sharks something."

"Can you keep the tag 'serial killer' out of this thing?"

"I'll try, but you know the press."

"Yeah, I know them. I wish they would end up on our tote board occasionally, maybe then they would be a little more sympathetic."

"You don't really believe that do you?"

"No."

"Listen, right now the heat isn't turned up too high. We only have two bodies and that's still a far cry from a serial killer's rampage. Now, if the Sorenson girl turns up mutilated like the others with another warning then the shit is going to hit the fan. And you know what they say about shit."

"Yeah, I know, it rolls downhill."

"I know this has nothing to do with you two or your abilities as detectives, but the brass, the politicians and the press are going to go headhunting if this thing plays out the way I think it is going to. Try not to give them an easy target. Cover your asses," Karen advised, stepping back into her office to answer the ringing phone.

"Point taken," Vito said, turning away from the lieutenant's office and swallowing hard to force the bile back down into the boiling pit of his stomach.

"We caught a shitty one, didn't we?" Haskell asked.

"This case is a career breaker, a real career breaker. You want out? I'm sure I could put in a word with the LT."

"No, I'm afraid I'm in this one for the long haul."

"It's your neck, you can stick it out if you want to," he shrugged. "Let's go back down to Hollywood and bump elbows with the rich and famous. Maybe they'll be a little more accommodating this time."

The day was bleak and ugly outside. Bruised storm clouds hung over the mountains threatening to wreak havoc at a moment's notice. Distant thunder rumbled in the valley, causing both men to look towards the sky. They both knew a cold, hard rain was coming, and soon. Vito didn't mind much; it couldn't be any worse than the storm brewing inside him. Paradise had just become a living hell. He pulled away from the curb even before Haskell had a chance to close his door.

One would have thought they were driving through some Midwestern city during the worst bite of winter the way the pedestrians were bundled up against the encroaching weather. Fan palms along the street bowed in reverence to the onslaught of the wind. Broken fronds littered the gutters giving the city the appearance of Miami during hurricane season.

"It's a bad one," Haskell said, craning his head so he could look out the windshield glass and up into the sullen storm clouds.

"It's good to wash the filth away once in a while."

"Too bad it never quite gets all of it, huh?"

"You got that right."

All at once the clouds let loose and a torrential rain began falling in an angular sweeping pattern across the blacktop. It felt as if they were driving through an endless car wash. Haskell's anxiety level rose as Vito drove through the streets without turning on his wipers. The sheets of rain blanketed the windshield, obscuring their view and bringing the visibility down the nil.

"Kind of nice, isn't it?" Lorenz asked.

"What is?"

"Driving in a storm like this. It's peaceful."

"I don't quite see it that way."

"It's like we're the only two people left on earth. It's the ultimate solitude."

"Until we crash into something or someone."

"How can we crash into anyone if we're the last ones left?"

"But we're not the last ones left."

"Prove it. Do you see anyone else?"

"Not if you don't turn the damned wipers on."

"Sometimes it's better not to see where you are going."

"Are you trying to get philosophical with me?"

"Not at all. Just trying to point out the fact that sometimes our instincts are better to follow than what is in plain view," he said, easing the car to the curb.

"Are you trying to make a point?"

"Sometimes book smarts and formal education are great things, but other times simple common sense, gut instinct and street logic make all the difference in detective work."

"Listen here, Lorenz, I know you think of me as some kind of green rookie, but I've done my time on the street. I've seen my share of crime scenes while dressed in blue and I've paid my dues. I'm a damned good detective whether you think so or not."

"Are you going to get out?" he asked, reaching for his door handle.

"What? Why?"

"Because we're here Sherlock," he laughed and stepped out of the car into the driving rain. He ran for the shelter of the building's awning as best as his abused body would allow him to.

"Asshole," Haskell said as he splashed passed him and ducked under the awning out of the driving rain.

"You've just got too short of a chain."

"And you're just too big of an asshole."

"Yeah, well that's what my mother says too," he said, opening the door and allowing his partner walk into the lobby in front of him.

*   *   *

Rita smelled the gruel long before she tasted the repugnant slop. Her mind swam through her daily rituals of feeding, extricating and bathing. Nineteen X's were screaming at her from the facing of her Plexiglas prison. Nineteen days. Nineteen times the pervert had come into the room and fondled her breasts. Nineteen times she had screamed at him without any result. And yet, as bad as the nineteen visits had been, she would endure them forever if it meant there were more than a mere twelve visits left.

She began to cry. If her calculations were correct, she only had twelve more days of life. She prayed through her tears. She wondered if her parents were helplessly looking down on her from heaven. What about her Aunt Maren? Was anyone concerned with her predicament? And what about the living? Were the police even looking for her, or had her life been written off a long time ago?

The lighting in the room changed and Rita was able to see even more of her surroundings. She could see the fractal images of other plastic chambers in the room with her. Several more than she had first imagined. She could see the two empty chambers which stood caddy corner from her and soon realized the room was full of chambers, arranged in a circular pattern, a circle of friends sharing a tragic friendship.

Pinch after pinch, grope after grope only served to incense her, not arouse her as her captor surely must be hoping for. Rita couldn't see the man's eyes. However, she could still imagine his lustful stare as he fondled her breasts. The cretin had lobster claws for hands and no clue as to how to treat a woman tenderly. She visualized this beast as Quasimodo without all the sympathetic endearing qualities the storybook monster possessed, merely his brutishness and repugnance. Assuredly while standing in a pool of his drool this creature manhandled her breasts for no more than fifteen minutes, a lifetime to Rita, and then withdrew his hands from her body. She chortled to herself, he was a quick draw artist as well. He was nothing more than a pathetic, sickening beast.

She could see the shroud of his figure drifting around the room. She attempted to raise her arm to shield her eyes from the harsh fluorescent overhead lights, but she was too weak and sore to move. She forced her eyes to strain down her body until she could see the crook of her arm. She gasped at the sight of her arm. It was purple and shiny like a freshly licked grape flavored sucker, but the edges were faded into an ugly yellowish color. It was a color that reminded her of mustard drying on a paper plate. She worked the muscles over and over trying to get her arm to work. She desperately wanted to bang on the face of her Plexiglas tomb to get her captor's attention. She wanted him to know what she thought of him. That he was a chicken shit coward and a waste of human life. Rita watched the figure glide out of the room and darkness fell about her once more.

She screamed inside of her chamber until she was hoarse. Too hoarse to even cry out in pain. The mysterious figure had entertained her long enough to feed, bathe, humiliate, and inform her that her life had dwindled by yet another twenty-four hours. All without one, single, solitary word.

*   *   *

"It's been a long week, do you want to swing by Gus's and get a couple of drinks?" Vito asked.

"I'd love to, but I promised someone a little bit of my time this afternoon. If you could just drop me off at my car, I'd appreciate it," Haskell replied.

"Ooh, a girlfriend I don't know anything about," his voice was alarmingly juvenile as was the sharp jab to Gregg's ribs.

"And you never will if I have my say. She already thinks I'm a shithead, if she discovers the kind of company, I am keeping she'll definitely believe that," he laughed.

"Fair enough."

"Sorry to disappoint you, Vito, no girlfriend so there won't be any juicy stories in the morning. Evy has a game tonight."

"How is the team doing?"

"Still undefeated."

"Great! Hope she's not letting it go to her head."

"Oh no, of course not, remember she learned everything about humility from you," Gregg sighed.

Vito laughed, "Hard to live with huh?"

"Sometimes impossible."

Vito dropped his partner off at the precinct and made his way the few short blocks to Gus's place. The bar was actually named The Shield, but the name had never quite caught on as everyone just called it Gus's. Vito was blinded by the darkness of the place as he stepped in off the street. A thick blanket of cigarette smog hung head high across the entire place. It made him remember why he had given up the nasty habit. The closer he got to the bar the more his nose was assaulted by the astringent odor of stale beer and bourbon, compelling him to remember why he had given up yet another of his nasty habits.

He made his way past several fat-assed retired cops telling bullshit stories they had relived more times than they had changed their underwear, with a different version emerging with every retelling. Customary "Charlie's", "Milt's", and "Bob's" were accompanied by head nods to those he didn't know but would defend to the death just the same. They weren't much to look at, but they were family, his family. Vito made his way to the back booth where he had sat almost every night for the past twenty years.

"Christ Vito, don't you ever give it a rest?" Gus, the bar owner asked, eyeing the file folders under Vito's arm while bending over to wipe a day's worth of greasy crud off the table. He flicked the stained bar rag over his shoulder and stared down at Vito with nothing but concern in his gray, tired eyes.

"It's a bad one, Gus," he replied, glancing at the files he had set on the table after Gus had cleaned it off for him.

"The usual?"

"Yeah, and how about a bowl of your chili too."

"Only if you promise to leave within the hour," Gus smiled.

"Don't worry Gus, pipes are clean," Vito said, patting his protruding belly.

"That's what I'm worried about. Don't need you cleaning them in here."

They both laughed. Vito watched Gus disappear through the haze before flipping open one of the folders. He read through the notes he had taken during his second interview of Oslo Rademacher. Clinking glasses and kissing pool balls echoed in his brain while he studied the case file. The voices of dozens of conversations melded into one comforting sound. Some may have found the cacophony quite unnerving and distracting, but to Vito it was soothing, it was home. It made him feel like he was someplace where he was unconditionally welcome, even if the chili got the better of him.

Vito's nose twitched from the onslaught of odors drifting about the room. The distinct smells of stale cigarettes and spilled Jack Daniels teased his will power, beckoning him toward the blackness of his recently tamed vices. And then came the unmistakable, out of place smell of White Diamonds, another wisely discarded vice.

"What are you doing here?" he asked bitterly as he looked up to see Karen Stoddard invading the realm of his sanctuary.

"Well, it's good to see you too," she huffed, cleared a place and sat down in the booth across from him.

Vito was about to lash out when Gus came walking up with his order.

"Would the lady like something to drink?" he asked, looking at Vito instead of his guest. Gus set a steaming bowl of chili down in front of Vito followed by a tall glass of chocolate milk. Once his hands were free he reached into the front pouch of his apron and withdrew several packages of cellophane wrapped saltines and set them in front of his customer.

"No, she was just leaving. And aren't you forgetting something?" Vito asked.

"Like hell I am. I'll have a Grand Marnier, warmed, in a snifter if you have one," she smiled warmly at Gus who was busy digging in the front of his apron and had no intention of returning her smile.

"Here you go," he said, placing a small plastic container of jalapeno pepper rings next to Vito's bowl of chili. He looked to Vito for confirmation on Karen's drink order.

Vito blinked his approval and sighed.

"I don't think I have a snifter ma'am, not much call for one in a place like this. Mostly just beer and shots of bourbon get served in this joint," he said, reaching across in front of Karen with a wet bar towel and wiping the table. She noticed his solid forearm that decried the now dumpy man had once been someone to contend with. A tattoo of a black panther seemed to stalk up his arm toward his shoulder. However, it had been on his arm so long it now more closely resembled an obscure Rorschach test image than a lithe jungle cat.

Karen smiled up at the man and said. "Whatever clean glass you have will be fine. Thank you."

Gus nodded his head covered in multi-shaded gray hair and gracefully bowed away from the table.

"He's kind of a strange looking man, isn't he?"

"Gus? I wouldn't care if he looked like a squirming maggot, I'd respect him just the same. The man took bullets for three different partners, one of them being me. The last time he was shot finally did him in and forced him to retire and I've felt guilty ever since. You just don't get it," Vito fumed.

"I didn't mean any disrespect by the comment," Karen recoiled from Vito's biting comments. "And just what is it I don't get?" Her voice raised a notch to match her rising anger.

"You don't understand what it is to be a cop. You've been behind a desk from damned near the very second you put on the blues."

"Hey, I can't help that. I tried to get out into the field but my father made damned sure I'd never see the streets."

"Your father was a good cop and a good man. More importantly, he was a good father. He did right by keeping you off the streets and safe. Los Angeles ain't no place to be a cop, especially if you're a female. And don't call me chauvinistic, it's just a fact. But you could have made the effort to get to know the troops, mingle, and get interested in their lives. Treat them like something more than liabilities or photo ops. These guys are not just folders in your filing cabinet," he said, sweeping his eyes around the room to indicate all of the cops in the place.

"I do care about these guys, and I do get interested," she defended.

"Sure you do, but only when they are in trouble or up for a commendation."

"That's not true."

"Isn't it? Who is that guy, right there?" he asked, pointing to a blonde haired young man in his early twenties.

"I can't say I recognize him."

"Of course you don't, because you don't take the time. That's Pete McCloud, his wife has been diagnosed with terminal brain cancer. The kid is going through a rough time but he's too damned proud to ask for help."

"How the hell am I supposed to know things like that? He talks to you guys. A kid like that won't come to me with his problems. You're not being very fair, Vito," she said, her voice betraying her attempt not to appear angry.

"He didn't come to me either, Karen. I overheard him talking on his phone in the break room."

"So, you want me to eavesdrop on the men's private lives, is that what you're saying?" her face took on a hard, combative edge.

"When it is warranted, yes. McCloud had been bouncing around the precinct like a puppy with a new toy for the past year and a half. Every day all I heard was the young man bragging up his beautiful wife to the other guys in the squad room. Then unexpectedly he started coming to work with tear stained eyes and seemed a million miles away. And he never talked about his wife. I thought the poor kid was having some marital problems and quite frankly I was concerned not only for his safety but the officers around him as well. So yes, I eavesdropped on his conversation. I took his case to the squad chaplain and let him approach the kid about the problem," Vito explained.

"How is she?" Karen asked. Vito sensed her concern was genuine and that she was thawing out up just a little.

"Day to day she's fine, but the prognosis is still the same. Worst of it is the doctors have told him she could be fine one minute and dead the next. The poor guy is living his life under a shadow of doubt and fear."

"That's terrible."

"Yes, it is. And there are dozens of McCloud's in the department, under your direct supervision and you don't seem to know it. At least not until they finally snap and take it out on a perp, or worse and then they're in front of you and the IAB review board for discipline."

"I am sorry if I don't seem sympathetic enough for you, but I just wasn't brought up that way."

"Yes, you were, and that's the sad part of it."

"Well, damn it, Vito, I didn't choose to be a supervisor. My career path was chosen for me and you damned well know it."

"You're right. It was, and I do know that. But that doesn't mean you can hide behind that excuse. If you don't like your career, choose a different one. The men need you to be something more than just a shit screen, Karen, they need your attention."

"What can I do?" she asked, blinking the tears away from her eyes.

"Come on, let's get out of here," he said, tossing a twenty onto the table and chugging down the last of his chocolate milk.

Karen finished her drink and followed him out the door. The grayness of the day had passed into the thick blackness of night. Out on the street the two of them stood next to Karen's car and continued their conversation. A light drizzle had begun to mist the night air and the temperature was dropping like a rock. Karen pulled her coat tighter around her and folded her arms across her chest.

There was a long silence between them allowing the sounds of the night to invade Vito's thoughts. Muffled laughter and conversation from the bar mingled with the melody of a distant Christmas carol echoing from some electronic source. The coldness of his empty house last Christmas Eve was still fresh in his memory. Cold pizza and warm chocolate milk for dinner, trying to pretend it was just another day. Loneliness began chewing at his soul like a Rottweiler on a rawhide bone. He hoped she didn't recognize the pain in his eyes.

"Can you help me?" she asked, breaking the agonizing silence.

"Help you what?"

"Teach me how to be more understanding and open with the men."

"I don't think that's anything I can teach you," Vito replied.

"You don't even want to try?" she asked, sliding teasingly close to him.

Vito fought against her allure. He tried to ignore her enticing scent and warmth as it radiated from her body. "Karen, you know we can't do this. Not anymore."

"Why not?"

"Because you're married, damn it!"

"I was married before."

"But he was just a jerk then."

"And now he's a jerk with political influence. Does that scare you?"

"You are damned right it does. Besides, I never felt right about you being married anyway."

"You know damned good and well it's only a marriage of convenience."

"But it is still a marriage."

She put her arms around his waist and moved in closer. "Vito, I've missed you," she said, nuzzling his ear.

"Karen, we can't do this. Damn it, don't you care we're right out in the open for everyone to see? How many drinks have you had tonight?"

"Not enough. And no, I don't give a damn who sees us. That rat bastard is probably fucking some little teenage whore right now. He's already taken her out for some fine, expensive dinner and dancing, parading her around like some prize trophy. And he sure the hell doesn't give a damn who sees him," her anger had turned to tears.

"Karen, keep it down before you draw too much more attention to us," Vito pushed her away from him.

"Look who the fuck is being cold and uncaring. When did you become so damned self-righteous?" She glared back at him with anger and frustration in her eyes.

"I'm not being self-righteous, Karen. We both know what happened between us was a mistake. It was a mistake then and it would be an even bigger mistake now."

"A mistake? No, a mistake is something that happens once, not continually for six months Vito."

"You're being unreasonable."

"I loved you, Vito. I think I still do," she said, no longer able to hold back her tears.

"I'm sorry, Karen. Let's go somewhere and talk about this."

"Do you have anything to drink at your place?"

"No, but we can stop and get something," he reluctantly relented.

"Okay. I'll follow you," she said, walking around the car and unlocking the driver side door. She closed the door and fired up the engine without unlocking the passenger door, a direct cue for Vito to go and get his car.

A heavier rain began to fall, and Vito switched on his wipers. He glanced between the road in front of him and the headlights bearing down on him from behind. He was hoping the next time he glanced into his rearview mirror Karen would be gone, having changed her mind. However, her lights never faded, in fact, she had closed the gap between them considerably after he drove away from the liquor store with a bottle of brandy.

Vito and his unwelcome shadow wound their way through the quiet streets of West Covina until finally pulling into the driveway of a modest two-bedroom ranch. The lawn was overgrown and long overdue for grooming. Even in the dark of night, brown spots of dead grass screamed out their thirst. A lone nectarine tree sagged in the front yard. A motion detector sensed their presence and turned on the porch and walkway lights for them. Karen noticed more than half of the lights lining the driveway and short walkway were either broken or burned out.

Vito opened the door and they stepped wordlessly inside. There was no tail-wagging pet to greet Vito at the door, only the long, lingering smell to remind him of the past.

"Vito, you can have your carpets cleaned and that smell will eventually go away," Karen suggested as she stepped across the threshold and was slapped in the face by the odor of Vito's bachelorhood.

"I kind of like it."

"It's not healthy hanging onto the past."

"Listen, if you're in the mood to lecture me you can leave right now."

"No, I'm sorry, I was out of line."

"They didn't have any of that Grand Marnier shit you like so I got you some Christian Brothers," he said, setting a brown paper sack on the counter. He pulled the bottle out, cracked the top and poured about two fingers worth of brandy into a McDonald's glass with the Hamburglar acting out a different mischievous act on each of the sides. He took a pack of Marlboro's out of the sack and tossed them into the trash without opening them. The urge to abuse his body had passed, knowing Karen would be all the abuse his body could handle for one night.

"That's fine," she said, dusting off a place on the couch and sitting down. The couch was the type that folds out into a bed, however, a severe list on the left side warned if it were ever pulled out it would never fold back away again. The arms were a ratty and torn multi-colored striped fabric that felt like rough burlap. Undoubtedly the rest of the couch was in as bad shape as the arms, a fact Vito tried to mask by covering the decrepit piece of furniture with an L.A. Lakers throw blanket. However, the blanket was just as old and ratty as the furniture so his efforts were all for naught.

"Sorry, it's the maid's year off," he said coolly as he handed the plastic glass to her.

"Year? That's all," she laughed.

Karen glanced around the room. Nothing had changed in all the years she had known Vito. The same poster of Magic Johnson being guarded by Larry Bird hung tilted, in the same place it always had. The contrasting outline of dirt and smoke stains against semi-clean paint decried the fact the poster had shifted ever so slightly quite recently. Karen thought back and remembered there had been a small earthquake a few months ago. It hadn't been very strong, but it had taken her a good couple of days to straighten out the knickknacks and paintings in her house. She chuckled to herself, certain the only reason Vito hadn't righted things was that he was waiting for the next quake to come along and put things back where they belonged.

"Wanna watch TV?"

"Not particularly."

The room fell into the kind of silence that seeped into Vito's soul. The walls were screaming at him to say something. To show some kind of life. He desperately wanted Karen to finish her drink and leave, but then, he also wanted her to finish her drink, take off her clothes and stay.

Karen seductively crossed her legs and licked the rim of her glass as she sipped the nectar from within. Her eyes sparkled in anticipation of the proclivities to come. She never broke eye contact with him as she unpinned her hair and let it spill around her shoulders in long golden rays of sunshine, a move she knew from past experiences would send his hormones raging into overdrive. She got up from the couch, walked over to where Vito was sitting and reached down to take his hand. Weakly he stood up and faced her, his body shaking with apprehension. He still loved her deeply. Always had, and probably always would.

Her enticing aroma lured him into the crook of her neck. Karen moaned lightly and eased her head to the side as his lips met the softness of her skin. His hot breath tickled her earlobe and she secretly hoped he would suck it into his mouth. She slowly worked her hands up his body to his chest where she dug her fingernails firmly into his flesh. A guttural moan escaped his lips and he grabbed her face in both of his hands and kissed her deeply for several minutes before allowing her to lead him back to his bedroom.

Vito stood in the doorway of his bedroom, lost in the surreal aura of the moment. On one hand, he knew this was so wrong and wanted nothing to do with her. Yet on the other, feelings were stirring inside him he hadn't felt in many years. Karen made eye contact with him before slowly moving her hands to the front of her blouse. One by one she unfastened the buttons until her shirt fell open, exposing the lacy, black bra underneath. Her nipples were visibly hard through the sheer fabric and it was more than Vito could endure. Any and all reservations he had about their tryst disappeared from his mind without so much as another thought.

Karen smiled, recognizing his lustful stare she reached out, grabbed his hand and pulled him down onto the bed with her. Vito buried his nose in her hair and breathed in deeply. White Diamonds enveloped him and his transformation into a lusting animal was complete. Several deep passionate kisses later and the idea of making love to her was replaced by raw, passionate sex.

The morning sun was as hazy, gray and awkward as the air in Vito's bedroom. Wordlessly he and Karen showered in turn, with her going first. By the time he finished with his shower, she was gone. A short note sat for him on the kitchen table. He read it over while sipping his morning coffee.

You were wonderful as always. See you at the office. And in case you're wondering, George won't be back from Sacramento until Monday. She signed the note with X's, O's and a smiley face. He threw the note in a kitchen drawer with the rest of them. For some sick reason he just couldn't bring himself to throw any of them away.

The week that followed was nothing short of a roller coaster ride for Vito. Cold days at the office coupled with searing hot nights at home. Feelings he had long since buried were starting to resurface, and that scared him. Scared the living hell right out of him in fact. His feelings about Karen Stoddard scared him almost as badly as his feelings for Rita Sorenson. Day after day he and Haskell had run themselves ragged trying to find a break in the case. And night after night they went home with a hollow empty feeling eating away at their souls. Vito had Karen to try and ease his guilt, even though it only replaced it with something much more ominous. He hoped Evy was keeping Haskell busy enough that he was able to forget about his impotence at work.

Vito had been out driving and thinking late in the afternoon. The sun was blazing even though the air was still chilly, or at least what they called chilly in southern California. Tired and weary he rounded the corner and his heart sank. Karen's car was in his driveway.

"How did you get in?" he asked, stepping through the door and throwing his keys onto the kitchen table.

"With my key."

"You still have a key?"

"You never asked for it back."

"Fair enough. Isn't George going to miss you?"

"Nope, not tonight. He's taking his trophy piece somewhere tonight."

George Masarick was Karen's husband. She had been his trophy piece, someone to look good on his arm, until the tarnish of years robbed her of her fresh, young appearance. Karen had realized she wasn't in love with her husband almost immediately into their marriage. Although she had been infatuated with his good looks and uncompromising drive to succeed at first, that infatuation quickly waned when those same attributes proved to occupy most of his time. The more Masarick succeeded, the more he pushed her into the background. This forced her to pursue her political aspirations as a substitute for her husband's companionship. Between the two of them they couldn't find a spare moment to share together, or so George continually used that as an excuse.

"I'm sorry to hear that."

"No you're not," she smiled and finally turned to face him. She was wearing one of his old patrolman shirts and had left most of the buttons unbuttoned. Her breasts teased and peeked at him from the polyester uniform. He soon felt his arousal taking control of his rational thought.

They had fallen back into a comfort zone they had felt during their brief, tumultuous affair two years earlier. Vito began to like having her around and she enjoyed being around. He smiled as she enticingly unbuttoned the remaining buttons on his uniform shirt and allowed the fabric to fall away from her body. Vito stepped into her, sliding his arm under the shirt and around her waist. Her warm, soft skin felt good to his touch. He kissed her neck softly and became intoxicated by her aroma. They cleared the kitchen table with their bodies and made passionate love to one another while the kitchen filled with smells of charring meat.

They finished their session and sat down to an oddly satisfying meal of burned meat loaf and scorched potatoes. Retiring to the living room they sat, still disheveled, and watched the evening news followed by some very unrealistic cops shows. Vito sat on the couch torn between guilt and lust. His thoughts had turned to Rita Sorenson. Her time was rapidly running out and he had failed her miserably. And between each thought of young Rita, White Diamonds coupled with female lust teased his senses. He grabbed Karen by the hand and led her back to his bedroom. He needed something to ease the pain he feared the morning would bring. The pain of an empty pillow, because Karen would eventually slip out sometime during the night. And the pain of knowing it was Rita Sorenson's last day.

*   *   *

Rita's morning began as it had every morning for what seemed an eternity. She was in the midst of having herself blown dry when her mysterious abductor floated into the room through the shadows. The entity paused in front of the Plexiglas tomb for several minutes before skirting across the room to busy itself with some unseen task.

Rita's stomach exploded with a flurry of nervous spasms. The last open box remained unchecked, but for how long? Was this the last day? She couldn't determine whether or not twenty-four hours had elapsed since the last X screamed ominously back at her. She recalled the last thirty days, or what she had perceived as the last month. Daily the dark figure would appear in front of her and daily the maniac would squeeze and fondle her breasts. And while the assault was disturbing to her, she was still relieved her captor was seemingly sated by this perverse activity. He had yet to break open her tomb and fondle her in any other way. She shuddered at the thought of this person forcing himself upon her. Forcing his hot, fetid breath into her lungs until she suffocated. She felt a sharp pinch in her left arm and strained to turn her head to the side. All she could see were snakelike tubes being dragged across the floor leaving a trail of her bodily fluids behind them. She could feel a trickle running down her arm around her elbow. The rivulet formed an epicenter of a droplet that grew in size until it was too heavy to fight the forces of gravity and it ripped loosed from her elbow and splashed onto the floor. The chamber seemed to echo with the sounds of the droplets slapping the tile floor. She could feel the residual splashes of cooling fluids against her shins.

Rita pumped her fists open and closed in hopes of chasing away the tingling feeling in her arms. Her shoulders ached and burned from the effects of atrophy, as did her knees and calves. The realization of her body's deterioration was bringing on the darkness of melancholia once more. Images of her almost forgotten life flashed through her battered mind and tears began to flow down her cheeks. Rita was entertaining a happy memory when movement across the room jerked her out of her reverie.

The ghostlike figure moved ominously closer to Rita's chamber. She heard several loud clicks and felt the vacuum of her chamber escaping as her captor opened the case. The lighting in the room cast flickering rays of light upon the secretive figure allowing Rita to make out some of the person's features. She almost breathed a sigh of relief when she realized this phantom was actually a person, a living, breathing entity and not some storybook monster. Not some specter who could drift in and out of her life on a mist of misery. She might be able to reason with a human being. Maybe she could even reconcile with them for whatever she may have done to deserve such punishment.

Her captor wheeled Rita's gurney out of her Plexiglas chamber, down a long dimly lit corridor and into a small, dark room. Goosebumps erupted on her skin under the assault of a cold breeze. She could smell the fresh air of the outside world and her heart began to race with anticipation. Maybe she was being set free. Maybe soon she would be back with the people she loved, and those who loved her. Although the winter air was cold, biting, it was exhilarating compared to the dead air that surrounded her for what seemed an endless tide of time. Rita began to relax. She felt as if her ordeal may be coming to a close. She had been punished long enough. She would be a good girl from now on, she promised.

And then the brutality of her horrific reality came crashing down around her. Suddenly the room was aglow with blinding light and Rita found herself staring into the bottomless pit that was now her soul. Indescribable waves of emotions raged through her as she began to understand what had been happening to her day after day. She now knew this person, her captor, was a savage animal. Tears of hopelessness flooded her visions and blurred the image of her staring back at herself from a full-length mirror. She tried to look away from the horrific display, but there were mirrors everywhere. Everywhere she looked, there she was. On the ceiling, on the floor, twisted, mangled and broken. Rita Sorenson's transformation to the living dead was complete. Freedom was no longer a burning desire. Life was no longer an option.

With her last desire for breath Rita whispered, "You bastard!"

Her captor, being satisfied with her period of suffering, laid the gurney back into the prone position. Rita's mind swam with consternation and indifference. She didn't even flinch against the initial assault but then the pain grew too intense to ignore. Her skin was aflame with searing hot pain, jerking her from her self-induced trance. Rita screamed, inhaling a lung full of acrid smoke rising from the surface of her own burning flesh. Her eyes were fixed open, staring up at the blinding lights in the ceiling. She watched plumes of smoke curling toward the ceiling in obscene tendrils. The pain intensified as it spread across her tender stomach. Wave after wave of nausea wracked her body and she convulsed violently with dry heaves. The smell of her own flesh burning etched itself into her brain, which was now screaming out for mercy. Mercy she knew she would never be shown. Her eyes glazed over as she prayed, no, begged for death. She watched the lights of the corridor passing by overhead. Hearing the sound of doors being opened she felt herself being wheeled out into the frigid air of the outside world. She was gaining her freedom. A freedom she no longer craved.

Chapter Four

Vito rolled to his side and rubbed his hand across the wrinkled sheet next to him. It was still slightly warm. He leaned over, put his face to her pillow and breathed in deeply. He felt the pit of his stomach twist with the recognition of Karen's lingering scent. He sighed and shook his head; he was completely entangled in her web once more.

Vito staggered out to the kitchen like a drunken sailor. He grabbed the carafe of yesterday's cold coffee from the Mr. Coffee and poured himself a cup. He waited for the microwave to get halfway through its cycle for warming up a beverage before pulling the lukewarm mug out. He turned and headed for the bathroom with only one thing pressing on his mind, making sure he didn't soil the carpet on the way to the bathroom. Vito froze in his tracks. He was standing face to face with a calendar hanging on the wall under his phone. Glancing up at the clock and then back to the calendar, he sighed apprehensively. It was five in the morning on March first and he had yet to receive a grim message concerning Rita Sorenson.

"Maybe you're all right, kid," he said aloud, hoping that hearing the words might help him to believe them and ease the pain burrowing into his soul.

The rattling of his pager vibrating on the Formica vanity caught his attention even over the din of the shower. The first time he had heard it he let it pass, hoping it was just his imagination. Less than a minute later, it was vibrating again. He quickly rinsed his hair and turned off the water before it went completely cold.

"Lorenz," he said, stopping Haskell before he could go through his entire spiel announcing which division of which police department, he was answering phones for. Vito had given up sounding like a receptionist a long time ago.

"Just got a call from Anaheim General. I'm rolling now," Haskell said.

"Rita?"

"I'm afraid so." Vito could almost hear the man's neck creak as his chin dropped to his chest.

"Damn it. I was hoping this one might have a happy ending."

"Me too. There is some good news, though. I didn't get all of the particulars on her condition, but the hospital liaison who called informed Lucy the patient was still very much alive."

There was a long silence before Vito finally responded, "I'm on my way," and hung up the phone.

He swallowed the last of his cold, nuked coffee, grabbed his jacket and headed out the door. A thousand gruesome scenarios played out in his mind during the lonely drive to the hospital. The truth of the matter was he couldn't truly begin to imagine what they were going to find once they got to the hospital and saw Rita Sorenson for the first time. He entertained a fantasy of walking into the hospital and finding her in perfect health, having escaped unharmed from her kidnapper. Dirty, a little disheveled but alive, she would hand him a manila folder brimming with a year's worth of evidence she had been able to collect, compile, and conceal from her captor. The file would contain photos of both her abductor and the place where she had been kept. A perfect set of fingerprints. The name, address and complete medical history of the maniac. And finally, a nice, neat handwritten note explaining why the killer committed the dastardly crimes and he would be turning himself in to the police, post haste.

Vito pulled his car into a space reserved for doctors and broke free of his perfect script. Haskell was waiting for him at the emergency entrance door. His charcoal gray suit matched his shirt and tie perfectly and was so fresh Vito half expected to see a dry cleaner's bag draped over Haskell's head like a poncho. There wasn't a hair out of place and his eyes sparkled with energy. Vito caught his own reflection in the hospital doors and couldn't help but notice he looked like a homeless street creeper on a bad day next to his partner. They greeted each other with a somber nod and headed for the elevator to take them up to Rita's room.

"Have you seen her yet?"

"No, I just got here myself. I got the room number from the nurse and came back outside to wait for you."

"Looks like the press hasn't gotten wind of this yet," Vito shared his observation.

"Not that they haven't tried. But to the nursing staff's credit, they have been tight-lipped with everyone, including me."

"Thank God for that. The last thing we need is another media circus."

They stepped off the elevator and walked down to the nurse's station where a grim-faced man in a white lab coat stood waiting for them. He held a clipboard in his white knuckled grip. Vito was sure it was Rita's medical chart explaining in detail the horrors the poor young woman had endured. Relief washed over him as Vito realized this was the third victim, in a third hospital, with yet a third attending physician. At least this doctor hadn't been exposed to the wicked atrocities of this killer, which meant he might not hold Vito personally responsible.

"Detectives," he greeted them with a handshake that was strictly professional.

"Doctor. What have we got?"

"I've got a much-traumatized young lady, is what I've got. What is going on here detectives?"

"I'm not sure I get your meaning?"

"A colleague of mine, Sumbal Sayid, works at County General and he told me about a case he had earlier this year. It made quite an impression on him. In fact, it sounded a lot like what I've got here. And detectives, I must admit, I don't think I've ever seen anything this horrendous," he sighed.

"How so?"

"This girl has been kept alive, just barely, for months on end. She has been tortured repeatedly over a long period of time as well as being grossly disfigured. I'm not so sure she'll make it through this ordeal, physically that is. And I know for a fact she will never completely recover mentally," he said, eyeing Vito with disdain.

"Can you give me the details, please?" Vito asked, feeling the trappings of a headache starting at the base of his neck.

"From my preliminary investigation of the patient I would have to say whoever did this to this poor woman has been performing minor surgeries on her every day for at least a month. I stopped counting the scars after I got to a couple dozen or so."

"Awe, Christ," Haskell gasped. "How bad is her face?"

"Her face? It's fine, except for the effects of being subjected to malnutrition for months on end."

"But you said there were dozens of surgeries?" Vito was clearly confused.

"Not on her face detectives, on her breasts. At first glance, I thought it was some hack job's attempt at covering up a bad augmentation job. But once I was able to assess her condition further, I realized these surgeries were a direct effort to maim and disfigure this poor girl. And then there was the message of course."

"The message?" they asked in unison.

"Yes, there was a," he paused. "A note, I'll call it, for lack of a better word, scrawled across her stomach with what I believe was a type of surgical laser. This is the work of a serial killer, isn't it detectives?"

"We can't really speculate on that without examining at all of the evidence," Vito began.

"Don't bullshit me, detective, I'm really not in the mood."

"Doctor," Vito paused and bent forward to look at the man's ID badge. "Underhill, I can't stress enough how sensitive this case is. We need to keep this out of the press for as long as possible to give us the best possible chance of catching this guy."

"But by keeping it out of the press, you also endanger an indeterminate number of young women," his rising anger was becoming quite apparent.

"No, I don't think so."

"And what makes you so damned sure about that?"

"Because, I'm afraid we're already too late for that," Vito sighed in defeat.

He opened his mouth to say something, but before Doctor Underhill could grill the detectives any further, all hell broke loose. A flurry of voices on the very brink of panic echoed down the stark corridors. Nurses called for doctors over the intercom and from their cupped mouths. The orders and requests being barked were all in enigmatic code, not unlike police radio jargon. He had heard the words "code blue" spoken over the intercom many times during his career and although he wasn't completely sure of its exact meaning, Vito knew it couldn't be very good. It was never a good sign when one chose to use a number or code phrase rather than come right out and say what one meant. Hearing a sanitized code crackle over his radio was always much easier to stomach than "We have a corpse lying naked in the middle of MacArthur Park."

Wordlessly, but with a grave look of concern, Underhill bounded down the hallway. It took Vito and Haskell several moments to catch up mentally with the rest of the well-honed trauma staff. They darted after the doctor, somehow knowing the situation had just deteriorated from bad to worse.

They were still running toward the commotion when the first nurse's scream reached their ears. It was quickly followed by several more which were then accompanied by the sound of shattering glass. And then, just like after a tornado or hurricane, all was calm. Nothing above a murmur was heard from the crowd of more than a dozen hospital personnel. Vito felt his heart sag as head after head dropped in a show of defeat.

"What's going on?" he heard himself ask the first person he came within earshot of.

It was a young, doe-eyed candy striper. "She killed herself," she replied in a daze.

"Who?"

"The girl who was in that room. She was sleeping just a few minutes ago, when I checked on her, and now she's," the girl never finished her sentence. She darted past the two detectives and down the hallway, disappearing into the ladies restroom.

Underhill spun from the interior of the hospital room and pushed passed the detectives at the doorway. He walked briskly toward the elevator and was several steps away before he turned back around.

"You gentlemen had better follow me," he said, stepping into the elevator. He held his arm across the electronic eye to give the detectives time to shut their gaping maws and join him in the elevator.

Doctor Underhill was a rugged, athletic looking man with a barrel chest, who would look just as at home in a pair of logging chaps and a flannel shirt as doctor's scrubs. He was Vito's age, but in much better health so he looked like he might pass for Haskell's. His hands were powerful looking, not the soft, gentle hands of a doctor. And the way he had them clasped tightly together at that moment added to his Paul Bunyan persona.

Once the doors to the elevator closed, he spun around to face Vito. "I hope I don't need to explain to you what just happened, because I don't think I could find the words," he said, fighting back his tears of frustration and anger.

"No, I don't think you have to explain what happened, but I'd sure like to know why?"

"Once you see her, you might understand," his jaws clenched and unclenched in rhythm with his giant hands.

The silence within the elevator was deafening. The whir of the cables seemed to be coming from miles away. From another world. A world where Vito wished he could step into and away from this madness. Less than a minute later the stainless-steel doors opened and the three men stepped out into pandemonium. A paramedic unit getting ready to roll was unluckily idling in the emergency entrance turnaround when Rita Sorenson's body slammed into the asphalt in front of them. The windshield of the deep red rescue truck was splattered with Rita's blood the very second she impacted the hard asphalt. And although everyone on the scene knew the girl was dead, they weren't finished trying to save her. Vito walked over to where a young paramedic was rapidly running out of energy from doing CPR and put a gentle hand on his shoulder. The two remaining paramedics had given up the battle for the girl's life and were sitting white-faced on the pavement.

Vito looked down at Rita's corpse for the first time and gasped. She was lying face down on the pavement with her arms and legs twisted at perverted angles. Memories of Vito's childhood rushed back at him. He vividly recalled a mistreated Barbie doll of Lizbeth's when he was considered her evil brother. Rita's bare feet lay sideways with the toes pointing outward on each foot. Her blue paisley hospital gown had bunched up around her waist, exposing her bare buttocks to onlookers who had started to gather. Most of the onlookers had gasped and turned away at the sight the young woman's vermiculated body. Others only stared. Vito figured it was because they were really sure what it was they were seeing. This was Tinseltown after all, anything was possible.

Vito bent down and tenderly pulled her gown back down around her to cover her nakedness. His eyes wandered up her body to her head. His stomach lurched at the sight and he averted his eyes from the gruesome sight. Quickly Vito put the images of a smashed cantaloupe in his mind's eye. This wasn't a young girl's brains all over the tarmac, it was only fruit. The mental chicanery sufficed and Vito was able to face the girl's corpse once more. Haskell on the other hand didn't have the years of experience to have learned these little tricks and he was busy tossing his breakfast into a receptacle in the back of an ambulance. Vito wiped the tears from his eyes and got up from his kneeling position to go check on his partner.

"You okay?" he asked, putting a fatherly arm around the young man.

"Yeah," he replied between gasps for air. "Sorry about that."

"It happens. Why don't you get some uniformed help and move these people back away from here before we have a gawking crowd. And don't let the press get any pictures, especially not of her," he instructed.

Haskell simply nodded his head and swirled a mouthful of sterile water around in his mouth. He spit the water into the designated puke bucket, took a few deep breaths and moved on the gathering crowd.

"Hey, can I get you guys to give me a hand here?" he asked the group of paramedics who had been first on the scene. They were still dazed, and Vito knew giving them something to do to make them feel useful was the best thing for them.

"Yeah, sure," one of the paramedics gladly responded. He wasn't sure who the shabbily dressed man was, but he seemed to be in charge and looked as though he knew what he was doing. Besides, any excuse to escape this carnage would be a blessing.

"Go into the hospital and find me some portable screens and set them up around this young girl's body. I don't want any of her loved ones seeing any of this on television. And make sure you block everything, including the stain on the tarmac. Also, make sure one of you guys gets your windshield cleaned off, ASAP," he said. He felt a little better himself now that he had something to occupy his thoughts. Rita Sorenson was gone. There was nothing he could do to help her now except preserve her good memory. Vito's automatic pilot kicked in, forcing the battered corpse to the back of his mind.

A coldness swept over Vito; this poor girl had no mother. No family to be heartbroken if the press happened to air pictures of her battered corpse. He wiped a tear from his eye and wondered if he counted as someone who cared about her so she wouldn't have died so utterly and completely alone. Would she be looking at him from wherever her soul rested, knowing he truly cared? That he truly regretted not being able to stop this monster from destroying her every essence.

Within a few minutes Haskell had moved everyone at least a block away from the scene and the emergency crew had set up portable white privacy screens all around the battered corpse. One of the young men trembled as he sponged off the spattered windshield. But he kept at it. He kept at it because he had to. It was the only thing keeping him from stripping out of his uniform and walking home and away from this life forever.

Doctor Underhill stood shoulder to shoulder with Vito as they watched their people busying themselves with somber tasks. Once the screens were in place the two men stepped inside the makeshift cubicle alone.

"How in the hell are they ever going to make this poor girl presentable?" Underhill stated as they rolled her over onto a backboard. She was so frail from malnutrition the two of them were able to lift her up onto a gurney without any exertion whatsoever.

"I afraid this one's going to be a closed casket affair. But," Vito stopped before finishing his thought.

"But what?"

"Her remains will have to be positively identified, and even then, I won't be able to release the body until the crime unit is finished with her."

The two of them chatted as if they were doing laundry or fixing a car as they reshaped the body on the gurney so it would fit. They looked each other in the eye as they talk, glancing down only when absolutely necessary to get their bearings on what they were doing. Both men had been around dead bodies and blood for a good portion of their lives, but this was only a fraction away from being too much to endure.

Once Rita was straightened out, they belted her legs to keep them from flopping off the gurney. Doctor Underhill carefully unfolded a clean, white sheet and draped it over her broken form. Vito was struggling to keep the tears at bay.

"I guess I have to do my job now," he said, and carefully folded the sheet down to her waist. Underhill knew what he was after and pulled a pair of surgeon's scissors from his pocket. He slowly cut away the blue paisley fabric to the neck and pulled both sides of the gown away from her torso. Once her naked trunk was exposed, Doctor Underhill began tenderly, almost lovingly, wiping the blood away from the wounds made by the laser.

Vito found himself staring at what he supposed were the woman's breasts. They were completely mutilated and deformed. The skin had been cut and sewn into awkward, jutting angles and wide sweeping arcs. An image of a child's toy flashed in his mind. A deflated punching balloon with a long yellow rubber band tied to it as a tether. But even as bad as her disfigurement was, it was the crimson lettering being revealed on her stomach as Underhill cleaned her off that repulsed Lorenz the most.

Christina Douglas will be seeing you soon, Detective Lorenz.

The killer's taunting tone could be felt through the written words and Vito felt his anger swelling beyond compare. He pulled the flaps of her gown back over her exposed flesh.

"Seems like he knows you," Underhill hissed in contempt.

"Yes, it does seem that way, doesn't it? I wish I had the same pleasure," He said, running his fingers through his hair. He placed the heels of his hands firmly against his temples and pressed as hard as he could.

"Here," Underhill handed him a small sample package of painkillers he pulled out of his pocket. "You don't have any allergies, do you?" he added.

"Only to this job. Thanks," he said, tearing the end off the package and dumping two pills into his mouth. He swallowed hard several times to force the dry pills down his throat. Their bitter taste lingered in his mouth long after the pills themselves had disappeared.

"Can I take her back inside now, detective?" Underhill asked.

"I wish I could say yes, but we can't do that until the crime scene investigators have a look around. In fact, I shouldn't have even moved her body."

"Crime scene investigators? Why would they need to look around? This isn't a crime scene. I don't want this poor, young girl out here any longer than necessary," Underhill's emotions began to overwhelm him and he felt himself losing control. He knew there was no hurried reason to take the body inside, but he just wanted her out of his sight so he could begin to push her out of his mind.

"Neither do I doctor, but we need to preserve as much evidence as possible from her body. I'm sure most of it has been tainted, but there may be something. A hair, a fiber, anything that might give us a clue as to who is doing this. You can go back inside if you're too busy," Vito offered the man a way out.

"I'd rather stay here with here, if that's all right with you," he said, his anger simmering down to a slow boil.

"That is a preferable option. I might have some questions for you once we start going over things. But I feel it's only fair to warn you, things are going to get ugly in a few minutes."

"Get ugly? How could they possibly get any uglier?"

"I take it you've never seen a crime unit gather evidence at a homicide scene."

"No, I can't say that I have. It's not one of those things high up on my to-do list."

"It's not very pretty."

Before Underhill could respond, Haskell walked through one of the screens and into the makeshift cubicle. Lieutenant Stoddard and Mertyl Stumpf, the city's Chief Medical Examiner followed closely on his heels. Mertyl was a large woman, not fat mind you, but large. Her shoulders were thick, broad and solid. The squad detectives swore up and down she moonlighted as a linebacker for the Raiders, and there were more than a few outstanding bets just waiting for confirmation of that rumor.

Mertyl Stumpf was an ugly woman as well. In fact, she was as ugly as her name. Her nose bore the scars of being broken more than once and was mashed almost completely flat against her pinkish cheeks. Her eyes were a cold, unfeeling shade of gray and her face bore the battle scars of a long, losing war with teenage acne Vito could tell there was a lot of repressed anger in that woman and he hadn't a shred of a desire to see it loosed.

"Lieutenant, Mertyl," Vito acknowledged with a head bob. He glanced at Underhill who was doing a double take on Mertyl. The look of denial on the man's face almost bought Vito a world of hurt, but he suppressed his chuckles and turned his attention back to the two women.

"Vito," Mertyl returned his greeting in kind. Her voice was not too unlike that of an angered sea lion defending her young. She took three, or four quick, long drags from her cigarette without exhaling and tossed the flaming cinder beyond the perimeter of the scene. The cherry burst into a mini firework when it struck the concrete curb ten feet away. She held the smoke in her lungs so long Vito was waiting for her to blow smoke rings out of her ass. When she finally spoke only a whisper of blue haze escaped from between her lips. Tiny wisps escaped her nostrils and clawed their way up her face, disappearing into her mangy locks.

"I take it this one is like the others?" she barked, running her fingers through her long, stringy hair. The raven colored hair had been infused with so much gray it was now the same dirty shade of gray billowing from factory smokestacks.

Vito nodded.

"Okay. I've got my best people on their way over. We'll bag and tag everything that can be moved and photograph that which can't. Everything I collect will have priority once it gets to the lab. I can probably have a preliminary report within twenty-four hours," she rattled off mechanically.

"Thank you," Vito replied.

"You're welcome, but I'm not doing this for you, I'm doing it for her," she nodded at the figure lying on the gurney.

"Understandable," Vito replied, unnerved by the look of sadness and defeat in the woman's eyes.

Mertyl Stumpf glared at the homicide detectives until they got the hint and stepped out into the open air. Underhill needed no prodding to follow. Contrary to her bulky, stalwart appearance she was very tender to the deceased. Vito had no concerns this poor woman would be treated as delicately as possible and put back together with the utmost of care.

"I guess I better get back to work," he said, nervously fumbling around in the pockets of his blood stained smock.

"I have just a few questions for you, if you don't mind," Vito stopped him.

"Of course."

"When was Miss Sorenson brought into the hospital?"

"Around four this morning. No knows for sure."

"Why not?" Vito asked, already knowing the answer.

"One of the off-going orderlies saw her in the waiting room as he was leaving. He said he was walking by just like any other morning and normally a patient in the waiting room wouldn't have caught his eye. But she was different."

"How so?"

"He told me she was staring off into space when he first noticed her sitting there. After several minutes he moved around to get a better look at her. That's when he realized she was naked and saw the damage to her body. The orderly then ran to the nurse's reception desk and asked about the patient, but he was informed no patients had checked in. He and the nurse went back and checked on her and quickly decided to call me down here."

"Did she say anything to you?"

"Not as much as a whisper. I should have had her sedated," he said, starting to second-guess his actions.

"She wasn't violent, was she?"

"No, quite the contrary in fact."

"Then why would you have ever even given a thought as if you needed to sedate her? Don't beat yourself up over this one, doc, there was nothing you could have done."

"Oh yes there was. There was plenty I could have done. There was plenty you could have done. Now, are there any more questions, I'm not feeling too great right now?"

"No, that's it for now. But I might have a few questions for you later."

"That's fine. And I'm sorry if I'm sounding short right now, but this has been quite a traumatic experience and a bit overwhelming to say the least," Underhill said.

"I understand completely, and I'm sorry you've had to go through something like this," Vito replied.

The detectives watched the doctor walk back through the emergency room doors. Vito hoped the man would eventually be able to put this all out of his mind. Although, deep down, he knew that was just wishful thinking. It was going to be something the man carried with him to his grave, and quite possibly beyond.

Vito stepped toward Karen and raised his arm to put it around her shoulder but thought better of it and dropped it quickly to his side. Haskell could feel a certain amount of tension in the air between the two of them and moved a safe distance away. He wasn't sure what the problem was, but if there was going to be an explosion, he wanted as far away from the blast zone as possible.

"Why did you come down here?" Vito asked, a little harsher than he would have liked.

"I thought you might have wanted my assistance, and I wasn't aware I needed your permission, I am the boss, remember," she snapped back.

"Sorry, I didn't mean it to sound the way it did. I think the pressure is getting to me," he sighed.

"That's okay, what have we got?"

"It's the same guy all right. Poor girl must not have been able to endure the monumental amount of abuse this bastard had been heaped on her. She jumped out of the window the minute no one was around to watch her," Vito said.

"You said it was the same guy?" Karen questioned without really wanting an answer.

"Yes, there was another message. It's getting personal too. This one was written to me."

"So that just adds one more angle to this puzzle," Haskell blurted.

"I'm afraid so. Now, not only are we looking for someone who might have a beef with these girls, but someone who has a beef with me as well," Vito said.

"No offense, but I'm sure that's a long list," the lieutenant interjected.

"None taken. I don't mind having a reputation for not getting along with vermin, but I just can't think of anyone with a grudge like this. It's not like I have a lot of outstanding serial killer cases on record."

"I'll get a printout of every homicide case you've worked on since you made detective run it against a list of recent parolees." I'm not sure what it will turn up, but right now, any angle is worth looking into," Karen offered.

"That will be helpful. Come on, you and I have got to see what we can dig up on this Christina Douglas," he grabbed Haskell by the elbow and led him toward the doctor's parking lot.

"I'm parked around front," Haskell said with a smile and a shake of his head.

"Start taking notes," Vito said, and headed for his car. "Thanks again, Mertyl," he called out as he passed by the screens. She growled some incomprehensive response causing Vito to crack a small smile. He turned and blew Karen a kiss once he saw Haskell go around the corner of the building and drop out of sight. He wanted to ask her where in the hell she had disappeared to in the middle of the night, but he was certain he wouldn't like her answer. George Masarick most assuredly didn't wake up next to a cold pillow. Vito sighed, got into his car and drove out of the parking lot in the direction of the precinct.

Chapter Five

Today was a good day for Judge Blue Morgan. He had
awakened this morning for starters, which was always a good
thing, but today he also remembered who he was. Even though
old age had gotten the better part of his brain, Blue Morgan still
had a voracious appetite for life. His body was holding out
pretty well in spite of his years of abuse. It was the damned
Alzheimer's that was going to be able to finally claim him as its
prize. Today, the judge even had the presence of mind to be
aware of the fact he was losing the battle between the gray cells.
Not only was knowing what affliction ailed you extremely
frustrating, it was ten-fold knowing there wasn't a damned thing
either you, or anyone else could do about it. Of course, he
always knew he was going to die someday, he just didn't like
accepting the fact he was doing it piece-by-piece, day-by-day.

The old man shrugged off his bitterness and negativity.
Eager to start the day, he powered up his laptop and hurriedly
logged onto the Internet while he still remembered how. He
knew he had to hurry up and read his e-mail and scan the news
before his mind decided it needed a vacation. And even though
he might not remember what it was he had read later; he wanted
the satisfaction of knowing the information right then and later
be damned.

Being a retired Circuit Court Justice, he was privy to
certain bits of information not available to the general public
without moving a mountain of red tape. Mainly it came in the
form of e-mails from friends and colleagues who were still
sitting judges. And although most of it had died off to a slow
trickle once word of his disease spread, there were still a few
die-hard friends who kept him apprised of the goings on in the
judicial world.

He scanned through a few court docket listings, shaking his head whenever he ran across the familiar name of a repeat offender. Morgan had been a caring judge who was more than fair most of the time. But he had also been a strict judge when it came to repeat offenders and of course the sick, pathetic animals who preyed on innocent children.

"Morning Judge," Clarence, his caretaker, greeted and set his breakfast in front of him. It was the same every morning. Two pieces of lightly buttered rye toast, cinnamon-raisin oatmeal, homemade of course, a banana and a glass of pineapple juice. Sometimes Clarence would surprise him with V-8 juice or one of his own special concoctions, but mostly it was pineapple. Or at least Blue Morgan thought he remembered it being pineapple. For all he knew, it might be something different every day. He felt his frustrations welling up inside him once more and turned his attentions back to his computer screen. His milky-blue eyes darted back and forth across the screen, absorbing information in a race against time.

He finished reading the court reports and moved on to the low point of the morning, the obituaries. The first hint of his mortality had come to him years before while reading the obituary of a child actor he had grown up watching who died from liver failure. The actor wasn't but a few years older than Blue and they were close enough to the same age to put them into the same age demographic. That was the year Blue Morgan gave up bourbon.

The following year one of his best friends from high school passed on. Sure, there had been others before him, but none of them had been from natural causes. Car accidents, drugs, alcohol and the occasional suicide had plagued his graduating class like any other. But to have a classmate die due to congenital heart failure struck a nerve. That was the year Blue gave up smoking. He was fifty-five then, and life suddenly seemed a lot shorter. Now, with Alzheimer's chewing away at his brain, it seemed so cruelly long and arduous.

Today's obituaries struck him significantly hard. Another young girl was dead. And although the four-paragraph blurb didn't explain what had caused the cessation of her life force, he still felt the weight of her death. She was just like the other two.

Rita Sorenson, the girl's name tumbled around in his head like a circus clown on crack. She was so familiar, yet so foreign. Something inside of his eroding brain screamed little bits and pieces about the girl, except for the details of why he was remembering her so vividly. He could see her young, innocent face staring back at him from the gallery of his courtroom, but for the life of him, he couldn't recall why she was there. On either side of her were two other girls, Kendra Jenkins and Evangelique Martens, but again, everything but their names and faces were a blur.

The more Blue Morgan pondered this conundrum the more he began to believe the only reason he even knew the girl's faces and names was because he had seen them on his computer screen. And that would have satisfied his curiosity had his mind's eye not seen them distinctly sitting in his gallery. He had seen them before, when his mind was still whole and uncluttered. The more he brooded over the subject, the more he became convinced this wasn't his old age getting even with him for years of bad living. This was real.

"Clarence, can you come here for a minute, please," he called out.

"Yes, sir," the man replied, stepping into his boss's study a couple of minutes later.

"I'm afraid I have some information I will probably forget, and I fear this information may be too important to be forgotten.

"What would you like me to do?"

"These three girls seem familiar to me, but for the life of me I cannot remember why," he explained as he pushed a pad of paper toward his caretaker with the girl's names scribbled across the face of the yellow paper. The handwriting looked like that of a child just learning how to write. Full circle. He spent the better part of his life learning how to perform certain tasks and now, he was destined to spend the rest of his days forgetting how to do them.

"Yes sir."

"And can you get me my medication, please, my head is starting to throb."

Clarence disappeared for a couple of minutes and returned with an Imitrex tablet and a cool glass of water. Blue Morgan popped the pills into his mouth and finished off the tumbler of water.

"Is there anyone in particular you'd like me to contact about these girls, sir?"

"What girls?"

Clarence opened his mouth to say something, but then thought better of it. He knew it would be useless now. The man had slipped back into his other being, the one who didn't even realize it when he had to urinate. Clarence left the beleaguered old man to stare out the window in thoughtless abandon. Gripping sadness crept over Clarence like a gray cloud. Every time his charge faded off into this "other" it scared the hell out of him by exposing his own mortality to him.

Lines of sadness sprouted from the corners of Clarence's deep, dark eyes. He rubbed a large hand across his closely cropped salt and pepper hair and sighed. This man was not only his employer, but a lifelong friend as well. He had no idea what he would do with the rest of his life once Blue passed into the next. He wiped away his tears before they had a chance to start and let his melancholy mood subside into thoughts of chores that needed tending to.

"Gray Morgan's office," the receptionist chimed.

"Good Morning, Phoebe, this is Clarence. May I speak with Gray, please, that is if he's not too busy."

"Nothing wrong with Blue I hope," she responded caringly.

"Nothing serious, but I would like to talk to Gray about something important."

"Of course."

The line went dead for a few seconds and then it started to ring again. Gray Morgan, Blue Morgan's son, was a very prominent prosecuting attorney for Los Angeles County. Although the pay wasn't the greatest, the job made him feel like he was making a difference in his community. He would one day follow in his father's footsteps and don the black robe of justice.

Gray's mother had become pregnant during Blue's heavier drinking days and came to term in the middle of winter; the heart of football season. She had gone into labor during a college football game, the Blue-Gray Classic to be exact, and

Blue was forced to miss the second half. He had decided on the name Gray on the way to the hospital. He thought it was kind of catchy and was quite satisfied with it. His wife wasn't nearly as thrilled. They argued about the name for several days until she was ready to be released from the hospital and they had to make their son's name official. They both won the argument and named their son, Ezekial Gray Morgan. As a young adult Gray decided he liked the colorful moniker and chose to use it as his proper name.

"Gray Morgan," his strong, deep voice greeted.

"Good morning, Gray, this is Clarence."

"Is Pops okay?" he blurted as soon as he recognized the voice.

"Medically, yes. But there has been something nagging at him though. And I'm beginning to think it might really be of some importance."

"What makes you think that?"

"You know your father. He is like a pit bull when he gets onto something. Well, he's been tugging at this one for a couple of months now."

"What is it, Clarence?" he asked curtly. Gray had always felt Clarence would have made a much better actor than a caretaker. He always seemed to want to embellish and expound every little conversation, but the man was very good to his father, so he was allowed quite a bit of latitude.

"Your father has become obsessed with a few obituaries he has read."

"Friends of his?"

"No sir. These are young girls. He doesn't seem to know why he recognizes them, but he really feels it is important he does."

"Do you have any clue why he thinks he recognizes these girls?"

"Not really, except he told me he can see them all sitting in his courtroom. Normally I would just blow this off as another of his ramblings, but I saw two of these girls on the news. They were murdered Gray. I think there may be some significance to what your father is saying," Clarence explained, his voice clearly expressing his anxiety.

"Interesting. Fax me over the information you have, and I will look into it as soon as I have a free moment," Gray said.

"Sorry to bother you with this."

"No bother at all. In fact, I'm pleased my father still has some of his penchant for mystery and intrigue left in him."

"He's in one of his moods, but I will tell him that I have talked to you when he comes around."

"You do that, Clarence. You also tell him I love him, and I will get back to you on this as soon as I possibly can," he said, hanging up the phone. Gray absolutely abhorred it when Clarence used the term 'moods' to describe his father's loss of memory. He might have admonished the man for it had he been able to think of a better term for it himself.

As soon as he was off the phone Gray began flipping through his appointment book to see what was on the agenda for the day. Glancing down at his watch he realized he was due in court in less than half an hour. He put the phone conversation with Clarence in the back of his mind and prepared himself for the battle at hand. Whatever was disturbing his father would have to wait until he had the time to investigate it. Whatever it was couldn't possibly be that important.

*   *   *

Through her peripheral vision Christina could watch rise and fall of her breasts as they swayed ever so slightly back and forth with her sashaying movements. The light spring jacket she wore was opened to the midriff and cut to accentuate the fullness of her breasts sloping down to her narrow waist and then flaring out again at her curvy hips. While her gold slacks were snug and form fitting, they were extremely comfortable as well. She knew the flashing cameras were capturing her voluptuous posterior for posterity. Strobes popped around her like fireworks during a hero's welcome home celebration. The customized outfit formed to her curves so well because it had been especially designed for her and her alone. No one else on earth would ever look quite as good in it as she did.

Her vibrant blue eyes scanned the crowd on either side of the runway. All the famous photographers were there, as well as agents, scouts and casting directors. She took special care and attention to make eye contact with each and every one of them. They were special. They were her ticket to the big time. No man could resist the allure of her eyes.

She felt her belly give a slight rumble and hoped no one but herself had heard the hunger pangs growling. She was forced to skip breakfast in order to fit into the snug pants and now her body was telling her just how angry it was because of her abuse. And the hot dog vender wasn't making things any better.

Hot dog vender? She wondered what on earth a hot dog vender was doing inside the auditorium. Surely the people responsible for putting on a show of this magnitude would never have allowed a mere hot dog vender into the venue. Christina couldn't help but scan the audience for the source of the tantalizing aromas. She really didn't care who had let the vendor into the fashion show, the smells were reminding her of home. A smile broke over her face as she realized she was back in the city. The Big Apple. Broadway. The Gardens. Home at last.

The long runway was constructed solely of mirrors. Pieces of reflective glass were arranged in sharp, geometric patterns sucking light in and shooting it directly at Christina until she exploded in an array of dazzling prisms. The faces of the photographers lining the glittered path were all focused on her. Their eyes twinkled with her brilliance. She had finally made it to the big time. She was a star desired by all.

As she drew nearer to the end of the catwalk, she spied the vendor responsible for her hunger growing out of control. Her heart iced over with fear when she noticed a shrouded figure standing next to the stainless-steel cart. Why would the hot dog vendor be hiding his face from his customers? And then he looked up at her, directly into her beautiful blue eyes. She gasped. He was as faceless as a Movado clock.

As she took her last few steps toward the end of the catwalk the tantalizing aroma had changed. He was burning the hot dogs. It wasn't the kind of smell that would be emitted by his steam table merely running out of water. This was much different. This was nauseating. The dogs were already charred, and they were burning up until there was nothing left of them.

The acrid smoke stung her nose and cause tears to start rolling down her cheeks. She scrunched up her face and rubbed her tongue against the roof of her mouth. The bitter taste began making her gag.

She made her way back down the runway, gagging and convulsing with every step. She noticed all heads turning and all eyes falling upon her as she staggered. Their eyes were burning holes through her soul. Christina wanted nothing more than to make it back to the thick, luxurious curtain where she could duck behind, out of sight.

She gagged once more and jerked her eyes open as the gruel spilled out of her mouth and ran down her chest. She was back in hell. She was no longer on the catwalk where she longed to be but trapped inside of a glass box instead. She was home again, but not to the home she had always known, the home she had so desperately been struggling to endure.

She noticed a hypodermic needle moving away from the IV bag hanging to the side of her chamber. That was why she had come back to reality. Not because she had wanted to, but because the bastard had ripped her back.

Shadows danced in front of her face, but they were too close for her to be able to recognize what was causing them. A flash of red light sparked in front of her eyes for the briefest moment of time. And then there were more shadowy movements. She struggled to focus in the darkness but was unable. She fought against the drugs and forced her brain to function.

An army of memories goose-stepped their way back into her consciousness. Now she recognized the smell her dream was symbolic of. It was that poor girl's flesh, the one who used to occupy a now empty chamber. Christina glanced down at the face of her see-through tomb. Although the word MARCH was written across the top of the box, S'LOOF LIRPA, was written in big block letters across the bottom of the calendar. Her brain hurt and she had to struggle to make sense of the lettering. "April fools, my ass," she spat. This was no April fool's gag; this was real and it was terrifying to try and imagine what was coming next.

The pinprick of red light exploded in front of her again, but this time it remained lit. She watched it inching closer and closer. A strange sensation of heat began irritating her eye, she tried to close it but found it impossible. Christina rolled her eye toward the back of her head to see what may be keeping her from closing her eyes. Something shiny, metallic, hovered at the very edge of her peripheral vision. She assumed it was some sort of clamp forcing her eyes to remain open.

The pinprick of light continued to inch closer while the irritation it caused grew in intensity. Every nerve in Christina's body suddenly screamed out in pain. Her eyeball felt like it was on fire, as if the fluid inside were boiling. She could hear the popping and hissing of her ocular fluid as it tried to escape the fiery wrath of the laser beam. She arched her back and curled her toes in extreme agony. She screamed in fear, she screamed in pain, she screamed to drown out the sound of her eyeball frying.

The pinprick of light disappeared like the flame of a blown-out match, but the pain it had caused remained. Christina's depth perception had been completely destroyed. With one eye she saw the blackness through destroyed flesh, with the other she saw a brief flash of red and began to whimper.

Once more the laser attacked tender flesh. The pain was inescapable. She screamed until she no longer possessed the strength to even breathe. She prayed for mercy and then she begged for death.

*   *   *

The days peeled off the calendar like leaves on a blustery fall day. Both Haskell and Lorenz were stupefied by the lack of direction this case was affording them. Sure, they had checked out the Douglas girl, but they had come up as nearly empty-handed as they had with Rita Sorenson.

Christina Douglas was a model from New York City. She was nineteen years old and had been living away from home a mere eight months. Her mother and father had suspected no trouble whatsoever. In fact, the girl was upbeat and positive every time she had called home. And the last time they had spoken to her, her mood had been even better. Christina had been chosen to model for a famous designer in a world premier gala show opening in Paris. She had been excited about the trip and couldn't wait to experience her childhood dream of going to Europe. But that was when things seemed to sour.

She had simply vanished on her way to the airport. No phone calls. No note. Her luggage never even made it onto the airplane. And never once during the year long absence had there been a ransom note.

The detectives had interviewed the designer directly and had come up with nothing to connect her with the other three girls. They had even enlisted the help of the FBI whose vast database failed to reveal anything other than what Vito and Gregg had already learned. They had run into an impassable brick wall. So they were once again relegated to waiting. And the more they waited; the ornerier Vito became. The case had turned into a festering boil that continued to swell and fill with angry puss. As each day ground to a close, the threat of the boil exploding became ever greater.

Vito left Haskell at the precinct and drove over to his sister's place for his weekly obligatory punishment. He didn't think his system could handle any more cumin or jalapenos, but he figured a little self-imposed punishment was in order.

"Vito," Lizbeth cried and threw her arms around his neck. He focused on a spot all the way to the back wall. A place he always paid homage to when he visited his sister. Freddie's badge hung in a glass display box above the mantle. He had really enjoyed Freddie's company. He was a good man and he had always treated Lizbeth the way she deserved to be treated.

"Hi, Lizbeth," he broke from her grasp and smiled at her. "You're looking good tonight."

Vito's sister was a good five inches shorter than his own average stature. Candlelight sparkled off her long, flowing black hair. The flickering light cascading down her shoulders in luminescent sheets. She was a slender woman, but healthy, with just enough meat on her bones to make her shapely, cuddly and soft. Her smile was warmth in the purest sense, and she shared it often.

"I wish I could say the same for you. Pardon my language, Vito, but you look like hell."

He laughed. "Yeah, well I feel a lot worse than I look."

"Would you like to talk about it?" Her deep, brown eyes were attentive and sympathetic.

"I don't want to bring you down, sis."

"That's all right. Lord knows, I've cried on your shoulder enough."

"Maybe you're right, it might help if I got a few things off my chest."

"Then it's a deal. After dinner I'll send Freddie Junior to a friend's house and we can talk."

"Speaking of dinner, what's that I smell? It smells wonderful," Vito asked, truly impressed with the aromas and not just being gracious for his sister's sake. His stomach gurgled and echoed its desire for food. And there wasn't even as much as a hint of cumin in the air.

"Pasta fagioli. I hope you like it," she cooed playfully.

"Thank God, you remembered you're Italian," he said and they both burst into a short round of sincere laughter.

He petered around in the kitchen with Lizbeth, performing menial tasks like chopping vegetables for the salad and mincing the garlic. After the second time she had to administer first aid his sister took the knife away from him and put him in charge of brewing a pot of coffee. The fagioli was simmering and emitting some of the most seductive aromas Vito had ever smelled. The garlic bread in the oven had just started to toast and would be ready for freshly grated Parmigiano-Reggiano in just a few minutes. Vito salivated heavily and his thoughts mercifully drifted away from Christina Douglas.

He helped set the table, with Lizbeth going behind him and doing it correctly of course. Freddie Junior had burst through the door fifteen minutes earlier and was still washing up for dinner as per his mother's instructions, which had been nothing more than a finger pointed toward the general vicinity of the bathroom.

Vito set the steaming crock of pasta fagioli on the table while Lizbeth sliced the bread. Between mouthfuls of food and grunts of satisfaction, Vito and Lizbeth were brought up to speed on Freddie's day at school. Vito learned about the new girl he was dating, how he had passed driver's training, and how he had recently moved up in the pitching rotation on the baseball team. He was always stunned by how much more the boy looked like a man every time he saw him, even if it were only from one week to the next. It warmed his heart knowing what a good job his sister was doing with him despite the bad pitches life had thrown at them. Freddie was going to grow into one hell of a man one day. Vito could only pray for the boy's sake he didn't choose law enforcement as a career path.

"So, what's eating you up this time, Vito?" Lizbeth asked as they cleared the table. Freddie Junior had disappeared as quickly as he had appeared, and it was time for him to bear his soul.

"A lot of things really. No, that's a lie. There are only two things I can think of."

"Let me guess, a case, and either another case, or you've been sleeping with Karen Stoddard again," she said with a smile that was merely masking her frustration with him.

"Do women tell each other everything? Is there some sort of secret club where every woman in the world gathers to share information? Some huge database with a wealth of information on every male on the planet?"

"I'd tell you the truth, but then you'd have to sleep with the fishes," she said in a bad imitation of DeNiro and laughed. "It's not really that big of a secret, Vito, men are just an open book is all. So, am I right?"

"Yeah, you're right. And you do realize DeNiro wasn't in the Godfather? That was DeNiro you were attempting wasn't it?"

"So what would you like to discuss first?" she asked, completely ignoring his comments as though he had never even uttered the words.

"I think I love her, Lizbeth."

"That's never been a secret either. You've always loved her."

"Yeah, but this time is different. I want her to leave her husband and come live with me."

"In your dump?" She almost screamed with laughter.

"Well, not exactly come and live with me. I mean we could get a different place together. Besides, what's wrong with my place?"

"Oh, nothing the CDC couldn't fix. Hell, Vito, I'm sure you could get some assistance from FEMA if you applied for it," she laughed. "There are things growing in your apartment that would strike fear into the heart of even the bravest adventurer."

"It's not that bad," he defended.

"Vito, your clothes have come over here by themselves to get washed. They've even learned how to drive," she laughed again.

"Cute."

"And have you even bothered to buy any dishes yet? Gloria has been gone a long time now, Vito. You can start living your life again."

"One more Slurpee and I'll have a matching set. And Styrofoam has been scientifically proven to be the best thing to drink coffee out of," he ignored her reference to the worst heartache of his life.

The wounds on Vito's heart still bled every night when he tried to fall asleep and Gloria's face, or smell, or voice would invade the silence of his room. She haunted his sleep until morning when she haunted his day. Her memory tortured him every single day of his life since losing her.

"Do you think Karen will leave George this time?"

"Honestly? No, I don't."

"Then why put yourself through the heartache?"

"Because I'm so smart?"

"Now listen to who's trying to be funny. Would you like a bit of advice?"

"Sure. I probably won't listen, but you can give it anyway."

"Give her an ultimatum, with a deadline attached."

"Like what?"

"I don't know, something like, either you leave your husband by the first of June or we can never see each other again, ever. And, then sweeten the pot, tell her that because of your relationship, you feel she will be unable to treat you fairly so you will also be putting in for a transfer."

"Oh, you mean really piss her off," Vito's face scrunched into a scowl. The last thing he wanted was to have to deal with an enraged Karen Stoddard. The pleasant side of her was hard enough to cope with.

They finished drying and putting away the dishes and moved into the living room with two steaming mugs of Highlander Grog. Vito wasn't much for flavored coffees, but he tolerated it when his sister made it for him. In fact, between her and Haskell he was starting to develop a taste for it.

"Sometimes you have to break a few eggs."

"I know, I know," he cut her off. "Why did you have to pick up all of ma's stupid little sayings?"

"Are you trying to say I am just like my mother? Oh, I know you didn't just compare me with mother," she said while snapping her fingers at him and her eyes took on an angry, almost lupine glow.

"No, not at all," he quickly retreated, having crossed that bridge one too many times before.

"So, what else is bothering you?"

"A case of course."

"A bad one?"

"The worst. But I don't think I should be discussing it with you."

"You always discuss the bad ones with me."

"Like I said, this one is the worst. And it's becoming personal."

"How so?"

"We've got a serial killer loose in the city, Lizzy," he blurted.

Lizbeth couldn't stifle her surprise.

"I don't think you have to worry about anything, he targets pretty, young girls," Vito said before thinking about how his sister might take his words.

"Well thanks a lot, Vito," she huffed and retaliated for the comment.

"No, no, I didn't mean it like that," he laughed and rubbed the spot on his arm where she had punched him. It was sore enough already he knew there would certainly be one hell of a bruise by morning.

"Sure, you didn't."

He could tell by the look on her face he was going to have to endure several jalapeno and cumin laced dinners for his last comment.

"So why do you think it's personal?"

"This guy has been leaving notes on the bodies of his victims. The last one was directed personally to me."

"So, you think this is someone you've rubbed the wrong way somewhere during your travels?"

"It looks that way on the surface, but I'm afraid that angle just doesn't seem to be panning out. I don't believe the killer ever intended to make this personal with anyone in particular, but now that he has an audience, he has decided to make a game of this. It's always impossible to judge what these wackos are thinking. I've got an FBI profiler helping us, but she stated so far, the evidence is not giving her a clear enough picture to draw any concise conclusions. And it doesn't help matters these girls are coming from all parts of the country, but they are being dumped on our doorstep for some reason."

"Wow, this does sound like it could be pretty bad."

"I don't know how you people do it day after day," Vito said.

"I don't quite understand what you mean," Lizbeth replied

"Nurses, doctors, anyone in the health care field. I mean, ever since this case started it has been like I have been sitting back waiting for these girls to die so I can gather evidence from their murder and hopefully catch this guy before he kills too many more. How can you treat a patient day after day, knowing ultimately they are going to die?"

"It's kind of like your job, Vito, you just get numb to it after a while. You save the ones you can, and you try to make passing as comfortable you possibly can for those you can't. You said you sit back and wait? Is there something going on you haven't told me?"

"The notes, they all have the name of the next victim and inform me there is only one month until the next body shows up."

"Oh, my God. That must be terrible for you." Lizbeth reached across the sofa and put a hand over Vito's. He looked up and smiled weakly at her comforting gesture.

"Tomorrow is the first of April, it's only going to get worse. One of the hardest things about this case is that we cannot find even the slimmest of threads bonding these victims together, and yet, we know they're connected and not just random killings. I've spared you a lot of the gory details," he sighed heavily.

"I've got the feeling I should probably thank you for that one."

Freddie came barreling through the door, effectively putting a halt to their conversation. Lizbeth looked deeply into her big brother's eyes and her heart palpitated with sympathy for his grief. She had always hated his job, but so much more so since her husband had been killed in the line of duty. She found it hard to believe Freddie had been gone for almost ten years. Ten years and she had yet to even come close to getting over his death.

She handed Vito a Tupperware bowl full of Fagioli and a brown paper sack with the remnants of the garlic loaf. They gave each other a long hug and a couple of quick pecks on the cheek. Vito thought about going up to Freddie's room and telling him goodbye, but he didn't have the energy.

On the way home Vito stopped at a twenty-four-hour grocery for a pint of Ben and Jerry's Cherry Garcia ice cream and a plastic ice cream scoop to eat it with. His ten-carat plastic silverware never stood up to the test of frozen foods. Two pretty, young girls stood idly at the cash registers waiting for him to pick out his purchases and get the hell out of their store. He was certain he was giving them the heebeejeebies after glancing at his own reflection in the freezer glass. He found himself looking at the two girls, wondering how old they were and where they went after work. Did they go out to parties? Did they go to the dance clubs and pick up strange men who would eventually take them home to maim and mutilate them? A shudder rippled through him and he closed the freezer door. He kept from looking the girl in the eye while she cashed him out. He didn't even want to take the chance on getting to know her.

"Strange dude," he heard her comment as he stepped out into the chilly night air.

He was cruising down Wilshire Boulevard when the clock in his car rolled its numbers and told him it was now April Fool's Day. He had just turned onto Alameda when the little black monster clipped to his belt began telling him the killer knew what day it was as well. He didn't even look down at the number to know who it was. Vito pulled into a gas station with a pay phone set at a height to accommodate drivers and called the precinct. Less than a minute later he was back on the road driving toward the county morgue with a severe case of indigestion threatening to ruin a perfectly shitty evening.

Chapter Six

Vito experienced a strong sense of déjà vu as he stepped through the automatic portal opening up into the hospital's emergency room. He swiveled his head around for several minutes before spying the back of Haskell's head next to a uniformed officer.

"Gregg," he said softly as he walked up on them.

"Vito," he replied, his eyes were bloodshot and swollen from the lack of sleep. "This is Patrolman Dodge. He's the one who found the Douglas girl."

"Where?" Vito asked shortly.

"She was at the drive-in," he choked. Kevin Dodge was a young cop. And although he wasn't a rookie in the true sense of the word, this was his first homicide. He was visibly shaken, nervous and stumbling over his words. "Do you mean you saw her outside the emergency entrance here at the hospital?"

"No, sir, I mean the drive-in theater. The Starlight, out on Interstate Five."

"Was she just lying in the entrance?" Vito asked. Normally the young man's failure to get to the point would have perturbed him and would have ultimately provoked him into yelling, but he could sense this young officer was teetering on the brink and needed to be handled with kid gloves. This fact gravely disturbed him, mainly because it alluded to the fact the scene must have been gruesome.

"I'm sorry, sir, I'm just nervous. I've never had to do anything like this before."

"That's okay, son, just take it slow and explain everything in detail."

"I responded to a call of a possible four fifty-nine in progress at the Starlight. When I arrived, I began patrolling the perimeter to check for any signs of foul play. As I approached the entrance, I noticed fresh tire tracks, so I called it in and continued on into the interior of the drive-in. Once I got around the fence and into the interior, I saw a flashlight beam shining in the distance. By the time I got close enough to see anything, I realized the beam was coming from a parked car near the center of the lot. I could see there was someone sitting in the driver's seat, so I called out several times with no reply. I thought maybe they had fallen asleep watching the movie or were possibly having car trouble. I moved closer and called out again, identifying myself as a police officer several times while walking toward the car but I never got any response. I took an angle on the vehicle and continued my approach. It was then I saw the light was coming from a flashlight sitting on the dashboard with the beam pointing toward the entrance."

He took a deep breath and continued. "I watched the driver carefully for several minutes before it became apparent, they weren't moving. Not even a little. I couldn't even be sure if they were breathing or not. I approached the car from the rear quarter panel and when I looked inside, I found the victim. Her eyes, they were gone, detective." He choked violently at the remembrance.

"Excuse me?"

"Her eyes were gone. There were two black holes in her face. My God, who would do such a thing?"

"Was she dead?"

"Yes, sir. But not for very long I don't think."

"Her skin was still a little warm to the touch, but that could have been from car heater, I guess."

"The heater was running?"

"Yes, sir. And the radio was playing. It must have been a cassette though, because it ended while I was waiting for back up and the coroner to arrive."

"Okay, thank you, Dodge. Why don't you get with the Watch Commander and see about taking a few days off? If I need anything else from you, I can always get it from you later."

"Thank you, sir. I'm sorry."

"Sorry? For what?"

"For not being quicker. For not getting to her before she was killed," pools of tears formed in the corners of his eyes.

Vito pulled him to the side, away from the mayhem to console him. "Son, you couldn't have prevented it. If anything, you might have gotten yourself killed if you hadn't been as cautious as you had. You did the right thing," Vito explained with a rock sitting in the bottom of his gullet.

"Mertyl just got here. I saw her get on the elevator," Haskell broke in.

"I guess it's down in the hole we go," Vito said, taking a step toward the elevator.

Haskell pressed the small green arrow pointing down and said, "I've got an observation if you'd like to hear it."

"Well, hell yes, I'm game for anything at this point," he replied a little too exuberantly.

"Okay," he chuckled nervously. "Although we don't know much, we do know this. Kendra Jenkins was burned, not just burned but cooked to death. I think the killer was destroying her skin, or her complexion. And then there was Evangelique Martens. Her lips were burned off. While Rita Sorenson's breasts were mutilated. And now we have a girl, Christina Douglas, who has apparently had her eyes burned in their sockets."

"I assume you are trying to make a point, Gregg."

"I am. All of the pictures we have of these girls confirm they were once very beautiful. Drop dead gorgeous in fact. And the killer went to great lengths to destroy their looks. I'll bet if we study those pictures, we're liable to find out whatever part of their bodies were damaged will have also been their best physical attribute."

"By this theory, you think that Rita Sorenson was once quite buxom?"

"And Evangelique had very sexy lips."

"So, Christina Douglas must have had pretty eyes?"

"Exactly. The killer is taking his retribution on these girls because of their good looks. We could be dealing with some kind of ugly duckling. A man, who as a boy, never went on a date, never went to the prom. He was apt to have been teased, picked on and ridiculed throughout his school years. He may have even dropped out of school because of the torment."

"So, he probably never got laid, and could be stupid," Vito interrupted.

"Well, theoretically yes."

"But what?"

"But, in keeping with that scenario, these girls should have been raped and/or sexually mutilated. And at the very least, our perp should have had some type of sexual release. This aspect of his crimes makes absolutely no sense at all. There should have been some sort of sexual deviation. As for stupid, just because he may have dropped out of school does not mean he wouldn't be intelligent. I would wager he was academically fit for school, just not socially. In fact, we should assume he is at or near genius levels."

They both pondered this latest theory as the elevator slowed to a halt. The doors chimed opened and they stepped out into the cold, stark corridor. They made their way down to the morgue and stepped through the double doors into the examination room together.

"Hail, hail, the gang's all here," Mertyl Stumpf said in her gravelly voice. She was her typically good-natured self.

Vito looked around the room and saw Mertyl was right. Karen Stoddard was standing at the foot of the examination table with Chief of Police Wilkinson on her right and San Diego County Sheriff Philip Glasgow to the right of him. Not a one of them looked pleased. Vito knew he had better get his shots in early.

"Who gave the authorization to move the body?" he asked as both he and Haskell strode into the room like they owned the place.

Lieutenant Stoddard stammered a few seconds before answering. "Honestly, I'm not sure. I got a page from dispatch and was told to meet you here."

They all started looking suspiciously at one another.

"Easy people, I authorized it," Barry Wilkinson, the chief of police said. He was large, overbearing man who would most likely die at an early age from congestive heart failure. He adjusted his belt to pour his belly back into his pants and dabbed his forehead with a handkerchief.

"And might I ask why?" Vito said in a tone of voice that instantly submerged him in hot water.

"First of all, I don't think I need to answer to the likes of you. It's no wonder why you never make lieutenant with that attitude. And secondly, the Starlight drive-in isn't in our jurisdiction. It is in San Diego County. Their people showed up on the scene and began investigating the homicide. As soon as their people noticed your name carved into the victim's body they called Sheriff Glasgow who in turn called me."

Vito could have kicked himself for not noticing Patrolman Dodge was wearing a San Diego County Sheriff's Department uniform and not one from Los Angeles.

"First, let me apologize, and secondly, I haven't made Lieutenant because I have never tried," his anger seethed. He never liked Barry Wilkinson, he was a pompous, good for nothing politician, not a cop. He never was a cop. The moment he joined the force he had effectively applied his lips to someone's ass and rode them all the way to the top. As chiefs go, he wasn't too bad, as long as he played chief and stayed the hell out of the way. And to complicate things even further, Wilkinson was George Masarick's best friend and he seemed to take it as a personal affront Vito was banging his best friend's wife, regardless of who George was out diddling.

"Listen, we've got too much to be worrying about to be bickering amongst ourselves," Wilkinson gave a sickly sneer that sent ice water trickling through Vito's veins. The sneer was meant as a reminder that this wasn't over, not by a long shot. He was going to pay for his insubordination, and dearly. But it would come in the form of some backstabbing, paper-filing motion Vito wouldn't be able to defend himself against. Maybe he would find himself temporarily loaned out to the border patrol or something else just as humiliating.

"Okay, Phil, Mertyl, what can you tell us?" Karen separated the testosterone twins before things got any uglier and brought the meeting back to where it belonged.

"I've already sent a team of investigators down to San Diego to work with their people on the evidence. It will probably take me a day or two before I can process a report for you. As for the girl, Mertyl here will know more about the specifics," the crime scene investigator said.

Mertyl coughed up half a lung before giving her report, "A core temperature reading tells me she's be dead about three or four hours give or take an hour. There is no doubt in my mind that the same person who killed the other three girls has murdered this poor girl as well. And again, there have been extensive efforts to keep this girl alive during her captivity."

"How was she killed?" Haskell jumped in.

"In a nutshell, her brain was cooked. The same surgical laser that has been used to write the messages on the other girls was also used to burn out her eyes. After the eyes were destroyed, the beam went to work on her brain matter. However, I believe that was accidental."

"Why do you feel it was accidental?" Gregg asked.

"There wasn't much damage to the brain tissue, but enough to kill her. I think this monster just didn't realize the damage this laser can do, which leads me to believe if this person has limited medical training."

"Christ Almighty!" Vito blurted.

"And whoever did this left this for you, detective," she jerked back the sheet exposing Christina Douglas's body to them for the first time.

All in the room recoiled except for Mertyl Stumpf. She had already done that, privately, when the body first came in. Two hollow pits stared up at the stark white ceiling. Her once vibrant blue eyes were now nothing more than horrific black shadows. They reminded Vito of bullet holes in paper targets, the edges jagged frayed and scorched. If one could ignore her accusing eyes, her face was surprisingly peaceful.

Vito's eyes passed quickly over her naked form until he got to the abhorrent lettering burned into her flesh.

Tick, Tock Detective Lorenz. Tick, Tock, Amber Reese is on the clock!

Vito visibly cringed at the message. Karen shot him a sympathetic look, as did Philip Glasgow. Both Wilkinson and Christina Douglas shot him glances nothing short of reproachful. He spun on his heels and marched out of the room. The world felt like it was closing in on him and he suddenly found it extremely hard to breathe.

"Shit, damn, hell," he said as he waited for the elevator to get to the basement and rescue him from bowels of hell.

"Easy, man, it's not your fault," Haskell said, hooking Vito's arm and stopping him just short of punching the wall.

"Why me?" he turned and asked his partner.

"If we knew, we'd be one step closer to solving this thing."

"Man, I haven't slept for shit ever since Rita Sorenson jumped from her window."

"To tell you the truth, neither have I. Neither of us is going to get much action looking like this," Haskell said with a weak smile.

The doors to the elevator opened up on the lobby and the two detectives headed for the doors leading to the outside world.

"Vito," a voice called from out of the hustle and hurry world of the hospital.

Vito and Haskell both turned around and scanned the sea of people flowing in and around them. When they didn't see anyone they recognized they turned with a shrug and continued down the corridor.

"Vito," the voice called again.

"Lizbeth?" Vito said to no one in particular. He had recognized her voice, but he didn't see her anywhere.

"Over here," she said, waving her hand at the two of them from a nurse's station.

A huge specimen of a woman had been standing in front of her, obscuring their view of her. As soon as Vito spied her he walked over to where she was working with Haskell in tow.

"Boy, what great detectives you two turned out to be," Lizbeth smiled. Haskell felt himself melt a little beneath her smile. It was the first time he had met his partner's sister. He knew she was pretty from the pictures Vito had shown him, but Gregg never imagined she was this exotically beautiful. He smiled back at her, trying not to let his racing heart command his mouth and force him to say something stupid. He just gave her a silly grin and chose to remain quiet.

"Aren't you going to introduce us?" Lizbeth asked.

"Hi, I'm Gregg Haskell," he reached his hand out to Lizbeth.

Hearing the tone of Haskell's voice Vito said, "Easy cowboy, that's my sister."

Gregg blushed and Lizbeth giggled.

"I forgot this was the hospital you work at," Vito smiled awkwardly.

"Why are you two here? Oh," she said, after realizing they must have come up from the basement where the morgue was. She shuddered internally, remembering her and Vito's earlier conversation.

"I'm afraid this bastard isn't missing a beat," Vito snarled.

"I'm sorry to hear that, for both of you."

"It's not us I'm worried about," Haskell said.

All three of them just nodded in a gesture of sympathy for the dead girl.

"Well, don't you two make a cute couple?" Karen Stoddard commented as she walked upon the trio. Haskell had been standing next to Lizbeth and Karen couldn't resist the comment.

"What? Oh," Haskell blushed and moved a step away from his partner's sister.

"Good morning, Karen," Lizbeth greeted, not even making a weak attempt to mask the contempt in her voice.

"How have you been Lizbeth?" Her own voice was sour with contempt.

"Great. You're looking good this morning."

"Never as good as you, I'm afraid."

"How's George?" Lizbeth asked venomously.

"Never better. I'm sure he'll win his election this year."

"That's nice to hear, maybe then the two of you will be able to spend more time together. I'm sure it's very difficult having him gone politicking all the time."

"I'm sure we'll think of some way to celebrate."

Vito and Gregg watched the verbal tennis match, neither one of them too sure of exactly what it was they were witnessing. On the surface it looked as though the two women were getting along just fine, but they were certain a catfight was merely one hiss away.

"I will see you two back at the precinct," Karen said while turning to leave.

"It was a pleasure seeing you again, Karen," Lizbeth called after her.

"Likewise," she spat in rebuttal.

Lizbeth stood steely eyed with a smug smile painted on her face.

"I'm glad to see you two are getting along as well as ever," Vito commented.

"Don't start with me," she smiled and feigned another blow to his arm.

Vito flinched, as did Haskell.

"Well, sis, we had better get going."

"Okay. I love you," she blew a kiss at him causing Haskell to blush.

They turned to leave and she called out, "Vito," before they made it to the door.

"Yeah," he turned around.

"Talk to her, today," she mouthed. "It was nice meeting you, Gregg," she cooed.

He just grinned and nodded stupidly. "What does she mean, talk to her?"

"None of your damned business," he ended the discussion even before it began.

*   *   *

Vito brewed a fresh pot of coffee and began working at putting all of Christina Douglas's new information into the computer. He meticulously outlined the details of the girl's death and tried to reconstruct her days in captivity as best as possible. He transmitted the information to the FBI along with requests for information on Amber Reese.

Haskell was busy on the telephone trying to find out who the person was connected to the name on Christina Douglas's stomach. Who was Amber Reese? Where had she come from? Where had she been going when she disappeared? All of the same questions and answers they had asked and received about the other girls resulted in more of the same vague, general information that brought them to the exact same place, nowhere.

Vito brought them each a fresh cup of coffee, setting one front of Haskell and the other next to his keyboard. He stared at the computer screen hoping for something, some key point of information to jump out at him. But nothing did. They had drawn a chart for each of the girls. It was a timeline of the last few hours of their free lives, or at least as much of it as the detectives had been able to piece together. Who it was they had last been seen with? Who they had talked to? Where were their favorite places to eat? What they had eaten? Lines connected boxes of information which were then connected to other boxes of information with even more lines. The only inescapable fact was only two of the lines ever crossed, Kendra's and Evangelique's. And Vito was certain this was only dumb luck. There was something else connecting these girls to one another, something they just couldn't see yet. Something they weren't being allowed to see.

Tick Tock! The phrase echoed in Vito's head. He couldn't for the life of him, figure out why this thing had become personal. He had gone over all of his case files and not a one of them even hinted at the fact this was a recent parolee or someone he may have pissed off. In fact, there was nothing even remotely suggesting that possibility.

He closed the computer file on Kendra Jenkins and opened Evangelique Martens' file. After fifteen minutes he closed her file and opened Rita Sorenson's. He repeated this process fifteen minutes later, opening Christina Douglas's file.

"I think you're on to something, Gregg," he blurted.

"What?" he asked, pulling himself away from a bevy of files he was scanning through.

"You speculated the killer was pinpointing the girl's strong points as if he had some personal vendetta against them. And after looking over all of this, I'd have to agree with you and this fact is the only common thread binding each of these girls together."

The fax machine rumbled to life.

"So, if we find out what Amber Reese's best physical attribute is, we might have a clue as to how to help her," Haskell interjected.

"Theoretically, yes," Vito responded.

"And practically?"

"We will only have an educated guess as to how the killer is going to mutilate her before we get to see firsthand for ourselves."

"That's comforting," Haskell's sarcasm was bitterer than his coffee.

"Amen to that," Vito added, reaching into the basket and grabbing out the transmitted fax.

He looked over the paper for several minutes before passing it over to his partner. Haskell studied the innocent young face smiling back at him. Nothing stood out. There was nothing about the young woman setting her apart from the other girls.

"What do you make of it?" Vito asked.

"I'm not sure. She seems kind of plain Jane compared to the other girls, don't you think?"

"That was my first impression."

"So, what now?"

"We think. We read. We wait."

"I don't much like those options."

"Well, they're the only ones we have right now."

They both paused for a minute and took long, hard sips of their coffee. Haskell dropped the faxed picture of Amber Reese on his desk. The girl's eyes seemed to be pleading with the two detectives.

"Vito, let's assumed you are correct and the way this killer is grouping these girls together is what binds them together in this case, right."

"Yeah, so."

"Why?"

"Why what?"

"Why do all of these girls have some special attribute setting them apart from each other?"

"I don't think I quite get what you're trying to say."

"I would say they had all attended the same high school, but that wasn't the case. You know, voted best smile or best eyes or biggest breasts for that matter," Haskell explained.

"Yeah, now I got you. But they weren't in high school together, or college for that matter. What about a beauty pageant?"

"Could be, it's a definite possibility."

"And maybe they weren't even in the same beauty pageant together," Vito added.

"Exactly, random, yet with a pattern. The killer may have just yanked their names out of a directory somewhere."

"Or, he works for a pageant touring the country. Maybe each of these girls rejected him or made fun of him at some point."

"I'm on it," Haskell blurted, spinning his chair around to face his computer. Instantly the squad room exploded with the sound of him clicking away at the computer keyboard.

Vito smiled, more of a grimace, and got up from his desk. He would never find the nerve again, so he headed for the glass palace. He opened the door without knocking and stepped inside. Once in her office, he locked the door behind him.

"Vito, what are you doing?"

"We need to talk."

"About what?"

"Us," he breathed.

"What about us?"

"Exactly. What about us?"

"Vito, I don't have time to play twenty questions with you right now. Can we please have this discussion later tonight, at home?"

"Whose home, yours or mine?"

"That's a pretty stupid question don't you think?"

"Not at all. Listen Karen, I am going to be perfectly blunt with you. I love you," he paused long enough to see the reaction on her face. It wasn't so much shock from his saying the words but shock he had said them so soon into their rekindled relationship.

"Vito," she said, her voice was condescending, apologetic and loving all in the same breath.

"No, no Vito. Listen. I love you, I know I do and I also know there is no changing that fact. However, I can't allow this relationship to continue with the way things have been going. Either I get to love you on my terms, or no terms at all."

"What are you trying to say, Vito?"

"I'm saying I want you to leave your husband."

"And if I don't?" She took a defensive stance.

"Then there can be nothing more between us."

"That's not fair, Vito."

"The hell it's not. The way it stands right now this isn't being fair to me. And if you chose to end our relationship, I'm afraid I will have to ask for a transfer under the circumstance."

"Oh really? And what makes you think for one minute I would grant your request?"

"You're a politician Karen, you couldn't have the bad publicity of our relationship making it to the press. And I don't think you could be fair with me if I were to break things off with you."

"Are you threatening me, Vito?"

"Not at all, I'm just giving you the facts the way I see them."

"Are you sure this is the way you want this, and not your sister's?" She spat.

"You can leave Lizbeth out of this. This is my decision, and mine alone."

"I'm sure she put the ideas in your head, you could never think of this on your own," her tone was acerbic and biting. Karen was stung by Vito's request. Mainly because she felt a certain kind of love for him as well, but she also knew she would never leave her husband, no matter if he was a cold, heartless son of a bitch. She couldn't, it would prove much too harmful for her career.

"I said, leave Lizbeth out of this. I think we could have a good thing together, Karen, but not like this. I don't want to be sneaking around and only getting to be with you when your husband is out of town or out entertaining or whatever. I want you, when I want you for as long as I want you."

"I'm not sure you could have that even if I were to leave my husband."

Vito fought the sour knot balling up in his stomach. Tears were just below the surface and he knew if he didn't get out of her office, away from her, he would break down right in front of her. Silently he kicked himself for ever falling this far down again.

"Your partner wants you," she broke the uneasy silence.

"What?"

"Haskell, he's waving for you," she said, staring out the glass separating her world from theirs. She wore a forced smile and waved back at the beckoning detective.

"Well, I guess I had better go see what he wants."

"Is this your final decision?"

"Yes, I'm afraid it is," Vito replied, stepping out of her office without looking back.

His legs were wobbly, and it took great effort to walk straight. He swallowed hard several times and got control of his nerves. He could feel Karen's eyes burning into his back and down into his soul. He fought the urge to turn around, run back to her office and tell her he was just joking.

"Yeah, what's up?" he asked, sitting back down at his desk.

"I just got a call from Gray Morgan."

"The prosecutor?"

"Yes. He claims to have some information he thinks we might be interested in. He thinks it might help us with this case. He wants to meet with us tomorrow morning, early, if that's all right with you."

"Sure, what time?"

"Five o'clock in the morning, at his father's place. He gave me directions."

"Any particular reason why so early?"

"I didn't ask, I thought any break in this case was a good break, even at five am," Haskell smiled.

"I see your point. Besides, neither of us is getting much sleep anyway," he grimaced as he drunk the last of his cold coffee in one gulp.

Tick Tock, Detective Lorenz!

Chapter Seven

Amber stared, teary eyed, at the encrusted face of her transparent sarcophagus. Coagulating rivers of gruel were oozing down the plastic and had begun to dry in grotesque patterns. Her arm stung where the third needle had been forced through her skin and into her bruised vein. She could taste the vitamins, proteins and sugars being pumped through her blood. She wondered why the bastard continually tried to feed her the disgusting slop, especially when she spat it out every time.

There was even a time early in her captivity when he had opened her chamber and used a device to pry open her clenched jaws. He locked her mouth into an open position with a surgical clamp and forced the tube down her throat. Nevertheless, in spite of his efforts the minute the rancid tasting gruel hit the pit of her stomach, she regurgitated it back out onto herself.

She sensed her subjugator was becoming increasingly frustrated. It was clear to her he wasn't accustomed to encountering such defiance. Amber had even been able to bite him, hard, while he was removing the vise-like device from her jaws. It hurt like hell, but she bit down with all the force she could muster. Of her endless months of captivity, it was the only time she could remember seeing the bastard angry. But she immediately recognized his uncontrolled emotions as a good sign. He was human, and humans bleed. And humans die!

Her captor had tried to keep her in a stupor most of the time, but she fought the drugs as hard as she could. She fought against them so hard he doubled her dosage, which resulted in her becoming addicted to the narcotics. When he cut them back, she went through severe withdrawals. That was when Amber understood this animal wasn't trying to kill her. Quite the contrary, he was doing everything within his power to keep her alive. He had actually tried to feed her solid food at one point but her jaw muscles were too sore to chew and her stomach was too volatile to keep anything down.

This fact was quite disturbing to Amber. As was the fact aside from his fondling the redhead, he had done nothing sexual to her or to the others as far as she could tell. She had absorbed every nuance of her surroundings. She knew how many bags of saline had run through her, as well as how many bags of vitamin laced glucose. She used her untrimmed thumbnail to scratch marks into her armrest to help her keep track of time. Amber didn't need the perverse calendar on her chamber to keep track of time. She knew exactly how long she had been held captive. Eleven months and seven days to be exact.

She still remembered the day she was taken hostage. May first, one year ago. In Chicago's O'Hare airport, awaiting a flight to Barcelona. She remembered being so excited. So pumped. She was sure to make the cover. There had been at least a dozen girls in all waiting to go on the Sports Illustrated Swimsuit Edition photo shoot.

Tears rolled down Amber's face as she recalled her past. At first she had thought her kidnapping must have been a case of mistaken identity and her captor had simply made a mistake. He must have been after someone else, someone with a hell of a lot more than the twenty bucks she had to her name. But then, as time went on, she began thinking it was someone who didn't want her on the Sports Illustrated photo shoot for one reason or another. She found it hard to believe a rival model would go to all the trouble of having her kidnapped just to keep her from making the cover and stealing the spotlight, but stranger things had happened. Cheerleader's mothers killing other cheerleaders, a teacher seducing her students and coercing them into killing her husband. There was no end to the depravity of humanity. But the photo shoot would have been over six months ago. If any of her theories were truly the case, then she should have been freed, or even killed by now. What's more, she wasn't the only one held in captivity.

And then she began thinking, maybe all of these girls were going on the shoot with her. Maybe the entire crew of models was being held for ransom. But why had they all been held for so long? Surely if the ransom demands hadn't been met, they would have been killed long, long ago.

Amber continually took note of her surroundings whenever she was coherent enough. She had already deduced her captor was somewhere between five foot six and five foot eight according to the shadows he cast. He was a smaller man, maybe one hundred and fifty pounds, soaking wet and with a twenty-pound sack of flour on his shoulder. And as far as she could tell, he was white, not to mention, extremely intelligent and cunning.

Amber had tried every trick she could think of to get the man to speak, but nothing worked. She wanted to hear his voice. Was it deep and manly? Or was a he a milquetoast with a falsetto voice and lack of balls to boot? She had tried to engage him in conversation, just for conversation's sake. However, he seemed to be so immune to her voice she had to wonder if her voice even carried outside the walls of her tomb.

Each time Amber had learned something new about this monster she worked hard to commit it to memory, so the tidbit wasn't lost once the drugs began flowing through her veins again. She only focused on one piece of information at a time. She had chanted his estimated height repeatedly for hours until it was firmly imbedded in her gray matter before moving on to his weight. She had practiced this technique so often she now had a complete mental picture of the creep. She had even painted a face on him. Granted, it would probably turn out to be completely off base, but it helped her to cope with her daily struggles. She needed someone to hate. Not just a blank face. A real person.

Her captor had become a conglomeration of every man who had ever done her wrong, dating all the way back to Billy Foster, who in third grade tickled her so hard she wet her pants in front of everyone on the playground. He was also a little bit of Chuck Proctor, who in her senior year decided to force himself upon her despite her repeated pleas for him to stop. Luckily for her, Chuck had been more adept at football than sex and only managed to soil the front of her prom dress. And he was a little bit of her father, who chose his career and his new wife over her.

Amber felt her tears tickling her face as they streamed down in remembrance. At the present the sins of Billy, Chuck and her father didn't seem so appalling. They had only taken little pieces of her this maniac wanted the whole damned thing.

Another taste began invading her mouth. It was bitter and rancorous. She watched the shadowy figure float away from her as the drugs began invading her system. Her mind slipped from its precarious perch on reality leaving her to contend with her nightmares once again.

*   *   *

"Morning sunshine," Haskell greeted Lorenz and he slid into the passenger seat.

Vito responded with a guttural grunt reminiscent of a Cro-Magnon late for dinner.

"There's coffee in the thermos," he said, nodding to a silver cylinder sitting on the seat between them.

Haskell grinned internally as he watched Vito's nose turn up at the odor of cinnamon hazelnut when he poured a cup full of the foo foo coffee. He was glad he was driving for a change, he actually felt safe. They made their way through the Hollywood hills out to the modest suburb of Sherman Oaks. Gregg sipped at his Colombian Supreme while Vito suffered through his cup of crap coffee. It was one small step in his plan of retribution for the cinnamon doughnuts. Gregg had several Post-It notes on his refrigerator door reminding him of the little pokes he had planned for his partner.

Haskell slowed down enough to read the mailboxes lining the road and turned into the driveway belonging to retired Circuit Court Judge, Blue Morgan. They eased up the winding driveway lined with a variety of spring blooms. Flaming Parrot tulips, brilliant white Ismene Festalis and Pineapple Lilies brush-stroked the landscape with vibrant color. Bougainvillea vines splashed nature's paint along the lengths of four ionic columns propping up the porch roof like robust sentinels.

Clarence stood stately on the sprawling porch to greet the pair. His dark gray suit and maroon tie were a proud testament to his alma mater. An NCAA National Championship ring from nineteen forty-two adorned his right hand, his only jewelry save for a simple USN tie tack in the center of his chest. Gregg sensed the man was an athlete and a veteran by the way he carried himself so proudly. He reached out for the man's hand with great respect.

"Detective's Gregg Haskell and Vito Lorenz," he greeted.

"We weren't expecting anyone else at this hour," he droned and showed them into the house. Vito thought he caught a hint of a smirk wrinkle the man's face.

As they walked through the house, Vito couldn't help but notice the odor permeating the air. Behind all the masks of wild berry, pine and vanilla air fresheners was the unmistakable odor of old people. It wasn't a single scent, but a conglomeration of smells blending into something hinting of death creeping just beyond the horizon.

Clarence led them through the foyer, passed the dining room and into the study where the judge sat behind his laptop in an oversized brown leather chair. Vito wasn't sure which was older, the judge or the chair. Ornate brass studs accented the seams of the cracking leather and the red oak legs shimmered with a lifetime worth of polish. The chair seemed to envelop the shrinking man. The image of Lily Tomlin's character Edith Anne sitting in her giant rocker flashed through Vito's mind and he had to suppress a chuckle by biting the inside of his lip.

A large man, obviously closely related to the judge, stood up to greet them. "Gray Morgan, you must be detective's Lorenz and Haskell," the man greeted, knowing full well who they were. He shoved a hand at Vito so large he had first thought the man was wearing a catcher's mitt.

"Lorenz, Vito Lorenz," he said while the man tried to shake his arm free from its socket.

"Greg Haskell," he said, trying to quell the pain induced scowl perched on his lips.

"I'm glad you two could make it so early in the morning. Let me apologize for that, but this seems to be the only time of the day when I am worth a damn," Blue's voice was still strong and commanding of respect yet laced with fatherly qualities.

"Perfectly fine, Your Honor," Vito replied.

"My father has told me much of everything he knows, and I will be able to fill in the blanks if it comes to that," Gray said.

"I'm afraid to say you have me at a loss here," Vito replied.

"I have Alzheimer's detective. My mind is not a stable creature, I'm afraid."

"Now that, I understand," Vito smiled weakly at his poor attempt at humor.

An awkward hush fell over the room and Vito silently berated himself for his shitty sense of humor and even shittier sense of timing.

"Would you like some coffee, detectives?" Clarence asked bitingly.

They both nodded.

"Excuse me, Your Honor, I don't mean to be rude . . . "

"You wish to know why I've called you two here?" he interrupted Vito.

"Frankly, yes, sir."

"Call me Blue," he said with a glance of his hazy, smoke blue eyes. "Let me cut to the chase before my old age starts kicking me in the ass. You are working on a case involving the murder of several young girls, am I correct?"

They both looked at each other with puzzled looks and then turned to the judge with an affirmative nod.

He laughed a dry throated chortle. "I have my ways of finding things out. Is this a serial killer? And be straight with me, I don't have enough time left in this life to be wasting it on BS."

"We believe so, sir," Vito replied honestly without hesitation out of a sincere respect for the man. Blue Morgan had a reputation that would forever stand the test of time. He was a fair, good man with an unfaltering sense of justice.

"I was afraid of that. Let me start by saying I am not sure how much I can actually help you, or even what I know about this case. But I can tell you what I do know. About two months ago, after two of these girls, Kendra Jenkins and Evangelique Martens had found their way into the obituaries. I started having this gut feeling I knew the girls. And when the third girl, Rita Sorenson, joined them I was certain I knew they were connected to one another somehow. But damned if I could remember exactly why I knew this. I contacted my son, who, as a prosecutor, has access to NCIC and he ran their names. By this time, the Douglas girl had also turned up in the morgue."

He paused to look at his computer screen where he had amassed meticulous notes about the case. He read through the information for several minutes before proceeding.

"Like I said, I had asked my son to look into this for me and by the time he was able to get back with me on this, Christina Douglas's name had been added to the list of girls. The very minute Gray mentioned her name to me, I could see her, with all of the others, sitting in my courtroom. Up until this point I thought my mind might be playing tricks on me and making me see things that had never really been. I thought maybe my seeing their pictures helped to create this illusion. That was until Gray brought up this Douglas girl's name to me. Even though he hadn't shown me her picture, I saw her face just the same. By then I was convinced not only were these five girls connected, but I had seen them in an official capacity as well."

"Please tell me you remember," Vito said, almost pleading.

"At first, I had no clue. But I have maintained meticulous records throughout my years on the bench and I knew the information had to be in there. My son and I," his speech had begun to slow at first and then abruptly he stopped talking altogether and began rubbing his temples. Vito noticed the man's hands were trembling.

"Are you all right, sir?" Haskell asked.

"Damn, damn, damn," he pounded his fists on the arms of the chair. Clarence quickly stepped into the room and fed the man two blue pills with a tall glass of water. The detectives stared at the old man, waiting for him to continue with his soliloquy. It was the last they would see of Judge Blue Morgan for the day.

"I'm sorry, gentlemen, but I think my father has slipped out of our world for a while. Not to worry, I have all the information you'll need right here. However, he will be quite disappointed he wasn't able to tell you himself."

"Maybe we can humor him later," Vito offered.

"Keeping him informed as to what you uncover in this case will humor him just fine."

"You've got yourself a deal."

"Okay," Gray said, opening a large manila folder and sorting through several pieces of paper. "It seems these girls, along with thirteen others were involved with the making of a calendar several years ago. They were the models. This was a nude calendar strictly intended for an extremely select European market. Somehow a couple of the copies slipped into the mainstream and one of the girl's estranged parents got a look at it. Immediately they brought a lawsuit against the company and the photographer as well as filing criminal charges," he explained.

"They were underage?" Vito asked, seeing the direction of the conversation.

"Most of them, sadly enough, yes. The majority of the girls were between the ages of fourteen and sixteen, but there were a couple as old as eighteen and if these notes are accurate, as young as twelve. The eighteen-year old girls were among a group of six who had been designated as alternates. Their pictures probably wouldn't even have been used unless something happened to one of the primary twelve. Once the lawsuit was filed seven of the other girls signed on as well. Ultimately the listed owner of the company who was merely an unwitting fall guy and two of the photographers were convicted on child pornography charges. But the convictions came with a long list of strings attached."

"I take it a civil case followed," Haskell interjected.

"Exactly. The girls were eventually awarded seven point two million dollars in damages."

"Seven million dollars? How in hell could a fly by night calendar producer have that kind of money?" Vito blurted.

"Have you ever heard of Raymond Kyser?"

"The billionaire real estate tycoon? Sure, hasn't everybody?"

Gray Morgan gave the detectives a moment to mull over the information and waited for the light to go on.

"Raymond Kyser. Involved in a child pornography ring? I can't believe it. This would have ruined him had it gotten out to the public," Haskell commented.

"Exactly."

"So, why didn't it get out?"

"Because my father had the records sealed."

"Why on earth would he do that?" Vito asked.

"His hands were tied, and he felt, despite the circumstances, it was the right thing to do."

"I don't understand," Haskell said.

"Several of the families petitioned the court to have the records sealed. They claimed the young girls' careers were taking off and to have something like a nude calendar coming back to haunt them could ruin them. Not to mention the emotional scarring of such an ordeal. My father agreed with that assumption and felt the greater good would be served by sealing the records. He had tried several different angles to keep Kyser's name from being washed away with the rest of the file, but he just couldn't do it. In the end he exhausted every resource and avenue to put these sick men away for life."

"What kept him from getting to Kyser?"

"The man has enough money to hire the best lawyers in the country. Their argument was that if Kyser were going to be able to defend himself in court, then the calendar, along with all of the photos of the girls, would have to be submitted into evidence during his trial. He all but threatened to drag each and every one of the girls through the mud and ruin their lives and their careers before he was finished. He even had the audacity to present the families and the courts with mockup press releases they would run in several newspapers and tabloids, which of course he holds controlling interests in. Finally, all parties involved agreed upon an undisclosed amount of money and a list of stipulations designed to satisfy all parties, except my father of course."

"I can tell from your tone of voice something just wasn't kosher about the deal," Vito said.

He nodded his head and looked at the floor. "My father was certain Kyser's people had somehow manipulated the families into petitioning the court to seal the records. He was convinced Kyser bought his way out of one hell of a hornet's nest. After the records were sealed my father wanted a task force assigned to investigate Kyser, but the man had somehow bought his way out of that as well."

"Did your father suspect him of something else?"

"Yes. While the police were investigating the case, they confiscated some materials from the photographer's loft. The place had been well sanitized, but there were a few videos in his private collection. They had been altered but the lab was able to clean them up. There were several different styles of illegal films. Most of them were chicken films, involving young boys, mostly Asian. There was also several involving bondage, which exploited little girls as young as six or seven years old."

"Christ," Haskell choked.

"What else," Vito sighed.

"These weren't just porno films for the depraved they were advertisements for retreats, getaways where the rich could indulge in their fantasies far from the prying eyes of authorities. The FBI was able to link Kyser to the corporate address listed in the videos, however, he fled the country long before they had a chance to arrest him on suspicion."

"Damn the bad luck. Any ideas where he might be?"

"The last known whereabouts was Thailand, but Interpol was closing in on him there when he disappeared again and hasn't been seen since."

"So, he could be anywhere?" Haskell asked.

"Including Los Angeles," Vito added.

"Including Los Angeles," Morgan agreed with a nod, his face sullen and dark.

The three men contemplated this information while drinking fresh coffee Clarence had brought for them. Vito walked over to a window facing the south. He stared out at a plot of recently tilled plot of ground ready for planting. The wheels in his brain were screeching and grinding against one another. Something about this just wasn't making sense.

He spun around to face Gray Morgan. "But none of the girls who were murdered had been sexually assaulted," he said.

"That's true, if this were some kind of slavery ring it seems there would be evidence of sexual abuse," Haskell added.

"And what if it is nothing more than good old-fashioned retribution? Kyser was forced to give up his home here in the states and live abroad," Morgan countered.

"Well, I am sure he's living quite comfortably wherever he is. It hardly seems like it would be worth the risk," Vito said.

"Who knows what goes on in a sick, twisted mind like his," Haskell added.

"True. Did the judge maintain a file on this case?" Vito turned back around to face Gray.

"Yes. I can print you out a hard copy of his notes. All the girl's names have been removed, however, but the details are there, including the photographer's name as well as a few others who worked on the calendar project. It's not much, but I hope it helps."

"We really appreciate this. Our case was absolutely dead in the water up until now."

"I wish my father would have kept a list of the girl's names, but he didn't."

"I wish he had too, but I can understand why he didn't. We've already got a list of missing women from around the country who fit the age profile. There are hundreds of names on the list, but hell, maybe we'll get lucky. At least now we know of what we should be looking for," Vito said.

"I'd love to help you more if I could," Gray offered.

"Keep talking with your father, maybe he'll remember something more than he already has," Haskell said.

"You can count on that. You can also count on me taking on this case personally, if and when you catch this creep."

"Hopefully that will be soon. I can't begin to thank you enough for your time. I hate to be rude, but we had better get back to the precinct with this information. I think we need to track down this photographer, and fast," Vito said.

"Think nothing of it, I understand completely. It was nice meeting you two, I only wish it was under better circumstances," Gray said as he escorted them through the house to the front door.

"The pleasure was ours, I assure you," Haskell said. He was containing his excitement about getting the first real break in the case, but only because something didn't feel right. He knew Vito was right about the girls not being sexually assaulted having a lot to do with the perp's motives. And he was also right about Kyser not having anything to gain by killing these girls, and if there was one thing he knew about Raymond Kyser's type was they were the kind of men who never did anything unless there was something to gain from it.

"Oh, detectives, one more thing," Gray Morgan called out from the porch as they were getting into the car.

Vito and Haskell turned and acknowledged him.

"Please make damn certain you get all your ducks in a row for this one. Cross and the T's and dot all the I's, I don't want this bastard sneaking out of this one on a technicality. In fact, I damn sure plan on seeking the death penalty."

"Yes, sir, you can count on that. And death certainly sounds like a plan to me," Vito said, throwing the car into gear and pulling away from the sprawling estate of Judge Blue Morgan.

Although neither one of them showed it, they were both quite excited about the turn of events. All they needed to do was locate the photographer, get him to give up the goods on Raymond Kyser. Then they would simply track the tycoon down and save the remaining girls from a fate worse than death. It was simple. They both knew differently. It felt as if they were only one step away from the beginning. Now they knew a little more than they had the day before, but only very little.

*   *   *

They spent the rest of the day gathering as much information as possible on Raymond Kyser and his holdings. Sadly, the only thing they had learned was that before the trial he had been able to effectively transfer all his assets into trust funds for his young children, all of whom were still minors. The children were in the custody of his conveniently drug and alcohol addicted ex-wife who spent more time in detox centers than she did at home, leaving him in full control of the children until she was clean. His dirty money was sitting in accounts, drawing interest, waiting for him to collect once the children came of age. They had also uncovered several offshore accounts linked to Kyser as well, but those accounts had all been closed out days before the trials began. It looked as though he may have been planning to skip the country even before making it to court. Kyser had it all figured out which strongly suggested premeditation, a key element in a death penalty case. Every aspect. Every angle, as though he had been through this ordeal more than once in his twisted lifetime.

They had run the photographer's name through NCIC and were waiting on confirmation of his whereabouts. Luckily, his probationary period was not over and being a prior sex offender he was required by law to report his whereabouts. Now, if he only chose to obey the law they would be in luck. For the first time during the investigation did they no longer feel they were trapped in a long, dark tunnel with no exit in sight. Judge Morgan had given them a crumb it was up to them to turn it into a meal.

*   *   *

Greg Haskell sat in the bleachers, darting his eyes between a cute, blonde power forward and the case files sitting in his lap. He beamed with pride as number thirty-four drove to the basket and made her shot. She recovered and quickly set herself up on defense where she took the opportunity to steal the inbound pass and lay it up for a quick two points, putting her team up by twelve with one-minute remaining in the half. Red faced and flush she looked up to the bleachers, spied her Uncle Gregg and beamed from ear to ear, but only for a brief second. She blinked and her mind was back on the game.

Haskell closed the folder and began making his way down the bleachers. He caught a glimpse of his niece as the buzzer sounded and she bounded off the court with her teammates. With cheeks flush with adrenaline she turned and gave him a vigorous wave before disappearing into the locker room with the rest of her team. Gregg ambled over to the concession stand, bought a cup of coffee and walked outside to enjoy the brisk evening air.

He listened to seagulls squawking and the low roar of passing cars on a nearby freeway. The cars almost sounded like the waves of high tide crashing against the yellow sands of the beach. Before long, Gregg realized he was no longer alone. He turned around and saw an attractive woman tapping a cigarette out of a pack she had pulled from her purse.

"I hope you don't mind," she said, more as a courtesy than an option.

"No, not at all, I'm standing upwind," he smiled, but was clearly agitated at the intrusion into his sanctuary.

She flicked her lighter and touched it to the end a long, slender cigarette until the tip glowed cherry red. Gregg watched as a fourth of the cigarette's tip was reduced to ashes in one drag. She exhaled quickly and ground the cigarette out under her shoe. She picked up the remnants and tossed it into a trashcan.

"I'm trying to quit," she said with a nervous smile, noticing Haskell reaction to her odd behavior.

"Never started myself, but I imagine it can be pretty tough to quit."

Gregg couldn't quite put a finger on why he felt so moody, or why he was being so short with the woman. The woman was much prettier than Gregg's first impression seeing her in the flickering light of her cigarette lighter. She had thick, puffy red lips pulled back slightly from her perfectly polished teeth when she smiled. Her thick brown, almost black hair, fell in ringlets around her shoulders. She reminded him of Vito's sister, Lizbeth. She had the same exotic look about her, the same deep brown eyes, but this woman was taller and more catlike. And then suddenly it dawned on Gregg, he was being curt with the woman because she looked like the others. Not in any overt semblance, but in individual particulars. She had the sexy lips Evangelique Martens had once pursed and pouted. She had the smooth, supple skin Kendra had enjoyed at one time. And she was buxom, quite buxom in fact. Subconsciously he was trying to set up barriers against this woman.

"It's a lot tougher to keep smoking these days. It's amazing what a little knowledge can do to a bad habit. Amanda Lyons," she said, offering a gentle hand to Haskell. She detected him staring at her chest and found it a little uncomfortable at first. But hell, he was cute, and most men stared at her breasts. But she couldn't help but get the feeling he wasn't seeing what most other men saw. His wasn't a look of lust, the lip licking, drool on the chin kind of look. No, his expression was almost sad.

"Oh, is your girl the center?" Gregg asked, jerking himself out of his trance, hoping the woman hadn't noticed him staring at her wares.

She nodded.

"I'm Gregg Haskell, my niece, Evy, plays forward. She's the blonde," he explained.

"The cute one who scores all the points?"

"Yes, on and off the court I'm afraid," they both laughed.

"They grow up fast, don't they?"

"Too fast. Much too fast."

The two of them talked about nothing for the entire second half and before they knew it, their charges were coming out the school, freshly showered and famished.

"Did you see me score that last point, Uncle Gregg?" Evelyn asked, knowing all too well he hadn't been in the gym when the third period began. She had been miffed too, at least until she saw him talking to a pretty girl and decided to forgive him.

"Uhm, no, I think I missed that one, honey, I'm sorry," he replied nervously.

"That's okay," she winked at him several times, quite obviously pleased with his excuse.

"Mom, I'm starving," Corrina Lyons complained, rocking back and forth on the heels of both feet. She had never been one to understand adults, and she certainly didn't understand them when they got that peculiar look in their eyes.

Corrina was a gangly girl with long brown hair dangling past her waist. Her nose had outgrown her face years ago, but it was looking like her face might eventually catch up and she would eventually grow into quite a stunning young woman. Her attitude was that of a typical teen's, hate everyone and everything all the time.

"Okay, honey, we can leave in a minute. Well, Gregg, it was certainly nice meeting you." Amanda Lyons offered her hand once more. This time he smelled her delicate fragrance wafting up from her wrist. He was certain she had somehow reapplied her perfume without him seeing her do it. What a great detective he was.

"The pleasure was certainly all mine," he replied with a smile. "Maybe I will see you at another game."

Evy jabbed an elbow into her uncle's ribcage, eliciting both a grunt and a scowl. She cocked her head in the direction of Corrina's mother several times, hoping desperately he would get the hint before she had to draw him a picture. She sighed disgustedly when he just stood there with a stupid grin on his face.

"I'm hungry too, Uncle Gregg," she prodded.

"You are? But you're never hungry after a game," he said. He grunted a second time and rubbed the spot where she was elbowing him. It was starting to get tender and he was starting to get the idea she might be trying to tell him something.

"Mom," Corrina whined and stomped her foot. Her belly suddenly grumbled loud enough for them all to hear, letting them know she meant business. They all snickered and she clicked her tongue, folded her arms across her chest and stormed off in the direction of her mother's vehicle.

"I had better get going," Amanda smiled.

Gregg grunted once more and the light bulb finally went on. "How about we all go somewhere and get something to eat? Maybe pizza or something, my treat."

Both girls squealed with delight, Evy a little more enthusiastically.

"Sure, why not," Amanda responded.

"Where would you girls like to go?" he asked.

They both crammed their heads together like a two-girl football team in the huddle discussing the last play of a knotted-up ball game. "How about Henri's?" Evy emoted a thick French accent, pronouncing the restaurant's name as 'Ohn'rees' and folded her hands beneath her chin while fluttering her eyelashes at her uncle.

Gregg stood shell-shocked like a deer caught in the evil clutches of a set of headlight beams. He was oblivious as to the restaurant the girls were talking about, but it sounded pretty fancy.

"Don't you girls think Henri's is a little too formal for an after game get together?" Amanda asked with a grin spread across her face as smoothly as peanut butter on hot toast.

"But it's so romantic," they both giggled in unison and ran skipping toward the parking lot.

The adults followed them, stopping at Gregg's car, which just happened to be the closest to them.

"Okay, you two have got your choice, burgers or pizza," Amanda said with the authority of practice.

"Pizza," Corrina chimed.

"Yeah, at Henri's," Evy laughed and fluttered her eyelashes even more pronounced than she had earlier.

"Not at Henri's," Gregg heard himself say with a loud sigh.

"Don Provolone's is pretty good for pizza, and they have a pretty good dinner menu besides," Amanda suggested.

"Sounds great to me, but I don't a clue where it is," he admitted.

"Follow me," she laughed and relented to her daughter tugging at her arm.

Gregg waited until Amanda had gotten herself and her daughter buckled into their minivan. She gave a short blast of her horn as she passed by the back of his car, signaling him it was time to fall in line.

"She's cute," Evy smiled at him with his sister's smile, transporting him back to another day for a brief whisper.

"Yeah, well, she probably thinks I'm a doofus. And what was up with all those shots to the ribs back there? Take it easy on me, I'm an old man."

"You are a doofus, and you're clueless." She rolled her piercing blue eyes at him and giggled.

Evy was a vibrant fourteen-year-old who had just started budding into womanhood, a realm Gregg found as alien as the Martian landscape. When she was a girl, she was easy to deal with. Admittedly, he had turned her into somewhat of a tomboy, but Mother Nature had already shown she was going to undo any damage he may have caused. Evy's rapidly budding breasts scared Gregg almost as much as her budding interest in boys. Nevertheless, no matter how difficult it was raising his niece, every time she smiled, he saw his baby sister and he wouldn't change that for the world.

As he pulled into the parking lot behind the bright red Chevy Traverse he could see Corrina had already bolted from the passenger side and was standing with one hand on the restaurant door and the other on her hip. It was glaringly obvious the girl needed more than a few lessons in patience.

"I hope I don't get lost trying to get home from here," Gregg said, walking up to the driver door and opening it for Amanda.

She had touched up her make up while driving to Don Provolone's and looked delicious. Gregg found himself struggling to keep from staring at her breasts, and this time he wouldn't be thinking about Rita Sorenson.

To Gregg's chagrin the women ordered a blasphemous pizza complete with pineapple, asparagus, or artichoke, Gregg wasn't too certain, and some distant cousin of meat. By the way things had been going that evening he was sure it was probably tofu. He was mighty grateful for the basket of breadsticks the waitress was keeping mercifully filled. With more than half a pizza left the girls disappeared into the game room with a pandered roll of quarters. The disappearing act was all part of Evy's master plan, a plan in which Corrina didn't even realize she was an accomplice.

"So, Evy is your niece. It is so sweet you take her out and do things with her."

"Actually, I have to," he bemoaned parentally.

"Why do you say that?" she chuckled, completely empathizing his exasperation.

"She lives with me."

"Oh?" Amanda's one syllable response spoke volumes of questions.

"Her mother was my sister," Gregg started to explain. He felt his throat constricting like it did every time he mentioned or even thought of his sister Brenda.

"Was? Is she . . . "

"Dead? To tell you the truth, I can't honestly answer that question."

"Not to be rude, but did she just up and walk out on her daughter?"

"I only wish that were the case, then I would at least know the truth. No, Brenda never made home after going out on the town to celebrate her twenty first birthday. She had left Evy with me for the night and I expected her home sometime after the bars closed. I was a doting brother and I made her promise to go out with friends and not to drive, you know, the whole mother hen spiel. She did exactly that, and still, she never came home."

"Oh my," Amanda gasped.

Gregg was on a roll. It felt good to get some of it off his chest and be able to talk it out. "I spoke with her friends and they said she had been perfectly fine. She had left to go to the bathroom and never came back to the table. One of them said she thought Brenda might have ducked out with some cute guy she had been talking to. I didn't argue, but I knew that wasn't like Brenda at all. If she left with a guy, it wasn't because she wanted to. Brenda would have never left with anyone without telling her friends she was leaving. And there was no way she would have gone anywhere without, at the very least, leaving me a voice mail or text. Evy was not yet three years old when her mother disappeared. I petitioned the courts for temporary custody at first, and then full custody once a year had passed and it was getting closer to having to enroll her in school."

"Did the police ever find out what happened to your sister?" she asked with compassion clouding her eyes.

"I'm afraid not. There were only two suspects in the case. One, a man in the bar she had a few drinks with. But that never panned out because the police were never able to positively identify him. And secondly, Evy's father was a main suspect. His alibi was shaky at best, but without a body there is no way to prove he had anything to do with her disappearance."

"Wow, I'm sorry," she sighed.

"No, I'm sorry. I am always amazed at how fresh the pain feels whenever I talk about her, like it happened only yesterday. I should have never burdened you with this. I guess I'm being a bit of a buzz kill," he said, using every bit of his concentration to keep his tears at bay. As it was, he could feel them welling up and knew his eyes must be showing the signs.

She smiled warmly. "In your defense, I asked."

"But I didn't have to tell."

"What? And start our relationship out with a lie." Amanda winked and reached across the table to take his hand in hers.

Her touch was electric. He felt a ripple start in his stomach and soon it grew into a wave of queasiness and his best doofus grin uncontrollably broadened across his face.

Gregg heard a muffled giggle and looked toward the game room. Evy was peeking around the corner watching every move he and Amanda made. Amanda laughed and squeezed his hand.

"You sure have one hell of a fan club president," she said.

"She's always looking out for me, just like her mother used to do," Gregg felt a tear try to shine in the light.

Amanda glowed.

"So, what do you do?" he asked, desperately wanting to change the subject.

"Believe it or not, I'm a cop," she smiled weakly. It was the kind of smile waiting for an anticipated response.

"No shit, where?" he blurted and the look on her face changed drastically. It wasn't the response she was accustomed to.

"I must admit, I've gotten a lot of responses when someone learns my profession, but never that one."

"I'm a cop too."

"No shit?"

"Yep. L.A., homicide division. I'm a detective."

"Wow, a prima donna. Ooh, can I see your gold shield?" she laughed.

"I wouldn't go that far. What do you do?"

"I'm an instructor, at the academy."

"Really? What do you teach?"

"Criminal investigations and profiling are my forte, but I dabble in a bit of everything."

"What made you choose to be an instructor?"

"You know the old saying, those who can't do, teach."

"Somehow I don't buy into that," Gregg replied with a smile.

"In my case, it's true. But only because I really can't stand the sight of blood. I can handle it in an instructional, classroom kind of scenario, like teaching blood spatters and things of that nature, mainly because I know the blood is either simulated or came from a butcher's shop, not a human. I just can't seem to catch my breath when I am in the same room with a real corpse," she laughed.

"I don't think I'm very far behind you on that one," Gregg joined her in laughter.

They both looked at each other even starrier eyed than before. Corrina tugged at Evy while she watched and giggled. And the rest of the world, it just seemed to stop.

Chapter Eight

"Where did you go after Evy's game last night, I called your place several times?" Vito asked Gregg as he scooted into his desk.

"I was enjoying some personal time, if you must know."

"Did you get any?" he asked, his sneer making him look like a lecherous old man.

"I don't really think that's any of your business," he replied, ignoring Vito's rude gestures. As much as Haskell hated to admit it, this case was bringing the two of them closer together and Vito was starting to wear off on him. He felt himself starting to enjoy the juvenile camaraderie they shared.

"Come on share the gory details with me. I'll share mine," Vito laughed.

"No thanks. I have no desire to hear about your wild night on the sofa with a twenty year old, grainy porno in your VCR and an industrial size jar of Vaseline," he said with a grin and nodded toward the glass palace where Karen was scowling out at the two of them.

"Low blow, partner, but let's not forget the cat."

"Yeah, well, it's the only blow you're getting right now, so you'd better appreciate it," Gregg laughed even harder. "What did you do to piss her off this time?"

"I don't know, probably left the toilet seat up or something," he grumbled.

The squad room had begun to fill with the rest of the day shift detectives and the din had risen to near riotous levels. The combination of computer keyboards clacking, telephones ringing and various bodily functions was already getting on Vito's last nerve. Haskell could tell he was agitated and wished he had some devious plan to hatch upon his partner, but his mind was on other things this morning when he had left the house.

"What's on the agenda this morning?" he asked.

"Damn, I almost forgot with all this chatter," Vito spun his head to the side and let his words rise in volume and accusing tone. "We got a hit on Roger Merrill, one of the photographers Judge Morgan mentioned."

"Oh yeah, great."

"Oh, it gets even better. Seems our little pervert couldn't stay clean through his probation. He's a guest of ours, in Chino. It seems his penchant for little girls was stronger than his common sense. A family friend who just happens to be an off duty cop spotted him picking up a young girl outside of a junior high school. The patrolman pulled them over with the intentions of merely chewing the kid's ass out for getting into a car with someone she didn't know. Lucky for her the officer came along when he did, there was a rape kit in the trunk along with a bunch of video camera equipment."

"Damn, no shit. And he was only on the street because of the other records having been sealed. What did they give him this time?"

"He's doing seven to fifteen, but that means he'll be out in less than three if he behaves himself."

"Why is he in Chino? I thought that was a minimum-security facility."

"It is, but they do the processing and quarantine there. They are probably going to ship him out to San Quentin or Folsom before too long."

"A creep like him is liable to have a hard time adjusting to a place like San Quentin. He's probably going to want to try and cut a deal with us, but I am sure you already know that."

"I'm fully aware, and I have a plan."

"Do I want to know what it is?"

"Probably not," Vito responded. "How's your rainy-day fund?"

"Great," he sighed.

"Let's take a cruise over to Chino and see what this guy has to say first, maybe we'll get lucky and he'll be a real charmer."

"I highly doubt that," Haskell said, grabbing his jacket off the back of his chair and falling into line behind his partner.

"I've already given the prison a heads-up call so they're expecting us," Vito said over his shoulder as they exited the precinct. The two of them split like a pair of June Taylor dancers as they neared Vito's car.

The weeklong bout of stormy weather seemed to be drawing to a close, and with it, California's wet spring weather. The air had become still, and the sun was at least ten degrees warmer than it had been a week earlier. Soon the beaches would be teeming with young, vivacious teenagers with nothing else to do but get themselves into trouble. Vito cringed at the thought. He hated the warmer seasons when young, naïve girls would flock to the city with the twinkling stars of Hollywood in their eyes. A large percentage of the disillusioned girls ended up on his streets, in his gutters and on his morgue slabs. They never seemed to understand pretty girls were a dime a dozen out here, sometimes even cheaper. He had always likened it to what a young college football player must feel like the first time he sets foot on a NFL playing field and finds out he isn't the star player anymore. He's just another dumb ass jock with his balls tucked into a plastic cup. With the girls it was the same, except they had their plastically enhanced tits tucked into undersized cups of Lycra.

"How did Evy's game go last night?" Vito asked.

"They won pretty big."

"Was she the leading scorer again?"

"Yes. You know, the more that girl scores, the more she wants to. It's almost as if she's out there on the court competing against herself."

"You're welcome."

"For?"

"Teaching her everything I know," he smiled wickedly.

"Everything you teach that young girl I spend the next two weeks undoing."

"Are you implying I am a bad influence?"

"I'm not implying anything, you're a slob." They both laughed.

Vito pulled up to the prison gates and honked twice, just as the sign outside instructed him to do. Instantly their mood was infused with the dreariness radiating from the prison's shadow. A corrections officer at the gate checked their credentials and waved them through. After checking in at the prison reception area, Lorenz and Haskell were instructed to take a seat in the lobby and wait for the prison's administrative director to come and speak with them.

Both men shivered at their surroundings. Vito thought to himself, this wasn't a correctional institution; this was a den of evil. This was a gathering place. A fortress where some of the state's most corrupt and twisted minds would congregate, take a little time off from the drudgery and hard work of a criminal lifestyle and compare notes.

Rapists traded the names and locations of rape victims who would be too embarrassed or scared to testify like they were baseball cards. The same with B and E specialists who would share the names of marks who loved to travel and would always leave their precious belongings behind, entrusted only to the ineptitude of some fly by night security company. Murderers bragged of their exploits. Drug dealers bragged even louder. And pimps bragged the loudest of all of them. And in the quiet darkness, the child molesters whacked off and prayed no one learned of their evils, lest they be instantly made someone's bitch. A bitch who would be passed around like a bag of jujubes at a Saturday double feature until they were able to shit a bowling ball. It was this specific fear Vito was going to rely upon, heavily.

"Good morning, detectives," an overly enthusiastic red head with a bad dye job, stepped quickly upon them with her tiny hand extended. Vito thought she would have looked more at place addressing a kindergarten class or working in a library.

"Morning," Vito offered her his hand as he creaked up out of the hard-plastic chair. "I'm Lorenz, he's Haskell," he said, his introduction no more than a thumb poked in the general direction of his partner.

"Sylvia Quincy, I'm in charge of all the public relations work around here, it lets the warden keep his focus on more important things," she said with such a smile it made her eyes completely disappear.

Vito assumed she was of Asian descent, or at least had Asian blood in her lineage somewhere. Or even maybe Inuit Indian. Her face was round and cherubic and her cheeks as rosy as Santa Claus on Christmas Eve after a few nips of brandy. Her eyes, when they were visible, were two little dots of gleaming onyx. Her hand was freezing cold where she touched Vito's and he flinched involuntarily.

"Is it always this cold in here?" he asked.

"It's better to be too cold than too hot, the complaints are a lot fewer. And with inmate rights the way they are, if the cons even as much as break a sweat they can sue the state," her face had soured slightly with the thought. Vito admired her already, even though she was a little too bubbly for his tastes.

They walked down a long, white, brightly lit corridor. Their shoes squeaked against the cold tile floor, while her high heels kept a clickety-clack rhythm with her swaying hips.

"In here, gentlemen. I've already taken the liberty of Mirandizing Mr. Merrill, as well as informing him this conversation will be recorded," she said, putting her hand on the doorknob, but not turning it.

"Thank you, I'm sure his lawyer appreciates the effort," Vito chuckled weakly.

"Oh, and a friendly word of warning, Mr. Merrill doesn't have a lawyer present, and although we don't have all the amenities you might be accustomed to, such as two-way mirrors and the likes, he will have a health and human services representative listening in on your conversation," she said, her eyes no longer the tiny slits of happiness they had so recently been.

"Thanks for the warning," Vito said.

She smiled and opened the door for the detectives. They stepped into a small cubicle used as an interrogation room. Roger Merrill eyed them nervously. It was obvious the man had no clue as to who they were or why they were there, which was exactly the way Vito wanted it.

Both detectives casually strolled across the room to a long, battle scarred table and took their seats directly across from

Roger Merrill. The table's surface was a myriad of initials, lewd comments and prior inmate's versions of the Statue of David, when aroused of course. The guest's attitudes toward the police department were also painfully obvious from their carved sentiments.

Their chairs screeched across the tile floor as they drug them away from the table and both detectives took notice of Merrill cringing at the sound. He was scared. Not so much of what the men seated across from him could do to him, but of what they could have done to him once he was back in the general population. They were cops, that he was sure of, and talking to cops was never a good idea. He was looking at less than three years if he behaved himself, and whoever these two guys were, he was sure they weren't there to change his life for the better.

"What's the matter Roger, you look a little nervous?" Haskell smirked.

"Yeah, it must be sixty degrees in here and you're sweating like stuck pig," Vito sneered.

"Who are you?" Roger Merrill asked, struggling with the quiver in his voice.

They didn't respond to his question. Instead, they just glared back at him like the little weasel he was. They both had hatred and condemnation burning in their eyes. They wanted to reach down to his scrawny, weasel base and jerk him free from humanity like an annoying patch of ragweed.

"Who do you think we are?" Vito asked.

"I don't know, but it's obvious you're not comedians," he smiled and gave a short, nervous chuckle.

Again, they glared back at him without any reaction. Roger Merrill was about as ugly and contemptible looking as a man could get. Maybe it was just life behind bars, but Vito could see the maggot in his genes as clear as day. How a young junior high school girl could ever get into a car with the likes of him was beyond his comprehension.

His eyes were big and bulging, with twice as much white as they should have had. He was taller than Vito, but weighed at least fifty pounds less. His extremities were so skinny he would have made a skeleton look obese. What little hair that remained on his balding head had receded so far back his sloping, misshapen skull, that his hair was nothing more than a three-colored ring of fluff encircling the back of his head in varying degrees of smoky black, gray and yellow. It was shaggy, greasy and hung to his collar. Vito couldn't help but think if he were cursed with having only one hair left, he would at least wash it. The man's head looked bulbous on top of his scrawny, leathery neck. And when he stretched, he looked like a tortoise poking its head out of its shell for a quick look around. Red, inflamed sores dotted his forearms and bare scalp leading Vito to draw the conclusion the man was so ugly he was probably saved from a life as a cellblock bitch. If ugliness were a virtue, Roger Merrill would have been a saint.

"No, we're far from being comedians or even the slightest bit humorous at this point. We're homicide detectives."

The air was so still Roger Merrill choked on it.

"From Los Angeles," Haskell added.

"What could you possibly want with me?"

"We have some questions about your relationship with Raymond Kyser," Vito said, finally destroying the air of mystery.

"I have nothing to say," Roger Merrill stiffened up harder than a Christmas fruitcake on the Fourth of July.

"If it is immunity you want," Haskell started.

"I said, I have nothing to say," Merrill interrupted him.

"Listen, all we want to know is what your relationship was with Mr. Kyser," Vito's voice growled with growing frustration.

"No, you listen, I want a fucking lawyer and I want one now," his eyes narrowed, and his nostrils flared in an attempt to wear an angry mask. The fact of the matter was he was scared enough to shit his pants. He had thought the business with Kyser was over, way over. Now that these bastards were poking around, dredging up the past, Kyser would also be sending his people to pay Ol' Rog a visit.

"Why you little son of a bitch," Vito stood up and began crossing the room with a vengeance. He had one mission and one mission only, make the man talk, or make the man bleed.

"Detective!" a disembodied voice crackled over the intercom system. "This interview is over. The man has requested a lawyer."

"Shit, damn, sonofabitchin' hell," Vito took his frustrations out on his chair and stomped toward the door with Haskell right behind him.

Vito put his hand on the doorknob but stopped and turned back around.

"Since you won't talk to us about Mr. Kyser, I guess I will have to ask Mr. Kyser all about you instead," he said in a contemptuous tone of voice.

Having said his piece, Vito twisted the doorknob and stepped outside into the hallway. They were a dozen paces away from the room before he cracked a grin thoroughly confusing his partner.

"What in the hell are you so happy about?"

"I think that went rather well."

"Were you in the same room I was? It went like shit, Vito."

"Are you a gambling man. Gregg?"

"On occasion, but I like to bet on a sure thing."

"Oh, this is a sure thing."

"Really?"

"I'll lay you ten to one odds Mr. Merrill gives us a call before the week is out. He'll be begging to talk to us."

"You're on," he shook his partner's hand, somehow quite aware of the fact he had probably just taken a sucker's bet.

*   *   *

Amber Reese floated back into reality from a sea of fog onboard a vessel piloted by a sick, perverse captain. The more she came back into focus, the more she became aware of the fact she was not alone. He was in there with her, them, again. She could smell him. Taste him. Taste her very loathing of him.

She tried to concentrate on feeling sensations in her skin receptors, but everything felt numb. It was ludicrous to even imagine her head was missing from her shoulders, yet she had no cognizance of it existence. Amber focused intently, searching for some shred of sensation in her skull, there was none. No twitching, throbbing, or pulsating from blood coursing through her veins. Not even as much as a tingle from her hair follicles.

Rolling her eyes from side to side she scanned the room. Although she could feel his presence, there was no physical sign of him anywhere in the room. She could see several different orbs about the room of assorted shapes and colors. They were heads, the heads of the other girls who were being held captive with her.

A loud click sounded in her chamber. It didn't echo like sound usually did, but died like a cry for help in the vacuum of space. A wave of relief washed over her as she felt something pressing against the back of her head. It was liberating to have finally felt something. But then the more she thought about it the more she realized she was only aware of this because her head was being forced forward. Almost immediately her mouth was flooded with a foreign taste. Something tinny, like she was chewing on a ball of aluminum foil invaded her mouth. Suddenly, her tongue began to go numb and her brain, the actual tissue of her brain, began to burn. The wave of relief was quickly replaced by panic.

What in the hell had the bastard given her? What kind of a trip was he taking her on now? The shapes and angles of the shadows began to warp into paisley swirls of psychedelic color. Amber had never even as much as taken one toke from a joint in her entire life. But even without having experienced the effects of drugs before she was certain she was starting to trip on something now. She giggled, even though she felt like crying. She could feel the muscles in her mouth constricting, twisting her face into a permanent grin. The last thing she noticed before succumbing to the vile solution being pumped through her veins were the twelve red X's on the front of her tomb.

*   *   *

"Christ, did a bomb go off in here or something?" Haskell asked, stepping into a small, rarely used lunchroom.

Vito had papers, folders, index cards, pencils and chairs strewn all about the small room. He was rapidly moving from one cluttered chair to the next.

"Morning," he said, barely glancing up from the folder he was reading.

"What are you working on?"

"Morbid shit."

Vito looked up at Haskell and the man nearly gasped. His partner looked like he had aged ten years in one night. His eyes were red and puffy and the bags beneath them could have held a week's worth of bus tokens. Gregg wasn't sure if it were the case, Stoddard, or both that was wearing the man down. He thought about saying something, but then just let it go.

Haskell looked over the information Vito had been scrawling onto a dry erase easel. There were twelve names written across the top, the first four had been scratched out with a red pen. Beneath each name was the date when the girl had first been reported missing. Then came the dates when their bodies were discovered, then their ages and general appearances. And finally, the last column was something Vito had been formulating with his best educated guesses. It was a column dedicated to figuring out the girls' best physical attributes. Kendra, Evangelique, Rita and Christina's ordeals were the basis for this hypothesis.

"You're right, this is morbid shit."

"I thought it might help. It might give us some kind of understanding where the killer is coming from."

"You still don't think Kyser has anything to do with this do you?"

"Sorry to disappoint you, but no, I don't. It just doesn't make sense, not good sense anyway."

"I tend to agree with you, but we can't rule him out," Gregg said.

"Oh, no, quite the contrary. I don't think he's responsible for these girls' deaths, but I think he knows who is, or he is linked to whomever is responsible in some way. Kyser may not even be privy to who this killer is or what he is doing either, but I'm sure they're acquainted in some sick way or another.

Another thing I am certain of is we will be a hell of a lot closer to solving this case once we have the pleasure of his company."

Gregg nodded. "I see you have best legs, prettiest hands, sexy smile, sounds like we might be in for some really nasty stuff."

"Nothing to look forward to, I can assure you."

"What about Amber Reese, you don't have anything written down for her?"

"I don't know enough about her to draw any conclusions. After looking over all of the pictures of all of the girls, nothing about her stands out."

Haskell thought about this for a minute. "What if it isn't something we can see?"

"What do you mean?" Vito asked softly, fearing the worst possible answer.

"I don't know, something like sexiest voice, sweetest personality."

"Or smartest? She did graduate valedictorian of her high school," Vito said, flipping through her sparse file.

Haskell shuddered visibly. "Yes, or the smartest."

"Help me put this shit away. I don't want to think about it anymore."

"Good idea," Gregg said, stuffing papers and photos into their corresponding manila folders and tossing those into a large banker's box with the case number written in big black numbers on the end.

They were back at their desks wordlessly suffering through cups of stale, cold coffee when the phone rang. Vito picked it up and began a series of nods as the caller talked. Gregg watched a shit-eating grin appear on his partner's haggard mug.

"What was that all about?"

"Are you ready for another tour of Chino?"

"No way."

"Oh, yes. Roger Merrill is begging to speak with us."

Vito could barely contain his laughter until they were on the road. Haskell had been staring at him as though he were the antichrist himself.

"Well?"

"Well what?"

"Are you going to tell me about your mojo or not?"

"It's not mojo, or magic or anything that lame. It's famiglia."

"You just took a left turn and dumped me into Duhsville, Vito," Haskell laughed at Evy's saying coming out of his mouth automatically.

"I've got a cousin who works for the department of corrections. He moonlights as a part-time actor, or at least he thinks he can act, so I gave him a call. I told him I needed a little harmless coercion done. He pretended to be a guard who was a little more than friendly with our Mr. Kyser. He let Mr. Merrill know in no uncertain terms Mr. Kyser was very unhappy with him and thought he was in need of some re-education. My cousin followed Merrill everywhere. He made certain the man was assigned to him every chance he could. He said Merrill was pissing himself before the first day was over. Joe, my cousin, even worked some overtime to make sure he was on the night shift. He paid Merrill a lengthy visit last night, and voila, a phone call this morning," Vito grinned at Haskell until Greg was certain the man's mouth was going to open so wide he would swallow his own head.

"I guess there's nothing immoral or illegal about that," he said, shaking his head.

"That was our bubbly little administrative director on the phone. She seems to be quite pleased Mr. Merrill has decided to see things our way as well," Vito said. "You up for another scenic cruise?" he asked, grabbing his car keys off the desk.

"I take it I don't get to drive?"

"You got that right, you drive like old people fuck, slow and sloppy."

"At least I get us there alive."

"I don't know about all that, I almost died of boredom the last time you drove," he laughed.

"If you're driving, I get to pick where we go for lunch. There's no way my bowels can endure anymore fast food crap you're always forcing me to eat. Haven't you ever heard of vegetables?"

"Yeah, they're what you feed rabbits right?"

"There's this neat little place in Pomona I think you'll get a kick out of," he grinned. It was the kind of grin that made Vito nervous.

Within minutes they were on Interstate Ten heading east. Traffic was more congested than usual, and Haskell opted to keep his mouth shut and let Vito concentrate on driving. And still, the man continually fumbled around for something instead of concentrating on the road. He messed with the radio for several agonizing seconds while merging into congested freeway traffic, a brief moment when Haskell swore he saw his life passing before his eyes. And if things couldn't get any worse, Vito chose to use this time to check his pager for messages and return calls using his cell phone, which he would dial without bothering to look up at the road. Haskell couldn't have thought less of the man's driving skills until, while arguing with the dry cleaner, Vito searched through all his pockets for his laundry ticket. He caught himself wondering just what in the hell it could have possible been that Vito dropped off at the dry cleaners. It surely wasn't anything the man wore to work.

During the nerve-wracking drive there were several moments when Gregg had contemplated opening his door and jumping out, taking his chances with the hard asphalt freeway. By the time the large, green sign announcing the Pomona exit came into view, his jaws were so sore from clenching his teeth he wasn't sure if he would be able to eat anything harder than tapioca pudding.

"Take this exit," he squeaked through clenched teeth.

"See, I got us here in one piece," Vito turned and smiled at his partner, allowing the car to drift off into the emergency lane as they careened down the exit ramp. A plume of dust rose up behind them and gravel ricocheted off the side of their car.

"Sorry about that," he laughed and jerked the car back onto the road.

"You're just not going to be satisfied until I shit my pants, are you?"

"Hey, I am in complete control of this beast at all times," he smiled and patted the dashboard. "Now, where is this joint?"

"It's over on Mission, just up the road a mile or so," he quavered.

The next few minutes of the drive were uneventful. As soon as Gregg spied a glint of neon on the horizon he pointed to his left.

"You've got to be fucking kidding me," Vito said, swinging the car into the gravel parking lot.

Perched atop a fifties style diner, glowing in glorious flesh colored neon, was a hot dog that looked suspiciously like part of the male anatomy. Below the pulsating frankfurter was the name "Franks-N-Steins," and below that, in putrid pink was the slogan, "Home of the Monster Wiener." A caricature of Frankenstein's monster lumbered near the fleshy, flashing tubular piece of neon meat holding an overly large, foaming mug of beer. The creature was positioned in such a way a person's imagination didn't have to work too hard at creating some very obscene imagery.

"Isn't anything sacred anymore?" Vito said, shaking his head slowly back and forth while looking down at the ground.

As they reached the front door, Haskell grabbed the handle and swung the door open for Vito who never saw the shit-eating grin spread across his partner's face. Instead, he saw a mural painted on the wall directly in front of them as they walked into the restaurant. It depicted the same likeness of Franky, only this time the hot dog wasn't flashing neon, but still just as fleshy and pink. There was another slogan, one that almost made Vito turn around and head for the nearest Taco Bell. This time Franky was smiling with a callout balloon over his head, which read, "Let us put a monster wiener between your buns."

"What is this place, some sort of Village People meat market?"

Haskell couldn't contain his laughter any longer. He sat down in the nearest booth, grabbed his ribs and hoped he remember how to breath before he suffocated himself to death.

"What's so damned funny? I hope you know, I don't plan on staying here a minute longer. I'll see you in the car when you're through having your fun," Vito huffed.

"Take it easy, Vito, this isn't what it appears to be."

"I'm not at all convinced I even have an idea as to what it appears to be."

"The owner is a recent immigrant from Pakistan, he doesn't have a very good grip on American slang and even less of a grip on our humor, but he does plump one hell of a mean wiener," Gregg burst into another round of short, hard laughter.

"You know, the more we work together, the more I realize you're just like me," Vito sighed.

"Oh really?" Gregg said between pants of laughter.

"Yeah, you're an asshole," he smiled and slapped his partner's shoulder.

They spent the next half an hour gorging themselves on Greek salad, franks and chili-cheese fries. During their meal the Pakistani born owner, Nasir, visited them no less than half a dozen times. The last time the man had started for their table, Vito reached into his jacket and put his hand on his gun. Nasir must have understood the gesture because he thought better about visit their table and quickly pivoted around on his heels. He hurried off toward the kitchen where something much safer was demanding his immediate attention.

After lunch and a brief drive, they made their way through the checkpoints at Chino without a hitch and were soon waiting for the bubbly administrative director to escort them to their prize. Haskell was glad to see Sylvia Quincy was her usual effervescent self, anything to detract from Vito's wealth of warmth.

Vito was still burping up Franks-N-Stein's when they were led into the interrogation room housing Roger Merrill. He looked like hell. It was painfully obvious the man hadn't slept much more than a wink at a time since the last time they had spoken with him.

"Afternoon, Rog, how are you." Vito was all smiles and handshakes.

Roger Merrill's eyes darted between the two detectives as he tried to decipher the plot of ground he stood on. He figured the steadiest the ground was going to get was still going to leave him doing a one-legged hop on the San Andreas Fault line.

"Afternoon," he choked.

Sylvia smiled and stepped back out into the hallway, closing the door behind her. The only sound in the room was the gentle hum of the ballasts in the overhead fluorescent light hanging above the table. Roger Merrill stared silently back at the two detectives who were staring him down. Sweat began pooling up at the base of his neck and streamed down his back in little rivulets.

"Well?" Vito finally broke the silence.

"Well what?" Roger squeaked.

"You're the one who called us here, remember?"

"We assumed you wanted to talk about your relationship with Kyser," Haskell nudged.

"Do I have a choice?"

"Sure, we can leave right now if you'd like," Vito said.

"But if we leave, we're not coming back again, ever," Haskell warned.

With that cue, they both stood up and moved for the door.

"Wait, I didn't say I wanted you to leave, but I'm confused. So damned confused," he eased back into his chair and dropped his face into his hands. Beads of sweat had formed on the top of his balding head and the bright fluorescent lights reflected off his skin like it was a disco ball.

"Well then talk, Rog, or we're leaving," Vito barked and both detectives took their seats. "We don't have time for your shit."

The man took several long, deep breaths and then said. "You know he's crazy, right?"

"Who?"

"Kyser, man. Raymond fucking Kyser that's who. He's a complete psycho," his eyes darted wildly back and forth between the two detectives. He was wringing his hands nervously beneath the table. Gregg couldn't help but think about how cruel this was, but effective, very effective.

"Why don't you tell us about it."

"What do you want to know?"

"How did the two of you meet for starters?"

He took a deep breath and moaned. "I had a friend who knew Kyser was looking for a photographer, someone who knew the importance of being discreet. I had my buddy drop my name to Kyser and I got a call from the man's people less than a week later. I went to his office and we haggled over price and I guess mine was the best."

"As easy as that?"

"As easy as that."

"So, then what happened?" Haskell asked.

"He gave me his business card with an address on the back and told me to show up the following Saturday."

"And did you?"

"Of course," he shrugged, "He was paying me damned good money."

"But you didn't even know what you were supposed to do yet?"

"I didn't give a rat's ass. Like I said, he was paying me good money."

"Too much for a photo shoot?"

"Maybe," he answered nervously.

"And that didn't send up any red flags?" Haskell asked.

"Sure it did. But I didn't give a damn. Look around you, detective, I'm not the most upstanding, civic minded individual."

"Go on," Vito prodded.

"Like I was saying, I had this business card with an address and a date to be there. When I showed up to the address on the card I found a vacant warehouse. There were a couple of big, mean looking dudes waiting outside. When I pulled up, they unlocked the door to the warehouse and let me in. I told them I had a lot of camera equipment to carry in, but they said I didn't have to worry about that. They weren't the type to be argued with, so I just followed their instructions. One of the men stayed outside while the other one led me in to meet with Mr. Kyser. As soon as Kyser saw me, he nodded and motioned for his gorilla to go back outside."

"Is there a point to all of this?"

"I thought you wanted to know everything?"

"Are we going to be here all night?"

"Okay, I get your point. To make a long story short, Kyser already had all of the equipment I would need, and it was already set up just the way he wanted it. Man, it was top of the line shit too. Stuff I could never afford to work with. There were twelve different muslin backdrops arranged around the warehouse. He strongly expressed a desire to get this shoot over with as soon as possible. I figured I might be able to squeeze a little more money out of this rich bastard so I told him it would take a few weeks, at least, if he wanted things done right. He said that was unacceptable, that he needed me to finish the shoot that day. I argued I didn't think it was possible. I told him the shoot would be involved and would probably take two days, maybe three. And since he was paying me by the piece and not the day, I didn't understand why it would matter if I took my time. That's when Kyser explained the delicate nature of the shoot and said under no circumstances was it to take longer than one day."

"What you mean to say is he let you in on his dirty little secret about these girls being underage models and he didn't want to get caught taking their pictures," Vito spat.

"Something to that effect," he nodded guiltily.

"Go on," Haskell said. Suddenly images of Evy flooded his mind and he found it nearly impossible to control his anger. He placed one hand over the other on the tabletop to keep them from shaking.

"As I was checking out the equipment, I reached into a cooler thinking there might be some sodas or something, but there was nothing but wine coolers, beer and an assortment of liquor. Kyser claimed it helped things along, loosened the girls up. I saw several sno-seals of cocaine and a small baggie on a table with I thought looked a lot like cooked up drugs, GHB, or maybe it was ecstasy. Kyser slipped it into his pocket before I could see exactly what it was. I could hear the girls laughing and giggling from another room in the warehouse. It sounded like they were all pretty wasted.

"Once my equipment was all set up I told Kyser I was all ready to start shooting pictures. That was when he showed me four video cameras and wanted them set up to capture the shoot as well. He said the 'making of' videos sold better than the calendars themselves. This took me about another half an hour to set things up and Kyser disappeared into the room where the other girls were. Just as I was finishing up, he brought one of the girls out. She was a cute black girl with a pretty smile."

"Kendra Jenkins?"

"I'm not too sure about the names, I mean, he had given them all fake names and profiles for the calendars, so getting to know their real names wasn't necessary."

"Oh, isn't that convenient?" Gregg said while gripping the side of his chair to keep from punching the man in the mouth.

Roger Merrill continued his story without once looking up from the table. "We shot these girls one by one without any problems until we got to one of the last girls. She had sobered up and was claiming she had changed her mind and didn't want to do the shoot anymore. Well this really pissed Kyser off. I don't know if she was the youngest, but she certainly looked the youngest. She barely had any breasts and she had such a pretty face," a lustful smirk slipped up from his dark depths and subconsciously creased his face.

"Just give me a reason, asshole," Haskell started to stand up.

"I strongly suggest you stick to the details, but not that closely," Vito said, gripping his partner's forearm and pulling him back into his chair.

Merrill flashed his eyes between the two detectives, cleared his throat nervously and said, "Yeah, I guess you're right. As I was saying, this girl argued and refused to take her robe off. Kyser tried to get her to take a drink, but she refused. He was about to give up and use one of the alternates when one of the other girls starting playfully tugging at the sash holding the girl's robe together. She fought back and soon a couple of the other girls joined in. I think the girls were just stoned enough to think this was all just in fun and there was nothing serious about it. But the girl who didn't want her robe taken off was really starting to get upset. I looked over at Kyser and I noticed he was really enjoying this. He glanced up at the video cameras, looking for the indicator light to make sure cameras were recording. I was taking pictures and just watching, but I started to get nervous about the direction this thing was taking. Anyway, eventually the girls finally stripped the other girl's robe off and she got really pissed. That's when I noticed Kyser had done two things that really kinda shocked me."

"What?" Vito asked.

Merrill looked over at Haskell to check his anger level before continuing. "He had gotten a good grip on himself, if you know what I mean. And he had put on this strange looking leather mask, like those bondage freaks wear. I heard him tell two of the girls to hold her down. It was kind of like watching a dream, or a movie. It was like it wasn't really happening. After a few minutes Kyser started fondling the girl and it was getting pretty clear as to what he intended to do. That's when he looked over at me and told me to join him. I shook my head no. I mean, I don't mind looking, and hell, I don't even mind doing, but not if the girl ain't willing. I mean completely willing. He yelled at me and told me I had better leave then, so I did. On my way out I noticed two of his goons had also joined him on the floor with the girls. I just got into my car and got the hell out of there."

"Being the upstanding, civic minded individual you are I suppose you ran straight to the police?" Vito asked, ignoring his urge to ask the man why he had been caught with a rape kit in his car if he only wanted a girl who was willing.

"No. I was scared. Kyser has a way of making things happen."

"So, why didn't this girl press charges against him?"

"She did. But the way I understand it, she committed suicide before the grand jury had a chance to indict him."

"Or you," Haskell added accusingly.

"Was that the extent of your involvement with Kyser?"

"Unfortunately, no, I came home from doing a shoot about three weeks later and Raymond Kyser was sitting in my living room with two of his less than pleasant sidekicks."

"What were they doing there?"

"Let's just say they convinced me to take a little trip with them. We went to a condo out in the hills. I think it was Kyser's, but I don't think it was his everyday place. The more I think about it, I'll bet the place wasn't even in his name. Mr. Kyser spent the better part of the evening showing me all his enterprises, which all seemed to include his own fetishes as well. I think he was his own best customer."

"Things like what?"

"Video tapes, magazines, mostly kiddie porn and snuff films. I have got to tell you, I think those snuff films were real too. Let's just say they had me pissing in my pants," Merrill's eyes revealed the fact he had an unadulterated fear of this man Kyser.

"What else did he show you?"

"He had some little flip out brochures that were pretty amateurishly done, obviously made on someone's home computer. They were for vacations, the kind rich men take when they want young stuff. Mostly they were in Thailand, but there were a couple from Canada, and one from right here in Los Angeles. He also showed me these ashtrays, they were little hands. Like when you made an ashtray for your mom and pops back in kindergarten art class by pressing your hand into some clay concoction the teacher made out of flour or something. He said these were of some boys he had 'done'," he said, shifting uncomfortably in his chair throughout his explanation.

"What do you mean, done?" Haskell grumbled.

"To tell you the truth, I wasn't really sure what he meant by that, but I wasn't about to ask either. By this time I figured the less I knew, the better."

"But what do you think he meant?" Vito asked.

"I think he meant, done, as in both done them, and then done them," he said, making a slicing gesture across his throat. His eyes nervously darted between the two detectives. He could tell the blond cop was getting more and more agitated as the conversation progressed. He hoped the fat one would be able to save his ass if his partner exploded. Sweat beaded up on his upper lip and Roger suddenly wished he had never opened his mouth.

"So, you think he killed them?"

"I only say yes because of some shirts I saw."

"What shirts?"

"At one point Kyser excused himself to go to the bathroom. He was in there forever, so I started poking around. I looked in this drawer and there were a several white T-shirts, with reddish-black handprints all over them. Little handprints, just like the ashtrays. They were the kind of shirts I've seen grandparents wearing, you know, the kind where their grand kids will use finger paints and put handprints all over the shirts and each grand kid will sign their names and put their ages underneath. These shirts were like that too, only, there was only one size of handprint on each shirt, and I don't think it was finger paints. In hindsight, I think Kyser left me alone so I would find those shirts."

"If it wasn't paint, what do you think it was?"

"Blood. Dried, crusty blood. I've never been so scared in my life. I was lucky to have gotten out of there with my life. The message he was sending was pretty damned clear."

"Where is this secret hideaway of his?" Haskell hissed through clenched teeth.

"Gone."

"What do you mean gone?" Haskell said, spraying spittle across the table.

"It burned up. By the time the police had connected it to Kyser, he had already paid to have it torched. He's a smart man who has a lot of friends in high places and knows how to cover his ass."

"So, where is Kyser now?" Vito asked.

"I don't have a clue, but he knows I'm in here, and he knows you two are poking around," Merrill responded in a panic, sensing the young cop's growing hostility towards him.

"What makes you so sure of that?" Haskell asked.

"I've been told he's watching me. You gotta help, you gotta get me out of the general population," he begged.

"But Chino is a minimum-security prison, you'll be safe here."

"Like hell I will, you don't know Raymond Kyser. Besides, they'll be transferring me soon enough and then he sure as hell will be able to get to me."

"Apparently, I don't know him, at least not like I thought I did. And don't worry, we're going to make sure you are well taken care of," Vito responded.

"Somehow that doesn't make me feel any better."

"What else do you know?" Haskell asked through gritted teeth.

"Nothing, that's all I know."

"You better come up with something," Vito warned, grabbing Haskell's forearm once more, stopping just short of lunging across the table.

"Wait, there is this one guy, he was some kind of accountant. He was there at the shoot when I got there. He and Kyser were arguing about something, but when I walked over to them they quit and the other man left. I think I heard Kyser call him Stallworth, Stillwell, something like that."

"Okay, we'll have to look into that. And you have no idea the names of these other girls who were involved with the shoot?"

"Sorry, no, I just didn't pay attention. I was, distracted," he quickly averted his eyes from the glaring detectives.

"We'll be in touch, don't go anywhere, okay?" Vito smiled sarcastically as he stood up from the table. Haskell glowered at Roger Merrill for several seconds before getting up from the table.

They said their good-byes to Sylvia and promised to come back when they had more time. The drive back to Los Angeles was all but silent. Vito's driving was a testament to the fact he had a lot of things on his mind. Luckily for him, Haskell had a lot on his mind as well.

*   *   *

Vito dropped Haskell off at his car and headed for Gus's. He needed the comfort of normalcy, or at least as close to it as he could get. The bourbon smelled almost as good as the cigarette smoke and he cringed at the thought of traveling down those two paths again. He picked a wilted leaf of lettuce off the faded red Naugahyde covered bench and slid into his usual booth. He forgot about the broken spring and it poked him sharply in his right cheek, making his ass sting like the rest of him.

"What'll it be today," Gus said, with what could only pass for a smile on his embattled face.

"Just some soda with a twist would be nice, thanks," he replied without looking up.

"Nothing to eat?"

"No thanks, Gus, I don't think I'll even be able to hold down the soda right now," he smiled and rubbed his stomach.

"Thanks for the warning," he grumbled with a pained look on his face while wiping the table with a bar rag Vito was certain was dirtier than the table top itself.

Vito played with the ice cubes in his drink with his finger and contemplated the things they had learned from Roger Merrill. His stomach had finally begun to settle when a hauntingly familiar sense of dread washed over him.

"Evening Karen," he said without looking up.

"So, did you learn anything new?" she asked, smiling as she slid into the booth across from him.

"Is this conversation going to be strictly professional?"

"Why do you ask that?"

"Because, if it is, then I am off the clock and I will gladly discuss the case with you in the morning. And if it's not, then I don't want to talk to you at all, unless of course you've resolved that little matter we discussed."

"Well, aren't you just the little prick today," her mood did a complete one-hundred-and-eighty-degree turn.

"Maybe I wasn't clear, or you thought I was joking, but until you make a decision, this is over Karen. Now, please leave me alone, I have a lot on my mind."

Without another word, she grabbed her pocketbook and stormed out of Gus's. He dreaded even thinking about what their morning conversation was going to be like.

He grabbed his coat and hoped he had given Karen enough time to get bored with waiting in ambush outside the bar. He flipped a ten at Gus, waved and walked out into the cold night. Vito was still thinking about their interview with Merrill and the things he had disclosed. The things revealed in that discussion sickened him, but not nearly as badly as it had his partner. In fact, Vito was sure Haskell was still down at the church talking to the priest in confessional. The man had certainly worked up a lot of anger during the interrogation, justifiable and damned near impossible to control.

Vito barely remembered the drive home he was so tired. He fumbled around in the kitchen for a few minutes getting the coffee pot ready for morning. He flicked on the television but then flicked it back off even before he had a chance to see what was on. He had turned it on more out of habit than anything else. The one thing he could never get over about being single was the fact the house was always so deathly quiet at night. Most nights he left the television running but tonight he needed the silence. He needed to have a clear head.

Vito didn't bother turning on his bedroom light before stripping down and climbing into bed, a decision he regretted almost immediately. He wasn't sure why he hadn't smelled her scent long before climbing into bed with her. Maybe he didn't want to. Or maybe he had thought it was her scent lingering on his sheets. Either way, he was naked, and Karen was all over him. He had never even stood a chance.

Breakfast conversation was about as cheery as a mortician's convention. Not too many words were spoken, just a few tongue clicks and nods when the coffee pot was offered. Vito was surprised Karen had spent the entire night. Her husband must have been out of town.

"Where's George this week?"

"What makes you think he's not home?"

"The sun is up and you're still here."

"Oh. He's in Frisco, some seminar thing up there," she answered while cupping her mug of coffee with both hands.

"He still thinking about running for re-election?"

"Yup."

"You sound excited," Vito said.

"Wonderful," Karen grunted.

"Some things never change."

"What?" she snapped.

"Nothing. Listen, I'm heading down to the precinct now, we've got a lot of work to do, and as you know we're kind of on a tight schedule."

"I'll be there as soon as I take a shower."

"Make sure you lock up, and leave the key on the table when you go," Vito said, stepping outside before she had a chance to respond. He heard the crash of her coffee mug against the door even before he made it off the first step of the porch.

Chapter Nine

"Wake up, sunshine," Gregg called from outside Evy's door.

She mumbled something incoherent in reply and threw "cuddles", a large stuffed bear at the door.

"Billy Baker is waiting downstairs for you," he joked.

"What?" she screamed and bolted out of bed. By the time she reached her bedroom door she realized her uncle must have been pulling her leg. "That was a dirty trick," she scowled and pushed passed him on her way to the bathroom.

"What do you want for breakfast?"

"Coffee and donuts," she grumbled.

"You're starting to sound like Lorenz. How does granola and apple juice sound?"

"Like crap," she slammed the bathroom door.

Gregg chuckled to himself on the way down to the kitchen. She really was starting to sound like his partner in the mornings. If she wasn't such a cute girl the rest of the day, she might offend him with her less than cheery sunrise disposition. He busied himself with pouring each of them bowls of cereal from a box that hadn't nary a cartoon character on it and peeled her a banana. He poured out two glasses of juice, apple for her, and grapefruit for him. He hid the fact he drank coffee and ate donuts at work, a fact he was certain Vito had revealed to her in sworn secrecy.

Evy and Vito had hit it off almost immediately. She thought he was a slob, and he agreed with a hearty laugh. Vito didn't discuss Haskell's situation much, he knew what it was like to love a sister and he was certain he completely understood the kind of heartache constantly gnawing away at his partner.

Besides, Vito wasn't the arm around the shoulder, consoling kind of guy.

The real Evy bounded down the stairs and scooted up to the table. She gave the fare the once over, shrugged and poured some skim milk on her cereal.

"So, are we feeling better now we've had a shower?"

"What are you talking about, Uncle Gregg, I was feeling fine before my shower," she grinned devilishly.

He mulled over the conversation he wanted to have with her in his mind. He wanted the words to come out right. He didn't want to sound like he was preaching or condescending to her, but he knew he needed to say something. If for nothing more than his own piece of mind.

"So, I heard you on the phone last night. Was it Amanda?" she giggled.

"Yes, in fact it was."

"I think she's sweet on you."

"You think so, huh?"

"Uh, huh. And I *know* you're sweet on her."

"What makes you so sure?"

"We women just know those sort of things."

"We women? You're not a woman yet," Gregg argued as his heart skipped a beat.

"Close enough, I'm almost fifteen."

"That's a lifetime away from being grown up."

"So you say."

He took a deep breath and regrouped. He knew she was only jerking his chain, something she seemed to do a lot more since Vito had been introduced into her life.

"Listen, Evy, I've got something really important I'd like to discuss with you."

"Oh no, not the sex talk. I don't need the sex talk. Besides, I've already learned everything I need to know about sex from Vito." The pained expression on Gregg's face caused her to throw back her head and squeal out a raucous peal of laughter.

"Oh great, that makes me feel much better. But I don't think I'm ready for the sex talk to be honest with you."

"Then what, Uncle Gregg?"

"I know this is going to sound like I am treating you like a child, and nothing is further from my mind, but I feel I need to say this. If for nothing else than for my own piece of mind."

"Can you please spit it out before I'm too old to go to college?" she grinned.

"Cute. Listen, I know you are smart enough to know not to take rides from people you don't know, but I just want you to promise me you'll never do such a thing. And also, if anyone approaches you for any reason, I want you to give either Vito or me a call right away. You have our numbers in your purse and cell phone, right?"

"Uh huh," she replied solemnly. She sensed something wasn't quite right with her uncle. And even though she knew what he was telling her was something she had known since she was just a little girl, she knew it was not something to be joked around about. He was sincere, as sincere as she ever wanted to see him. In fact, the look on his face scared her. A fleeting memory of her mother danced through her brain and she completely understood where her uncle was coming from.

"Promise?"

"Cross my heart and hope to have to kiss Wayne Windleham if I'm lying," she smiled, but weakly enough that he would know she had taken what he said to heart.

"Good, that makes me feel better."

"Uncle Gregg, is something going on I should know about?"

"No, honey. We are working on a case involving a lot of creepy guys and it's got me spooked is all. I guess I'm just being a worry wart old fart."

"You don't need to worry about me, Uncle Gregg, I know better."

"Oh yes I do," he stared down into his bowl of cereal and lost himself in thought. He never even heard her get up from the table. "I worry about you every minute of every day."

"Uncle Gregg," she called from the doorway with an armload of books.

"What honey?"

"It wasn't your fault, about mom, I mean. There was nothing you could have done, oh, and I love you," she smiled and darted for the school bus.

Gregg got up and went to the kitchen window. He watched the little blonde-haired teenager bounding down the aisle of the bus; her head bobbing passed each of the windows. He wiped a tear from his eye as the putrid yellow vehicle shut its doors and pulled away from the curb.

"When the hell did she grow up?" he commented to the wind as he pulled his jacket on and left for the day.

*   *   *

"Good morning, sexy," Lucy Davenport cooed from behind her dispatcher's desk. She had a smile that could light up even the darkest room and her round, cherubic face glowed as it always seemed to do. Her onyx eyes grabbed every ray of light and reflected them back into the room with sincere warmth.

"Hey, gorgeous," Vito mumbled.

"There's some guy waiting for you in squad room."

"Who is it?"

"Some inspector from Scotland Yard or something like that."

"Interpol maybe?"

"Yeah, that's it."

"Thanks Davenport, I could kiss you."

"Oh, don't get me started honey, I might not want to stop," her cackling laughter followed him down the corridor and into the squad room.

Standing with Haskell was a tall, thin gentleman with just enough peppering of gray in his hair to make him look distinguished. His face was narrow and chiseled, broken only by his warm smile and friendly eyes.

"Vito, this is Chief Inspector McNaughton, from Interpol," Haskell said once his partner was within their proximics.

"Good morning, sir. It's a pleasure," Vito reached out and heartily shook the man's hand.

"Glad I could be of assistance."

"I do have to ask why Interpol would send someone over, let alone a Chief Inspector. I simply sent out a request for some information," Vito said.

"Oh, Chief Inspector is just a title, really," his thick brogue grumbled like distant thunder. "And as for the information you've requested, let's just say we have mutual concerns. We've been interested in this Kyser fellow for quite some time. Quite some time indeed."

"I didn't think Interpol got involved with this sort of thing."

"On the contrary, missing, abused and exploited children are one of our main concerns. And let me tell you something, what you think you know about Raymond Kyser is only a fraction of what he's actually involved in. The things I could show you would curl your hair," he stumbled on the words as he noticed Vito's greased hair trying to spring back to its naturally curly state.

Vito laughed at the man's twisted facial expression. "Well hopefully you'll have some information that will help us get this character off the streets for good."

"I believe I might just have that. However, we understand you want to question him in connection with a series of murders."

"That's correct."

"Well, that is going to pose a bit of a problem. You see, my superiors would like to talk with him about certain crimes he may have committed against children in Thailand, Taiwan and a few other places."

"Okay, that's perfectly legitimate."

"How can I put this delicately?"

"Just spit it out," Vito huffed, quickly tiring of the cat and mouse game.

"We would like an agreement between your organization and ours."

"What kind of agreement?"

"That we can question him before you take him into custody. We don't want him protected by American laws. The laws governing our methods of interrogation are, shall we say, quite a bit more lenient than yours. No disrespect intended."

"Certainly, none taken. I couldn't agree with you more. Nevertheless, I don't think the bureaucrats who run this stinkhole will agree to something like that."

"I was afraid you were going to say that," McNaughton said, lowering his eyes to the floor.

"So, what does that mean, that you're not willing to share the information you have with us?"

"In due time, but not until we've been able to clear a few things up. Good day," he said and started for the door.

"Wait just a damned minute," Vito bellowed. "There is no way you are going to waltz in here with information that can save the lives of more than half a dozen women and then not give it up."

"My hands are tied."

"Well, so are mine. I don't run the show around here."

"Wait a minute," Haskell broke into the argument. "You seem to know where Kyser is right now."

"I do."

"Where is he?" Haskell asked.

McNaughton glanced around the room. All eyes were on him and he hated being in this position.

"Come on, you don't have to tell me exactly, just get me in the ballpark."

He waited several minutes before answering. "Vancouver."

After digesting this information for several moments Gregg replied, "Great, then I'm sure we can work something out."

"What are you talking about?" McNaughton and Lorenz asked in tandem.

"Vito, we couldn't go up into Canada to arrest him without going through a shitload of paperwork and red tape that would take us months, maybe years to wade through anyway. McNaughton here can cross any international boundary, as long as they recognize Interpol and its governing bodies. Canada is one of those countries. And being out of the country, we have no jurisdiction until we have him back here."

"So?"

"So, whatever may happen to him in Canada won't be any of our concern. If he ends up with a few bumps and bruises, falls up and down a few flights of stairs, or ends up completely beat to shit, that isn't our concern until he crosses into the United States. All we need is a U.S. Customs agent at the airport to give us an affidavit attesting to Kyser's condition when he entered the country."

"So, what do you suggest?" Vito asked.

"I suggest that McNaughton here give the Vancouver authorities a ring and let them know what we are up to. Then the three of us can go pay the man a visit. McNaughton can interrogate him the way he sees fit and then when he is finished, he can release him into our custody. We might even get some answers to our questions a little easier this way."

"Sounds agreeable to me," McNaughton said.

"Then that's settled," Vito said and plopped down in his chair with a satisfied smile.

"Not hardly," Haskell rained.

"What do you mean?"

"We still have to get authorization to go to Vancouver, meaning we have to get passed her," he nosed in the direction of the glass palace. Lieutenant Stoddard was jamming her key in the keyhole. She fumbled with the lock for several seconds, then jerked the door open, stormed inside and slammed the door behind her hard enough to make the windows rumble and threaten to shatter.

"I don't envy you," McNaughton laughed. "Where can a guy get some Earl Grey?" he said, turning his attention toward Haskell.

Reading the look on Vito's face Haskell said, "I'm not sure if they have any tea bags in the break room or not. Let's go see," he finished, taking a step in the direction of the break room.

"Don't even think about it. You two are coming with me," Vito snorted.

"Like hell we are. You riled her up, you can get her unriled," Haskell laughed.

"Is he, you know," McNaughton nodded toward Stoddard's office.

Haskell nodded in agreement.

"Well, laddy, I must say you're not doing something right," he and Haskell broke out into uncontrollable guffaws.

Lieutenant Stoddard bolted out of her office and glared at the two men who were trying to compose themselves lest they incur her wrath. She casually sauntered over to the group of men without even so much as a glance in Vito's direction.

"What's so funny out here?"

"Nothing important," Vito replied.

"Who is this?"

"The name is Roland McNaughton, ma'am."

"No need for formalities, the name's Karen, Karen Stoddard," she offered her hand to him.

"Charmed, I'm sure," he responded with a gentle handshake.

"Yeah, well, I'm sure you're charmed, but who the hell are you?" she asked, not buying his gentlemanly routine for one second.

"Yes, well, uhm, I'm Roland McNaughton."

"Yes, well, uhm, we've already established that," she mimicked him.

"From Interpol," Haskell interjected.

"Thanks Gregg, at least one of you doesn't have their head up their asses this morning."

Vito bit his tongue to keep from responding.

"What's going on?"

"McNaughton here thinks he might know where Raymond Kyser is."

"Who is Raymond Kyser and where might he be?"

"I'm sorry, I haven't finished the report yet. I can have it for you later in the week if you'd like," Vito said.

"How about you tell me right now."

"Fine. Raymond Kyser is our main, and only suspect in the case we've been working on."

"Raymond Kyser? The real estate tycoon? The man who owns half of this city?"

"One in the same," Vito said.

"What in God's little acre makes you think Raymond Kyser has anything to do with this case?"

"An eyewitness places him with the girls, each of them, long before the kidnappings. He has plenty of motives. He's deeply involved with child pornography, pedophilia as well smuggling, just to name a few of the charges Interpol has lodged against him. And this," Vito handed her a fax.

"What this?"

"It just came back from the lab. It's a fingerprint match. Apparently as neat and thorough as Mr. Kyser has been, he forgot something."

"And what might that be?"

"He must have gotten himself a little too worked up with Rita Sorenson, he left his fingerprints on her breasts. We almost missed the prints the first go around. They weren't on the surface of her breasts per se, but in one of the valleys this maniac created during one of his deviant surgeries."

"And let's not forget the man is wealthy beyond compare. He has plenty enough money to have pulled this thing off without any problems," Haskell added.

"Let's just assume for a minute you are correct, and Kyser is in Vancouver, what now?"

"We go to Vancouver and get him," Vito said.

"We will need to get authorization for that, from both the Canadian authorities as well as our own people," the lieutenant said.

"No, ma'am, you don't," McNaughton interjected. "The only thing these boys need is a credit card to travel on."

"You can arrange things?" she asked suspiciously.

"Without a problem. My organization has been keeping tabs on your Mr. Kyser for quite some time now. We would be more than happy to oblige."

"And what do you want in return?"

"My, you're a suspicious lass, aren't you?"

"If there's one thing I've learned in this lifetime, it's nothing is free. Absolutely nothing."

"I simply want to talk to Kyser. He has the names of some people I'd really like to meet," McNaughton answered.

"So, this is legit? You really believe this is our guy?" she softened and turned to face Vito.

"I'm positive Karen," he dropped his hard ass routine as well.

"In that case, I've got an expense card for just such emergencies. Now listen, this is all highly unorthodox and it will probably get my ass in a sling if anything goes wrong, so do this as quickly and quietly as you can."

"We'll be like church mice," Vito smiled.

"Yeah, speedy little church mice," Haskell added.

"This is going to be on the QT until you return so if you need anything from me, don't call me," she smiled.

"You Americans are some really queer folks," McNaughton laughed.

"You think that now and you've never even been to Franks-N-Steins," Vito droned and let loose a deep sigh, causing Haskell to burst forth into another gush of laughter.

*   *   *

Her mind was traveling through a snowstorm at night, flakes screaming toward her face rapidly disappearing somewhere in the darkness behind her. Amber giggled and extended her tongue hoping to catch an icy treat on the tip. Suddenly the storm erupted into a dazzling volcanic explosion of color. She clamped her eyes shut reflexively.

Slowly she opened her eyes to a sea of swirling colors. Spinning and whirling she was caught up in the whirlpool. She reached her hand out to dip it beneath the vibrant waves.

Like fireflies in a summer's night sky her thoughts flashed and then were gone, never in the same place twice. A part of her brain screamed at her to focus while the remaining cells merely wanted to play. To enjoy the brief moments of pleasure as they fleeted by.

In a sober moment she realized the tinny taste was still in her mouth. She watched the shadows flickering and she felt her head being prodded. For a hiccup of time she remembered who she was and recalled she was trapped in a nightmare, but those few precious seconds faded rapidly.

*   *   *

Their plane touched down at Vancouver International Airport at roughly three that afternoon. They picked up a rental car McNaughton had already reserved and drove to the small town of Pemberton where a hotel room was also reserved for them. Their plan was to spring on Kyser first thing in the morning, after tea and coffee of course.

The road led them through the snow-capped Coast

Mountains. And although the drive was quite scenic, no one paid any particular attention.

"So, inspector, if you've known about Kyser for this long, why wait until now to move on him?" Vito asked.

"This is a thankless profession, as you gentlemen I'm sure are aware of. And sometimes small sacrifices have to be made for the greater good."

"Would you please just cut to the chase? Why is it you Europeans take so damned long to explain anything?" Vito grunted.

"Let's just say he's a little fish in a great big pond. An ocean to be exact. And until he was linked to these murders, we felt his indiscretions weren't quite as sinful as those with whom he was doing business. It is those people we are after. The people at the top. The people with the money."

"Doesn't hardly seem fitting to let a child molester roam the streets preying on innocent children," Haskell said, his anger beginning to rise like steam from freshly pissed in snow.

"I understand your sentiments exactly, detective, but even you must admit that sometimes, when you know you can't win them all, you have to make sure you win the good ones."

"Most of the time I don't have the perplexing task of making those kinds of decisions, thank God," Gregg replied.

"If it makes you feel any better, we have enough on Kyser now we think we can make him talk. These people burrow so far down into the underground you'd have to be a retched sand flea to find them."

"And you think Kyser is that parasite?"

"I know he is. I also know he has been peddling his ghastly wares to these people. Although, for a long time after the nasty business with the calendar and all, he laid low. But he has started to run out of his liquid assets. We tracked him here to Vancouver where he has been relatively quiet for some time now, a couple of months at least. Maybe he has something to do your girls."

"He's been keeping himself occupied," Vito said.

"More or less, I think it's possible."

They checked into the motel and ordered pizzas so terrible they were left contemplating whether or not to eat the box instead. After choking down their dinner the three of them began devising their battle plan using satellite maps of Kyser's property McNaughton brought with him. Before turning in for the night he placed a call to the local authorities and set up a time and place to meet in the morning. Vito and Haskell were so pumped they barely slept at all. It seemed this nightmare was finally ending. All Vito could think about was the look on Amber Reese's face when the cavalry finally showed up to rescue her.

Chapter Ten

Lizbeth splashed cold water on her face and sighed deeply. Her shift was nearly over, and she was more than grateful. Three gunshot wounds and a juvenile traffic fatality all in one shift. Vito's despondent words about their careers echoed in her head. In truth, she didn't know how she managed to do her job day after day, tragedy after tragedy without going completely insane.

She was worried about her brother. She always worried about how long it was taking him to recover from Gloria's death. But now he was getting himself mixed up with that parasite of a woman, Stoddard, she was even more concerned for his mental welfare. She was no good for him, for anyone, and Lizbeth knew it with every fiber of her being. Freddie had known it too. But Vito was as stubborn as he was stupid so there was no talking to him about it. She could only hope and pray he had taken her advice and told Karen to hit the bricks.

Lizbeth looked in the mirror and didn't like what she saw. Lines creased her face in places that had once been as smooth as a baby's bottom. She was getting much too old for the constant stress of her job. There was so much more in life she wanted to do. Places she wanted to see. It was getting high time she herself got on with her life. One of the bathroom stall doors opened behind her with a loud bang.

Lizbeth jumped and spun around, "Oh, damn, you scared me half to death."

She saw the TASER but by the time her brain processed the information it was much too late for her to be able to react. Her body convulsed and crashed to the floor as a result of the voltage running rampant through her. Lizbeth felt her muscles relax and tried to catch her breath but before she could spasms coursed through her body once more. The fourth time her assailant pulled the trigger was the charm. Lizbeth cried out weakly for Vito before all went black.

*   *   *

Dawn came much too early, yet, somehow not early enough for Vito. He was tired, dead tired, but he was also ready to get the show on the road. He could always sleep later.

Growing up in Los Angeles Vito had been exposed his share of the mountains. He had even been introduced to trees, other than palms, once or twice when he did a short stint as a Boy Scout. His troop had embarked upon a couple of excursions into the San Bernadino National Forest and Vito had somewhat enjoyed himself, but not as much as he did in the city. The city was his home, his life and eventually, it became his prison. Nevertheless, the Canadian countryside they were currently traveling through simply took his breath away. Not only was the air crisper, cleaner and easier to breathe, it seemed to affect the entire surroundings in the same way. The grass was greener, the water bluer, and trees, they even seemed to be taller. It took Vito several minutes of contemplation to put his finger on what the exact difference was, but then it hit him like brick. Life was going on in this place, vibrantly and systematically forging ahead. Whereas in the city, life was only happening, merely passing time until death's inevitable knock upon the door.

McNaughton eased the rental car into a parking spot next to a Mounted Police cruiser. Two uniformed officers were already sitting in the diner waiting for them. The five of them grabbed a table in the back and began discussing their plans over breakfast. The Canadians were pretty much indifferent to the whole affair. People much higher ranking than them had already given the green light on this operation and they knew they were only there for tactical support, and to have someone to blame if something went awry.

"You seem to be preoccupied, detective," McNaughton interrupted Vito's soul searching.

Vito continued to stare out the diner's long, clear window. He was still amazed at how different things were here. Different enough to make him want to stay, forever. There was no Karen Stoddard to have to deal with. No child molesters lurking around the schoolhouses and no serial killers passing time like ticking bombs. He burped up the previous night's pizza and was forced to realize evil lurked everywhere, even in this pristine paradise. No matter where he ran to, men like Raymond Kyser would be there to greet him with a painted smile and a knife concealed behind their backs.

"Detective?" McNaughton said again.

"Yeah, what is it?" Vito replied without turning around to face him.

"I said, you seem to be quite preoccupied."

"I am."

"May I ask why?"

"I don't think we're going to find what we're after."

"You think Kyser may not be at his cabin?"

"No, he'll be there, if your information is correct. But he won't be the guy we're looking for."

"What makes you say that?" Gregg asked.

"I don't know really, it's just a gut feeling I guess. I can't explain it."

"I think I know what you're feeling, detective. But sometimes a case can end quicker and easier than we anticipate. Especially a case of such a gruesome, horrific nature as you've described to me. A case like this one has the ability to eat away at your very soul, consuming you until your every waking moment is spent tormented by your lack of progress. You feel impotent. Trust me, I've been there."

"Great, now I'm depressed too," Gregg quipped lightly.

"I'm sure you have inspector. And you're right. I'm just foolishly rambling on, I guess," Vito sighed and turned back around to face them. "You sure have some beautiful country up here fellas," he smiled at the troopers.

"Thank you."

"But it's nothing like the beaches of LA with all those bronze skinned beauties running around in tiny bikinis I'll bet," the younger of two said with a wink.

"Trust me son, this is much better."

"Are we ready to do this thing?" McNaughton asked everyone.

All heads nodded in agreement. The police officers stood up, gathered their jackets and settled up their tab. Vito was still feeling uncomfortable as they pulled away from the diner. He shrugged it off to old age and cynicism. He let the scenery wisp him away from the case just long enough to get a mental breather as they followed the troopers through the curvaceous mountain roads.

"We will pull up to a spot about a half mile from Kyser's cabin. From there we will hike in through the woods and take a good look around before committing ourselves to anything. I learned my lesson a long time ago with some crazy Belgian bastard who was holed up like this."

"Really? What happened?" Gregg asked, more out of boredom than actual interest.

"Dogs. The man had a pack of vicious, wild dogs running around guarding his place. Four officers and I were all bitten pretty badly that day. And of course it didn't end there."

"No?"

"No. Then there were the bleeding rabies shots," McNaughton said, sucking air through his teeth in a hiss of remembrance.

"Couldn't you have just tested the dogs?" Vito heard himself ask absent-mindedly.

"We could have, had the other officers not shot them to death. Actually, a few of the mangy beasts happened to escape into the forest, but we had no way of tracking them down."

"I for one can tell you I feel much better about this now," Vito said.

The brake lights on the trooper's car in front of them came on, effectively putting an end to their conversation. They eased up behind the car and McNaughton turned the engine off. They spent the next few minutes double checking their gear and rehashing their plan. For the time being, Vito and Gregg had only one plan, sticking as close to the troopers as possible so they didn't end up lost in the seemingly endless woods.

The musty smell of wet leaves and thriving fungi drifted up

from the forest floor. The air was wet and cold, but nice. Most of the trees were towering pines with the power to obscure the light of day lending an otherworldly feel to the trail. The deeper they dove into the greenery, the darker it became. Vito felt a little spooked. He didn't like being in a place he didn't know, in the dark, with a potential killer hiding somewhere over the next ridge. His mind played tricks on him with each shadow that crossed his path.

The half-mile trek through the dense forest was a lot harder than Vito could have ever imagined. Every step he took reminded him of how long it had been since he last visited the gym in the basement of the precinct. Every time he stumbled, he vehemently cursed Krispy Kreme under his breath. And every time he fell, panting from the lack of oxygen, he felt like kicking the shit out of the Marlboro Man.

Mercifully, they came to rest near the edge of a clearing about a half an hour after entering the bug-infested wilderness. Vito's perception of Canada's glorious beauty was diminishing with each gallon of blood the black flies, super-sized mosquitoes and chiggers commandeered from him. These were amenities he could rest assured weren't mentioned in any Canadian tourism brochure.

"Ouch, son-of-a-bitch! What in the hell is that?" Vito screamed, thrusting his arm out to one of the Canadian troopers, his eyes wide with fear.

The trooper looked down at a brown spot on Vito's arm about the size of a pumpkin seed. Eight brown legs spread out across Vito's skin, feeling for the perfect place to burrow their grip.

He laughed, "That's a wood tick. Pretty big one too."

"Well get it the hell off me."

"Hold still, this might hurt a little."

"It already hurts a lot. Just yank the damned thing off."

"Can't, if the head stays behind in your skin you could get a nasty infection."

"Oh, great, just my dumb luck."

The trooper worked at getting a good grip on the tick's head and body and then gave a quick jerk ripping it away from Vito's flesh.

"Holy shit! What is that?"

"Your skin in its mouth."

"I'm really starting to hate this place," Vito commented while rubbing the tender spot on his arm.

They finally came upon a small break in the trees revealing the modest cabin resting peacefully in a secluded valley. The homestead sat on a small clearing with only a two-track dirt path leading up to the front door. It was an original log cabin made of hewn trees, not a prefabricated kit and its rustic appearance made it seem warm and inviting. The landscaping had the appearance of being well groomed even though it was overgrown at the present time. The group of police officers watched the place from a small ridge overlooking the back of the property. Vito felt his anger swelling up inside of him. The place was absolutely gorgeous, even in its rudimentary state. This bastard went about his daily life, never once giving thought to the pain he caused throughout his miserable existence.

After several minutes of surveillance, the younger of the troopers said, "Something's not right."

"What do you mean?" Vito asked, suddenly getting a queasy feeling in his gut again.

"It's kind of a cold morning, don't you agree?" He said, rubbing his red hands together and blowing into them. Plumes of white mist rose in the air as an exclamation point.

"Yeah, so?"

"There's no smoke coming from the chimney."

"I think he's got a point," McNaughton agreed, blowing into his cupped hands to ease the chill.

"That could mean anything. Maybe he's got a gas furnace," Haskell argued.

"There would still be vapors coming out of the chimney. Besides, there's no gas this far up here in these mountains," the older trooper put his two cents in. "No way to get it up here. Only wood burners in any of these cabins," he sniffed the air. "And there isn't any wood burning for miles."

"It has got to be less than 40 degrees out here, why wouldn't he have a fire going?" Trooper Bakker asked.

"There's only one way to find out," Vito replied and started down the small hillside toward the cabin.

"Vito," Haskell called out.

"What?"

"What about dogs?"

"Fuck 'em," he said, drawing his service revolver from his shoulder holster.

With Vito crashing through the woods like a rutting buck the other officers dispensed with the idea of a stealthy approach and plowed after him. Little saplings whipped and snapped at him vengefully as he forged his way down the winding, nondescript path. Stumbling, he lost his balance the last few steps and tumbled headlong down the hillside. Vito went sprawling across the wet grass carpeting of Kyser's lawn as gracefully as a cat trying to run on greased linoleum.

"You all right?" McNaughton laughed and helped Vito back to his feet.

"Guess I still have my city legs on," he smiled awkwardly.

"I got a feeling our young trooper is right."

"About what?"

"Something just isn't right about this place. There's no sound at all, other than those made by you of course," he grinned toothily.

"I hate to tell you this, that was my graceful, quiet side," Vito laughed off his embarrassment.

The small assemblage of police officers regrouped at the bottom of the hill. They were only a couple of hundred feet or so away from the back door of the cabin, and as much as Vito hated to admit it, they still had to proceed with caution. There would be no way for them to know if anyone were laying in ambush until it was too late. The path to the back door was completely clear. And anyone inside would have easy, clean shots at all of them if they walked up in a group. They still had to proceed by the book. Vito and Haskell took the direct route and headed straight for the back door, praying with each step. McNaughton and the others made a beeline for the corner of the cabin where they would eventually head around to the front of the place.

Vito and his partner crouched as low as they possibly could while still being able to move. There were still a good twenty feet away from the cabin when Haskell got his first whiff.

"What in the hell is that?" Haskell asked while his nose involuntarily twitched and wrinkled.

Vito stiffened and took a deep breath.

"What is that smell, Vito?"

Without a word Lorenz dug his trusty little blue jar out of his pocket and handed it to his partner. "It's going to get ugly from here on out."

"I'll take that as a bad sign."

"Yeah, it is partner. That's the smell of death, very old death."

"Shit. What do you think is in there?" Haskell gagged and covered his face with his shirt collar, not wanting an answer to his question.

"I really don't think you want to know what I'm thinking," Vito said, himself gagging reflexively at the assaulting stench and his mind's visualization of what the girls must look like behind that closed door. He took the jar back from Haskell and wiped two fingers worth of Vick's into his thick, salt and pepper mustache, put the jar back in his pocket and started making his way toward the back door. Vito's brain churned with gruesome thoughts of Kyser getting spooked months earlier due to Interpol's pressure and hauling out of there, leaving the girls behind to starve to death.

Vito was standing up now, no longer concerned with the possibility of a hidden gunman. If there were someone alive in the cabin, they wouldn't be in any condition to be doing any shooting. He cupped his hands and peered through the filthy windows trying to locate the source of the stench before walking directly into it. Seeing nothing he braced himself and tested the knob on the door. He had expected it to be locked, but instead it turned easily. Vito took one deep breath before pushing the door open.

Haskell doubled over at the knees immediately and thrust a finger up into the air. He went through a series of dry heaves before standing upright and wiping off his lips. He gave a gentle nod and the two of them proceeded into the house. Sounds of someone gagging echoed from the front of the house. Vito thought he recognized the chortled voice as that of the young trooper.

The back door opened up into a breezeway passing through to the kitchen. Vito took quick mental notes of the condition of the room. There were two place settings on the kitchen table and dirty dishes in the sink. There had been something cooking on the stove and by the looks of the pans the fire in the wood stove had burned itself out while they were still cooking. Their contents were blackened and scorched. The cupboards were full of food. Not just the staples, as if someone had been living in the place for quite some time and intended to keep doing so for even longer. Vito pulled down a couple of cans, tuna, corned beef hash, and took note of their dates. They were recent as far as he could tell.

A further inspection of the kitchen revealed further signs life here had ended abruptly. The garbage was half-full and quite rancid even in the cool, crisp air of the cabin. The level of dust on the surfaces varied, less on the table and floor, but there was more on the surfaces higher up. Neglected cleaning of a bachelor? The signs pointed to the fact the cabin had been lived in not long ago. Vito took note of the fact there were two distinctive sets of footprints on the wooden floor, one set much larger than the other.

"McNaughton," he called out weakly.

"Yes, laddy," his voice echoed through the cabin from the front porch.

"You guys might want to steer clear of this place for a few minutes. Preserve the evidence and all that."

"No arguments here."

"Trooper Bakker."

"Yes, detective," he called out.

Haskell and Lorenz had moved through the kitchen toward the front of the house and were now standing near the door where they could all see each other.

"Do you have a crime scene investigative unit in this burg?"

"Not here, but there is one back in Vancouver. Shall I give them a call?"

"Yes, I strongly suggest you do that right away."

"I'll have to go back up to the car. It may take a while," he said, not wanting any part of what was in the cabin.

"That's perfectly fine."

"What do you think is in there inspector?" the young trooper asked.

"You don't want to know, laddy," McNaughton answered with a pat on the young man's back. "You need my help in there?" he called out through a broken window, grateful the breeze was blowing toward the back of the cabin, sparing him the brunt of the fetid stench.

"Not right yet. Until we know what we're looking at, the fewer feet trampling evidence the better."

"Understood."

With that Vito and his partner began a methodical, painfully slow search of the cabin. They moved from the living room area down a narrow corridor. There the smell grew stronger with each step and Vito knew what they sought lay in front of them. Haskell stopped at the bathroom, but Vito pressed forward, toward what he believed to be a back bedroom.

"Don't you want to look in here?"

"No need," he put his hand on the doorknob and took several deep breaths before opening the door. "Listen, Gregg," Vito's voice took on a fatherly tone. "It's liable to be quite ugly in there, I wouldn't blame you if you wanted to wait out here."

"No. I've come this far, there's no turning back now. If I don't walk in there with you right now, I'm likely to go back to being a patrolman and never be able to walk into another homicide scene ever again."

Vito nodded. It had become painfully obvious whatever was causing the stench permeating throughout the cabin was behind that door. The disgusting odor was so strong it almost visibly leaked out from the crack beneath the door. Vito braved himself and flung open the door.

Both detectives immediately and instinctively turned away from the gruesome carnage. It was almost like the game where an image would be flashed across the screen for a millisecond and then the contestants would be asked questions about what they had seen. But Vito and Gregg didn't want to play that game. They didn't want to remember even a fraction of what they had just observed, but they couldn't ignore it either.

The only furniture in the room was a rustic bed made from

hewn pine trees centered in the room with the head of the bed pushed against the far wall. A small-unfinished pine dresser with two small top drawers and two wider drawers below sat against the west wall. Next to the bed was a small bedside table with a kerosene lamp and a pack of matches sitting in the center. A set of powder blue curtains hung loosely from the only window in the room. The window offered a gorgeous view of the forest with the mountain as a backdrop. Everything looked peaceful and normal. Everything except for the rotting corpse trussed up over the bed. Chains stretched from anchors fastened in opposite corners of the room, firmly holding the body aloft by its decaying wrists. The feet were bound to the bedposts by nylon rope. The person, they were unable to determine gender due to decomposition, had been eviscerated and their entrails streamed down onto the bed in oozing streaks of thick, sappy liquid. The head was rolled to one side and the mouth frozen open in a tormented scream of agony.

"Oh, Jesus Christ, Vito. What the hell happened here?" Gregg gasped.

"It looks like whoever this person was had been tortured and left here to slowly die. Inspector," he called out weakly.

The corpse's skin had begun to sag on its frame and looked as though someone were pouring out the last of the congealed Thanksgiving gravy. The eyes had all but disappeared, forming dried riverbeds of encrusted ocular fluids on their blackened cheeks.

"My God," McNaughton exclaimed as he walked into the room behind the awestruck detectives.

"What do you think?" Vito asked.

"I think you found the source of this stench."

"Do you think that is Kyser?"

"Hell, I can't even tell what it is, let alone who it is," McNaughton choked.

They started rotating around the room to get different angles on the mutilated corpse. Just how much of the damage had been done to this person while they were still alive was unclear. It was hard to decipher which of the gaping wounds a sharp instrument had created, or which had been caused by the normal splitting of the skin during decomposition. That was something the coroner was going to have to determine. A job Vito didn't envy in the least.

"What do you gentlemen make of this?" McNaughton asked, pointing upward at a blackened stump that had once been attached to a hand. At first glance they had thought both of the man's arms had been bound the same. However, because there was no longer a hand on the right arm, the chain had been threaded through the flesh between the ulna and the radius and was wrapped around the bones several times.

"His hand is gone."

"Why on earth would the killer take his hand?"

"Explains the fingerprints we found on Rita Sorenson's body," Vito said somberly.

"I think your man is playing with you, if you ask my opinion," McNaughton commented.

Vito didn't reply verbally, only a nod of agreement. He had no doubts that for some reason he had been sucked into some sick fuck's twisted mind game, a game he was losing with every roll of the dice.

"Vito," Haskell called out from the other side of the room. He was peering down into the drawer of the bedside table.

"What did you find?"

"I think we can determine the gender now," he said, gagging and pointing to a piece of blackened flesh pinned to a piece of poster board. The man's organ had been traced onto the paper when it had been in a much healthier state. The shriveled raisin that had once been the source of the owner's pride was shocking enough a find, but not nearly as shocking as what they found next. In the drawer with the deformed penis was a note, a note with the names of every one of the girls who had posed for the calendar. The note was in fact, itself a calendar. January was crossed off, as well as every month up until May. In the box devoted to the current month were three, hand scrawled sentences. First, across the top of the box was the name "Amber Reese." Below that was "Detective Lorenz meets Raymond Kyser." And finally, below that, read the line "Detective Lorenz removed from the case."

"It's starting to look more and more like we might have found Mr. Kyser," McNaughton said.

"Not soon enough, I'm afraid," Vito huffed.

"What in the hell does he mean, Detective Lorenz removed from the case?" Haskell asked.

"I really don't have a clue, Gregg, but I've got a good feeling we're going to find out sooner than later."

The three of them slowly backed out of the room and carefully retraced their paths back out of the house. Once outside, they all met together in the front yard, far away from the front door where the Canadian air was fresh once more. They passed around the little blue jar of Vick's like a joint at a frat party, but still, they couldn't get the stench out of their noses. The raw stink of rotting flesh had burned itself into their sensors. It would be with them for a long, long time.

"How long before your investigators get here, son?" Vito asked.

"I suspect it will take them at least an hour or so. But they were coming straight away, so we should expect to see them sometime around noon," he said while glancing at his watch.

Vito nodded and lost himself in thought. There was something about the killer's message that really disturbed him. It was familiar, but not in the everyday kind of sense of familiar. It wasn't a memory he could just pluck from his brain, scrutinize it and throw it back where it belonged. This was more of a feeling. A sense of déjà vu.

The sun had begun to warm them and despite the horror inside the cabin, outside it was quite pleasant. Haskell found himself thinking about Amanda. He was questioning his feelings for her. Was it a schoolboy crush, a simple infatuation with her beauty? Or was there a little budding of what could grow into love hidden somewhere beneath the surface. He realized he was missing her more and more as the days went by. And he eagerly looked forward to the times when they were able to talk on the phone, and even more so when they were finally able to spend a few moments together. He had even marked every one of Evy's games on his calendar. He never missed them often anyway, but now, it seemed he was looking forward to them a lot more. They were no longer an obligation he had to his niece they were a special time for him as well.

The hillside erupted with the sounds of people crashing

down the narrow deer path. Several seconds later a group of men burst from the shadows of the forest and into the clearing. Two men struggled with a gurney loaded with gear while two others lugged even more equipment. They were red-faced and winded by the time they got to the awaiting group of police officers.

While the investigators disappeared into the cabin Vito found himself wondering how much experience they had up here in the great white north with murders of this magnitude. His thoughts were answered almost immediately. Three men in Tyvek suits hunkered down along the bushes relieving themselves of whatever lunch they had decided to wolf down on their way to the scene.

Vito jumped at the sound of his cell phone ringing. No one ever called him, and he wouldn't even have carried the damn thing had his sister not insisted on it. His stomach knotted when it dawned on him only three people knew his cell phone number and one of them was with him now.

"Lorenz," he barked once he figured out how to answer the intimidating device.

"Uncle Vito?" a young voice squeaked. It wasn't the manly voice Freddie used when he regaled Vito with his on-field prowess or escapades with members of the opposite sex. It was the same voice he had used when he talked to Vito about his father. Immediately Vito felt like someone had kicked him in the balls while someone else drove several punches into his stomach.

"What's wrong Freddie?" he asked sternly. His mouth was so dry his words clicked as they came out.

"Justice is dead. Someone killed him," he sniffled.

Justice was Freddie Senior's golden retriever. They had actually named him Justice, after Dave Justice the long time Braves outfielder, but given Freddie's profession the name seemed even more apropos.

"What do you mean someone killed him?"

"When I got home from school, he was laying in the yard all bloody," the boy's speech was rapid and interspersed with sobbing and sucks of air. "And mom's gone."

"Freddie, slow down and tell me exactly what you are

talking about," Vito tried to sound firm, but didn't want the boy to get the impression he was chewing him out or yelling at him.

"I came home, and Justice was in the front yard. I reached down to touch him that's when I realized he was all bloody. I ran in the house yelling for mom, but she didn't answer," he broke down and started sobbing even louder.

"Did she leave a note, Freddie?"

"No, she didn't, but someone else did."

"Who left a note, Freddie?"

"I don't know."

"Was the note on the table?" Vito asked. He could sense the boy was drifting away from him. There was something terribly wrong and he was certain Freddie didn't want to face whatever it was.

"No, it was in the yard."

"On the ground next to Justice?"

"No, Uncle Vito, it was Justice. Somebody carved him up," the boy's voice was laced with fear and subtle hints of growing anger.

Vito took several quick seconds to gather his composure. "Freddie, can you read the note?"

"Sort of, but it doesn't make any sense. It's for you. It says 'Detective Lorenz, tick tock, your sister's on the clock.' What does that mean, Uncle Vito? Does that mean my mom?"

Vito's stomach soured instantly. He choked back the bile and concentrated hard on his next few words.

"I don't know what it means either, Freddie," Vito choked out the lie to protect his nephew.

"What am I going to do, Uncle Vito?"

"Freddie, don't worry about anything. Go back in the house, lock the doors and just stay put. You call me if you hear anything from your mother. I'm out of the country right now, but I'll get back there as soon as I can. As soon as I hang up call my precinct and ask for Lieutenant Karen Stoddard. Tell her who you are and what has happened. Now, this is very important, Freddie, do not move Justice. Not even a little bit."

"But shouldn't I bury him? I don't want mom to see him the way he is. She loves him so much."

"I know she does, Freddie. But Lieutenant Stoddard will

take care of Justice for you. And Freddie, don't worry, we'll figure out where your mom went. She probably went shopping and will be home in the next few minutes," Vito told another lie. He knew what had happened to his sister. She had just become a pawn in this vicious game.

*   *   *

Amber Reese tried to keep her eyes open, but she was simply too tired. She had been watching a kaleidoscope of dancing colors for what seemed like an eternity. She had not remembered to notch her armrest for days, or maybe even weeks. In fact, she couldn't even remember what her last coherent thought had been.

She thought she could hear voices echoing in the distance. But then she thought they might be in her own head. Screams. Screams of anger. Screams of terror. Screams of laughter.

The swirling patterns began to slowly dissipate from her vision and her mind began to clear. It was like looking out of the window of a jetliner as it passed from one cloudbank and into another. It was crystal clear and openly blue for one moment and then simply white the next. In one of her clear moments she realized the drugs must have been wearing off. She was suddenly able to feel herself again, solidly, not from the ethereal realm she had been living in for the past couple of weeks.

Fear settled in on Amber when she realized her mind wasn't working like it used to. Some of her memories were gone. Not simply forgotten where with the right impetus they would come rushing back but gone forever. She could sense big blank spaces in her mind. The spaces where her thoughts had once occupied her brain and were now hollow. They were now empty spaces echoing erroneous thoughts and ideas. She searched for a memory she could hang onto, but found nothing familiar, nothing comforting. She was drifting aimlessly within her own mind, adrift on a sea of confusion.

Between bouts of incessant giggling Amber caught fleeting glimpses of reality. She felt thick strands of drool oozing from the corners of her mouth. For a moment fear gripped her tightly, almost aware of what was happening to her brain. But then it tickled, and then she giggled, and the coherent thoughts disappeared.

Once more she became aware of the voices in the distance. These were not the voices of schizophrenic characters living within her own mind, these were real voices. Real screams. Her screams.

Chapter Eleven

"Take some more from that angle," Vito directed the crime scene investigator who was currently recording the crime scene. He kept his hands in his pockets to hide the fact they were shaking. He wasn't sure what was affecting him more, his anger, his frustration, or his fear.

It had taken Vito nearly twelve hours to get back to Los Angeles from Vancouver and Justice had already begun his degradation back into the earth. The poor dog had been shaved entirely on one side and the grim message had been etched into the creature's skin with the same surgical laser used to convey each of the killer's previous messages. The dog's tongue was now blue, swollen and jutted obscenely out from between its teeth in death's permanent snarl. The message had definitely been for him, and it was definitely meant as a threat. "Tick tock, your sister is on the clock," he said aloud, burying his face into his hands.

"What was that, Vito?" Karen asked sympathetically.

"Why the fuck doesn't this chicken shitted bastard come after me? If he's got a fucking beef with me, then let's settle it. Why do this?" he said, thrusting a finger at the mutilated family friend.

Karen and Vito stood shoulder to shoulder, watching the crime scene investigators as they wrapped things up. They carried away shards of Vito's family in a nice, neat, tidy package.

"You want me to stick around?" Karen asked, putting her arm around Vito's shoulder.

As enticing as her offer was, he just shook his head. He didn't know what he wanted to do. And he didn't know where to begin, but he was certain she wouldn't be the answer to his problems, merely another aspect of them. Karen slowly let her arm fall away from him when it became clear she wasn't going to get any more of a response out of him.

"Vito, I'm going to need to talk to you in the morning, in my office," she said, opening her car door and sliding into the front seat. Her voice was that of a parent preparing to scold a child. He could almost hear her saying, "This is going to hurt me a lot more than it is going to hurt you."

"Yeah, I know," he replied, fighting the urge to tell her to fuck off and get it over with right then.

"Vito, I'm truly sorry."

He simply nodded and thought about the calendar in Raymond Kyser's cabin. *Detective Lorenz taken off the case.*

Vito waved back at her weakly as she pulled away from the curb. He knew what she was going to have to say in the morning, and he couldn't blame her. It was strictly adhered to departmental policy. He was quite certain the lieutenant was going to take him off the case. It had gotten too close to him, much too personal for him to be able to remain objective, let alone be of any use. Vito knew he had less than twelve hours to find his sister, or he would have to leave it in someone else's hands.

He went through the motions of helping Freddie gather a few changes of clothes and pack them into a suitcase and then he drove him over to the Bouchard's. They were good people and Vito knew he would feel a lot better if Freddie were with people who could be more sympathetic than he ever could be. Besides, Freddie needed someone compassionate, and Vito just wasn't that person right now.

He drove around for more than an hour after dropping his nephew off. He couldn't believe what was happening, nor could he even begin to fathom being at such a loss of what to do next. He tossed an empty pint bottle onto the floor of his car and sprayed several blasts of breath spray into his mouth.

When Vito stepped through the door at Gus's, he was a man on a mission. He ignored his usual booth and bellied up to the bar. The bartender was in the process of pouring him a double Dewar's when Gus stopped him by putting his gorilla-sized hand over the mouth of the rocks glass.

Gus eyed the bartender and said, "He don't drink in here, ever. You got that?"

The younger man nodded obediently.

"What are you doing Vito?" the old cop admonished him with a sad look in his eye.

"I don't want to hear it, Gus."

"Listen, son, word travels fast around a joint like this. I know all about what happened, and I sympathize with you. It's a terrible thing and I'm sure it's gnawing at you, but that's still no reason to do this," he nodded toward the bottle the bartender had left on the bar. The man had wisely retreated as soon as their conversation started heating up, wanting no part of Vito's or Gus's wrath if and when either of them exploded.

"Gus, I said, leave me the fuck alone, please."

"Sure, Vito, I'll leave you alone. But I'm taking this with me," he said, grabbing the bottle by the neck. "You're welcome here anytime, you know that, but I'll be damned if you'll get a drink in here. At least not like this."

"Damn it, Gus, quit being such a hard ass."

"I haven't even started, Vito. Do you think you're the only one who has ever had any tragedy in their lives? And Vito, you won't do Lizbeth any good by disappearing back into that bottle."

"Fuck you Gus, what the hell do you know?" he screamed, throwing his bar stool down and storming out of the place.

Vito stopped at a corner store for a refill and headed across town to another place he used to hang out at. It wasn't like Gus's place at all, they didn't give a rat's ass about a person in this place and Vito was certain to get what he wanted. He was already feeling two sheets to the wind when he sat down at the bar and ordered two doubles and a beer back. He took a deep breath and slammed the two shots and grabbed his chaser off the bar and made his way to a booth in a dark corner at the back of the room. He sat in the booth and waited for the whiskey to kick in while ignoring everything else. It was then Vito remembered something that had slipped his mind since Vancouver.

He reached into his jacket and pulled out a wallet from his

breast pocket. Instantly, Vito was taken aback by lingering stench of Raymond Kyser's death stained wallet. He gagged on his lukewarm beer several times while rifling through the dead man's belongings. There were all of the basic essentials one would expect to find. His driver's license, a couple of video rental cards, although none of them were from Sick Fuck Rentals, a roadside assistance card, a medical insurance card as well as a few suspect photographs. But there were no credit cards. Vito found this quite strange. The man had been going about daily life as if there was nothing to set him apart from any other Canadian citizen, so why no credit cards? Not even a bankcard, or Automated Teller Machine card for that matter. Vito's head was too cloudy from the effects of alcohol and stress, making it impossible for him to think clearly. He tossed the wallet onto the table and stood up. His drinks were empty, and a gnawing urge told him he needed more.

As Vito was sitting back down with another double shot of scotch and a fresh beer, something caught his eye. When he had tossed the wallet onto the table a couple of the pictures had slid out of their clear sleeves. There was a business card stuck in between two of them and it was now lying on the table. Vito half recognized the name, but his advancing stupor wouldn't allow him to place it. He flipped the card repeatedly in his fingers, trying to coax his deductive memory into kicking in. And then it dawned on him, this was one of the names that photographer, Robert, Roland, Rog, some shit had dropped during their interrogation. This guy, Aubrey Stillwater, had been pretty close to Kyser, according to ol' Rog anyway. Vito tossed the double into his mouth, washed it down with the last of his beer and stood up from the table. He looked over the business card one more time to commit the handwritten address on the back to memory before slipping it back into the wallet. He tucked the wallet back into his pocket and staggered for the door.

Outside in his car Vito did two very important things before driving over to what he hoped was Aubrey Stillwater's personal address. First, he puked with all the fury of an addict going through withdrawal and secondly, he made sure both his weapons were loaded. After nearly taking out a fire hydrant,

Vito stopped at an all-night doughnut shop and had two horrendously old cups of coffee while he waited for the waitress to make a fresh pot and bring him two more cups to go. His head was already starting to pound, and he was sure within a few hours he would be incapacitated from the ill effects of having succumbed to his demons.

Vito drove slowly down Magnolia counting out the addresses several houses ahead of him. He was genuinely pleased to see both the name and address on the business card matched the name and address on the mailbox. He drove around the block and parked his car out of sight of his intended target. Stillwater lived in an upscale neighborhood where one rarely heard the bark of a dog because most of the people owned security systems and their pets were of the variety that yipped. Vito crept around to the back of Stillwater's house and peered through the patio door. He immediately saw what he was looking for. The alarm system control panel was blinking with a green light, indicating it was armed. He crept around to the side of the garage and stole a glance inside. There were two vehicles in the garage, a Cadillac Escalade and a black Porsche 911. So far, he was batting a thousand. The man was home.

Vito finished his coffee and polished off the remainder of a roll of wintergreen Certs. He walked brazenly around to the front of the house and rang the doorbell. When no one answered immediately, he rang it again, and then once more for good measure. After several minutes a voice called out groggily from behind the closed door.

"Who is it?"

"Edison," he mumbled.

"Who?"

"Edison Power Company, Mr., uhm, Stillwater. Aubrey Stillwater?"

"Do you know what time it is?" his voice bore a definitive measure of annoyance.

"Yes, sir, sorry for interrupting your sleep, sir. But we've had reports of a gas leak and according to my equipment it is coming from your residence."

"I don't smell anything," Stillwater barked suspiciously.

"You wouldn't sir," Vito hoped he wasn't slurring his

speech too much. He didn't think he was, because the lies were coming too easily. "The leak is outside of the residence, underground, but according to my schematics, the shut off valve should be inside your residence, sir."

"Can't you come back in the morning?"

"Believe me, sir, if I could, I would. I really don't much care for being out here this late at night myself. But this leak is pretty bad, might cause some really big problems if there was to be a spark out here or something. And you never know, if it backs up and starts leaking into your house while you're sleeping, you'll never wake up to know it."

There was complete silence behind the door. Then, the subtle tones of the alarm being disabled. Vito knew he was going to have to act fast, there was liable to be a panic button on the panel as well.

"I'll be out your hair just as soon as I locate and shut off the valve, no more than five minutes, Mr. Stillwater."

There were still no sounds from the other side of the door.

"Mr. Stillwater?" Vito called out once more. He was starting to get nervous. There was a distinct possibility the man had simply gone to the nearest phone and called the power company, the police, or both.

"Yeah, keep your pants on, I had to get my robe," he said, jerking open the door and exposing the sour look on his face. Vito immediately erased the scowl when he shoved his revolver into the man's mouth and forced him back inside.

Stillwater was a tall man who seemed dwarfed by Vito's angry posture. Vito quickly backed the man up to the couch and shoved him down into the seat. Stillwater's eyes screamed in disagreement, but wisely, his mouth stayed shut. His teeth hurt and his gums were bleeding from having been force fed Vito's gun. But as uncomfortable as he was, he was certain things could get worse.

With his gun buried in man's mouth all the way up to the cylinder, Vito stared hatefully into his eyes. He could see the confusion and fear, but also a twinkle of defiance. This was a man who was not used to being treated in this manner, especially not in his own home. Vito found he enjoyed shattering the man's illusion of safety, no amount of money in the world could save his sorry ass right now, and both of them knew it.

"First, let me start by saying this is in no way, shape or form a robbery. So, that being said, you know money is not an issue with me so bribery won't sway my decision to pull this trigger either way. And lastly, and most importantly, I hate being lied to almost as much as I hate having to repeat myself. So, if you find me getting angry, you can rest assured it's because I've either had to ask the same question twice, or I don't think I'm getting a straight answer. Do you understand?"

Stillwater nodded his head. His nose twitched in disagreement of Vito's stale bourbon laced breath.

"I'll bet you're wondering why I'm here."

Again, he nodded, slowly, without ever taking his eyes away from Vito's except to steal a glance at the gun pointed at his face.

"We have a mutual acquaintance, you and I, only you've had the pleasure of meeting the man while he was still alive. I on the other hand, I only got to see his dick in a drawer," Vito emphasized his words for effect.

Stillwater flinched at the imagery.

"I can tell by the look on your face you don't have a clue who I am talking about. Does the name Raymond Kyser ring a bell?" Vito asked, sliding the barrel of his gun out of the man's mouth.

"It most certainly does, he's a client of mine," Stillwater replied a long minute later after he had finally found his voice. It felt like he had a bucket of sand in his throat, and he was certain it sounded that way as well.

"And when was the last time you had words with your client," Vito emphasized the last word with sarcasm.

"It has been a while. I can't honestly say for certain when it was."

"And when might the last time have been you spoke to him on a less than professional level?"

"I'm not sure I really understand what it is you are referring to. Raymond Kyser and I have always maintained a purely professional relationship."

Vito gave no warning whatsoever, just a faint little flicker of anger in his eye the instant before delivering a hard punch to the man's forehead. Stillwater's eyes rolled up into his head and he fell out of consciousness for a brief moment. Reaching over with his free hand, Vito grabbed a tuft of the man's hair and jerked him back upright again.

"I thought we agreed upon the fact I don't like to ask questions more than once," he spat.

"Really, I don't understand what you are talking about?" his voice was panicky, and he flinched in anticipation of another blow to the forehead.

"Are you trying to tell me you don't enjoy the same, let's say, recreational pastimes as Mr. Kyser? And keep in mind I hate being lied to much worse than I dislike having to repeat myself."

Stillwater thought long and hard before answering. "No. The only recreational activity Mr. Kyser and I have ever participated in together was an occasional round of golf."

"What about your play dates?"

"Excuse me?"

"Don't jerk me around, I know all about Kyser and his penchant for little boys and I know all about your involvement as well."

"Wait just a damned minute, I don't know who the hell you are, or where you are getting your information from, but Raymond Kyser and I have never shared those tastes."

Vito softened a little. He had interrogated enough people during his career, both guilty and innocent, to know when someone was telling the truth. But his desire for more information, and a possible link to his missing sister was clouding his judgment.

"I have an eyewitness who places you at the scene of a perverted calendar shoot of Mr. Kyser's some time ago. Are you trying to tell me you weren't there?"

"Yes, I was there," his head dropped, and his defiant stance waned considerably.

Vito let him brood over this for several minutes. He could feel his own anger rising to the point where he would soon no longer be able to control it. His every muscle was tense with the growing desire to strangle this son of a bitch.

"Are you that young girl's father?" Stillwater asked, the images of that ruinous day rushing at him like the raging waters of the Colorado after a spring thaw.

Vito saw no reason not to mislead the scumbag, so he simply nodded.

"I didn't touch her, I swear," Stillwater seemed more afraid now he understood the reason for the intruder's visit. Right or wrong, at least now he could place some tangible reason for the man's animus feelings towards him.

"Liar," Vito let loose some of his pent up anger and slapped the man across the face hard enough to draw a trickle of blood from his nose.

"No, I swear, I didn't touch her. I told Kyser I didn't approve of that sort of thing."

"But you didn't stop him, and I'd feel safe in wagering you didn't call the police or drop him as a client either."

The man eyes sank to his lap in reply.

"When was the last time you saw Raymond Kyser, alive?"

"Alive? Raymond is dead?" Stillwater's head snapped up to look at Vito.

"Yes, he's dead, and I have a good reason to believe you killed him."

"Me? What reason on Earth would I possibly have to kill Raymond Kyser? Who the hell are you? And why do you care so much about Raymond Kyser?" He reverted to being on the defensive.

Vito heard several cars screech to a halt outside and assumed the man had somehow been able to trigger the panic alarm before he could stop him. He knew he only had a matter of moments to extract any useful information from the man.

"What does my sister have to do with all of this?"

"Your sister? I don't even know who you are, so how in the hell should I know anything about your sister?" Stillwater asked in a loud tone, his courage returning now the cavalry had arrived.

Vito brought his fist crashing into the man's mouth, snapping his head back hard enough to cause him to briefly lose consciousness. "I don't have time to play with you. I want to know where my sister is," he drew his fist back and readied himself to deliver another bone crushing blow. Had Vito been sober, or even close to it, he would have realized the man didn't have any clue what Vito was talking about. And in fact, a part of him did realize he wasn't going to get the answers he sought, so it was time to extract a little personal satisfaction from this piece of human garbage.

Vito untied the last knot of his self-control and straddled the man on the couch with his knees on either side of his legs. He grabbed him by the throat and began shaking his head violently back and forth while screaming at him.

"Get off my husband," a woman's voice pealed frantically from out of the darkness.

Vito spun his head in time to see a muzzle flash. The bullet ripped through his upper arm. Seconds later the police burst through the door and the next several minutes were a blur. When things finally settled down, the sight of Karen hovering above him deflated Vito.

"Well?" Karen's voice sounded like turn number two at Talladega.

"Well what?" he asked, flinching as a paramedic tended to his wound.

"What in the fuck were you thinking," she leaned down and hissed in his ear.

"Listen, I had good reason to believe Stillwater might have knowledge of Lizbeth's whereabouts."

"So, you broke into his house and held him at gun point while you kicked the ever loving shit out of him, not to mention, scaring the bejesus out of his wife."

"I don't recall asking you to understand," he spat, his head was throbbing now, and he definitely didn't need her to tell him how badly he had screwed up. Vito knew that well enough for himself.

"I was going to wait until morning to discuss taking you off this case. But now, you leave me no choice. Considering everything that has happened tonight, I'm going to have to suspend you, Vito. Damn it, why did you have to go and do something stupid like this for?"

"You know me, lieutenant," he shrugged. The truth be known, he didn't have any excuse, and especially not a good one. Hell, he didn't even have a good reason.

"Don't get smug with me, you're damned lucky I'm not having you arrested. And you're damned lucky our Mr. Stillwater here is a less than honorable man. He's willing to make a deal with you. He won't press charges, if you keep your mouth shut about everything that happened in that warehouse. You're lucky Stillwater agrees with me that this kind of exposure could be damaging to his professional reputation, let alone his relationship with his wife. And of course, there's always the threat of his indiscretions leaking out to the press."

"Poor baby. Screw him, let him come after me, I'd love to drag his name through the mud."

"Vito, I mean it. He has your balls in a vice. Now I want you to go home, sleep off whatever it is that is ailing you, and I will stop by sometime tomorrow afternoon."

"Yeah, whatever," he said.

"I mean it, that's an order," Karen said. She walked over to where a couple of uniformed patrol officers were waiting. She said something to them and they both nodded and looked over at Vito. He knew they had been relegated to being his babysitters for the remainder of the evening.

Just a few shorts hours after being winged by a piss poor shot, Vito was sitting on his couch, alone, in the dark and much more sober than he wanted to be. There were at least seven messages from his partner on his answering machine. He had left Haskell at Los Angeles International Airport while the man was using the restroom. It wasn't the right thing to do, but it was the Lorenz thing to do.

Vito could see the outline of a patrol car outside next to the curb. They had just replaced the crew who had been sitting there so they were fresh. He needed to sneak out and get a bottle. It would be morning soon and he didn't want to face the sun without a little bourbon in him.

He knew all the tricks of the trade. Vito hung up the phone, grabbed his jacket and waited for the commotion. There was nothing like a good 911 emergency call to start everyone's day. He heard the squad car squeal away from the curb and waited for them to turn the corner at the end of the block before walking out the back door. He would be back before long, but he wouldn't be empty handed.

*   *   *

"Don't you think you're being a little too hard on the guy?" Amanda asked with a look of consternation.

"Not at all. I went over to talk to him the other day and he's a mess. It's like he has just given up on himself and everything else. If the killer's established pattern holds true, then Amber Reese will be in our care in less than forty-eight hours, and Vito doesn't seem to give a damn. Man, it seems the more you get to know people, the less you find you actually know about them," Gregg said, standing up and refilling his coffee. "Would you like some more?"

"No thank you. Gregg, you have to admit, the situation has changed quite a bit. Put yourself in his position."

"I know, honey, but damn it, he just crumbled. You ought to see the guy, he looks like a completely different person."

"Have you gotten any leads on where his sister might be?"

"None, and that really scares me."

"Why is that?"

"Because, whoever did this, knows exactly what they're doing. There's no telling how long they have been at this game, or for how long they'll be able to continue for that matter. We might end up with one hell of an enormous body count by the time this is all said and done."

"I don't think so."

"You don't, huh?"

"No, I don't. I've been going over some of the files you left here," she smiled.

"Oh really? I never knew you wanted to be a detective, I thought you just trained them," he smirked.

"Sometimes the teacher enjoys being the student as well," she smiled and gave him a tender kiss.

"What are you thinking?"

"I'm starting to believe you were right all along. These killings are fueled by an insatiable motivation for revenge, the pieces fit too well for them not to be. The main question is, who is the ultimate payee?"

"So, is this someone with something against these girls? Vito? Kyser? Or God only knows who else? That's where it all starts to cloud up for me. There doesn't seem to be a common denominator linking all three pieces together."

"There may not be one, Gregg. At least not one linking everyone together. I believe Vito and his sister are only residuals of this killer's true intentions. I think this monster has read something in the press or saw Vito at one of the scenes and has decided to bond with the detective. It sometimes happens. It heightens the game, the thrill of chase for the killer. It makes it much more personal, especially for a madman as ruthless and cunning as this one."

"But you still think this person is crazy?"

"Oh, God yes, as loony as they come. But loony doesn't mean a lack of motivation, concentration and especially not intelligence. And quite honestly, I can see how Vito has gotten so frustrated with this case. There are no right answers. And to make things worse, this person seems to be changing their pattern virtually at will to throw off the profilers and investigators," Amanda said, taking a drink of coffee and reaching into her make-up bag for her eyeliner.

"I wish you didn't have to go; I miss you when we're apart. I realized that when I was in Vancouver," Gregg said.

"That's so sweet of you," she blushed.

"It's the truth."

"I wish I didn't have to go either, but this is a very important seminar and my boss would have my head if I tried to beg off."

"I understand, but that doesn't mean I will miss you any less."

"Tell you what, I will so make it up to you when I get back."

"And what am I supposed to do while you're gone?" Gregg pouted playfully.

"Why don't you pay Vito another visit, I'm sure he could use your company, as well as your friendship," Amanda looked up at him over top of her mirror while stabbing something into her eye, or at least that's what it appeared like she was doing to Gregg. "And that's not a request, it's an order," she smiled.

"Somehow I knew you were going to say that."

Chapter Twelve

Gregg tapped lightly on the door at first, but then rapped a little harder once it became apparent Lieutenant Stoddard hadn't heard him. He almost turned and walked away when she didn't look up after several attempts. He even had the notion that subconsciously he hadn't even knocked hard enough for her to hear him. And he wouldn't even be standing there now, had it not been for Amanda's words ringing in his head.

She waved a friendly hand and Haskell walked into his boss's office. He stood there staring at her like a nervous schoolboy.

"Can I help you with something, detective?" she asked with a smile. He couldn't help but notice there was something different about her. She was looking more like a woman than a hard-assed police lieutenant.

"I'm not sure," he replied, never looking up from his shoes.

"Is there something on your mind?" Karen found it hard not to snigger at his awkwardness.

She had always found it amazing how differently men reacted toward her position of authority. Some were threatened by her and felt their masculinity was in question whenever she gave them an order. Vito was one of those types. They were hard to get along with no matter what. The type that demanded she be an even bigger bitch than she already was. And then there was the types who were oddly aroused by her power, they were the inanest as far as she was concerned. They followed her around wanting to do everything for her. She had distanced herself from those types, and in the police department, that wasn't an easy feat, there were far too many ass kissers. And then there were the Haskell's of the world. The ones who felt intimidated but weren't even sure why they felt that way. They weren't threatened enough to act out, only enough to become tongue-tied and unsure of themselves in her presence.

"Spit it out Haskell," she smiled in an effort to set him a little more at ease.

"Yes, ma'am."

"You don't have to call me ma'am all the time, you know. I'm a cop, just like you."

"Yes, ma'am," he replied before he could correct himself.

"Gregg, why don't you take a seat and tell me what's on your mind."

"Yes, ma'am. I was just wondering," he paused to think about what he wanted to say and exactly how to say it.

"Is this about Vito and I?"

The wideness of his eyes telegraphed his surprise. "Yes, ma'am. Well, sort of anyway."

"What would you like to know?"

"Honestly, I want to know where my partner went."

"I had to suspend him; you know that."

"That's not what I am talking about. If it were merely the suspension, I could live with that."

"I guess I don't quite follow you."

"When was the last time you saw Detective Lorenz?"

"The night I suspended him, why?" she lied.

Karen had gone over to Vito's place several times to check up on him after he wouldn't answer his phone. She had used a spare key she had made and let herself in. It wasn't a pretty sight. Had she been anyone else he would have shot her right there on the spot. As it was, he left one hell of a bruise on her thigh where he had kicked her during a well-timed leg sweep. Karen decided right then and there that their personal life was over. Vito didn't have to tell her twice.

"What do you know about his drinking?" Gregg almost choked on the words. If Vito had a drinking problem and had been hiding it from the department, then he had just let the cat out of the bag, and it was a screamer.

"I thought he had it under control. To my knowledge he hasn't touched a drop for at least five years or so. I'd be the first to admit he hit the bottle pretty hard after his wife died and I thought we were going to lose him. But his sister, Lizbeth, got him under control somehow. I think it was when his brother-in-law was killed. I think Freddie's death sparked a sense of responsibility in Vito. Maybe he realized he was the only one left to take care of his sister."

"Oh great, if this case wasn't bad enough, he's got a whole freight car worth of personal baggage to contend with."

"Is he drinking again?" Karen asked, more as a friend than a supervisor.

"I don't know. But I suspect he might be."

"I sure the hell hope he isn't. I would expect there to be an inquiry about his little episode sometime within the next few weeks and I am certain it will go a lot smoother for him if he isn't drunk when the board convenes," she said.

"I should probably go and have a talk with him, huh?"

"As a partner, that's your decision. As a friend, I think you owe him at least a valiant attempt. However, with that being said, any contact you have with Vito will have to be on an unofficial level. No discussing this case with him. Do you understand?" She asked.

Haskell nodded, stood up and took a step for the door.

"Gregg, help him get his shit together please. For him, and for me," she smiled.

Gregg grabbed his jacket off the back of his chair while wondering what in the hell just happened. Somehow, he had just been relegated to baby-sitter duty.

"Valiant effort my ass," he commented while slipping on his jacket.

"Excuse me?" Davenport swung a look in Haskell's direction.

"Nothing, just talking to myself."

"With words like that coming out of your mouth, you'd better be," she gave him a look that would melt the polar ice caps. And then she broke into a wide, devilish grin. "Just bustin' your balls, honey. I like to do that every so often."

"Great, Lucy, just great."

"Hey, lover boy," she called out before Gregg was able to escape outside into the waning sunlight.

"What?"

Her face was quite stern and somber. "What's up with our friend?"

"Vito?"

"Of course, Vito."

"I'm not sure. I don't know enough about him, not as much as I thought I did anyway."

"Have you talked to him recently?"

"No, not since sometime early last week. I am a bit busy you know."

She ignored his sarcasm as if the words had never even been uttered. "Are you planning on talking to him?" she asked in a tone that was more of a request than a question.

"I've thought about it, why?"

"What in the hell happened to taking care of each other, Christ Almighty. Ever since this thing with Vito happened, you all have been treating him like he has the plague or something."

"More like the brown bottle flu, if you're going to give it a name."

"That's not fair, detective. You don't know enough about the man to go saying something as cruel as that. And to think, I always thought you were one of the good guys," she turned her back on him.

"What in the hell do you want from me, Davenport?"

"I want you to be a friend to that man. He needs you right now."

"The only friend he wants is Jack Daniels."

"Come here," she said in a motherly tone not to be argued with.

"What?"

"Come in here," she said, opening the door to the women's bathroom behind her dispatch desk.

Haskell followed the woman, even though she scared the hell out of him, and she was leading him onto her turf. Once inside the small, porcelain enriched cubicle, Lucy Davenport locked the door behind her and turned on the water in the sink. Gregg immediately realized there wasn't enough room in there for her, let alone the two of them.

"What in the hell did you turn the water on for?"

"There are ears everywhere."

Gregg gave a quick glance around the minuscule room. "Don't you think you're being a little bit melodramatic?"

She just glared at him.

"Okay, maybe not. Might I be so bold as to ask why you brought me in here?"

"How much has Vito told you about his past?"

"Not much, and I'm finding out even less than I thought."

"The man has been through hell, and back, I want you to know. I don't know what has happened to make him act out like he has, but I know it must be something pretty awful."

"How much do you know about the case we've been working on?"

"Some serial killer shit, I don't know much about the details, but I do know there are young girls involved. But even with it being as bad as all that, it's not enough to make a man like Vito snap. He's been on the front lines a long time and has seen just about all there is to see."

"Maybe not," Gregg sighed. "While we were in Vancouver, someone kidnapped his sister," Gregg blurted out and for the first time, he realized the gravity of the situation. Suddenly it was real, not just another loose piece of paper in a folder on his desk. Lizbeth's face flashed into his mind and was quickly replaced by his sister Brenda's and then by Evy's. It was like a punch in his stomach. Suddenly he was acutely aware of what Vito must be feeling."

"Oh Lordy, how much crap can one man endure," she rolled her eyes toward the ceiling.

"What do you mean?"

"First his wife, then his brother-in-law and now his sister."

"What happened to his wife?"

"Gloria? My, she was a looker. And I'll be damned if Lorenz didn't love the stuffing right out of that woman," she said, a reminiscent spark twinkled in her eye as she recalled how fond she had been of Gloria.

"Davenport?"

"She was killed. Quite a few years back now, going on ten maybe."

"How was she killed?" Haskell asked, wondering if there

were a way to pry the information out of her a little quicker as he was feeling quite claustrophobic in the tiny cubicle.

"She was in a car accident. She was mad at Vito and had stormed out of the house in the middle of the night. She lost control and went over a cliff and into a ravine. It tore Vito up. He has blamed himself every single day since then for her death. That's why he's still single, he just won't let it go."

"I don't think it is any of my business, but I'll ask anyway. What pissed her off so badly?"

"She came home early from a visit with her mother and caught Vito in bed with another woman. From what I gathered, they attributed her accident to fatigue. She bolted out of the house before Vito could say anything to her and was in an accident later on that evening. The woman was Lieutenant Stoddard."

"Damn," was the only reply that Gregg could muster.

"You see, the man has eaten a guilt sandwich for breakfast every morning of his life ever since. Stoddard is a constant reminder of the worst night of his life."

"And washes it down with a shit milkshake. That explains a lot."

"The drinking?"

"Yeah, and why he's taking his sister's disappearance the way he is. He blames himself. The killer kidnapped Lizbeth because of him."

Lucy wiped her tears away and straightened herself up. She turned off the water and unlocked the door.

"Go over to his place detective, he needs you. And I mean that when I say it. Next to his sister the only thing he has in his life is this job. I have it on good authority Internal Affairs is going to call him in on Monday morning. Try to get him straightened out before then."

He nodded and they both struggled to squeeze out of the little room.

"Tell me something, Lucy. Who do you think might be listening in on us around here?"

She just shook her head and averted her attention back to her desk. Their conversation was over, and she expected Gregg to do as she asked. He was beginning to wonder if being a detective was really what he wanted to do with his life after all.

*   *   *

Haskell knew right away something wasn't right the moment he pulled up in front of Vito's house. The man was a slob, true, but had always managed to somehow contain most of his slovenliness within the four walls of his domicile. However, at the moment the place looked like it would have no trouble drawing FEMA disaster relief funds. The lawn hadn't been mowed in what Gregg figured to be at least a month, which actually didn't matter all that much because it hadn't been watered in at least two. There were empty liquor bottles next to the porch as well as a fresh patch of something he didn't want to learn the origins of. Vito had his drapes pulled so tightly across every window in the house so not even a sliver of light had a chance to pass through in either direction, in or out. Haskell shivered, Vito's place was far creepier than Thirteen-Thirteen Mockingbird Lane had ever hoped to be.

He knocked on the door until his knuckles were starting to get sore before trying the doorbell. After several minutes of nothing, he put his ear to the door while pressing the button and could hear the distinct sounds of chiming from within the house. The bell worked. He stood on the porch trying to ignore the curious glances from nosy neighbors who were undoubtedly wondering when the body snatchers would come for the rest of the neighborhood.

Once Haskell's knuckles became too sore to knock anymore, he decided upon a different approach. His heart thumped wildly in his chest as he walked cautiously around the perimeter of the house searching for a window he could peek through and see what was happening inside the house. He entertained visions of cupping his hands around his face and peering into a window just in time to see Vito raising his revolver. Gregg could make out the little imperfections in the bullet's nose cone as it traveled at super high velocity toward his face.

After quite some time Gregg finally found an unlocked window at the back of the house. He pressed his hands hard against the screen and worked the window loose in its frame and slid it carefully open. He took out his Gerber multi-tool and opened the knife blade. Quietly he slit the screen just wide enough to reach his hand inside and pull back the drapes. The bedroom door was open, and Gregg could see straight down the hallway and into the living room. He gasped at the horror he was confronted with. There was blood everywhere and he swore he could make out the outline of a person lying face down on the couch. Visions of suicide danced in his head and Gregg's heart leapt into his throat.

"Vito," he cried out as he ripped the screen open and began pulling himself through the window.

Gregg had to go through the window headfirst and came down hard on his wrists. Crouching in the darkness, he rubbed them gingerly and waited for his eyes to adjust to his new surroundings. As soon as he could make out the corners and distinguish shadows from reality, he drew his gun and slowly made his way down the uninviting corridor.

A variety of atrocious smells assaulted his senses like honeybees after mischievous, stick-wielding children. He wasn't sure if he was smelling his partner's decomposing corpse or his long-neglected trash. There were half eaten Whoppers, Big Mac's and pizza slices strewn across the floor of a bedroom Gregg assumed was Vito's combination bedroom/dining room. Hoping it wasn't also moonlighting as a bathroom he did a quick sweep of the room, found it unoccupied and continued down the corridor.

As he neared the entryway into the living room Gregg noticed an enormous dark stain on the wall. Even in the dim lighting he recognized the ugly brown stain as blood. There was a large splotch of it about the size of a small cantaloupe with spray patterns spreading out in all directions. There were spatters of blood on two adjacent walls as well as the ceiling. Haskell's heart nearly stopped. The person lying face down on the couch was covered with what appeared to be blood as well.

Haskell trained his weapon on the figure and called out lightly. "Vito," he said repeatedly as he inched closer to the man. His eyes had adjusted to the darkness enough to make out the person was in fact his partner. Once he drew within a couple of feet from the lump on the couch, he held his breath and listened. There was nothing, no wheezing, no snoring, and no clue as to whether or not the man was even alive. Gregg felt a lump welling up in his throat. He reached forward, using the muzzle of his gun as a prod, he stabbed it into the person with a gentle poke. Nothing, there was not even the slightest reaction to the intrusion. Gregg poked the person again, only harder this time. All at once Vito rolled over, grabbed the gun out of Haskell's hand and started poking the man with his own gun.

"Jesus Christ, Vito, you scared the shit out of me."

"I thought I smelled something," he replied.

"I thought you were dead."

"Sorry to disappoint you. Now, get the fuck out of here," he grunted and rolled over, putting his back to Haskell.

Haskell stood there in the blackness of the room and felt even more austere than his surroundings. He wanted to find the nearest hard object and club Vito over the head with it, at least until he felt better. He struggled with the urge to turn around and walk out of Vito's life and let the man cope with whatever cards were dealt him on his own.

"Vito, get your fucking ass up off that couch and explain what in the fuck happened here," he screamed so out of character he even shocked himself.

"Fuck off," Vito mumbled. "Go away or I'll fucking shoot you."

"It's not going to be that easy to get rid of me."

"Yes, it is."

"No, it's not. If I have to, I will call the department and get a team over here to investigate a possible homicide. Christ, look at all this blood," he said, his eyes having completely adjusted to the dark.

For being on the brink of death only moments before, Vito moved like a California wildfire during a Santa Ana windstorm. He had Haskell shoved back into the wall with his gun jammed up under his chin before the man knew what had hit him.

"Mind your own fucking business," Vito growled with bourbon-soaked breath.

"This is my fucking business, I'm your partner," Haskell choked and struggled against Vito's grip.

"Don't make me hurt you," he said.

"Vito, I've got a stake in this too."

"Do you? What in the fuck makes you think that?"

"Because, like I said, we're partners."

"Like hell we are," Vito reared back to launch a right cross. Haskell saw his chance and he took it. He gave a short, sharp punch to Vito's solar plexus, knocking the wind out of him and driving him to his knees. Gregg relaxed, but a little too soon. Vito lashed out and caught Haskell in the groin with a vicious backhand, sending the man sprawling to the carpet in pain. Haskell slowly opened his eyes and tried to ignore the searing pain.

Scrambling to his feet he cried out, "What in the hell is that?" he pointed to a bloody box with a chunk of decaying meat inside.

Vito was sitting on the couch with his head between his knees, gasping for breath.

"Vito, what in the hell is in that box, and why is there blood everywhere?"

"Lizbeth," he panted, sucking in deep sips of air.

"What?"

"It's my sister, or what's left of her," his last words trailed off into oblivion.

"Vito, what are you talking about?"

"There was a package waiting for me the day we got back here from Vancouver, that was in the box, with a note."

"What note?"

Vito just waved the gun toward a lamp table sitting next to his couch. Gregg couldn't believe what he was reading. *Detective Lorenz, is it too late to send you a valentine? Here, this was your sister's, she won't be needing it anymore!*

"What does that mean?"

"Lizbeth's heart was in the box. I killed her, I killed my fucking sister," he thumped himself in the side of the head with his gun hand as he talked.

"You didn't do anything of the sort."

"Just like Gloria, I drove her over the edge too. I killed them both."

"You didn't kill anyone."

"I might as well have pulled the trigger myself. Now, get the fuck out of here and leave me alone."

"Why?"

"I've got things to do."

"Like what?" he asked, not liking the way Vito was looking at his gun.

"None of your damned business."

"Okay, just give me my gun back and I'll be on my way," Gregg said, trying to test the water Vito was treading.

"I'm going to have to borrow it for a little while, they took mine and I'll be damned if I can find my back up piece in this shit hole. I think that bitch Stoddard swiped it. You can have this back when I'm finished."

"I'm not going to let you do that Vito."

"You don't have a choice."

"What about Freddie, Vito? What about your nephew? How's he supposed to handle all of this?"

"Don't you dare bring him into this," Vito looked up with bloodshot eyes screaming out the magnitude of his pain.

"I'm not bringing anyone into this, he's already into it whether you want to believe that or not. How long has it been since you've spoken with him?"

"I called the Bouchard's, he's all right."

"Physically, maybe, but just imagine what the kid is going through inside? If you are hurting this badly, then he must be going through hell, alone."

"Oh, damn, I forgot, my partner the psychologist," he spat sarcastically.

"You know what, fuck you, Vito. You're on your own, I don't need this shit," Haskell said, finally tired of the crap Vito was dishing out.

He was almost through the front door when Vito finally spoke. "Here, you're going to need this," he said, handing Haskell back his gun, butt first.

Gregg took the gun, checked the safety and slipped it back into his shoulder holster without a word. He looked Vito in his ragged eyes, shook his head and turned back for the door.

"I'm sorry," his words were almost inaudible. "What in the fuck am I doing?" Tears streamed down his face, dripping onto the carpet below.

The tone in Vito's voice immediately cooled Gregg's anger. His pain seeped from each syllable as he fought for the right words to say. He backed up several steps and sank into the couch, dropping his face into his hands. Gregg moved over to the couch and sat down next to the man. He put his arm around Vito's shoulder and struggled to hold back his own tears.

"What now?" Vito looked up at his partner through tear stained eyes.

"We get your shit together, that's what. We get you cleaned up and ready to face a firing squad, whenever they decide to call you. And we need to clean this place up," he said, looking around the room in disgust.

"Better get a team over here, all of this is evidence," Vito said, nodding his head at the walls.

"Do you know anyone who can be discreet about this? I think the less the department knows, the better off you'll be."

"There is a guy I did a few favors for a while back. If you explain the situation and tell him who it's for, he'll keep a lid on it for as long as he can. Name's Brent Goulding, he works in serology now, I believe."

"Okay, I'll call him as soon as I can. As for you, can you stay somewhere else for a while? This Goulding guy won't be able to do this alone and the less people who know this is your place the better."

"I can pick up Freddie and stay at his mother's place for a few days," Vito said, not wanting to say the words, *his sister's place.*

"Are you going to be all right with that?" Gregg asked, noticing the pained expression on Vito's face when he thought of the dead woman.

"Better than Freddie I suppose."

"Yeah, I suppose you're right about that."

"What's today?"

"It's the thirty-first," Gregg replied, already knowing the direction Vito was traveling with the conversation.

"No word?"

"None. But we did get an initial report back from the Canadians on Kyser."

"Yeah, what'd they have to say?"

"The man had definitely endured a lot of torture. Many of those cuts we saw were shallow. The lab report states the cuts were made by sawing into the flesh very slowly with a serrated knife. Great care had been taken not to strike any major arteries or do any mortal damage. They also suspect the torture went on for weeks, if not longer. The treatment was brutal, vindictive, purely of a vengeful nature," Gregg explained.

"Kyser had been sodomized repeatedly with a variety of objects, one of which perforated his colon. The ME assured me that would have been excruciatingly painful. This led to sepsis and eventually his death. The investigators found traces of his DNA on at least a dozen different objects throughout the cabin. And according to the lab boys, before the cut along his abdomen had been performed, he had been anesthetized locally with what they believed to be dry ice or liquid nitrogen. The tissue damage surrounding the incision was consistent with that of frostbite. This crude local anesthetic would have numbed the outer areas, but his organs would have had full use of their pain receptors. His internal organs had all been perforated with something. The lab wasn't sure what was used, but it was something like a crochet hook."

Vito cringed. "My God, not saying I feel sorry for the sick bastard, but that's just a bit overboard don't you think?"

"Very violent, yes. This is a very sick and angry individual we're dealing with here, Vito. I first thought this was a vengeance killer, and I still believe that, but I think their motives run much deeper than anything Kyser may have done. If the young woman were still alive, I might suspect her, but even then I think that would be a stretch."

"What about her father? Or maybe even a brother?"

"None I could find. I spoke with Gray Morgan again and he said there was nothing in Judge Morgan's records about the young girl's family, or her suicide. In fact, he didn't think his father even knew the girl had killed herself, and he would rather he didn't find out."

"That would be a lot of guilt to carry around, wouldn't it? A crochet hook, huh?"

"They said it wasn't a crochet hook, but a lot like it."

A visible tremor shuddered through Vito as he thought about the man's last few hours of life. "Kind of like what the Egyptians used during mummification."

"What?"

"Yeah, you know, the hook they would shove up the nose and yank out the brain with. Don't look at me like that, I watched a show on the Discovery Channel," he added after seeing the look on his partner's face.

"I suppose it might look a lot like that."

"Probably not a common item at the notions store," Vito said, mulling this information over in his head.

"I think you're right."

"You shouldn't be talking to me about this, you know."

"About what? I just brought you over some breakfast," Gregg smiled.

"Sorry about being such a prick."

"I didn't notice. Just promise you'll lay off the sauce."

"I think there's a coupla bottles out in the kitchen, get rid of them for me, would ya? I gotta go to the can," Vito said and struggled to get to his feet.

Gregg busied himself in the kitchen while Vito cleaned himself up a little. It was the first time he had been sober in at least two weeks and it didn't feel very good at all. He liked the indifference a good drunk could paint on him. He reached into the medicine cabinet and pulled down a half-pint of bourbon and twisted the cap off. He put the bottle to his lips and took a long hard pull of the liquor. Just as he was ready to swallow, he caught a glimpse of himself in the mirror. It wasn't the man he knew looking back at him. It was another monster, a demon who took control of his soul every time he touched alcohol. He could have lived with that, but what he couldn't live with was the fact it was his sister's eyes staring back at him, haunting him and filling him with shame. He spit the whiskey into the sink and turned on the water. He began pouring out the rest of the bottle when the smell of the sour mash suddenly made him nauseous and he was forced to say a little prayer to the porcelain god.

Gregg could hear Vito's retching all the way out into the kitchen. He knew things were going to be rough on the man for a little while, but he also knew Vito was strong enough to pull through all of this, or at least he hoped he was. Gregg was amazed at how quickly alcohol could steal a man's soul. Recalling his own personal demons, he remembered just how easily it could make a man revert back to his old habits in literally no time at all.

"Sorry about that," Vito said, wiping his face with a warm wet towel as he walked into the kitchen.

"Wasn't my shoes," Gregg smiled.

"I can't thank you enough, partner," Vito said, pools of tears welling up in his eyes once more. "I thought I was over this problem, I guess I was wrong."

"It's a lifelong struggle for some of us, I know, I've been sober now for a little more than ten years. My little Evy saved my life," Gregg said in confidence.

"Really?" Vito said, genuinely stunned.

Gregg laughed. "Am I such a tight ass you could never see me as a onetime hell raiser?"

"Yeah, you are. So, what sent you over the edge?"

"Genetics mainly, but my sister Brenda's disappearance had a lot to do with it," Gregg replied, using his sister's name instead of the title "Evy's mother" for the first time in a very long time.

A pained look spread across Vito's face. "Damn, looks like my boat is getting smaller all the time."

"That it does. I started drinking in high school and got into some binge drinking in college, but I had it under control, or so I thought. The academy helped me a lot there, it's a lot easier staying sober when you can't get any alcohol."

"That it is."

"But then I graduated the academy and started doing the cop thing, hanging out at the FOP bar after work. I was already drinking more than I should have been when Brenda disappeared sending me right over the edge. I damned near lost Evy over it too. But, I got lucky and had a pretty good caseworker at Child Protective Services and an even better union rep who both guided me through my problems and steered me in the right direction for help."

"Sounds familiar."

"So, what's your story?"

"What is this, an AA meeting?" Vito said, suddenly back on the defensive.

"Sorry, didn't mean to touch a nerve."

"You want some coffee?"

"If you're buying, sure."

Vito nodded and began fumbling around the kitchen for the coffee. The smell of alcohol emanating from the sink drain was both alluring and nauseating at the same time. The longer he was awake, the clearer his head became. Incidents of the past couple of weeks began forming themselves into pictures in his mind. Pictures he didn't care to see. He turned around to pour the water into the coffee maker and caught sight of his living room. The sight took his breath away and he had to catch himself on the counter. Gregg helped him over to the kitchen table and finished pouring the water into the pot.

Vito was waiting until the coffeepot was finished gurgling and spitting before he decided to talk. "My story is lot like yours, I guess," he finally said with a nod of thanks as Gregg set a cup of coffee in front of him.

Gregg sat down across from him and gave his full attention.

"Although, I didn't start drinking until I became one of the good 'ol boys in blue. But I quickly made up for lost time. Then I met my wife, Gloria and she straightened me out, turned me into a regular choirboy. Life seemed pretty damned good. I was on my way to earning my gold shield, I had a loving wife whom I absolutely adored, in fact I don't think things could have gotten better."

"What happened?"

"Gloria was killed in a car accident," he wiped a memory away from his eye.

"How?" Gregg asked, knowing the answer but lacking the details.

"I met Karen Stoddard, that's how," his voice was suddenly laced with anger.

"What did she have to do with anything?"

"I said before my life was picture perfect, but in truth, not quite. Gloria and I couldn't have children. She had something wrong with her ovaries, or something like that. Well, I had been obsessing about wanting children, a son, for quite some time when I met Karen. That was long before she made lieutenant. Her father was a captain at another precinct and had asked my captain for a favor. One which involved me baby-sitting her and teaching her the ropes. Well, we got to talking as partners do and things just developed. I started feeling sorry for myself which led a path straight back to the bottle, and Karen, well, she insisted on buying."

Haskell must have had a questionable look on his face because Vito laughed.

"I was a lot easier on the eyes back then."

"I kind of figured as much. Go on."

"Well, Karen talked me into a plan of me getting her pregnant. We we're both supposed to break the news to Gloria. It was a scheme which included her fully involved in the child's upbringing."

"And you went along with this?"

"It sounded good at the time. To make a long story short, Gloria caught Karen and me in bed together, trying to formulate our plan so to speak. Gloria stormed out of the house and drove off. I got a call around three in the morning, they found her car in a ravine off the Grapevine Highway." Tears were streaming down his face now.

"At the risk of sounding insensitive, why in the hell were you dumb enough to be with Karen in your wife's bed?"

"Gloria was supposed to be out of town, at her mother's. And like I said, Karen had me all screwed up in the head. In a sad way I really thought I was doing the right thing for my marriage."

"And Gloria came home unexpectedly?"

"Quite unexpectedly. I hit the bottle hard after that. Karen and I became a couple, even though I don't remember much of it. That's when my sister started getting involved with things. She didn't like Karen very much from the start, and she liked her a lot less once she married Freddie and he told her some horror stories."

"Freddie knew Karen Stoddard?"

"They went to the academy together and then ended up working for the same precinct. But that's not the point. I knew

Karen wasn't a saint, far from it in fact, but I was a grown man and capable of making my own decision, even if they were the wrong ones. Lizbeth and I had a falling out over the whole situation and I started drinking even heavier. I can't tell you much about that period in my life, because I really don't remember much about it."

"What finally brought you around?" Gregg asked, astonished at how their lives had paralleled each other's.

"Freddie was killed in a shootout with some drug dealers in South Central. Freddie junior was just a young boy then and Lizbeth really needed my help. I moved in with her for a little while to help her get on with her life. But I'd be the first one to admit she helped me a hell of a lot more than I helped her."

"Maybe by helping you, she was helping herself."

"Yeah, you might be right. She seemed to enjoy it. She was able to talk me into giving up two of my demons, cigarettes and alcohol, I gave up a third, Karen, on my own. She just wasn't the same person when I was sober, in fact, I sometimes wonder what it was I ever saw in her."

"What about now?"

"I don't follow you," Vito said, wanting to change the subject.

"You've been involved with her since then, haven't you?"

"Yeah, a little," he thought about their relationship for a few minutes, giving Gregg enough time to get up and pour them both some more coffee. "I guess she's like a drug for me, really cheap and easy to get," he couldn't help but laugh.

"If she heard you say that she'd have your balls in a jar," Gregg laughed too.

"She already does, partner. She already does."

Gregg spent another hour drinking coffee and talking about inner demons with his partner. When he left, he left with a warm sensation surrounding his heart. Vito was better, not healed, but better. He called the lab and made an appointment to speak with Brent Goulding as soon as possible. He wound his way through the city streets mulling over every aspect of the case, always coming back to one, single, inescapable fact, he could bet his life he was going to get a call sometime before dawn.

Chapter Thirteen

Gregg rolled over and grabbed his cell phone from the nightstand. He hadn't even bothered turning off his light when he had laid down sometime after midnight. He and Lieutenant Stoddard had spent half the night going over their game plan in the event Amber Reese's body was discovered as prophesied. They had posted stakeouts at every major hospital and medical center in the area including the San Diego County area just for good measure. He went to bed that night feeling optimistic about having all their bases covered. It was only a matter of time before they caught this guy dropping off the poor girl's mutilated body. It would definitely be a bittersweet victory.

"Hello," he said, barely getting any sound to come out.

"Haskell?" Stoddard's voice asked.

"Yeah, this is Haskell. What's up?"

"We've got her."

"How is she?" he asked, bolting upright in bed.

"I guess it all depends on your point of view."

"Should I ask?"

"I'd rather not say over the phone, especially not on an unsecured line."

"Understood. Where are you?"

"CMH. Down on South Vermont"

"County Mental Health? I'll be there as soon as possible," Gregg sighed.

Obviously, he hadn't covered the bases as well as he thought. This bastard was smart, smarter and more devious than he imagined. He felt sick for not having thought of this possibility. Stoddard was still talking but he hadn't heard a word of what she said.

"What?"

"I said, how about picking up some coffee and one of those cinnamon powdered sugar donuts you like so much on your way?" Her voice revealed her smile.

"Okay," he replied, wondering how she could be thinking about donuts and coffee at a time when they screwed up so badly.

The phone was silent for several moments before she asked, "How is he?"

"How is who?"

"Vito, of course."

"Better."

"Good. I want the details."

"Not many to give."

"I'll take all you've got."

"Okay, see you in a few," he turned the phone off before she could say anything more. His head was throbbing, and he was so tired even his hair hurt. He took a shower so quickly he could barely even remember getting wet. Grabbing yesterday's clothes from the top of the hamper and slipping them on he started to gain a little insight into Vito's constant choice of raggedy wardrobe. Before bolting out the door, Gregg scribbled a note for Evy and quickly set out her breakfast, which he knew she would bypass for something much less nutritious.

Gregg balanced the coffee and donuts while ducking under a banner of yellow crime scene tape. The red and blue flashing lights reflecting off the damp pavement stung his tired eyes terribly. He had the urge to grab a megaphone and tell everyone to turn off their damned lights, but he knew that was bound to do more damage than good. He felt like he was the sole survivor of a three-day frat party.

"You're a lifesaver," Karen said, taking the Styrofoam cup from him, snapping off the lid and sipping the strong hot liquid inside.

She gave him a wink as she pulled one of the donuts out of the bag and took a big bite, sprinkling flecks of powdered sugar all over her tight, black sweater. Karen then completely shocked him by brushing the powdered sugar from her noticeably braless breasts while smiling at him. Her nipples hardened visibly and

Gregg struggled not to react with testosterone.

"What have we got? I noticed there's no meat wagon here, does that mean she's alive?" he asked, rubbing his temple with one hand and holding his coffee with the other.

"She's alive all right, alive, but not very well."

"Great, finally a witness. We might be able to catch this bastard after all," Gregg's mood did a complete turnaround.

"Don't get your panties in a wad yet, soldier," she smiled. "She's not going to worth too much to us in the way of an eyewitness."

"What's wrong?"

"I think you had better take a look for yourself," Stoddard grabbed him by the elbow and led him toward the front door of the mental health clinic.

A dozen different scenarios with a dozen different outcomes were playing over in Haskell's mind like an endless ribbon of videotape. And not one single conclusion sported a happy ending. The double glass doors of the mental health clinic had been propped open in order to facilitate the ease of movement in and out of the building. Two uniformed officers were posted at the doors to keep out the press and any other curious bystanders. Gregg flashed his shield instinctively while Stoddard didn't even so much as glance up at the patrolmen.

The backwash of flashlights and the building's own emergency lighting dimly lighted the corridor which was quickly filling with investigators and their equipment. Obviously, no one knew where the breaker panels were for the lights and no one had bothered looking for them.

Thick, soundproof doors on either side, behind each of which were small counseling rooms, flanked the long passageway. At the end of the long corridor was a reception area bathed in a soft glow and Haskell could see a horde of official looking people scurrying around like mice looking for a hidden chunk of cheese. A small figure sitting in a wheelchair seemed to be at the center of everyone's attention. Gregg saw this and his pace quickened.

As Gregg came within sight of Amber for the first time, he felt his stomach roil, gripped by a childhood fear. She looked like Norman Bates' mother, the skeletal remains, sitting in her chair. Instantly his heart began to weep for this damaged young woman.

He knelt in front of the girl to get a better look at her. She stared right past him, concentrating on a spot in her mind that only she knew existed. A long strand of drool streamed down her chin onto a towel a thoughtful paramedic had placed across her chest. Gregg took her hand into his and felt nothing. She didn't even as much as flinch, let alone grip him back. He peered deeply into her eyes and saw nothing but his own reflection. The physical shell of Amber Reese was sitting there, but not a shred of anything more. In fact, he was certain she wasn't even aware of the fact she was sitting in her own excrement. Gregg endured the sour smell, if for nothing more than out of respect for the girl, and to allow yet another of the atrocities of this maniac to seep into his soul. Against everything he believed in, he began wanting the person responsible for this dead.

"What is wrong with her?" Gregg asked one of the medical personnel attending to the girl.

"I'm not a doctor, but I would suspect it has something to do with this," the man said, reaching around behind the girl and lifting up her hair. There were little scars all over her scalp from dozens of incisions.

Gregg just looked up at him inquisitively.

"Don't ask me, I've never seen anything like it before in my life," the man's jaw muscles were clenching and unclenching in rhythm with his fist. "Look at this," he said, moving around to the front of Amber Reese and carefully, compassionately pried open her clenched jaws.

Gregg recoiled. Her tongue was gone, and in its place was a chunk of flesh flicking in tiny, erratic movements, as if searching for the rest of itself. The meat was blackened at the end from having been cauterized. The remaining tissue was a swollen, angry red.

"Sick bastard," the paramedic hissed.

"Is this where she was found?"

"Don't know. Jerry over there, he was first on the scene," the man pointed to a young uniformed cop sitting in one of the reception chairs. Gregg could see his hands were trembling from across the room.

"Why don't you stay here," he said to Karen as she started to follow him over to where the young cop was sitting.

"Why?"

"You're an authority figure, the man is already screwed up enough, I don't want him thinking even for a minute he did anything wrong."

"You're the boss," she smiled and disappeared back down the corridor.

Gregg wished he had a cigarette to offer the nervous young man, maybe even a shot of Cuervo. The patrolman looked up at Gregg as soon as he saw his shadow creeping across the floor into his space. He saw the detective and started getting to his feet in a hurry.

"No, just have a seat," Gregg said, forcing a smile as he sat down next to the officer. "I'm Detective Gregg Haskell," he offered his hand with a forced smile.

"Duncan, Jerry Duncan," he returned a firm handshake.

"Pretty ugly stuff over there," Gregg nodded in the direction of Amber and her attendants.

Duncan just nodded.

"I understand you were first one on the scene."

Again, a nod.

"Where was she?"

"She was sitting over there, like she was looking out the window. In fact, that's what I thought was going on. I thought a patient had accidentally gotten locked in here when I saw her standing at the window."

"You saw her through the window?"

"Yes, she was just standing there, staring out into the night. I was making my usual rounds. Normally I swing down here and eat my lunch in the car, it's kind of peaceful back here. Don't think I'll be doing that much anymore."

"You said she was standing up. Are you certain about that?"

He nodded. "Why?"

"I only ask because I don't think she can stand up on her own. Someone must have been in here with her. Someone must have been holding her up."

"You think?"

"Yes, I do. How often do you come down here for lunch?"

"Most every night. Unless I decide to get a hot meal, but my wife usually does a pretty good job of feeding me. I'd say I come down here on an average, three or four nights a week. What are you getting at?"

"It's probably nothing," Gregg shrugged and jotted a few sentences in a small, brown notepad.

"Detective," a voice called out with a sliver of panic imbedded.

Gregg looked up to see a young paramedic waving him over to them. They had already loaded Amber onto a gurney. She was rolled to one side with her shirt pulled up over her shoulders. He had almost forgotten this part of the investigation. He was still a good ten feet away from her when he first spied the hauntingly familiar lettering scrawled into her back. Her skin was still oozing from the fresh wounds left by the laser.

"You," he pointed to an investigator carrying a video camera. "Do you have a still camera with a spare memory card?"

"Yes, out in the van."

"Go get it. I want photos of this I can take with me. And then take video footage from every angle. And make it fast, I don't want this girl here any longer than she needs to be," Gregg barked.

Suddenly he felt the weight Vito carried on his shoulders every day and could completely understand the man's somber mood. He was the one who was in charge now, not just following his partner around with a notebook and a smile. This was his investigation to solve or screw up.

The photographer captured dozens of images of the inscription on the girl's back from multiple angles. The very second Haskell reviewed the digital files from the camera's screen and once he was certain of what he had he waved his hand over the girl instructing the paramedics to cover her up and get her to a hospital. The good news was her prognosis for survival was optimistic; the bad news was she was never going to be able to help him find her attacker.

Gregg walked down the now lit corridor, someone had

obviously found the light panel, staring at the image on the camera back. The words screamed at him accusingly. *Thom Tran's life is in your hands now, Rookie!* Haskell pulled a folded-up sheet of paper out of his pocket and began scanning the list of names. His finger came to rest on Tran, Mia. He angrily folded up the sheet of paper and shoved it back into his breast pocket. It was the beginning of another long month he hoped wouldn't end all too soon.

*   *   *

Mia squirmed in pain, yet she actually only moved in untraceable amounts. She was tired, so very tired, but they wouldn't let her sleep. And how she wanted to just go right on sleeping. She figured, sooner or later, she was going to wake up from this nightmare.

Every muscle in her body ached and she was cold. So terribly cold she felt as if her skin were shrinking. She could still taste the remnants of her last meal recently force-fed her through a tube.

Her mind drifted as her captor guided her through her daily rituals. She was back on the movie set. It was a low budget martial arts film, but the star was becoming a household name, and she hoped she could ride along on his coat tails. She was pretty, exotically beautiful, one Hollywood producer had called her, but that was all he called her. After giving up her goods to him, he never called as he had promised. They were pigs, all of them.

She winced in pain and jerked back to reality. She felt a biting pinch near the corner of her right eye. It hurt badly enough to bring tears to her eyes. But then, the warm liquid didn't run down her cheeks like tears. Instead, the thick fluid oozed and seeped, like, like blood. She winced once more and then saw her blood spray all over the front of her Plexiglas coffin.

Mia's heart began to race wildly, and she fought to wake herself up. But she wouldn't come to. She couldn't escape her horrific nightmares. She couldn't escape, because they were real. Mia's tears mixed with her blood and she slipped back into the safety of blackness.

*   *   *

"Boy, you don't look so good," Amanda said as she climbed into the car.

"And I missed you too, gorgeous," Gregg winked.

"I'm sorry, I didn't mean it to sound like that," she laughed and leaned over to give him a consoling peck on the cheek.

"You're gone a week and that's all I get?"

"For free. Besides, what was it you were expecting?"

"At least a little tongue," he turned and stuck his tongue out and wagged it like a catfish stuck on a riverbank.

"You're just gross, Uncle Gregg," Evy laughed and made faces from the back seat.

Haskell pulled up to the gate guard, slipped the guy a five and waited for the black and white striped arm to rise, letting them out of the parking lot. He felt like showing his badge and not paying. He couldn't believe how badly the airports were screaming for people's business and constantly asking for federal aid, yet they still gouged their customers for parking. That would be like K-Mart or the Piggley Wiggley setting up shacks and charging for parking, they wouldn't be in business very long.

"Anything happen while I was gone?"

The car fell into an eerie hush.

"I made Uncle Gregg some cookies for his lunch at work, but I found them out in the trash this morning."

"Gregg!" Amanda turned on him like an angry pit viper.

"What?"

"You threw away cookies this sweet child made for you?"

"They were terrible. But not to worry, I saved you one," he reached over and popped open the glove box. A brown glob of something that may have resembled a cookie in another life tumbled out into her lap. She glanced over at Gregg and from the smirk on his face she knew in an instant she had been set up.

"They were pretty bad," Evy squealed from the back seat.

"But at least I tried them," Gregg sneered at Amanda.

"You set me up you little traitor," she turned to face Evy.

"You're too easy, Amanda," she laughed.

She slowly unwrapped the plastic wrap clinging to the cookie like a protective second skin. "So, what exactly is wrong with this?"

"I screwed up a couple of measurements is all, nothing too bad," she giggled.

Amanda held the cookie up to her lips and glanced at Gregg with a look eliciting mercy, mercy that wasn't going to come.

"Aren't you going to try it?" he asked with a chuckle.

Amanda held her breath and bit down into the cookie. She grunted at first, positive she had broken a tooth, and then she gagged once the wretched flavor hit her. "Mmm honey, better than even Ellie Mae Clampett could make," she coughed and spit shards of chocolate oatmeal chip cookie out into her hand.

"Who's Ellie Mae Clampett?" Evy asked, scrunching up her nose.

"Never mind. So, let me guess, salt and something else."

"Yeah, I sort of forgot which was the salt and which was the sugar. And those powder thingy's too."

"Baking powder and baking soda?"

"Yeah, that's them. I think I put too much of something in there."

"It's a darned good thing you're cute," Amanda laughed.

Gregg laughed so hard he almost had to pull over.

"Hey, what's that supposed to mean?" Evy folded her arms across her chest and stared at the two laughing adults.

"It means I'm stopping for pizza on the way home instead of letting you cook a welcome home meal."

"Ha, ha, very funny. But hey, I like pizza. Can we get enough so I can have some friends come over?"

"What about Corrina?" Gregg asked, glancing back through his rear-view mirror.

Amanda's daughter had been so quiet he had almost forgotten she was even with them. Corrina was a completely different monster than Evy was. Whereas Evy was always like a hive full of bees someone had just taken a stick to, Corrina was more like a contented lioness who only roared if her cubs became too rambunctious for her tastes.

"Well of course she'll be there," Evy looked back at her uncle as if he had just uttered the most preposterous statement she had ever heard. "But I meant like friends, she's almost like my sister," Evy squealed while Corrina merely clicked her tongue and rolled her eyes.

"You are silly."

"Hey," she turned on Corrina. "We can have a sleep over."

Before he could protest, the bricks had been laid.

"Can we Uncle Gregg, please?" she cooed.

"We'll see," he replied, taking Amanda's hand in his and giving it a gentle squeeze. Her fingers began tracing light circles of electricity across the skin of his knuckles.

"It will give us some time to talk by ourselves," Amanda smiled to keep from laughing.

The next couple of hours were hectic, mind numbing, and it was exactly what Gregg needed. Between running back and forth from Amber, Courtney and Sarah's homes, and the pizza parlor, twice, Gregg didn't have one second to spare thinking about the case. Life sort of seemed normal, as normal as life can be for a man trapped in a house with horde of half-crazed women.

By eight o'clock that evening the girls had devoured the better part of two pizzas and disappeared to Evy's room where cackles of delight echoed throughout the house like lovelorn banshees in a B grade horror movie. Gregg and Amanda helped each other clean up after the heathens and sat down on the couch to watch some chick flick she had picked out at the video store. Gregg didn't complain, he knew it was pointless. Besides, he could use the time to think about the whirlwind that had become his life.

"So, how was your day?"

"Unique, to say the least."

"What did you do?" Amanda asked. The coming attractions and commercials were starting on the video and Gregg knew that meant he had at least fifteen minutes to have to fill with discussion before the movie started and she cut him some slack.

"I went over to Vito's," he said, regretting the words as soon as they passed over his lips.

Amanda reached for the remote, pressed the power button

off and turned to face him on the couch. "Tell me all about it."

"I'd rather not."

"Let me check. Do you have a choice? Nope," she grinned and kissed him lightly on the cheek.

"I figured as much. Let's just say it wasn't the most pleasant experience I've ever had."

"Well, I know that."

"What's that supposed to mean?

"The most pleasurable experience you've ever had had better have been with me," she pinched his leg just above the knee, eliciting a tremendous leap from him.

"Ooh, I don't know, I think you're running a distant third," he flinched from a telegraphed punch.

"You're lucky I know better. Now, quit trying to change the subject and tell me what happened with Vito."

"It wasn't pretty, if that's what you're asking."

"Am I going to have to get rough with you?"

"No," he laughed. "In all actuality, I think I helped him get back on the right path. I found out we both have a lot more in common than I could have ever imagined."

"I'm not sure if that's such a good thing or not."

Gregg smiled weakly as he drifted away from the conversation and allowed other thoughts to invade his brain. He could hear Amanda's voice in the background, but her words were lost on his contemplation.

"Is something going on?" she asked.

"Huh? Yeah, sort of. We found Amber Reese this morning, or I should say, she found us."

"Oh," her one syllable response spoke volumes.

"She's not dead, but she may as well be."

"Are you wanting to pick my brain?"

"With a pickax."

"What's bothering you?"

"This whole damned case. It seems like this killer's profile in changing with each new victim, as if he has premeditated his every move in anticipation of our investigation."

"Sometimes that's the way it happens."

"True, but it seems very suspect to me, like his every action has been premeditated from the very beginning. I can't help but feel we're being led around by our noses."

"What was this girl's condition?"

"I'm not really sure what the technical medical term will end up being, but in a nutshell, I think she was lobotomized. Her tongue had been cut out as well."

Amanda shivered. "Oh my, how terrible." She thought about this for a few moments. "But, Gregg, leaving her alive might still be in keeping with the killer's pattern."

"How so?"

"From what you've told me, at least one of the girl's so far had also been left alive."

"You're right, Rita Sorenson actually killed herself after she found herself in our care."

"I don't think this person is getting their release from the killing of these girls, in fact, it is probably quite the opposite. I'm afraid the truth of the matter is this person is getting most of what they need from the act of torturing them. Now, in Raymond Kyser's case, I think there may have been several different factors at work."

"I'm listening," Gregg said, completely attentive to her theory.

"I think this person may have needed Kyser for something, otherwise, out of sheer anger, they would have killed him right off."

"So, you do believe this person is motivated by revenge. A hatred for Raymond Kyser?"

"There's no doubt in my mind but nailing down the motivating factors is going to be a lot harder I believe. I don't think this person is acting on one, single impulse."

"That damned calendar shoot is the only link binding all these women. Possibly a family member, or loved one of the girl who was raped?"

"That's one angle to look at."

"And another would be?"

"That's for you to figure out, I'm afraid."

"What's that supposed to mean?"

"It means I don't have all the answers, Gregg. I'm not the trained detective, you are. But if there's one thing I do know about detective work, it can't be closed-minded. If you start investigating this as only a family member or a friend, then you might lose sight of a bigger picture."

"Point well taken. Now, I thought I'd never say this, but can we watch the movie."

She smiled and pressed play on the DVD remote. He cringed as the credits started rolling. Clint Eastwood and Meryl Streep. "This ought to be really good. Clint, how could you do this to me?" He thought to himself cynically.

He contemplated telling Amanda about the way Stoddard was suddenly acting around him. He had an eerie feeling his boss had been hitting on him, but it was subtle enough to raise his doubts. He ignored the movie, his thoughts about his boss and allowed his mind to drift back to Amber Reese.

*   *   *

"Good morning, Freddie. Is your Uncle Vito here?"

"Yeah, he's upstairs stinking up the can as usual," the boy's semi-cheerful voice couldn't hide his pain, or the fact things were far from being normal.

Gregg busied himself around the kitchen making coffee while waiting for Vito to come downstairs. He had heard Freddie holler through the bathroom door, so he expected Vito to be down shortly. By the time the man made it down to the kitchen, Haskell had already polished off two cups of coffee.

"What in the hell took you so long?"

"You don't want to know," he smiled weakly. "What's up?"

Gregg glanced around the room, making sure they were alone.

"He's already left for school. I figured it was the best thing for him, to be around his friends."

"Probably. Listen, I've got some good news, and some bad news."

"How bad is the bad news," Vito readied himself to recoil from something he probably didn't want to hear.

"Nothing you couldn't stomach hearing," Gregg responded, having seen the sour look in Vito's eyes almost the instant the words came out of his mouth.

"Good," he sighed. "In that case, give me the good news

first."

"I got a call from Goulding early this morning. Apparently, he owes you big. Not only did he work through the night, he also called in several favors. But in any case, the verdict is a good one. None of the evidence they collected from your house belongs to Lizbeth."

"How did they find that out without her DNA to match it to?" Vito asked suspiciously.

"It turns out they didn't even need her DNA. Seems Lizbeth is a community minded individual. She has donated her blood several times at the hospital. They had her records on file and Goulding was able to type her and the evidence and they were not a match."

"If not from Lizbeth, where did it come from?"

"Goulding couldn't be certain. With no sample to check it against there's no way for him to know. It will be one of life's mysteries I guess, but as long as it's not your sister's then there's still hope she's alive," Gregg said.

"That makes things a little easier, I guess."

"It does add one more piece to the puzzle as well."

"What do you mean?"

"Sorry to be so morbid, but why wouldn't he have just killed her?"

"Maybe he has other plans for her," Vito shuddered.

"No, I don't think so. It wouldn't fit his pattern."

"Neither did Kyser."

"Oh, yes he did. In fact, he may have been the first to get the ax so to speak. I compiled a list of credit card charges applied to Kyser's credit cards and it looks like he was kept alive until all of his liquid assets had been depleted. And once his funds were depleted his fate was sealed."

"I can tell by your tone tracking the charges was a dead end."

"Not completely, but so far it hasn't panned out to any solid leads either. The charges were all for cash and I'm sure Raymond Kyser accompanied a guest to the sites where the cards were used. There were a variety of places, Western Union offices and some check cashing joints, both in and out of the US. However, on a brighter note, some of the places had surveillance video recorders in use and all I am waiting for is access to the memory cards."

Vito silently got up from the kitchen table and crossed the room to pour them two more cups of coffee. He dumped the remnants of the pot into the sink and put a fresh pot onto brew.

"What about Amber?" he asked, sliding a steaming mug in front of Haskell.

"She was found yesterday at the county mental health clinic, right on schedule I'm afraid."

"How bad was she?"

"We've seen worse."

"Meaning?"

"She's alive and will undoubtedly remain that way a good long time."

"Something in your voice tells me she's not going to make a very good witness."

"Not at all. Other than a few minuscule samples for trace she is pretty much useless to our investigation. For lack of a more politically correct explanation, she's a vegetable, Vito. It's far too early to know anything yet, the lab hasn't even collected all of the evidence yet."

"He's getting better at this."

"What?"

"This one didn't die. He successfully kept her alive to suffer and to serve as a gruesome reminder to whomever it is he is actually targeting."

A light knocking at the front door interrupted their conversation. Vito disappeared to answer it and returned several moments later with a smiling Karen Stoddard. To Gregg, it seemed Vito hadn't formally invited her in. It was more like she was just following him through the house like a puppy eager to please its master.

She walked over to the cupboard, grabbed a mug and poured herself some coffee.

"I stopped at your place and when I found you weren't there I figured this would be the next logical place to look for you. And quite frankly, I must say I am pleased to find you here and not down at Gus's," she turned around with a smile and sat down.

Vito grunted a reply.

"Morning, lieutenant."

"Good morning, Detective Haskell," she replied.

"Did you need me for something?" Vito asked.

"Do you need to be such a prick?"

"Yes."

"Then let me make this short and sweet. You are to appear before a review board Monday morning, eight am sharp. And I'd like to add my input has been requested by the board and I am sure they will consider everything I have to say about your current situation."

"And this means I am supposed to kiss your ass, talk sweet and let you come into my sister's house whenever you feel like?"

"No, but what it does mean, is when I take you off a case, I expect you to listen to me."

"I am off the case."

"Oh really. And just what were you two talking about?" she glared accusingly at Haskell.

"The weather," Vito shot back.

"Yeah, I'll bet."

"Prove otherwise."

"I don't need to Lorenz," her agitation echoed in her voice. "My impression is all that matters. If I believe you are disobeying orders, then you are disobeying orders. And Haskell, let me remind you of something, you work for me, not him. Maybe I wasn't too clear before, Detective Lorenz, you are officially off this case which includes discussing it in any capacity, official or otherwise. And Haskell, you are hereby forbidden to speak with him about this case on any level. Unless of course, you are looking forward to having a review board convene on your behalf. Am I clear?"

"Yes, ma'am," Haskell replied.

Her face softened and she stood up from the table. "Listen, fellas, I know all about your connection as partners and this unbreakable male bond thing, but I am trying to do the best thing for you Vito. The inquiry will go a hell of a lot better if I can truthfully tell them you're under a great deal of stress and you had a momentary lapse, one I am certain will never happen again."

"Sure, whatever."

"Damn it, Vito, I'm not the enemy. I just spent the last three days preparing my statements for your defense and you want to act like this?"

"Sorry, I'm still having a hard time dealing with all of this. My sister is still missing, or had you forgotten?"

"No, I haven't forgotten about Lizbeth. I've got plenty of people looking into her disappearance as we speak."

"What do you mean, people are looking into her disappearance?"

"Just what I said, what did you think I meant?"

"Never mind. I'm sorry, lieutenant, I'll try to behave."

"You do that, Vito. And you had better do the same," she turned on Haskell.

"Yes, ma'am."

"Good-bye, Karen, I'll call you later," Vito hoped his tone of voice let her know she had outstayed her welcome.

She glared back at him for several seconds before turning to leave.

"Well, Vito, I had better get going. Evy's got a game this afternoon," Haskell said as they both watched the lieutenant storm out of Vito's house. He made sure he said it loud enough for his voice to carry out to her ears.

"You probably better play things close to the vest for now, she's a real ball buster," Vito allowed his comment to drift out to her as well. She slammed the front door, announcing she had indeed heard their comments.

"I did some background checking on Stillwater and the man has enough concrete in his alibis to pave a road from here to the valley. We might as well forget about him completely. I was able to account for his whereabouts for most of the past year. The man's a workaholic, he didn't have enough time to be a kidnapper as well as a killer," Gregg said.

"I figured as much."

"I can even clear him of any wrongdoing in your sister's situation as well."

"Thanks"

"Not a problem. I also leaned a little on the man, you're not going to have any problems out of him."

"Not that I really give a shit anymore, but thanks."

"Well, hey, I do have to get running," he said, standing up and putting his cup in the sink with some other dirty dishes.

"Thanks for stopping by. And thanks for everything," Vito said.

Gregg nodded and started for the door. "Oh, I almost forgot. Has Lieutenant Stoddard ever been here before?"

Vito thought about it for a minute before answering. "No, I don't think so. Why?"

"Oh, nothing, she just seemed awfully comfortable."

"Yeah, she does, doesn't she," Vito laughed.

Gregg headed for the school. He was bound and determined to enjoy watching Evy's game, and some time away from this case. And with Amanda there he was certain he would himself, even if only briefly. The more he thought about it, the more he realized it was exactly what he needed. Sadly enough, he was beginning to understand Vito's cynical outlook on life as well as his graying coif.

Chapter Fourteen

The constant chatter of the surrounding crowd was quite refreshing. Gregg forced everything out of his mind and concentrated on nothing but Evy's game and Amanda's gentle touch. The gym echoed with squeaking tennis shoes and sharp, shrill whistles. The aroma of popcorn and hot dogs wove its way in and around the bleachers. Gregg had already downed two of the quarter pound monsters with all the fixings and a jumbo bag of popcorn, and yet, his stomach continued to growl for more.

Corrina and Evy had been working on their game in the driveway every night after school without even realizing what they were doing. They had developed what could only be construed as a sibling rivalry, which had produced some heated arguments over many things, the biggest of which being who was the better ball player of the two. Neither girl realized they each had their own specific talents to bring to the game, Corrina with her height and size and Evy with her speed and accuracy. And even though they weren't aware of it, they had developed one another into one hell of a team, which now showed in the twenty-point lead they enjoyed over their opponents, the best team in the state according to the local sports page. He suspected tomorrow's rankings might be quite a bit different.

"Gregg, is it just me, or are those two pretty darned good?"

"They're a lot better now than they were at the beginning of the season, that's for sure."

"So was your idea to have them settle their differences on the court planned, or just lucky?"

"Come on, give me some credit, I'm a lucky bastard," he laughed and squeezed Amanda's hand.

The bleachers erupted into a roar as Evy dished the ball off to Corrina who immediately proceeded to slam it home. Although the girl was barely fourteen, she stood a whopping six-foot one. When Gregg had first seen her on the court, before he had known her mother and her personally, he used to crack jokes about how awkward and out of place the girl seemed. She looked as though she were an adult playing with a bunch of children. However, she was so gangly she was also clumsy and not a very good ball player despite her size. The work her and Evy had done together had made a mountain of difference. At this rate, Gregg was certain they would both be all-Americans, state champs and be courted by college scouts by the time they finished their high school careers.

"Would you like another soda?" he asked.

"No, mine's still full, and at three fifty a pop, only you high priced detectives can afford them."

"Afford it, hell, I took out a second mortgage just to come to this game," he smiled and turned to make his way down the bleachers.

Gregg thought back to his high school days when the entrance fee to a football game was still less than a buck for students and soda was damned near free. But somewhere down the line some overzealous bean counter figured out a way to make the schools more money. But wasn't the state lottery system supposed to take care of that? No, that was why they had voted a millage increase in their property taxes. But weren't they supposed to be paying less in property taxes because of the lottery system? Gregg's head started to ache as he pondered the conundrum. There were even more loopholes, mismanagement and corruption within the lottery system than in the Internal Revenue Service.

Gregg was standing at the concession counter waiting for his Mountain Dew and large popcorn when he spied a familiar head of blonde hair. He paid for his indulgences, gathered them up and headed over to where his boss was sitting in the opposing school's bleachers.

"Fancy meeting you here," Gregg said, startling Karen and ripping her attention away from the game.

"Haskell? I mean, Gregg, what are you doing here?"

"My niece plays for the Yellowjackets," he pointed to Evy bounding down the court.

"Oh, one of the enemy," she smiled. "She's their leading scorer, isn't she?"

"Most of the time, I guess she is. You said enemy, does your daughter play for the Cougars?"

"Daughter? Oh, no, I don't have any children. My niece plays for the Cougars though. She's my brother's kid," she pointed to a brunette who was unsuccessfully trying to block one of Corrina's shots. The crowd roared as the basket was good and Corrina was fouled.

"They're pretty good together. You their coach?" Karen winked.

"Nope, I can't take the credit for that. They've worked at coaching each other."

"They might make the state finals this year."

"They haven't said much about it, but I think they're secretly hoping for it."

"Listen, Gregg, I'm sorry about that scene earlier at Vito's. I didn't mean to come across like a ball buster, but I am worried Vito is going to do something that will not be able to be undone."

"I understand."

"Do you?"

"I thought I did," Gregg replied, his brow raised in question.

"Vito has, let's say, some very sensitive documents in his file. He has, on occasion, been less than an exemplary employee. I'm afraid if IAD wants to, they can have his badge for this screw up. And truthfully, as much as he chaps my ass, I still wouldn't agree with that at all. He's a good cop."

"Neither would I. Look, lieutenant, this is something I would prefer not to talk about right now. I am here to enjoy my niece's game, and nothing more."

"Fine," she replied, turning her attention away from him and back to the game.

"I just need some time to clear my head," he said.

"I said, fine," she snapped without even looking at him.

Gregg made his way back through the crowd and was in his

seat just as the half time buzzer sounded. He had sat down next to Amanda without a sound and watched as the girls trotted off to the locker room.

"Is something wrong?" she asked, sensing his trepidation.

"Yeah, I think I saw Evy's coach colluding with the Russians," he smiled at her.

"You know what I mean," she swatted his arm playfully.

"Nothing much I guess. I just ran into Karen Stoddard."

"Your boss?"

"Yeah."

"What is she doing here?"

"Her niece plays for the Cougars. I guess that little brunette who is trying to guard Corrina is her brother's kid."

"Beth Parkinson?"

"You know her?"

"I know her mother, we work together. They live a few streets over from us. She's always trying to get me to send Corrina to private school with her daughter. I've always thought it was to get Corrina on their ball team. Chad Parkinson, Beth's father, is the coach of the Cougars and he has been salivating over her ever since her growth spurt two summers ago."

"You've got to be kidding me."

"I can't think of any other reason why Carol would suggest it, especially since Corrina and Beth don't get along with each other at all."

"You ever see Stoddard over there?"

"No, not that I can recall. But I don't go by their house very often. Why?"

"I don't know. You'd think if Stoddard had a niece she cared enough about to go to her school ball games she'd at least have a picture of the kid in her office."

"Do you have pictures of Evy and Corrina?" her tone was impishly sarcastic.

"Are you kidding me? I don't have room on my desk for anything else. I've even had to move your picture over to Vito's desk," he grinned. His smile only lasted for a millisecond and then his face quickly lost its happy edge. "But I noticed something peculiar while I was talking with Stoddard."

"What's that?"

"The kid never once looked up into the bleachers where Karen was sitting. Where is Beth's mother?"

Amanda scanned the opposing crowd and pointed. "Over there, to the left of the time keeper's table and three rows up."

"The pretty brunette?"

"You think she's pretty?"

"Hey now, let's not lose our focus," he laughed.

"Yes, the pretty brunette. I can see smoke bellowing out of your ears those wheels are turning so fast. What are you thinking?"

"If Lieutenant Stoddard came to watch her niece's game, why is she sitting on the other side of the gym from her sister-in-law?"

"Maybe they don't get along."

"Okay, then why hasn't the girl, Beth, looked in Stoddard's direction even once? I've seen her glancing at her mother repeatedly, but never her aunt."

"Maybe she doesn't know her aunt is even here."

"Sure seems like a lot of maybes, doesn't it?"

"I thought you weren't going to think about work today."

"Neither did I, honey, neither did I."

* * *

Sunrise came much too early for Gregg's tastes. He and Amanda had sat up half the evening discussing all of the twists and turns this case seemed to be taking, and yet it maintained the lack of physical evidence. It was getting harder and harder for him not to believe Karen Stoddard was a complete whack job. He wasn't sure how deeply her feelings for Vito ran and had yet to determine whether or not her intentions were good or bad when it came to his partner. On one hand she seemed sympathetic and helpful and on the other, full of nothing but spite.

Gregg had slipped into to the precinct during the predawn hours in order to use the computers without any interruptions. He pulled up several old files and began purging them for information. Files he was sure would ruffle more than a few feathers if it were known what he was up to. He spent three hours jotting down notes, recording dates and times of things that weren't quite jiving with what he had been told or what had been written elsewhere. Quickly he put things away once he realized Lieutenant Stoddard was in her palace.

"Detective Haskell," he answered his phone sometime around eight o'clock.

"Is Detective Lorenz, Vito Lorenz there?" a voice asked.

"Not at the moment, but I am covering his case load at the moment so you can talk to me."

After a long pause the man said, "This is Frankie Jewel, I'm Oslo Rademacher's personal assistant."

"Yes, sir, what can I do for you?"

"Detective Lorenz was here, to speak with my boss, some few months ago."

"Yes, I know, I was with him," Haskell replied a little more impatiently than he should have.

"I have some information regarding those girls you were asking about," he said nervously.

"I'm listening."

The man stammered for several seconds before saying, "I'd much rather meet in person, if that's all right with you."

"I don't see the need, but if it makes you feel better, certainly. Where would you like to meet?"

"There's a little coffee shop down on North Broadway, near Chinatown, they have this great little mustard and cress sprout sandwich with tahini on toasted pita. It's scrumptious, I mean to die for. I can be there in an hour."

"Okay, I'll see you then."

"Detective?"

"Yes," he said, pulling the phone back up to his ear.

"How will I know who you are?"

"I'll find you, trust me, I'm a detective."

The man laughed nervously as Gregg hung up the phone before he could say anything else. He suddenly envisioned himself sitting outside a little café with a man dressed in pink taffeta and sporting magenta pumps.

Gregg got to the coffee shop with about fifteen minutes to spare. He ordered a large Colombian Supremo with a shot of espresso and sat sipping the concoction while studying the crowd. After five minutes he came to two conclusions, people were strange, and he didn't get out into public nearly enough. It was a culture shock. When did young girls start walking the streets one thread from being naked? When did genders cross and combine until they were no longer discernible from one another? Gregg shook his head in despair and turned his attention back to his coffee where the world was still warm and fuzzy for him.

Gregg was getting impatient. The man was late, but finally he sauntered up. Haskell saw his pink taffeta creation strolling down the sidewalk toward the café. Gregg almost laughed out loud when he realized his mental picture of the caller was only a few minute details shy of being dead on. The man had some sort of fluffy brown animal attached to a leash extending up to his hand. The odd-looking beast sniffed at everything in his path, and the dog just seemed to be indifferent to the lowly commoners. Once he had entered the boundaries of the café the man began eyeing the crowd suspiciously. Gregg stuck a hand up in the air and flicked his wrist in a nondescript wave, hoping to get the freakish creature over to his table before anyone took too much notice. He slipped his sunglasses out of his pocket and put them on hoping to avoid a chance of recognition by any acquaintance who might happen to pass by. He almost laughed when he thought about having to explain his brunch company to Amanda.

"Detective Haskell?" the man stood at his table.

"Have a seat."

"Are you Detective Haskell?"

"Would I be asking you to sit down if I weren't?" Gregg replied, feeling somewhat violated by the way the man-thing eyed him up and down.

"In my dreams," he winked and pulled out two chairs. He set the fluffy little brown thing in one chair and he sat in the other. "I'm sorry for being late, but Oslo insisted I take Mitzi for a walk and I couldn't think of a good enough excuse to refuse."

"That's quite all right. You said you had some information for me," Gregg said, wanting to make this meeting as brief as possible.

"Oslo told me you had been asking questions about

Evangelique and Kendra."

"Yes, my partner and I were asking questions a few months ago."

"I think I might have some information for you."

"First of all, who are you, and why weren't you around when we first asked about them?"

"Oh, I'm sorry, forgive my manners. My name is Frankie Jewel and I work for Oslo Rademacher."

"Did you work for him five months ago?"

"Not exactly."

"What is it, exactly?"

"I worked for Oslo when the girls first disappeared. But about eight months ago, we had a falling out of sorts."

"What type of falling out?"

"That bitch of a pool boy, Ian, is what kind," he smacked his tongue and crossed his legs. "But I'm back now. It looks like Ian got tired of that fat, insensitive bastard a lot quicker than I imagined he would have."

"Can we please stick to the issue here?"

He rolled his eyes. "Of course, if we must. Well, I was setting up the office the way I like it. The way it should be. The way I left it. When I was cleaning Ian's things out of my drawers, I found a file with a copy of the affidavit Ian so thoughtlessly sent to you people. He didn't even bother to use the spell check program. The moron probably doesn't even know how. Since I didn't know what the affidavit was for, I was just going to throw it away. But then I got naturally curious, you know, I wanted to know what Mr. Fat Ass had been getting himself into while I was away."

Gregg began rubbing his temples, hoping beyond all hope this cretin would hurry up and make a point.

Frankie sensed Gregg's growing frustration and continued. "Like I said, out of curiosity's sake, I read through the file. And that's when I got to thinking I might know something more than I should. I think I know who the last person was to see Evangelique the day she disappeared. I asked Oslo about it and he told me about your little visit. I bet you guys damn near scared him straight," he pealed off an effeminate sounding laugh that seemed rehearsed.

"Who is this person you are talking about? The last one to see Evangelique," Gregg said, his attention fully on the organic organism sitting across from him.

Frankie looked around him suspiciously. He leaned close enough to kiss Gregg on the cheek, cupped his hands around his mouth and whispered, "A cop."

"Come on, quit jerking my chain. I don't have time for this crap," Gregg blurted and stood up.

"No, wait, I'm not joking," fear radiated from the man's eyes, sending a shiver up Gregg's spine. The man wasn't lying, or at least not knowingly.

Gregg saw something in the man's eyes he didn't want to see and sat back down. The man was telling the truth, or at least as what he perceived to be the truth.

"Tell me, what did you see, exactly?"

"I was watering Oslo's precious African violets out on the verandah and I saw a patrol car, LAPD, parked down in front of the studio. I noticed Evangelique leaning down, as if she were talking to the driver of the car. They seemed awfully friendly, like they might know each other, if you know what I mean?" He pursed his lips in a mock kiss.

"So, you think she might have been dating this cop?"

"It appeared that way, but then I remember, that same cop had been hanging around talking to Kendra too. Maybe he was tricking with both of them," he winked.

"How do you know it was the same cop?"

"I don't know, I just assumed it was," he delicately folded his hands in front of himself and rested his chin on his knuckles. Gregg caught a glint of color shimmering from an elegant ring on the man's pinky. He was obviously flashing it proudly. Probably something Oslo had purchased for him to make up for the *Ian* incident.

"Why would you assume that?" Gregg sighed.

"It was the same car."

"How did you know that?"

"The numbers on the roof. They're different on every car, aren't they?" he asked, jotting the number-letter combination down on a napkin and sliding it over to Gregg.

"Yes, as a matter of fact, they are. So far, you've been

invaluable and I only have one more question before I let you get back to whatever it was you were doing," Gregg said, ecstatic over this new development.

"It's your dime."

"Did you see Evangelique Martens get into the car with this patrolman?"

"Not in so many words, no."

Gregg sighed and his face sagged.

"But I wasn't watching them every single second, I turned around to give the thirsty little African violets their drink and when I turned back and she was gone. I looked away for no more than a few seconds. There was nowhere else she could have gone, detective."

"Okay, thank you," Gregg said, getting up from the table. He reached his hand across the table to receive a limp, sweaty handshake. The man's hands felt like a piece of cold, wet spaghetti wrapping around his hand and he had to suppress a shudder.

"Should I be worried?"

"About what?"

"I read the papers detective. If this serial killer is a cop."

Gregg quickly put up his hand to stop him from talking.

"Listen, the best way for me to be able to ensure your safety is for you to promise not to talk about this to anyone except Detective Lorenz or myself. Do you understand?"

"Yes," he replied sheepishly.

"That means no press, no friends, no, uhm, lovers. Not anyone, not even Oslo."

"I understand," he enthusiastically nodded his head for emphasis.

Gregg walked away from the café, resisting the urge to run to his car in unadulterated bliss. In his hot little hands was the information that might just break this case wide open and save the lives of at least seven women. He wanted to call Davenport and get her working on it right away, but he knew this information was much too sensitive to be discussed over the radio or a telephone.

The more he thought about his latest discovery coupled with the circumstantial evidence he had uncovered about Gloria and Freddie Mascho the more Gregg began feeling very uneasy about this case. If this killer were a cop, he knew they would stop at nothing to keep their secret safe. He spun the wheel and did a U-turn in the opposite direction of the precinct. He pulled into the post office and made two copies of his little brown notebook. He took one of the copies and put it in an overnight delivery envelope, addressed it to Vito and sent it on its way. Next, he rented a post office box for one month. He put the second copy in a self-addressed envelope addressed to the Los Angeles Times and slipped it into the post office box. He knew if the box went unattended or if the rent lapsed it would be cleaned out and the mail sent back to the sender, in this case, the LA Times.

Sweat coated his trembling hands as he closed the door to the post office box. He gave a nervous chuckle at the images of every political intrigue laced thriller he had ever seen flashing through his head. It was lightly amusing, possibly a bit sardonic, but not funny at all. He didn't need to remind himself just how serious and dangerous this investigation had become.

Gregg sat in the parking lot of the post office with his heart and mind racing in unison. Images of Kyser's tortured and mutilated body kept flashing through his memories. He hoped it wasn't a window into the future. An ominous portent of things to come.

He headed back toward the precinct. It was time to poke the snake to see if it was dead or just sleeping. He hoped his acting skills were up to the task at hand. He stopped along the way and picked up two cups of coffee and a couple of those cruller things Stoddard liked so much.

Less than an hour after leaving Mitzi and her pet at the café Gregg was strolling into the precinct with a nervous grin greasing his face. He was looking more like a Picasso than a Rembrandt. Haskell knocked at the lieutenant's door and waited for her to wave him in.

"Good Morning, Gregg, what can I do you for?"

"We need to talk about something."

"Okay. I hope one of those are for me," she said, eyeing the bag in his hand.

He handed her the bag, a cup of coffee and took a seat

across from her on the other side the desk. He watched as she pulled a pastry out of the bag and put it on a small, yellow and blue flower printed paper plate. He watched her intently as she cut the cruller into several bite size pieces, all symmetrical, and arranged them harmoniously on the plate just the way she wanted them. Nearly ten minutes later Karen stabbed a plastic fork into one of the chunks, dipped it into her coffee and popped it into her mouth.

"So, what's on your mind?" she asked once she had finished the delectable morsel.

"I've got a lead on the case, but it's not going to make you happy."

"Really? And what kind of lead would make me unhappy?"

"One pointing in the direction of a cop."

"What?" her voice raised several notches. "What in the world could possibly make you think a cop is involved in this? Do you understand the gravity of an implication such as this?"

"Of course I do. But I have an eyewitness who places a patrol car at the scene on the days when both Kendra Jenkins and Evangelique Martens were abducted. This eyewitness also stated the officer in the car spoke, in length, with each of the girls," Gregg related, watching Stoddard's face carefully.

"So, this doesn't prove anything. Our people patrol those studio lots quite often. You can't blame the men for wanting to sneak a peek at a pretty, young movie star."

Gregg found it odd this woman with a reputation as a ball-buster was suddenly making excuses for her men. Gregg watched her eyes intently as they spoke, watching for tell-tale signs of fabrication. Karen Stoddard was as well trained in interrogation tactics as Haskell was, but there was something below the surface betraying her. Her anger and he planned on pushing those buttons until he could learn everything he could about this woman. The more they talked, the more his ludicrous suspicions were being confirmed.

"It was the same car, both times, one month apart."

"So, we have a patrolman who has a thing for one of the girls. Something to discuss with him, explain our concerns, but certainly nothing to get all worked up over."

"Normally, I would have to agree with you. However, this

is a little different."

"Why, what makes this so special?" she spat out her words. Her eyes had become two piercing orbs shooting back at Haskell.

Gregg had made a cursory stop before trudging up to the lieutenant's office. To his chagrin the motor pool clerk confirmed his suspicions about the origin of the patrol car. This information gave even more credence to the rest of his suspicions.

"Because, this car was in the motor pool garage. All of the cars in the fleet we purchased that year were recalled due to a steering gear failure. This car just happened to be waiting for replacement parts and wasn't approved for duty on the street. There are only a handful of people authorized to sign those cars out."

"What are you trying to say?"

"Someone with brass on their collar signed out that car."

"What's his name?" she asked sardonically.

"I don't know that yet. The officer in charge of the records is out sick for the day and he has the only key to the cabinet with the archived records. As soon as he gets back to work tomorrow, I'll know the name of the person who signed out that patrol car," Gregg explained. He could see she was getting more and more agitated as the conversation progressed, just as he suspected she would.

"For the record, I think you are way off base here, detective."

"For the record, I hope I am," he wove an accusing tone into his voice.

"Is that all you have for me?" she asked, counting to ten over and over again in her head in an effort to let her anger subside. How dare this green detective accuse her of something so atrocious? She wanted nothing more than to slip an official reprimand into his service jacket and have his ass up in front of a review board. She should have done exactly that when she had caught him and that bastard Lorenz conspiring against her.

"Ma'am?" Gregg asked, reading the quandary written in her face and realizing he had struck a nerve with her. He didn't have enough ammunition to fire off all his guns yet, but soon.

"What!"

"Are we through?"

"Yes, we're through. Just one thing you need to remember though."

"What's that?"

"You had better make damned good and sure you have enough evidence against this person before taking it to the Attorney General's office, otherwise, I can assure you, it will blow up in your face."

"I understand completely ma'am. Now, if we're through, I have a lot of work requiring my attention," Gregg said as he stood up.

Lieutenant Stoddard merely waved a dismissing hand at him and ignored him as he left her office. Gregg knew the shit was about to hit the fan and he was standing directly in front of it.

*   *   *

Mia slowly drifted on a sea of her returning consciousness. The more she became aware of her surroundings, the more she realized something was wrong. Terribly, terribly wrong.

Mia was hearing sounds for the first time since her captivity, or least as far back as she could remember. They weren't distinct, identifiable sounds, but they were sounds. An icy fear gripped her heart, if she was hearing noise, then this wasn't a dream. She was never going to wake up and things would never be normal again. This was her life, her reality as foreign and dream-like as it seemed.

A shadow stormed into the room with her and her cellmates. The smoky apparition wildly flailed its arms in anger. Several tables full of equipment were sent crashing to the ground. Mia cringed at the sound of the clanging metals skidding across the hard, tile floor. Suddenly, the room was awash with blinding light. Mia began to panic. She clamped her eyes shut and struggled to keep from hyperventilating. At least in the darkness, with her captor concealing himself within the shadows, she had a chance for survival. But now the veil of secrecy was lifted, she knew she was left without a shred hope.

Mia glanced at the face of her Plexiglas chamber. There were only six boxes X'd out in red. Suddenly she felt an excruciating pain radiating up her left arm. Craning her neck, she strained to see what was happening to her. Mia could see the person, her abductor, no longer a mere shadow in the darkness, but a real, mortal being standing next to her. Without warning the IV tubes connected to the veins in the crook of her elbow were viciously ripped out. Blood ran freely down her arm and the clear plastic tubes dangled like translucent, lifeless snakes.

Mia jumped as the person flung the IV rack across the room and moved to the front of Mia's chamber. Her captor stood there, staring back at her with wild, angry, demonic eyes. The frightened young girl convulsed violently and regurgitated all over herself. Her captor began undoing the latches on the face of the chamber one by one. As each one popped open, a resounding click pierced Mia's nerves. She began crying out to the person, begging and pleading for mercy. It wasn't time damn it, she had twenty-four more X's. She wanted her X's.

The chamber front fell away and Mia was now face to face with her captor. She was helplessly trapped, suspended in midair by some type of framework platform. Her brain screamed at her to fight, to struggle for her life, but her body didn't have it in her.

Mia went crashing across the floor as the phantom yanked her free from her bonds and flung her across the room. The person bent down and dragged her to her feet by her hair and then flung her across the room once more sending her crashing into a table full of equipment. As she was being tossed about the room like a rag doll, Mia caught sight of the other chambers, each housing its own occupants. Most of the other girls were in the midst of a drug-induced slumber, but a couple of them seemed to be watching what was happening to her. Mia's body screamed out in agonizing pain. She was bleeding from several different places at once and hurt in more places than she could count.

"Please," she mouthed weakly and was rewarded with a sharp punch to the mouth.

Mia fell backward onto the floor, her head striking the cold tile. A dull thud resonated through her skull and her vision blurred. She forced herself up onto her knees and saw the frenzied maniac storming across the room after her. She turned to scramble away on her hands and knees but within seconds the person was on top of her and was bashing her head against the floor. Tufts of her hair ripped loose from her scalp each time her head was jerked back up from the floor.

Mia felt the weight of the person lifting off of her, but they were still there. She felt her pain begin to subside and darkness crept over her like a slow rolling fog. Her breathing began to grow shallower and Mia began to relax and let the warm, glowing feeling wash over her.

Thom Tran was dead long before her captor had finished bashing her brains out onto the floor. Her body was pummeled, beaten and kicked until all their energy was finally spent.

*   *   *

Karen Stoddard watched the doors of the school through a pair of binoculars. She held the field glasses in her left hand because the knuckles on her right were tender and starting to swell. The salty taste of her own blood permeated her mouth as it seeped from a hole bitten in the side of her cheek. Her brain was sending her in fifteen different directions at once. She knew what she was doing was wrong, but it had to be done. They had to pay for what they had done. All of them. Pay like Raymond Kyser had paid. Pay like the girls before them had paid. And pay like Vito and his bitch of a sister had to pay.

Karen felt a sliver of remorse over what she had been forced to do. Gregg Haskell had nothing to do with this, yet, now he had been drawn into it by mere circumstances. It was a regrettable but necessary fact. He was getting much too close to the truth and she wasn't ready for that yet. It was all Vito's fault. He was supposed to have known what to do. He was supposed to have figured all this out a long time ago. He could have stopped her and saved the girls, all of them. But he didn't want to. He didn't give a shit about her, about anyone but himself.

Karen bolted upright in her seat. Her target was on the move. She spied the little blond head bounding through the double doors near the school auditorium. Karen threw her car into gear and drove over to where the teen was waiting on the sidewalk for her ride.

"Evy," she called out.

The girl glanced over in her direction and Karen waved her over to the patrol car.

"Are you calling me, ma'am?" Evy asked, a little wary, but just as respectful as her uncle had taught her to be.

"Yes. Are you Evy Haskell?"

"No, my name is Evelyn Cooper. But people call me Evy. I didn't think there were two Evy's at this school. That's kind of neat," she babbled in her teenager sort of way.

"Do you have an uncle named Gregg Haskell?"

"Duh," she replied, thumping herself on the forehead. "Sometimes I can be so blonde. No offense ma'am," she said after spying Karen's blonde hair spilling out from beneath her patrolman's cap.

"No offense taken," she replied with a smile, even though deep down she wanted to pummel the girl right there on the spot and leave her bloody pulp for her uncle to find. But she had plans for her, just like she had plans for Vito's bitch sister. "So, are you Gregg Haskell's niece?"

"Yes ma'am."

"Great, my search is over. Come on around to the other side and get in," she directed while sporting a warm, friendly smile.

"Excuse me?"

"Get in the car," her tone came out much more gruffly than she would have liked, and her smile had all but disappeared. Why must she be forced to endure so much insolence?

"Why?" Evy backed away from the car a half a step.

"Your uncle sent me to pick you up, that's why."

"Why would he do that?"

"Do you know Detective Lorenz?" Karen asked, trying to think of some excuse to get the child into the car. It was kind of ironic, she had spent a good portion of her career speaking to children at schools about the dangers of getting into cars with strangers. But she was a cop damn it. This little brat was not supposed to be questioning her.

"Vito? Yeah, I know Vito," Evy replied, her wariness

forcing her politeness out the window.

"Well, it's his birthday today. We're throwing him a surprise birthday party and your Uncle Gregg sent me to pick you up."

"Why didn't he just come himself?"

"He's busy thinking of an excuse to get Vito down to Gus's."

A horn blared and ripped Evy's attention away from the police officer. She turned around to see Amanda waving her over to the van.

"There's my ride, I've got to go."

"What about the party?" Karen called after her in defeat.

"Amanda can take me there, she probably knows about it anyway," Evy called back.

Karen's hand trembled as she held the butt of her revolver in her hand. She wanted nothing more than to be able to swing her gun up and blow the little bitch's brains out all over pretty Miss Priss's minivan, but that wouldn't serve her purpose at all. In fact, she was becoming aware of the fact nothing was going to serve her purposes anymore. Her plan was a wash, it was time for a new one.

"Who was that?" Amanda asked Evy as she piled into the back seat.

"Some cop friend of Uncle Gregg's."

"What did she want?"

"She said something about a surprise birthday party for Vito. She said she was supposed to take me to see my Uncle Gregg."

"A party? For Vito? Gregg didn't say anything to me," Amanda questioned.

"Why should he?"

"What do you mean?"

"I don't know what that cop lady was talking about, but I think she's nuts."

"Why do you say that honey?"

"Because, mine and Vito's birthdays are the same, and it's not my birthday. Not even close to my birthday," Evy said, contemplating the meeting for several moments before reaching up and giving Corrina her customary pinch.

The two girls swatted at each other back and forth while Amanda tuned them out and thought about the strange occurrence. She thought of dialing Gregg several times and asking him what was going on, but decided she'd be seeing him soon enough and she would ask him about it then. It was probably nothing more than some little misunderstanding.

* * *

Gregg gasped when he caught his first glimpse of Vito. It looked as though the man hadn't slept since the last time he had seen him. And he knew he hadn't bathed from the smell of him.

"What going on?" he asked, his hand still perched on the doorjamb in an uninviting manner.

"I stopped by your sister's place and Freddie told me you were here. What's going on?" Gregg asked.

"Nothing, just going over a few things."

"Like what?" Gregg asked, ducking under Vito's arm.

Vito didn't answer. He knew Haskell wouldn't need him to.

"Christ almighty, did a tornado touch down in here?"

"What are you talking about, the maid just left," he gave a twisted smile.

"You need to fire her. I see you've been going over the case," Gregg commented, scanning the walls Vito had turned into an easel.

Black, red, blue and green marker streaked the walls in colored lettering. Vito had pretty much reconstructed the same mess he had had in the break room back at the precinct, only this time, his living room walls served as his canvas.

Glancing around the room Gregg was stunned at how much damage one man could do. There were no less than half a dozen Styrofoam cups with varying amounts of stale coffee sitting around the room. A two and a half foot tall ashtray in the shape of a horse's head sat with nearly an entire pack's worth of cigarette butts scattered in the bottom of the amber glass. Most of the cigarettes had been lit, set down and never touched again. Long strands of gray ash sat like zombie worms in a B grade horror movie.

Vito's hair was wild and clearly unwashed. His shirt bore

so many stains it reminded Haskell of a tie-dyed shirt from his hippie youth. He shook his head and laughed, unable to hold it back.

Vito glanced at him with a serious scowl. "Stoddard would have your ass if she knew you were here."

"Yeah, well, I think she wants a piece of my ass any way. And she definitely will once she realizes I didn't call her on this latest one."

Vito snapped his head around to face Gregg. "What do you mean, latest one."

"You can scratch Thom "Mia" Tran off your list," he pointed to a spot on Vito's wall, somewhere between Kareem Abdul Jabbar and a poster of DeNiro from Taxi Driver where Mia's name was written in red marker.

"What are you talking about, it's still way too early," he argued, snatching a small calendar off the wall.

"I guess something has changed our man's agenda. He's gone over the edge, Vito. She was completely beat to shit. I mean beaten literally to death. And there was no message on her body."

"He's freaking out. What could have pushed this maniac?"

"Me."

"What? How?" Vito asked.

"I can't really explain things right now. I'm not really too sure what is going on yet, but I have my suspicions. And if they pan out, it's really going to be ugly. I just came over to tell you to watch your ass. Don't trust anyone right now. No one."

"You're starting to make me nervous, partner," Vito said, a million and one scenarios tumbling around in his brain.

"That's the safest place to be right now, Vito."

Vito opened his mouth to say something but was cut off by Haskell's ringing cell phone.

"Haskell," he answered.

"Gregg, where are you?"

"Out checking up on a lead. Why?"

"I got that name for you."

"What name?"

"The name of the person who signed out the squad car you were interested in."

"Really? Who?"

"I'd rather not say over the phone. Where can I meet you? This is big Gregg, really big," Stoddard's voice was excited and rushed.

Haskell didn't want her knowing where he was so he had to think of something on the fly. "There's a little coffee shop on the corner of Alameda and Seventh. Meet me there in fifteen minutes."

"I'll be there in ten," she said.

Gregg flipped the lid of his phone back down once he heard a dial tone. He took a deep breath and got ready to dive into the cold, deep waves of a tumultuous ocean.

"What's up?"

"I've got to go meet Stoddard right now. But hey, I meant what I said about not trusting anyone, especially not the lieutenant."

"Okay, but promise me one thing," Vito said, his voice wavering.

"What's that?" Gregg tried to force a smile, which came out looking more like a baby with gas than anything else.

"Don't you trust anyone either."

"You can count on that," he replied. As he was walking down the walkway to his car, he popped the clip on his pistol and made sure it was fully loaded. He snapped the clip back in and holstered the weapon but didn't fasten the strap. He had a feeling he was going to need every second he could get.

Gregg saw Stoddard's Escalade parked near the entrance to the coffee shop. A thin plume of exhaust curled up from the tailpipe alerting him that the motor was running. He pulled up next to her, got out of his car and slipped into the passenger side of hers. Karen immediately threw the vehicle into gear and pulled out of the lot and out onto the street.

"There's a coffee there for you," she offered.

"Thanks," he replied, snapping off the lid and blowing at the steam while trying to act as normal as possible. His every nerve was tense, and his hands were on the verge of trembling uncontrollably.

The tension inside the car was nearly insurmountable. Gregg wanted to say something to her so badly he could taste it.

But what if he was wrong about her? What if she really did know who the killer was, and it wasn't herself?

"What happened to your hand?" he finally asked, pointing to her bandaged knuckles.

"I tripped and fell out in the parking lot. I'll never learn, I was wearing pumps," she laughed.

"So, who is this guy?"

"You're not going to believe it when I tell you."

Gregg put his coffee down and rested his hand on his gun inside his jacket. "Karen, pull over."

"What?"

"It's over Karen."

"What are you talking about?"

"Karen, I know it's you."

"What are you talking about Detective Haskell?" she tried to sound official.

"I can't even begin to tell you what your motives are for doing this, but I know you killed those girls. It's over," he tried to raise his voice, but suddenly his strength was waning. His vision began to blur, and he was finding it harder and harder to stave off sleep. It slowly dawned on Haskell there must have been something in his coffee. The narcotic was powerful, and fast, working so quickly he never even had the chance to admonish himself for his rookie mistake.

Karen looked over at him and grinned. She spun the steering wheel sharply to the right and struck the edge of a small utility pole with just enough force to deploy the passenger side air bag. Even though she had disconnected hers in anticipation of this moment, she still flinched expectantly when the car came to an abrupt halt. Gregg's airbag deployed, forcing his head back into the headrest and his hand away from his gun. Within seconds, Stoddard had a set of handcuffs on him and had secured both his Glock and his backup piece. Greg was still dazed and fuzzy when Stoddard pulled her Escalade back onto the road.

"This is far from over detective," she sneered and slammed the butt of his gun into his temple before he was able to fully recover.

Karen wound her way through the city streets, away from

the patrol officers who were responding to an accident on the boulevard. She turned her police scanner up and headed for the safety of her sanctuary where she could formulate her new plan and put it into motion.

Chapter Fifteen

Vito rolled over and grabbed his clock. He held the little black box close to his face until he was able to focus on the diminutive green luminescent numbers. He could almost hear Lizbeth's voice nagging in his ear telling him to abandon his vanity for a pair of glasses. Another round of loud rapping noise echoed through the house.

"Who the hell is knocking at my door at this hour?" Vito grumbled and threw the covers over the side of his bed.

He had ignored the doorbell ringing and the knocking for as long as he possibly could hoping the Jehovah's witnesses would just go away and leave him alone. But they didn't stop, in fact they only grew more persistent. Vito stomped through the house, contemplating a return trip to his bedroom to retrieve his sidearm from his nightstand, but then remembered he couldn't even find the damned thing. Whoever this was with balls big enough to even dare to disturb him at such an unruly hour was damned good and lucky he was in a good mood. He was convinced it was Karen pounding on his door and a few well-placed digs would chase her away soon enough, affording him the luxury of a few more minutes of much needed shut eye before attacking the world yet another day.

"This better be fucking good," he bellowed as he jerked open the door. His surprise must have been obvious because the moment Evy saw him she giggled with teenage delight.

"Hey, Vito, how's it hanging?" She smiled, covered her mouth and snickered.

Vito stared back dumbstruck at the child and her partner in crime. The morning was uncharacteristically chilly for that time of year and a gust of cold breeze made him instantly aware of his lack of clothing.

"You must be Amanda," Vito stammered, trying to be as nonchalant as humanly possible considering the circumstances.

She nodded. Her nose was glistening and her cheeks aglow from the biting morning wind. It was obvious she was cold, but Vito just stared back at the two girls.

"Hey, Vito, you gonna ask us in, or what?" Evy asked in a tone and manner her Uncle Gregg would have never approved of. In fact, Vito was certain Gregg would have chastised her for it. Vito brought out the best in the child.

"Yeah, sure. Sorry about that," he said, waving a welcoming arm across his threshold as he slowly emerged from his dream induced stupor.

"Sorry to barge in like this, but I didn't know where else to turn."

A creepy feeling of dread enveloped Vito as her words sunk in. "Where's Haskell? I mean, Gregg?"

"I don't know, Vito," Amanda replied, her face immediately dropping to the floor.

"He's missing, Vito, and all sorts of other weird stuff happened too," Evy gushed. She was excited with the prospect of being able to solve a real mystery, just like her uncle and failed to grasp the enormous gravity of what was actually happening.

"He's not missing, Evy, not really," Amanda said, her voice quivering with each syllable.

"This sounds like it might take more than a few minutes, should I get dressed?" he glanced down, hoping his thin boxers were keeping everything contained.

"I think you might want to."

"Yeah, and take a quick shower too," Evy pinched her nose and giggled.

Vito quickly disappeared down the darkened hallway to the bathroom. He took a U.S. Navy regulation three-minute shower and was back out to the kitchen before the coffee pot even finished brewing. He knew teaching Evy how to make coffee would pay off someday. He pulled a chair up across from Amanda. The lines around her eyes made it obvious she hadn't slept very much, and something was bothering her terribly.

"Now, what's going on?" he asked, still toweling his hair.

"Gregg didn't come home last night."

Vito thought about this for a minute, and as uncharacteristic as it was, he didn't feel it was anything to lose sleep over just quite yet.

"Maybe he worked all night. Did you call the precinct?"

"Yep, and Juicy Lucy said she ain't seen him all night," Evy interrupted.

"Evy, you know your uncle would never approve of you speaking in that manner," Amanda admonished with a suppressed grin.

"Yes, ma'am," she scrunched her face and crossed her arms across her chest in mock disgust.

Vito couldn't help but laugh. "So, Lucy didn't see him all night. That doesn't mean too much, the precinct can be pretty hectic at times. There are times when our paths never cross. Granted, those times are few and far between, but they do happen."

Evy opened her mouth to say something but a look from Amanda cut her off even before she began.

"Lucy asked around, no one has seen him all night. She even went as far as to call central dispatch. The last call from Gregg was before five yesterday evening."

"Yeah, he didn't even call in ten-ten," Evy blurted before she could be stopped.

"What? Now, that is a little strange. Gregg's a stickler for the rules. He would have never gone this long without calling in," Vito said, a sickly feeling invading the pit of his stomach.

"And there's something else too. When is your birthday?" Amanda asked.

"July twenty-third, same as Evy's. Why?"

"See, I told you. She didn't believe me when I told her."

"It's not that I didn't believe you, I just needed to check it out for myself."

"You didn't believe me," Evy huffed.

"What does our birthdays have to do with anything?" Vito asked.

"Somebody tried to kidnap me yesterday after school."

"What? No way, you've got to be kidding me."

"Yes, way."

"Who Evy? Why tried to kidnap you?"

"A cop."

"You don't know it was a cop, Evy," Amanda said.

"Yes, I do."

"No, you don't. It was just someone dressed up in a cop's uniform."

"Nope, she was too a cop," she argued.

"Whoa, whoa, whoa, you two. What are you talking about?" Vito asked, looking at Evy.

His head was suddenly throbbing. It wasn't he didn't respect Amanda's opinion, but he knew the girl, and he also knew she was seldom one to embellish or lie. And not only that, she was sharp as a whip.

Evy waited until she was certain Amanda wasn't going to interrupt her once she got going. "I was coming out of school yesterday, by the auditorium. I was late because the coach was giving me some diagrams of some new plays she was working on and she wanted me to study them. Well, anyway, I was late coming out and while I was waiting for Amanda and Corrina to pick me up, some lady cop called me over to her car."

"Do you know who she was?"

"No, I don't think so, but she certainly knew you, and Uncle Gregg."

"Why do you say that?"

"Because, she wanted me to get into the car with her. She said Uncle Gregg was taking you to Gus's and we were supposed to meet you there for a surprise birthday party. Your birthday party. Well, obviously I knew she was lying."

"I want you to think about this next question very carefully, Evy. Besides her being in uniform, and in a patrol car, what made you think she was a cop?" Vito's face was already criss-crossed with worry lines.

"I don't know exactly; it was in her eyes. And the way she smelled."

"What do you mean the way she smelled?"

"She smelled like the lotion you guys have down where Uncle Gregg works. The kind that smells sort of like suntan lotion."

Winn/Circle of Friends   282

"What lotion?"

"In the bathroom," she replied.

"There isn't any lotion in the bathroom, Evy, not unless someone accidentally left it there."

"Uh huh, there's a bottle of it on the counter."

"Maybe it's only in the women's bathroom, Vito," Amanda offered.

"Maybe, Which bathroom, Evy?"

"The one Juicy, I mean Sergeant Davenport lets me use."

Vito reached for the phone and quickly punched in a number. The blood running through his veins was colder than ice water.

"Davenport," he blurted, before she could get her whole spiel out.

"Lorenz?"

"Yeah, this is Lorenz."

"Where you been, baby, momma's been missing you," she cackled.

"Listen, Lucy, I don't mean to be rude, but I don't have much time here."

"What's on your mind sugar?"

"Two questions. Any word from Haskell yet?"

"Nope, not a peep."

"And do you have a lotion dispenser in your bathroom?"

"No, but I bring in a bottle and leave it on the counter. Why?" He sensed the inquisitiveness in her reply.

"What flavor?"

"Pina colada."

"And who besides you uses that bathroom?"

"Just the lieutenant, and the occasional visitor if they're special."

"Thanks," he replied and hung up.

"You going to tell me what this is all about?" she asked before she realized he had hung up. Lucy had been in the business long enough to know that something was up, and it wasn't good.

*   *   *

"Good morning, sunshine," Karen's voice echoed with a hollow callousness.

"Lieutenant? What's going on?" Gregg asked, riding a slow rolling wave back to consciousness.

The more he awakened the clearer his surroundings became. Karen moved out of his line of sight and Gregg tried to follow her movements, but his head was held fast by unseen restraints. He tried to move his arms, but they were restrained as well. It was then he became aware of the burning sensation in the crook of his arm. He clenched and unclenched his fist, constricting the muscles in his arm. There was a dull, constant pain in the crook from the IV needle buried in his flesh. When he concentrated hard enough, he could feel the cold, glucose solution entering his blood stream drop by drop. He closed his eyes and concentrated even harder and he could taste it.

"So, how do you like my little operation?" Karen broke the silence.

"Operation? Is that what you call this?"

"Do you have a better term?" she asked.

Gregg contemplated several replies before settling on a less abrasive approach. He tried to maintain his focus in order to compile mental notes of his surroundings. The size and shape of the Plexiglas chamber he was in. The electrical control panels on the wall in front of him. The smell of raw liver and soap gave the place an atmosphere somewhere between the morgue and a sleazy diner.

"Well?"

"No, I guess I don't have a better term."

"Let me say this, Gregg, I am very sorry it has had to come to this. You weren't supposed to be involved at all."

"Involved in what, Karen?"

"Don't patronize me, Gregg, I think you know exactly what is going on here."

"Karen, you're sick. You need help. I can help you, Karen."

She threw back her head and laughed, laughed harder than she had in years. It was true, unforced, unadulterated laughter.

"Help me? What in the hell makes you think I need any help? Look around you, look at what I've been able to accomplish on my own," she waved her arms like Moses parting the Red Sea.

"That's not what I meant, and you know it."

"What did you mean, then," her voice was wrought with sarcasm.

"This isn't like you, Karen. You don't really want to be doing this," Gregg let the syllables slip out in nice, soothing tones.

"What in the fuck are you talking about? You don't know me. You have never known me. You can't even begin to have a clue as to what I am like. And for your information, not to burst your bubble or anything, but this is exactly what I want to be doing."

Gregg paused to think. It was obvious he was agitating her, and he couldn't be certain what her response would be if he pushed her over the edge. He took a deep breath and hoped for the best. And more importantly, he hoped he was right.

"Would your daughter, Ashleigh, approve of your behavior?"

Gregg knew immediately he had struck a raw nerve from the look on Karen's face when she spun around to face him. The hatred in her eyes was terrifying and he could only imagine what was happening inside of her skewed mind.

"Why you insignificant piece of shit. How dare you try and use my love for my daughter against me? How dare you put words and thoughts into my little girl's mouth?"

Gregg saw the blow coming. He had even braced himself against its brutality, but there was nothing he could do to avoid her barbarous punch. Karen's fist slammed into his mouth and blood spewed forth in a torrent. His head snapped back even though his body was being restrained. He was amazed at her strength, and more than a little concerned. As she backed away from him her trembling was apparent. His prodding was extremely close to unleashing her fury.

"Should I take that as a no? Ashleigh would not approve of your behavior?" he spat from between his bloodied lips. Gregg ran his tongue around inside of his mouth, taking inventory on the damage her fist caused. Several gashes would need stitches.

Karen stormed forward and gripped him by his Adam's

apple. From the enormous amount of pressure, she was exerting it was apparent she wanted nothing more than to crush the very life out of him right then and there. Gregg swallowed hard and tried to keep from struggling. Instead, he stared into her enraged eyes and smiled crookedly.

"Don't you dare try to psychoanalyze me you prick," she leaned into him and spat into his ear.

Gregg ripped a page out of the Mike Tyson School of fighting and lashed out with the only weapon at his disposal. He bit down with everything he had. Karen ripped away from him, ripping the earring from her earlobe as he caught the metal between his teeth. Gregg said a quick prayer and braced for the onslaught he was sure was on its way. But instead, Karen stomped out of the room.

Haskell could hear her screaming and yelling from another room, but her words were muffled just enough so he couldn't make out what it was she was saying. He had a suspicion she was merely venting, trying to keep herself from hurting him. That fact alone gave him reason to suspect she had another use for him. Gregg wasn't sure what it was he had tried to accomplish by angering Stoddard, or if it had accomplished anything at all. He had just wanted to get some kind of reaction out of her, if for nothing more than to let him know whether or not she would be able to be reasoned with.

A shadow crossed the doorway seconds before Karen stepped back into the room. Haskell felt his stomach knot and wondered what was coming next. She was visibly shaken, frazzled, but smiling. Sweat dripped from the end of her nose and the tips of her ears glowed with a reddish hue.

"Nice try, detective. I'll have to admit, you almost had me there. You almost forced me to make a mistake, but I'm too smart for that. And just so you're not disappointed, when the time comes, I will get even with you for your rude comments. I can safely say your death will be quite long and painful. But that could be months, even years from now," she cackled as she slipped from the room.

*   *   *

Evy and Amanda were still at Vito's when the package arrived from Gregg. Vito turned the small white cardboard envelope over in his hands several times before opening it. He spilled the contents out onto the kitchen table and quickly glanced over them.

"What's that?" Evy asked. "It looks like my Uncle Gregg's handwriting."

"It is. It's a copy of his notebook," Vito replied, scanning through the first few pages.

"Vito, there's a note for you," Amanda pointed to the legal-size envelope with Vito's name hand written across the face of it. Shaking, he tore the envelope open and slipped out the note.

Vito, if you're reading this and I'm not there, then some very bad things have happened. I have learned some very disturbing things about this case, things that can get a man killed. In this package you'll find all my notes, I'm sure you'll know what to do with them. Do me a favor, make sure Amanda and Evy get as far away from Los Angeles as they possibly can. Thanks, and good luck. Gregg.

"What's it say, Vito?"

He paused, looking for something to be able to tell her. "Nothing squirt. Amanda, do you have someplace you can go? I mean the both of you."

"What are you talking about? Like shopping or out on the porch?"

"No, some place a bit further. A place you can stay for a while."

"For how long?" Amanda asked, uncomfortable with the waxen color washing over Vito's complexion as he read Gregg's note.

"Until I can get all of this sorted out."

"That's pretty vague, do you have some sort of time frame in mind?"

"None. But I would suspect things are going to start moving pretty quickly from here on out."

"Evy, can you please go in the other room," Amanda asked. She waited until Evy was well out of earshot before she leaned forward and whispered to Vito. "You think we're in danger, don't you?"

"Grave danger. And I don't think, I know."

"What's in that letter from Gregg?"

"He wants me to get you two out of town. And that was without his knowing about Evy's attempted abduction."

"Vito, what is going on?"

"I don't know, but I have a feeling all of the answers are in here," he patted the envelope full of secrets.

"I guess I could always take Evy to . . . "

"No, don't tell me, the less I know the better," Vito cut her off. "Once you get to where you're going, call Davenport and give her a number where I can contact you. That will be the safest."

"Vito, you're scaring me. Is Gregg all right?"

"No, I don't think so," Vito's voice trailed off.

*   *   *

Gregg's eyes darted open and he found himself stuck in the middle of a living nightmare. His thoughts were all jumbled and blind. He felt like he was playing a game of mental Marco Polo. His coherent mind would call to him from out of the darkness, teasing him with shards of reality.

"Coming back is always such a bitch," Karen smiled and spun a little pink thumb wheel in his IV bag to stop the drugs from flowing into his system. "Wouldn't want you to get too much of this stuff, now would we?"

"What are you doing, Karen?" Gregg asked. His swollen tongue and lips made his words were garbled and thick.

"I thought you might like some company," she commented while fiddling with a gurney she had wheeled in front of Gregg's chamber.

Gregg blinked his eyes several times and tried to focus. He estimated his clear coffin to be about three foot by three foot and had to be close to seven feet tall. There were thick beads of silicone caulking in the corners, more than likely to make the thing watertight. Gregg wondered if Karen knew he was deathly afraid of drowning. He watched Karen as she undid the straps and buckles on the gurney and dropped them to the sides. She then dropped the gurney into the prone position and began wheeling it out of the room.

She returned several minutes later, this time there was the shadowy lump of a human being on the gurney. A white hospital sheet covered the person and Gregg tried to prepare himself mentally for whatever show she had planned. Karen propped the head of the gurney up so Gregg and his mystery companion were as close to eye level as they could possibly get and then she pulled the sheet off.

Gregg gasped. It was Lizbeth. Her face was grotesquely swollen from having been beaten. Her olive complexion had darkened to a bitter yellow color and her eyes were so puffy Gregg doubted she would be able to see very much through the minuscule slits.

"What did you do to her?"

"She's a feisty one, I'll give her that much."

"Karen, what on earth are you doing?"

"Pay backs Gregg. I'm just taking what's mine."

"What did Lizbeth ever do to you?"

"See, there you go again, talking out of your ass. You don't even have a clue the kind of heartache this stupid bitch has caused me. But I'm going to let her tell you all of that herself. I'm going to let you hear her confession," she said, reaching over and roughly jabbing an IV needle into the woman's arm. Once the needle was taped into place, Karen turned the little wheel to start the IV drip flowing. "Just before I kill her."

Within thirty seconds Lizbeth was struggling to shake off the darkness of drug-induced hibernation. She let out a heart-stopping shriek and began thrashing around on the gurney.

"See what I mean, Gregg, she is just an unruly bitch," Karen said, unleashing a resounding slap across the woman's face.

"Karen, stop it!" he screamed and struggled against his bonds.

"The next time you feel like pushing my buttons to see how pissed off you can make me just imagine your pretty little niece keeping you company."

She spun on her heels to glare at him. He could tell by the look in her eyes he was a mere micron away from a personal meeting with the angel of death. Again, Gregg wondered what

Karen's motivation was for keeping him alive. What was stopping her from unleashing her fury upon him? She glared at him for several minutes before storming out of the room. He was sure she was standing there, contemplating her options, the least of them being was to cut him a new asshole. Suddenly the image of Raymond Kyser's trussed up corpse flashed into his mind, forcing Gregg to reevaluate pushing Karen any further toward the edge.

"Lizbeth," he called out softly. "Lizbeth, honey, can you hear me?"

"Gregg?" she replied, her voice a mangled conglomeration of wounded speech.

"Don't talk, just listen. Vito should be coming soon. He'll take care of everything. For now, I just want you to relax and quit fighting with Stoddard. Save yourself from the pain, fighting her is not doing any good, at least not for the time being."

She mumbled something so garbled it was incoherent.

"Just try to relax, this will all be over soon," Gregg's voice crackled over the two-way intercom.

"Sure it will, Haskell. Like I said before, it's just beginning," Karen said, turning up the volume on the intercom to enjoy the show.

*   *   *

Vito watched Amanda and Evy pulling away from the curb. He studied the deserted street for several minutes after they had gone, making sure no one had been watching his house and followed them once they left. He shook his head and chuckled to himself at the thought of being overly dramatic, but then all of the corpses came rushing back at him. Kendra, Evangelique, Rita, all of them, even Kyser. If this monster was able to cause that kind of damage to a human being, then they were capable of anything.

Vito sat down at the kitchen table and cracked open the copies of Gregg's notebook. There were four paper clips holding four separate sections together. Each of the sections had a blank page with only one word, a name, written on each of them as a title page. First was a name he wasn't familiar with, Ashleigh. The second was titled Gloria, the third, Freddie and finally the fourth was labeled Stoddard.

With trembling hands, Vito popped the paper clip holding the section labeled Gloria and began reading through the pages. There was a conglomeration of official documents such as phone records, accident reports, and medical documentation in addition to Gregg's hand written notes corresponding to each of the items. There had been no autopsy, at Vito's request, but the Medical Examiner had noted several points of interest in his report. Gregg had included those as well.

It also appeared as though his partner had ordered another, more thorough investigation of the vehicle Gloria had been driving on her ill-fated night. Vito had saved the vehicle from eminent destruction by listing it as evidence involved in an ongoing homicide investigation. But the truth of the matter was it had served as some sort of ghastly memorial over the years. He was never able to bring himself to visit Gloria's gravesite, but whenever the need for remembrance arose within him, he would go out to the vehicle lot where her mangled car was there to serve as a reminder.

The investigators had found signs Gloria's vehicle may have been tampered with, however, so many years had passed it was impossible to say for certain. Also, from the phone records, he was able to establish the fact someone had called Gloria at her mother's the night she had returned early to find Vito and Karen in bed. A comprehensive study of the phone records showed the same number had called Gloria's mother's residence multiple times in the past but had never once been contacted from the mother's home, not even once. The phone number traced back to a golf course equipment manager's office who, when questioned, swore he had no knowledge of the calls or even knowing how they would have been made. He claimed to have worked for the golf course for more than twenty years and was the only one with a key to his office. Gregg had annotated next to the phone records he believed the equipment manager, having found no reason to doubt him. A circle was drawn around the words "golf course" and the initials, K.S., B.S., G.M, and R.K. were scrawled along the edge of the page. Vito knew

Gregg was indicating there was some connection between the four sets of initials.

Gregg had scrawled out a hypothetical situation and timeline, giving Karen plenty of time to have tampered with Gloria's vehicle and then come back to Los Angles to make the phone call to Gloria mother's house. He was still checking on a lead that suggested Gloria's car had been ticketed and towed to the impound lot two months before her fatal accident. Haskell had also been convinced Karen's plan had been for Gloria to have never made it back to Los Angeles alive that night. She was supposed to have crashed on the way home, but for some reason, probably reasonable driving, Gloria had made it home in one piece. Haskell theorized Stoddard's intentions were to be the one who would be there to console Vito while he mourned his wife's tragic death.

Vito wiped his tears away and read some more. He felt like such an idiot for not having seen the signs back then. They were obvious. With trembling hands Vito set the section labeled Gloria off to the side and picked up the few pages dedicated to his brother-in-law.

Detective Haskell had reevaluated all of the evidence involving the shooting death of Officer Freddie Mascho. There were several different ballistics reports in the file. One report for each of the shooters, Freddie, Perp A, Perp B and Officer Karen Stoddard. As Vito read through the file, he began to realize how involved Karen had been in Freddie's death. He had always known she was one of the officers on the scene, but never realized she had been one of the primaries. According to the official findings, all rounds had been accounted for and had been assigned to each shooter. Freddie went through the door first and Karen quickly followed. Immediately they began taking fire. Freddie returned fire, striking Perp A in the leg. Freddie had been taking cover behind a partition wall when Perp B returned a barrage of fire. One of the rounds pierced the wall and struck Freddie in the throat. He staggered out from behind his cover and took two more rounds, both missing his vest, before Officer Stoddard had been able to reload and return fire. At this point Officer Stoddard was able to target Perp B and take him out with a clean shot to the head. All wrapped up nice and neat. It was ruled a justified shoot with an unfortunate outcome.

According to his notes, Haskell didn't have any faith in the validity of the officer involved shooting report. The detective had done some digging of his own and had come up with a completely different scenario. Haskell's findings alluded to the fact not all of the rounds had been accounted for, at least not according to the way the report had been written. By his count he felt two of Stoddard's had not been accounted for. And he was quite curious as to why the report had been signed off on so easily. He did some background checking and found out the IAD captain was in the same class at the academy with Stoddard's father, Captain Blake Stoddard. Things started falling into place, or more precisely, out of place.

The way Haskell saw it, for one reason or another, Stoddard froze on entry. She was either too scared, or quite possibly she never had any intention on entering the building at all. Freddie was quickly pinned down behind the dining room wall but had been able to keep the perps pinned down in the kitchen. At first Gregg had thought the reports had been fudged merely to cover up Karen's ineptitude and inability to react under duress, but then when the recovered round count was off by two rounds he became suspicious something much more ominous was going on. Gregg felt Karen's rounds had been too well placed to have been fired during the heat of a gun battle. Especially the kill shot. Haskell had taken the autopsy report to a private lab and had it analyzed. There were impressions in the paper suggesting there were two reports. The impressions in the paper also hinted there were more rounds in Freddie's corpse than were officially reported. Gregg had plans of submitting these findings to the state's attorney in hopes of exhuming Freddie's body to retrieve the missing rounds. At the very bottom of Gregg's notes was a handwritten scribble to himself. *Did Lizbeth suspect Stoddard had something to do with Freddie's death?*

Vito set the papers down and got up to pour himself another cup of stale coffee. He splashed some water on his face while waiting for the microwave to finish with its task.

"I'll be a son of a bitch," Vito commented and sat back

down. His head was throbbing with disbelief, but there it was, in black and white. In fact, some of it was so obvious Vito couldn't believe he had never seen it before.

Next, Vito spread the packet labeled Stoddard out across the kitchen table. It wasn't a conglomeration of reports, data and cold, hard evidence like the rest of the packets had been. It was merely a collection of Haskell's thoughts. On one of the pages he had drawn out a chart weighing the pros and cons of his assumptions. He continually came back to the same conclusion, there was no logical reason for Karen Stoddard to be killing these young women, no matter what the evidence suggested. Haskell had even pondered the fact he had accidentally stumbled upon Stoddard's dark secrets about Gloria and Freddie and there was absolutely no connection between her and these unfortunate girls' deaths whatsoever.

Vito began getting the feeling Haskell was grasping at straws. He couldn't explain away Karen's connections to both Gloria and Freddie's deaths, including damn good motives, but he couldn't even get close to connecting her to the other murders. He wondered what evidence Gregg had pointing him in that direction. His head throbbing, Vito began collecting the sheaves of paper and clipped them back together with the packet they belonged to. It was then the most damning evidence came to light.

The receipt was nothing more than a tiny scrap of paper Gregg had stapled to one of the pages with his handwritten explanation. Vito recognized it immediately as a chain of custody voucher from the motor pool. Gregg had circled the car's identifying number, the dates and times it was signed out and the signature of who signed it out. Vito grabbed his cell phone and dialed the number at the top of the voucher.

"Garage, Keeps, speaking," a voice echoed over the clamor of pneumatic tools and revving engines.

"Keeps, this is Detective Lorenz."

"Hey, Vito, how's it hanging?"

"A little too low and much too far to the left for my tastes," they both laughed at the warped sense of phallic humor.

"What can I do for you?"

"Check on a vehicle for me."

"Ours or theirs?"

"Ours."

"Okay, let me grab the book. Shoot."

"Eleven Adam Seventeen."

After several seconds of filling the telephone receiver with the sounds of shuffling paper Keeps came back on the line.

"That's one of those damned piece of shit cars we got two years ago. The ones they recalled because of bad steering gear and then the parts suppliers kept going bankrupt. It's been more than two years and we still haven't been able to get them all back on the road. To tell you the truth, we've sort of given up on it. We just wait until one of the rookie blue suits wrecks one of the others and then hopefully we can rob enough from Peter to pay Paul if you know what I mean."

"Okay," was all that Vito could think of in reply. He hadn't wanted the entire history of the fleet, just a little information.

"What's on your mind, Vito?"

"I just wondered how one of those cars has made it out onto the streets, and several times at that."

"The brass takes them out when they want to take a friend or a family member on a ride along or some shit like that. Most the time we don't have a car to loan them, so I let them take those."

"And they're allowed to do that?"

"Yes and no."

"What in the hell does that mean?"

"No, they're not supposed to take those cars on the road, but since the recall only mentioned high speed maneuvering problems, I figured a little ride along wouldn't hurt anything. Besides, they sign my paycheck if you know what I mean."

"Can you imagine ever getting a paycheck again if someone were to have an accident after you let them sign out one of those cars? Not to mention the lawsuits heaped on the city?"

"No, I guess not. I never thought about it."

"Well, you need to start thinking about it or you'll find your ass over the coals quicker than shit. Now, I got one more question for you."

"Shoot," he replied, his voice taking on a nervous edge.

Keeps pondered just how close he had come to giving up his pension.

"What do you do with the bad steering gear sets?"

"We scrap them."

"How do you do that?" Vito spoke very slowly and clearly, trying to get his point across.

"Oh, yeah. Honestly, we toss them out back in a bin. The vendors were supposed to be picking up the bad ones in trade, but like I said, they keep going bankrupt."

"Don't you get them mixed up?"

"No, the bin is clearly marked and each one of the steering gear has its own scrap tag on it."

"And what kind of car is that gear compatible with?"

"Any number of Dodge's or Chrysler's I'd suppose."

"Thanks a lot, Keeps, I owe you one."

Vito dropped his cell phone onto the kitchen table with a loud clunk and dropped his face into his hands. Although Haskell's package probably contained enough circumstantial as well as hard evidence to convince a jury, it was having a harder time with Vito. Mainly because he didn't want to believe it. If it were true, then he had missed these clues over and over again during the past several years. And if that were the case, then these girls died because he refused to see the truth.

Vito was going through Lizbeth's desk when he heard the front door open.

"Freddie, is that you?" he called out.

"Yeah," Freddie yelled out, even though he was standing less than a foot behind his uncle. He burst out into gut busting laughter until he saw the stoic look on Vito's face.

"Do you know the password to your mom's computer?"

Freddie thought about the consequences for a couple of seconds before reaching over to the keyboard and tapping in several keystrokes.

"I'm not even going to ask," Vito smiled.

After several minutes of snooping through Lizbeth's computer files he came up empty. Her computer was void of any personal information whatsoever.

"Well that was pretty much a dead end," he sighed

"She has a couple of flash drives to store her files on,"

Freddie revealed after several minutes of silence.

"Where does she keep those?"

"In there," he pointed to the bottom desk drawer.

"Is there a key?"

"You're not going to tell, are you?"

"Freddie, I need that key."

"Hang on," he sighed and bounded up the stairs to his bedroom. He returned within a couple of minutes and handed a key to Vito.

"I won't say anything about this, but I suggest you lose it, and never find it again."

Freddie nodded while Vito riffled through the desk drawer until he found the flash drives and slipped them into the USB ports on the front of the computer. Freddie stood beside him, watching curiously. He knew whatever his uncle was up to, it had something to do with finding his mother.

"Vito, why haven't I cried yet?" the boy asked, catching Vito completely off guard, literally stealing his breath away.

"What do you mean, Freddie?" he asked.

"I cried when my dad was killed, why not now?"

Vito had nothing to say.

"Does it mean I don't really love her?"

"Oh, God no, Freddie," he blurted and tugged the boy into his arms. "You know you love your mother, and she knows it too."

"But why haven't I cried?"

"You haven't cried because your mother's not dead. And she never will be, at least not before her time. You don't accept that fact, and neither do I."

"But Grandma says we never know when our time is gonna come."

"Well, I know it's not your mother's time. I'd love to discuss this with you Freddie, but right now, I really need your help. Now, where does she keep her secret drive, the one she doesn't let anyone see?"

"You mean the ones with her journal on it?"

"That might be a good place to start."

"She keeps that online in the cloud, at a secure storage service," the boy said, quickly signing onto the Internet.

Once they were logged onto the Internet and within a few more clicks they were at the web site where Lizbeth's deepest, darkest desires and secrets were stored away from prying eyes. Or so she thought.

"How do we get into her account?"

"You have to know the password."

"Do you know it?"

"I cracked it a couple of times, just messing around giving her some birthday present hints, but she got sneakier about it. Let me give it a try."

Freddie banged away at the keyboard for better than fifteen minutes. For every three wrong tries he entered he would have to log off, clear the computer cache, and restart everything all over again. The tedium was working on Vito's last nerve and watching Freddie struggle with the keyboard wasn't helping matters much.

"You want something to drink?"

"Is there pop?"

"Sure is, apple juice or orange juice flavored."

"Funny, ha, ha. Orange juice please."

Vito disappeared into the kitchen, leaving Freddie to face the trials and tribulations of computer hacking on his own. In the kitchen, Vito's mind drifted as he tried to piece together all the information Haskell had dropped into his lap. Orange juice spilled all over the counter as a result of Freddie's triumphant war whoop as he ran into the kitchen to share it with his uncle.

"And your mother wonders why I don't have any kids."

"I got it, I got it."

"Good, now let me get to work."

"You'll never guess what she used."

"I don't have a clue."

"My batting average and your initials."

"And you had a hard time with that?" Vito jabbed.

"Yeah, well at least I know how to spell your initials," Freddie laughed.

"Why don't you give me a few minutes to look through this stuff? I don't think she'll appreciate me reading it and I know she won't want you reading it."

"You're no fun," Freddie smiled as he left the room. Within

minutes Vito recognized the sounds of the boy's Playstation echoing through the house.

His hands trembled as he flipped through the electronic pages of his sister's secret life. There was more about Karen in Lizbeth's journal than Vito could have ever imagined. There were many references about Karen calling and threatening Lizbeth about many different things. Everything boiled down to one event, one tragic event. Karen's being partnered with Freddie Mascho. This was a tidbit Vito hadn't even known about.

Karen and Freddie had been partnered together just about the time he and Lizbeth started seeing each other regularly. He continually complained about Karen hitting on him at work. Lizbeth wanted him to file sexual harassment charges against her, but Freddie told her it wouldn't be a very good idea for two reasons. First, it would ruin his macho image, they laughed about that one. And two, Karen's father was a pretty powerful man and could really screw things up for Freddie, like making sure he was assigned to dangerous patrol areas. They didn't find that so funny. That was when Karen and Lizbeth had their first run in.

A couple of years went by and Karen asked to be transferred to another partner. Vito deduced this was about the same time he and Karen had met one another at some after hour's function at Gus's. Vito had more to drink than he should have and had almost succumbed to her temptations then. It wasn't much, but it was enough to endear him to her.

Lizbeth had never liked Karen, a fact she had never even tried to keep a secret. She had nagged Vito about his relationship with her so much he eventually quit going over to his sister's for dinner. He chose to ignore the guilt tearing at his soul and maintain his clandestine relationship with his co-worker.

That elicited round number two between Karen and his sister. Lizbeth, fed up with Vito's cheating on Gloria and his refusal to discuss it with her, was left with no other recourse and confronted Karen with her disapproval. According to her journal, this is where things started getting out of hand. Freddie claimed Karen had started coming onto him more and more at work, even going as far as to walk into the shower room when he was in there alone. When he jumped her about the incident and even threatened to go to human resources with it if she persisted, she became very combative.

Vito reflected on his relationship with Karen and tried to recollect the time frame. Most of it was a blur of alcohol and bad decisions, but it was clear enough for him to remember these confrontations between Karen, Freddie and Lizbeth were just around the same time Karen had begun planting the seeds for her plan of getting pregnant, something she would do for Vito.

Vito scanned through entry after entry in Lizbeth's electronic journal, taking a disturbing trip down memory lane. He froze when he came to a section written before Freddie had been killed. It was about a series of conversations her and her husband had shared together late at night. Vito was ready to flip through the section when something caught his eye. Freddie had responded to a bomb threat at a local abortion clinic and had run into Karen Stoddard, but not in uniform. She was a patient. This was right after Gloria had been killed and Vito had withdrawn into a shell, alienating everyone, including Karen. Freddie mentioned this meeting to Lizbeth who then confronted Karen about it.

Vito grabbed Haskell's notes and started comparing them with Lizbeth's journal. All the pieces seemed to fit. Vito was amazed at Karen's ability to cloud his mind so badly he was never able to see her for who she really was, a manipulating, self-serving killer. Vito grabbed his cell phone and dialed the precinct. Davenport answered.

"Lucy, I need you to do something for me."

"What's that?"

"I need you to check out something but be very discreet. Remember, I'm officially suspended, so you can't let anyone know you're running down leads for me. I'd hate to see you get your ass in a sling over me."

"Oh, oh, you're starting to sound like me," she laughed. "And I'd put my ass in a sling for you anytime. And I've got just the sling for you at home, baby," she laughed with a wink.

"I mean it, Luce, you not only have to keep this under

wraps, you have to be careful about who you talk to.'"

"What are you wanting to know?"

"I need to know everything you can find out about George Masarick. Everything. Specifically, any property he might own here in the city. And see if he had any dealings with Raymond Kyser or Blake Stoddard."

"Isn't that?"

"Yes, it is," he cut her off.

"Does this have anything to do with what you're working on?"

"I'm afraid it does."

"So then, I know who to look out for?"

"Exactly. How long do you think this will take?"

"Hard to tell, but I'm sure I will know something more by the end of the day."

"Good. Meet me at Gus's when you get out of work. I've got a few things I have to take care of but I can be there around six or a little after."

"Sounds good to me, Sugar."

"And Luce, can you procure me some protection?"

"I don't suppose you're talking about the fun kind."

"Sorry to disappoint you. Hey, I gotta go, someone's trying to call through," Vito said, pushing a button on the phone.

"What took you so long?" Karen's voice sang. She was in one of her moods.

"I was talking to someone."

"Davenport?"

"None of your business."

"Don't get smart with me Vito, you can't afford it right now."

Lorenz refused to say anything. He didn't want to play into her hands, nor did he want to spout off and say something he would regret due to his increasing anger. The last thing he wanted to do was to tip his hand and give her an advantage. He used Lizbeth and Gregg and the trouble they were in to keep from saying something antagonistic.

"Are you ready to listen?"

"Depends on what you've got to say, I guess."

"I'm tired of playing games with you, Vito. You've got until midnight, and then I start delivering bodies, one by one. And I can't promise you in which order they will come in. And Vito, you had better come alone or bring a lot of body bags."

"I don't know where I'm supposed to come to."

"That's one of the things you need to figure out for yourself. You're the great detective. This should be a piece of cake for you to solve."

"Karen, why are you doing this?"

"If you don't know, then you might as well pack it in right now."

"Let me talk to Lizbeth," he spat.

"If you insist," she set the phone down. Vito could hear a clamor of indistinguishable sounds echoing in the background. And then Lizbeth's voice. She was calling out to him and screaming, screaming in pain. "Would you like to talk to her again?" Karen taunted.

"Don't you fucking hurt her," he threatened.

Karen laughed thickly. "Hurt her? I'm going to kill her, Vito. You've got until midnight," Karen hung up the phone.

Chapter Sixteen

"You know I should just tell you to fuck off, right?" Gus said, his eyes flickering with fatherly disappointment and a tinge of anger.

"And I wouldn't blame you a bit."

"Tell you to eat shit and grin?"

"I'd understand completely."

"Tell ya not to let the door hit ya, where the good Lord split ya?"

"You tell me that all the time anyway, you old fart," Vito said and they both laughed. "Gus, I'm really sorry. I was way out of line."

"Yes, you were."

"And thank you."

"For all the good it did. I heard all about some of the shit you've pulled the last coupla weeks," his face was still stern and sour, but it quickly smoothed over. "But I also know your reasons. What can I do for ya, son?"

"More like bullshit excuses, Gus. One of these days I'll learn to listen to you. I need to use your place upstairs. I need some place I can trust."

"You got it," he replied and pulled a single key out of his pocket before handing it to Vito. "Anything else?"

"Yeah. How well did you know Captain Stoddard?"

"Blake? We had a few run ins, some good, some bad. Anything specific you want to know?"

"Why did he retire so early and give up half his pension? He always struck me as the lifer type. The kind the coroner retires."

"He was, but then he struck it rich."

"How'd he do that?"

"Real estate. Word has it he hooked up with that famous rich guy, Ray something or another. You know, the guy who owned all those hotels down along the waterfront."

"Kyser?"

"Yeah, Ray Kyser. I guess old Blake cut him some slack one time when he was younger, still a patrol officer, and Kyser never forgot about it."

"Interesting. Very interesting indeed."

Just then Lucy Davenport burst through the front door in her usually jovial mood. She hugged and kissed all the men she knew and plopped down on the laps of the ones she didn't. After several minutes she spied Vito at the back of the bar and made a beeline for where he and Gus stood talking.

"I gotta hand it to ya Lucy, ya sure know how to be discreet," Gus laughed, shook his head and disappeared back behind the bar.

"Honey, that was discreet," she smiled and winked at him.

"Follow me," Vito said, opening a door leading to the back storeroom.

Vito prayed the rickety staircase would hold both Davenport and his fat ass, at least until they were safely on the upper landing. He opened the door and then held it open for Lucy.

"My Lord, I've heard about this place, but I ain't never seen it," she exclaimed as she stepped into the tiny apartment.

The room was a small apartment Gus had "donated" to his comrades in blue to use as a safe house. If they were having troubles with the women in their lives, they were welcome to stay a night or two until they sorted things out. Mainly it was a place where CI's, confidential informants, could be stashed until the main players in a case could be rounded up. Occasionally, it was used to house a runaway or a battered wife when the shelters were full or closed. And it had, on occasion, been used as a hideaway for officers who might have found themselves on the wrong end of the book. Gus would negotiate their surrender, so things went peacefully. Vito preferred conducting his business there because it was completely electronics free. Gus, being an amateur CIA spook with more than a dozen conspiracy theories floating around in his head, was constantly sweeping the place for taps and bugs just to ensure its confidentiality. Vito doubted there was some great conspiracy going on, but he left Gus alone about his paranoid diversions. However, the more he learned about this case and the people involved the more he wondered if the old man really wasn't that far off base.

The apartment was about as basic as it could get. There was a small single bed in the middle of the floor, complete with dingy yellow sheets. An ancient thirteen-inch black and white television sat on a milk crate near the foot of the bed. It was small, but it was hooked up to the bar's cable television system so a guest would be able to receive all one hundred and fifty channels of shit. The bathroom had a tiled floor with a drain in the center and a handheld showerhead in a bracket super glued to the wall. The kitchen consisted of a couple of milk crates full of Styrofoam plates, cups and plastic silverware and a battered microwave sitting on the only counter. Vito pulled up a couple of milk crates for Lucy and him and invited her to sit down.

"Uh, uh honey, I am not walking out of here with waffle butt," she smiled.

"Suit yourself," he said and plopped noisily down onto the makeshift chair generously donated by McDonald's Dairy. "So, what did you find out?"

"I wasn't able to find out a whole lot, but the people I spoke with claim Masarick has had more than a few dealings with Raymond Kyser. And Blake Stoddard's name pops up more often than not in those same dealings. Cozy, huh?" she asked, seeing the look deep concern wash over Vito's face.

"A lot cozier than you can imagine. I'll bet Kyser also shared certain other interests with Captain Stoddard as well."

"How did you know?"

"I'm just starting to piece things together darling."

"There were three properties here in Los Angeles that all three of them, Kyser, Stoddard and Masarick had an equal interest in."

"Let me guess, a warehouse off Vernon is one of them. We've checked that place out thoroughly and came up empty. In fact, it was in the process of being sold when Kyser was killed."

"There's also a golf course and an abandoned

slaughterhouse out in the valley," she said, handing him a slip of paper with the addresses on them.

"Thanks."

"Something else kind of strange too."

"What's that?"

"No one has heard from George Masarick in several weeks. He was out of town on business and was due back a week ago last Monday, but Karen called in sick for him. She called back on Wednesday saying that he had a mild case of pneumonia and he would be out of work indefinitely. I checked with his doctor and that's the first he heard of George being ill."

"That's not good. That's not very good at all," Vito said, as he stood up and slipped his jacket on. "Boy, you're quite the detective, aren't you? And thanks a lot, Luce, you're the best," he walked over and put a nice wet peck on her cheek.

"Oh, I almost forgot. You better start watching your ass. Stoddard called the precinct."

"What did she have to say?"

"She gave a direct order to arrest you on site in connection to the murder of the Stillwater's."

"Shit, she got to him? Damn it, I never saw that coming."

"His wife too. It was ugly. Your gun was at the scene," her voice revealed that she was on the verge of tears.

"My gun was confiscated, you know that."

"Everyone else knows that as well, but an order is still an order."

"Yeah, I know."

"Don't worry about that too much. Most of the veterans, even the ones who hate your guts know you're not involved and aren't going to be looking too hard for you. And the younger guys sense the tension so they will probably try to stay out of this as well. By the way, here's a radio I swiped from dispatch so you can keep tabs on what's being said about you."

"Thanks, this will probably come in handy."

"Daddy's been poking into things too. He likes to use the private staff channel. Your radio can pick up any chatter on channel six."

"Daddy? As in Blake Stoddard?"

"Yes sir, the captain himself."

"Shit, what is that old ball buster up to?"

"Looking for a new set of balls to bust I assume. I also assume those will be your balls getting busted."

"Imagine so. Not good, not good at all."

"So, what do you do now?"

"I've got to find Karen, and I've got to do it before midnight."

"That gives you less than five hours."

"Oh, do I really have that much time?" Vito smiled, hiding the fact his throat was constricting to the point he thought he would suffocate.

*   *   *

The sun had all but set and dusk was settling in by the time Vito pulled up in front of Karen Stoddard's house. He didn't expect to find her there, but he had to start somewhere. Her house was in the same vicinity as the slaughterhouse, so Vito opted for the tried and true detective tactic of the process of elimination.

After knocking on both the front and back doors several times without any luck, Vito decided to look for an alternate way into the house. All of the windows were locked securely on the east and south sides of the house. Having helped Karen install the burglar alarm system, Vito knew the windows and doors were wired with alarms so breaking into them was not an option. There was only one viable way of entering the house undetected and he wasn't relishing the idea in the least.

Vito stared at the narrow slit of a window along the trailing edge of the house where the brick met the dirt. He knew his fat ass was probably not going to fit through the tiny portal, but he had to give it the old college try anyway. Taking off his jacket, he knelt down and pressed it firmly into the corner of the windowpane before gingerly getting back to his feet. He cursed growing old and rubbed his sore knees, trying to get the blood to return to his lower extremities. Once his legs quit tingling, Vito took aim and gave his jacket a swift, sharp kick. He felt the glass give, but the only sound was that of the broken glass shattering onto the concrete basement floor. He was relieved to find Karen hadn't installed an alarm on the basement windows like she had wanted to in the first place. He allowed himself a few minutes to rest and gather up his nerve before cleaning the window frame of the remaining shards and attempting a headfirst plunge through the rabbit's hole.

The slide into the house hadn't gone as smoothly as Vito would have liked. He ended up tumbling ass over tipple cart, landing on his palms in the shards of broken glass scattered across the basement floor. Now sore, bleeding and blinded by darkness, Vito staggered through the basement, cursing and looking for both a light switch and a rag to wrap around his bleeding palms. His search for a working light switch ended fruitlessly after ten minutes or so. For every wasted movement he made, another tick of the clock fell away into oblivion.

Vito pulled a small flashlight from his pocket and was quickly reminded of how lax he had become in his job. He should have been carrying a large, four D-cell battering ram sized flashlight instead of this hobby light. His miniature flashlight illuminated the room enough for him to see a good three inches in front of him. He crept up the basement stairs and cautiously moved from room to room throughout the rest of the house. After ensuring the house was clear he stood in the kitchen rubbing his battered shins. He was unsure as to what avenue he should follow next. He contemplated which of the two properties to check out next. Both of them would make perfect places for Karen to hole up, the golf course would be closed at that time of night and the slaughterhouse was abandoned.

Vito had hoped to speak with George Masarick, maybe get some insight into what in the hell was going on, but it appeared the Stoddard residence had been unoccupied for some time. There was no trash in the receptacle, nor was there any food in the refrigerator, not even as much as a quart of milk or a jar of pickles. There were no dirty dishes in the dishwasher and Vito hadn't seen any dirty clothes in the laundry room. Not to mention the fact the electricity wasn't working. And then an eerie feeling washed over him as it slowly dawned on Vito the electricity was in fact working. The light in the refrigerator hadn't come on, but there had been a minute gust of cold air when he had opened the door. He quickly checked the bulb and found it had been unscrewed. A few quick turns of the small bulb and Vito was blessed with light, and a gruesome thought. There was only one reason to leave the electricity running to the roomy side-by-side.

Vito propped open the self-closing door so he would have a little bit of light and opened the freezer door. It was stuffed. Crammed completely full of white butcher paper wrapped packages of what Vito could only assume was meat. Vito tore into one of the white packages and immediately dropped it on the floor. It was indeed meat. Ground meat. Ground meat with pigmentation unlike any ground meat Vito had ever seen in his life. Morbid thoughts raced through his head. Was this George Masarick, or what was left of him anyway? Did Karen do this? Was she eating this meat? Vito ran to the sink, barely making it in time. He thought of all the nice meals she had brought to him over the past several months. Chili, tacos, spaghetti, stroganoff, everything had been made with ground meat. Even though he doubted the two things had anything to do with one another, he couldn't keep his mind from painting the gruesome pictures and Vito blew chunks again.

Wiping his mouth with his jacket sleeve as he walked to his car, Vito double-checked the address to the slaughterhouse. It was the more plausible choice over the golf course. He highly doubted Karen's plans included the two of them getting in nine holes. Not to mention, she was becoming more and more obvious as things progressed. Vito trembled with understanding. She was the proverbial black widow drawing him into her web.

*   *   *

"Did you find what you were looking for?" Karen's voice echoed across his radio.

"I don't have a clue what you're talking about, Karen" Vito replied.

"Did you say hello to George for me?"

"Karen, what is wrong with you?" Vito's stomach continued to spasm.

"Nothing, sugar," she mimicked Sergeant Davenport's voice. "I'm just sitting here all alone, wondering where my man could be."

Vito didn't respond. He couldn't think of anything to say that wouldn't be just wasted breath.

"You still don't know what this is all about, do you?"

"You mean, besides the fact you are completely off your rocker?"

"Easy, Vito, don't piss the psychopath off," she cackled. "Especially not when your sister and your best friend are involved."

Vito chose to remain silent. He could taste a trickle of blood oozing from the raw spot he was chewing on the inside of his cheek.

"Pretty sad, isn't it?"

"What's that?"

"Haskell is your best friend."

"Don't know. I never gave it much thought."

"See, that's exactly what I am talking about, Vito. You don't give a thought to much of anything."

"I've never been good at solving riddles, Karen, you should know that. Christ, our entire relationship has been nothing but one big unsolved puzzle," he tried to maintain his smart-ass tone, hoping his arrogance would push her into spitting out a clue as to what he should expect once he got to the slaughterhouse.

"By my watch you've got a little time to spare. Maybe you'd like to slip on down to Gus's for a double," her tone was hateful and mocking.

"Not tonight, I've got plans," Vito disconnected the call and turned the power off on the phone as soon as he saw the furnace stacks of the slaughterhouse incinerator looming in the distance.

Vito pulled his car as far off the rural highway as possible and parked on the grass shoulder. He pulled out his shoulder piece, a nine-millimeter Glock Lucy had given him, and made sure it was loaded. He checked the spare clip as well before dropping it into the front pocket of his jacket. He popped the glove box open, hit the trunk release and walked around to the rear of the car. He had his suspicions Karen was watching him, whether it be from near or from far he wasn't too sure. She was a stickler for details so she would be covering all the bases of that he was certain. He listened to the day. Although the air was calm and still, he didn't hear anything out of the ordinary. He studied the open field surrounding the slaughterhouse and it didn't appear as though any wildlife were moving or scurrying about unnaturally so he assumed Karen must be inside the building, watching him through a pair of binoculars, or possibly even a riflescope. The thought sent icy chills rippling throughout his body.

Vito leaned into the trunk and loaded a Remington 870 twelve gauge with five shells, racking one into the chamber. Buckshot would have been his ammo of choice, but all Lucy could find was birdshot, making the gun damn near useless. He cringed at the thought of his having to be up close and personal for the shotgun to be even the least bit effective. He pondered various ways of concealing the shotgun, but short of sliding it down the front of his pants he didn't have too many places to hide it. Vito held the gun close to the side of his thigh and hoped for the best.

Wild blackberry bushes grabbed at his skin like crows picking at roadkill. He cursed the tangled underbrush with every half step he managed to take. For the life of him he didn't understand why he was putting himself through so much shit, she knew he was coming. And he knew she knew he was coming so why the pretentious façade of a sneak attack? As he was cursing yet another patch of pain rendering berry bushes, he realized he had moved close enough to the slaughterhouse to be in gun range.

Vito stared at the windowless north wall. The only signs humanity even knew this place still existed were the various graffiti gang tags spray painted along the wall. And even those were so faded it was obvious the place had even been abandoned by the city's finest youths long ago. A green "Chacho" with black outlining encircled the face of a clown who was never intended to entertain. Once a hopping meeting place for various gangs throughout the years, the slaughterhouse now stood like a structure left behind after filming a Stephen King movie.

After creeping through the underbrush and up to the wall, Vito began sliding down the bricks toward the northwest corner. The facing of the cinder block wall was crumbling in more places than he could count and as he scooted along the wall, he could feel the paint chips and decaying concrete dropping down the neck of his jacket. Vito had to struggle to keep from dropping his guns and tearing into his itching back with his fingernails. The edge of the building where the brick met the ground was spotted with green and black mildew splotches, infusing its musty, dead smell into the brick itself.

He hadn't a clue as to how long the place had been standing idle, but from the looks of things it had been more than a few years. There were several pieces of equipment that had long succumbed to the effects of time and weather and were now nothing more than angular pieces of jagged rust. A few large freezers without doors jutted out from patches of overgrown weeds, as did dozens of barrels Vito could only speculate at their contents. Truth be told, that's as far as he wanted to take the investigation.

As he neared the northwest corner of the building, he halted his progress. He listened intently to the wind, hoping to catch some glimmer of sound or movement to help him get a bearing or some clue as to what to expect next. But there was nothing, nothing but the sweet, gentle breeze of the impending summer. In fact, it was so quiet he swore he could hear the beating of the wings of a swallow-tailed butterfly as it floated passed his face. Slowly he peeked around the corner and took inventory of the new surroundings. On the western face of the wall, somewhere near the building's dead center, there was a large sliding door. Even from where he was standing, he could see the rollers at the top of the door looked rusty and unused. It wasn't going to afford him the quiet entry Vito had hoped for. Nevertheless, with wrought iron bars covering every window in the place he was fresh out of options.

He put his ear to the wall and listened for several minutes before committing himself to a walk out into the open around to the western side of the building. As he had feared, the sliding door was firmly stuck in place. The possibility it might even be nailed or locked from the other side entered his mind. The door appeared as though at one time or another it had been used as the stock entrance into the slaughterhouse. He was just about to give up using this door as his entry point into the slaughterhouse when on the last tug the bottom of the door moved ever so slightly. Vito began kicked at the thick clumps of weeds grown up around the base of the door. He was sweating profusely by the time he had kicked at the weeds enough to loosen the door. Once he realized he was making progress Vito began digging and pulling at the weed entangled door, tearing out tufts of canary grass and weeds with his hands. Before he knew it, his palms were raw and bleeding.

Vito cursed his way over to a decrepit stock corral and grabbed one of the metal fence posts. He bent the post back and forth several times until it broke free from the earth and then used this fence post to chip away at the weeds and hard clumps of dirt separating him from his destiny. With sweat dripping from his brow, he labored at the door until he had freed it enough to slide it open just far enough for him to slip inside. Vito sucked in his gut and prayed for the best.

Once inside the clammy, dank slaughterhouse, Vito decided he liked his situation even less than he had the minute before. The interior of the building was one half shade darker than pitch black. The only objects he was able to see were the shadows of indistinguishable shapes. Vito spied shafts of dim light suspended near the ceiling of the wall furthest away from him but the source was hidden behind a small wall. He didn't think the light was bright enough to be emanating from a light fixture so he assumed there was a transom window either in the wall or over a door somewhere out of his field of vision. Staying low to the ground he inched his way toward the source of the light. Although the slaughterhouse looked as though it hadn't seen any operation in a long time, the smell of fresh death hung in the air.

The closer Vito drew to the source of the light, the more he became aware of a nauseating smell permeating the air around him. At first, he couldn't place it, but then after several minutes he recognized it as an aroma he had learned to detest as a child. A smell that infused itself into his nostrils every Christmas when his grandmother would make fegato di vitello, a dish which completely ruined a good plate of fried polenta by putting calves liver all over it. It wasn't the finished meal that bothered Vito as much as have to look at the raw, purple organ meat marinating on the kitchen table for hours. The bowl of rubbery organs lent a smell of raw flesh to the house overpowering everything else, even the gingerbread baking in the oven.

It didn't take long for his suspicions to be confirmed. Hands out in front of him, groping the darkness, Vito knocked into a container, spilling chunks of raw liver out onto the floor. He slipped in the viscous fluid and crashed into utility table and then onto the floor, spilling yet another tray of mystery flesh all over himself. Instantly every bone in his body began to ache and throb.

Involuntarily Vito began to heave. The combination of the sickening odor along with the cold, sticky sensation of the sappy fluid clinging to his skin caused Vito to convulse in an episode of violent retching.

"So much for the stealthy approach," Vito said aloud to no one as he wiped the bile from his lips, hoping it was his own. He was surprised there was even anything left in his stomach after filling Karen's sink an hour earlier.

Several minutes passed before Vito was able to recover fully from his fall and subsequent fit of nausea. His head was spinning, and his stomach felt like the morning after an all-night sour mash tango. Every time he tried to get to his feet, he would catch another whiff of the nauseating aroma and again it would steal his breath away. Superman had his kryptonite and like the Fonz, Vito had his liver. He fumbled around in his pockets until he found his trusty blue jar. Two dabs under each nostril and he was ready to go.

Leery of more surprises, Vito tentatively made his way toward the slivers of light. The further away from the spilled organs he got the more his stomach settled down. The Vick's had thankfully overpowered the repulsive odors emanating from his clothing.

Vito caught the slightest shard of sound and froze in his tracks. He could now see the rays of light were indeed radiating from a transom above a door. It was a door leading to another part of the slaughterhouse. He could only hope it was a trifle more fun than the last room.

The transom was too tall for him to see in through and the room much too dark to find anything safe to stand on so, left with only one option, Vito laid down on the floor and peered through the crack beneath the door. There was less than an inch of clearance so the only thing he was able to make out were the shadows of objects in the next room. Or more accurately, the lack of shadows. The room seemed to be extremely well lit and completely empty, yet there were unfamiliar sounds coming from within the next room. A low, barely audible, hissing. It sounded like air escaping from a pipe. The more he inspected the door the more it became apparent the door's intended use was as an exit only. There wasn't even the slightest hint of a handle or knob on his side of the door.

As quietly as possible in his battered condition Vito dug his keys out of his pocket. He sorted through them until he found his house key. It was the strongest of the bunch and had the sharpest cut teeth. He slid the key beneath the small crack under the door and pried up with as much force as he dared to use. The first several tries netted nothing more than wood splinters and skinned knuckles, but then finally the door opened enough for Vito to grip the edge with his fingertips.

As soon as the door was open a barely a crack the hissing grew louder, and Vito felt a cool breeze emanating from the doorway. Ever so carefully he inched the door open far enough for him to be able to steal a quick glance into the next room. After ensuring a safe passage, he stepped through the door and found himself standing in a "clean room". He had only seen a room like this once before, while investigating a homicide in the paint department of an auto factory. The *clean room*, as it was called, was designed to rid workers of any contaminants they may transport with them into the paint booths, ensuring the cars would remain blemish free throughout the paint process.

The room was narrow, only about five feet wide. There were several archways constructed out of half inch diameter piping, each of which was connected to a compressed air line. Each of the archways had five air nozzles on either side and four across the top designed to jet streams of filtered, compressed air when someone or something passed in front of an electric eye designed to trigger the mechanism. Vito wasn't sure why the clean room was in the slaughterhouse, whether it was to clean the workers or the meat, but he was sure its intended use was not the reason it was still operational. He assumed Karen had been using the clean room to ensure Locard's Principle of Exchange was no longer the rule. As long as Stoddard passed herself and her victims through the clean room then little or no forensic evidence would remain on the bodies for investigators to find. No forensic evidence meant no clues, and no clues meant no suspects and no leads.

The hissing air Vito had heard from the other room was coming from a pressure relief valve in the filter, meaning the clean room was still in full operation. As loud as the hissing was, he could only imagine what kind of noise the apparatus would make when it blasted a jet of cleansing air. Scanning the room for the electronic eyes, Vito seized the moment to make a brief, but futile attempt at rubbing out the soreness in his muscles and bones. He hurt in more places than he could count.

After a diligent search of the surrounding walls and ceiling, Vito found himself at a loss. There were no electronic eyes hidden anywhere. There were no sensors whatsoever. He had no clue as to how the clean room air jets were triggered into operation. He shrugged and decided he didn't time to ponder the situation any longer and forged ahead toward the door at the other end of the tunnel shaped room.

Vito's mind recognized his faux pas even before he heard the click and felt the subsequent gush of compressed air. He stepped forward, off the pressure plate, but it was already too late, the warning shot had been sounded. Somewhere deep in the bowels of the building he heard the air compressor kick on to replace the lost air pressure. He was certain Karen had heard it too.

The entrance door to the clean room had a small one-foot square porthole type window in its face, but still no door handle from Vito's side. He fumbled for his keys but then got another idea. Since his stealthy approach had been foiled, he considered the option of going for the grand, beat your drum kind of entrance and let Karen know he meant business.

Vito used another one of his keys as a makeshift screwdriver and undid one of the support hangers from the ceiling. He grabbed the pipe archways at its weak upper corner and began rocking it back and forth. Within several bends the pipe creased and bent at a weak spot near the floor, which created a pinhole to form. The air rushing out of this pinhole created an ear-piercing shriek resonating throughout the clean room. Vito rushed to the get the pipe broken off the rest of the way before he went deaf from the pierce shriek of air. He shattered the window with the pipe and jerked the door open. The piece of pipe got hung up in the window as he was going through the doorway, which caused him to lose his balance and he stumbled forward down onto his knees.

Vito saw the muzzle flash milliseconds before he heard the bullet ricocheting inside of the clean room. His clumsiness had finally served him well. He rolled away from the direction of the gunshot and prayed he could quickly find some cover. The rushing air combined with the rumble of the air compressor's motor covered the sounds of his movements.

"Glad to see you're still as graceful as ever," Karen taunted him from the shadows.

"Yeah, well, it's nice to see you're still a crack shot," Vito retorted, moving the very instant he started talking.

She fired three more shots in the direction of where he had been crouching the very moment before he had responded to her. Vito was prepared for this move and countered by firing at her muzzle flashes. Karen screamed and crashed out of the room. Vito listened to the darkness until he was certain she had indeed fled the area. He took the time to reload his weapon and hoped his eyes would hurry up and adjust to his new surroundings.

As soon as he was no longer blinded from the change in lighting, Vito scooted over to where he judged Karen had been standing. Once the combination of stale cigarette odor, lingering White Diamonds and the smell of gunpowder became stronger he knew he was in the right area. He felt around in the darkness and found her cigarette butt smashed out on the floor, but no blood. He felt the floor, wall and some type of platform table but found nothing.

"In case you were wondering, you missed," an intercom speaker crackled. Vito jumped at the sound, thinking at first Karen had somehow been able to sneak up on him. "You win round one, but now the clock starts ticking."

Vito used the crackling intercom as a cover for his movements. He had gotten his bearings from the sound of the compressor motor and headed back toward the clean room. Once he stumbled across the broken piece of pipe, he knew he was close. Using his hands, he felt along the wall until he found a door. The door was vibrating, and it was slightly warmer than the surrounding air. Vito cautiously opened the door and was glad to see the room inside was fully illuminated. He darted inside and closed the door behind him.

He was standing in a room which housed the air compressor producing the air for the clean room. He was a little unnerved by the fact the compressor's motor drowned out all other sounds, making him vulnerable to attack. The tiny room was sweltering and within the first few minutes, Vito had begun to sweat profusely. The room was much hotter than he imagined it should be. He knew there was no possible way the air compressor's motor was throwing off as much heat as was radiating from that cubicle. And there was an odd smell in the room as well. It was the kind of smell one associates with heat. The musty, baking smell of an old schoolhouse radiator in early fall heating up the cracking paint and yearlong collection of dust for the first time of the season. Vito searched the floor until he found what he was looking for. There was a small hatchway with a ladder leading down.

Vito slowly opened the hatchway and cautiously peered down into the uninviting black hole below. The smell of dank, dusky darkness wafted up from the portal. He shone his little flashlight down into the hole and saw exactly what he expected to see, absolutely nothing. He turned himself around backward and poked at the darkness with the tip of his shoe until his toes connected with a metal ladder rung. Vito swung the next foot onto the ladder and grabbed the trap door for balance. Each descending step down the thin rungs echoed throughout the basement. Thirteen steps later and he found himself standing on the solid concrete floor of the sweltering basement.

Vito poked his hands carefully out in front of him until the tiny flashlight beam reflected back at him. He turned his palm outward and eased it closer to the gleaming metal. It was just as he suspected. A steam line ran through the guts of the building, providing heat, hot water and most likely sterilization. He was certain if he followed the steam pipe it would eventually lead him to where Karen was holding the others, if indeed she was keeping them here. He wrapped his jacket around the thick pipe as best he could in the darkness and grabbed hold of the sleeves. He used his jacket as a makeshift safety tether. As long as he knew where steam line was, he had his bearings. And, if he were to foolishly step into a hole or a pit, he might be able to stop himself before he plummeted to his death.

After following the steam pipe for what seemed like miles, Vito bumped into something, hard, square and steel. He directed the tiny flashlight beam over the surface of the object and concluded it was an electrical power panel. He ran his fingers across the multitude of buttons before choosing one to press. The click was followed by a loud bang, startling Vito even though he had anticipated the noise. But nothing happened. Or at least there were no visible results from his actions. It was then he noticed a small placard on the wall across from him. The placard was a map. An intricate layout of the steam tunnels and a crosscut view of what was above. Each of the sections had a number, letter combination to identify them. There was a big yellow arrow indicating Vito was "here," wherever the hell that was. He took note the quadrant was labeled B7. Vito turned back to the circuit breaker panel and ran his pint-size flashlight beam over the panel once more. This time he noticed the numbers on the face of the large round buttons. He pressed the button labeled B7 and suddenly the basement tunnel was flooded with light.

Vito used this unexpected turn for the better to his advantage. He took several minutes to study the map and commit a planned route of attack to memory. It was virtually a foolproof plan, if everything was exactly as he imagined and everything proceeded according to plan, with Karen's full cooperation of course. Vito chuckled to himself in disgust. He was no further ahead than he had been before stumbling across the map and the light panel. The only thing that had changed was now he could watch himself being shot, maimed or bludgeoned to death.

Vito couldn't believe how helpless and lost he was feeling. He knew he was always the cynic, but he was never one to just want to give up like he wanted to do right at that very moment. He struggled against his own internal negativity and tried to put a positive spin on the situation. He was going to get them all out of this sadistic place alive, or he was not going to be alive to remember his failure. Evy's cherubic face formed a mental image in his head and Vito knew he wasn't about to let her lose the only family she had left.

He sat down on the floor and began to ponder all the details about this case. One thing stuck out in Vito's mind. All the girls had been clean. Clean as a whistle in fact. And not a one of them had a rash or bed sore or any other wound that would hint they had been held captive in bed for months on end. In fact, quite the opposite. They were well cared for. And for them to be very well cared for they had to be near a clean water source. Karen would have had to have had access to enough water to bathe the girls, if not daily, then quite regularly. And the liver he had smelled upstairs, the more he thought about it, the more he convinced himself it must be what she was feeding them. High in protein and iron, just what little girls needed to survive.

Vito began studying the map once more. And although the map gave no indication as to what the layout of the upper level was, it did show a precise mapping of the nervous and circulatory systems of the building. All the wiring and piping was meticulously mapped out. He wasn't much of a tradesman, but even Vito could understand the simplicity of the map. There was a color-coded legend at the bottom of the map outlining the purposes of each separately colored pipe. The silver line was the condensed steam line, the largest of the pipes running through the entire building. The green lined pipes were the potable water, a necessity for Karen's grisly operation. Vito quickly crossed off each area of the map not covered by potable water. The blue lined pipes were compressed air lines. He wasn't sure if Karen was using compressed air for anything other than the clean rooms, so he put that information to the back of his brain.

Next there were a series of gray and black pipes running parallel to each other. These were the wastewater pipes, the black being the sewage. Vito crossed off all rooms containing only the black lines. He wasn't sure if she was using the sewage piping or not, but he was certain she had to have some wastewater flowing out.

Through his process of elimination, Vito was able to narrow the usable rooms upstairs down to a mere half a dozen. There were three smaller rooms, two large rooms and yet another extremely large room. Vito was sure the largest room was the processing plant and listed it as the bottom of his priorities. He felt it would prove much too difficult to sneak into a room of that magnitude with so much open space. On the map there were also three more basement access panels located in each of the four corners of the building. Small tunnels shared by the steam pipe connected each of these maintenance areas. After getting his bearings on which of the rooms above he thought she might be in, Vito tagged the buttons on the electrical panel by making deep gouges with his keys.

Once he had done all of this, Vito set his plan in motion by tripping the switches for the lights upstairs, including the breaker currently bathing the tunnels with light. Plunged into immediate darkness, Vito sat down and listened to the silence. The electrical circuits he cut were to all the power, including the air compressors, so the only sound in the tunnels was the gentle hiss of the steam careening through the pipes.

He could only imagine the frustration and anger Karen was experiencing. Not to mention, the anxiety and fear of his sister and his partner. Vito could hear minute echoes of sounds from somewhere upstairs. But because of the enormity of the place it was impossible for him to pinpoint where the sounds were coming from. His rusty Boy Scout skills told him they were to the east of his location. Vito began inching his way toward the southeastern corner where he hoped to eventually find the maintenance room and the hatch up to the innards of the slaughterhouse.

Vito couldn't be certain how well Karen knew the slaughterhouse or the tunnels, but he had to assume the worst. He listened to the steam pipe as it spit, knocked and hissed. He counted along with the pauses and jets of steam until he had the timing down pat. When the pipe hissed with another jet of steam, Vito slid across the floor, using the sound of the clanking pipes to mask his movements. And when the tunnel fell into silence, he stopped and held his breath. It was like running a marathon in super slow motion.

The further east Vito moved, the more he realized his first assumptions had been correct. There was someone or something moving almost directly overhead. He still wasn't able to decipher exactly what the noises were, but they certainly weren't anything caused accidentally, nor were they the incidental creaks and groans of a tired building.

"God damned, meddling, good for nothing son of a bitch," Karen's voice echoed throughout the tunnel causing Vito to freeze in his tracks.

There was a loud click, followed by a loud popping noise, which was immediately followed by the tunnel being flooded with blinding, fluorescent light. Vito and Karen stared agape at each other, neither one able to say a word. Vito was the first to move.

Quickly he drew his Glock and yelled, "Hold it, Karen, don't move."

"Or what, Vito?" she glowered at him. "Do you actually have the balls it takes to kill someone in cold blood?"

"Karen, don't make me shoot you."

"You sound so tough, but I'll bet you haven't even taken the safety off yet."

"Karen, I'm warning you," he said, ignoring the urge to look down and check the safety. He knew she was right. And she knew she was right.

"But I'm unarmed, Vito. Can you really shoot an unarmed person?" she mocked.

Vito chose not to reply. Instead, he used the time to judge the distance between them. He was still on his knees and was in no position to pursue her if she chose to run. And she on the other hand, was only a breath away from the ladder. He wished he hadn't opted to leave the bulky shotgun outside the damned slaughterhouse door. As useless as birdshot may have seemed, at least he could have used it to slow her down. But as it stood, he had several options and none of them good. He could shoot to kill her, but she was unarmed, or at least as far as he could tell. Or he could go for a leg or shoulder, but if he missed, his bullet would ricochet down into the tunnel until it would most likely end up hitting him knowing his dumb luck.

Karen didn't offer him any more time to contemplate his options. She reached over and popped the switch for the lights and bounded up the ladder in three leaps. Vito had almost fired once in her direction merely out of frustration. Nevertheless, she had moved much too nimbly for him to make any decision before she had disappeared. He could hear her grunting and working overhead and knew instantly what she was doing. He climbed cautiously up the ladder and pressed gently against the trap door. His suspicions were right it wouldn't budge.

Vito realized what a desperate situation he now found himself in. He should have shot her. Or at least shot at her, but he never even took the safety off. He didn't think he would have been able to shoot her even if she had been armed. And now he was trapped like a rat in a cage.

He could hear his name being called over and over again. And even though it was muffled, he knew it was much too loud to have been Karen standing near the portal. He climbed to the top of the ladder, cocked his head and put his ear to the door. He recognized it was an intercom system.

"You blew it Vito. You had your chance and you blew it," her voice rumbled in a low echo. "Since I'm feeling generous I am going to give you a gift, and another shot and ending this whole thing. You have ten minutes to make it to the maintenance entrance at the south end of the building. In eleven minutes poor Freddie Junior is going to be an orphan," her voice trailed off into nothingness.

Vito scrambled over to where the map of the catacombs was adhered to the wall. He studied the map and committed the turns and jogs he would have to make to memory. He considered turning the lights back on but decided against it. If Karen were to shut them off while he was halfway through the tunnels the sudden darkness might disorient him too badly.

Once Vito made it to a cross section of the tunnels, he quickly changed plans and opted to head to the west instead of where Karen was directing him to go. He prayed his decision wouldn't be a mistake costing his sister or his partner their lives, but it was a chance he had to take. He was running out of options and this seemed the best alternative to playing directly into her hands.

After Vito reached the maintenance room, he carefully climbed the ladder and listened at the trap door. As soon as he was satisfied there wasn't another one of Karen's ambushes waiting for him, he lifted the hatch and rolled out onto the main floor. The combination of things having been moving so chaotically and the darkened state of the room he was in had Vito disoriented as to whether or not he had ever been in the room before. In fact, he wasn't even sure of which area of the slaughterhouse he was in.

Vito was eavesdropping on the murkiness of the night when the first explosion of light sent him scurrying for cover. Several small bursts of light followed in succession before Vito realized Karen was turning the lights on in the building from one of the circuit breaker panels. A sudden assault of piercing light temporarily blinded him. When he was finally able to open his eyes again, Vito wanted nothing more than to squeeze them shut again, forever.

Standing in front of him was an assemblage of transparent sarcophagi, some were empty, but most were not. The living, breathing, near skeletal remains of Karen's victims stared back at him through hollow, accusing eyes. The strong, astringent smell of human waste forced Vito to turn his face away. It was obvious Karen's meticulous care of her victims had been lacking as of late.

He moved toward the vertical tombs, his reality melded with the surreal as if he were gliding through a bank of thick, dense fog. From the distance, the bodies in the tombs were just that, faceless entities of mutated shapes and form, no longer human. The neglected, dirty Plexiglas distorted their features. Vito's heart was pounding in his chest so hard it was taking his breath away. He moved from chamber to chamber, popping the latches and peering at the girls inside. Guilt washed over him every time he saw a new face and breathed a sigh of relief when he realized the tomb didn't contain his sister or his partner.

A creeping sense something was wrong invaded Vito's brain. Karen had been organized and methodical during this spree of hers, and that offered him some sense of comfort. She could still be reasoned with. However, the scene he was looking at now was not that of a rational person. She was over the edge, way over. Equipment, most of which he recognized as medical in nature from his being around hospitals and morgues a good portion of his career was strewn from one end of the room to the other. Splatters of blood the size of melons dotted the floor in a gruesome diary of Mia Tran's violent demise. Deep regret seeped into his soul. He knew this was not going to end pleasantly, for anyone.

Time seemed to lose all meaning and the sense of urgency he had been filled with earlier had graciously waned. He had now opened seven of the twelve chambers and had yet to find Lizbeth or Gregg. With five chambers remaining and two of those Vito could tell were empty, the odds were not looking in his favor.

"Are you looking for something?" Karen's voice rang out from behind him.

Vito started to turn around.

"Don't move," she warned, adding emphasis by racking a shell into the shotgun chamber. The dreaded sound reminded Vito once again what a stupid mistake it had been leaving the Remington outside. He carefully judged the distance and breathed a shallow sigh of relief. She was too far away from him for the birdshot to do any major damage, however, it was going to sting like a bitch and ruin a perfectly good shirt.

"Where's my sister?"

"Safe, for now. You couldn't have possibly thought it was going to be this easy," she mocked.

Vito tried to move for his shoulder holster without tipping her off. He moved so painfully slow his muscles twitched and screamed.

"I said, don't move."

At Karen's voice he quickly reached for his gun. Images of Wyatt Earp and the gunfight at the OK Corral flashed through his brain as he tried to beat his nemesis to the draw. Vito never had a chance. He could only hope she was too far away from him for the birdshot to do too much damage. The shotgun roared and Vito went down, hard. For a long time, he was dazed, so dazed he wasn't even sure what in the hell had happened. The pool of blood on the floor around him led him to believe he was bleeding profusely from several different places at once.

"It's a good thing I keep some buckshot lying around, isn't it?" she said, racking another shell into the chamber. "Don't worry, this one's your bird shot, it'll only sting a little," she pressed the barrel of the shotgun hard against his crotch and let out a wicked laugh.

Vito winced in pain and anticipation.

"On second thought," Karen said, slowly swinging the barrel away from Vito's groin. "Since you were too stupid to figure this one out on your own, I guess I owe you an explanation before I let you watch your sister die."

Vito closed his eyes and tried to focus on his multitude of pains. He needed to know just how badly he was hurt and in how many places. His chin was tilted down and he never saw the butt of the shotgun on a collision course with his skull.

Vito came to and found he had been duct taped to an office chair. The chair had a low back and every time Vito shifted his weight it threatened to topple over.

"Glad to see you're back amongst the living," Karen said. She stomped her foot on the seat of the chair right in the triangle of his crotch and kicked Vito across the room.

He careened out of control, spinning until he crashed into a small table and caromed to the floor. Karen took several long strides over to where he was lying helplessly on the concrete floor. She jerked him and the chair back upright and spun him around to face two gurneys propped into the seated position. His sister Lizbeth was strapped to one of the gurneys, his partner on the other. Neither one of them exhibited any signs of being conscious. Both were bleeding from the tender place in the crook of their arms where IV needles had been yanked out. Both their heads rolled listlessly to one side and thin streams of drool trickled down onto the sheets. They both looked dead. Like victims in a campy vampire flick, just waiting until the waxen moonlight would reanimate them into the world of the undead.

"You look like you've seen a ghost. Two in fact," Karen said, wheeling him ever closer to Lizbeth and Gregg. "But I can assure you, they are both quite alive, for now."

"Why are you doing this?" his voice struggled to be heard.

"Are we back to that? I was going to tell you everything, seeing how you were too stupid to figure it out on your own. But on second thought, I think it will torture you even more to know you are going to go to your grave never knowing the answers."

"What in the fuck is wrong with you, Karen?"

"I loved you Vito. So God damned much."

Vito sensed a deep sorrow in her voice. "And I loved you too, Karen."

"Not enough, Vito. Not enough."

Karen left the room briefly and returned dragging a huge piece of equipment with her. At first, Vito wasn't sure what it was, but then, after further scrutiny he realized it was the surgical laser unit she had been using to scrawl her grisly messages on her victims.

"What are you going to do with that?"

"Do you know what it is?"

"Why don't you enlighten me," he said, hoping to keep her talking long enough for him to be able to formulate a plan.

"Did you know this piece of equipment is so precise and sensitive I can use it to cauterize a paper cut? Or it could be used to sever something as well. Something like a carotid artery," she swung the laser over the neck of Vito's unconscious sister. Wisps of grayish smoke rose from her flesh and instantly the caustic stench attacked Vito's nostrils.

"Why Karen? Why?" he cried out, only being able to see Karen's back.

"I never liked the bitch much, that's why. And she insisted on meddling in my affairs," she laughed. She spun around to face Vito and said, "Don't worry, I'm only marking where I want to make my final cut. I want her to be awake when I do this for real."

Vito breathed a short-lived sigh of relief once he realized Lizbeth hadn't been harmed too severely.

"You're never going to get away with this Karen."

"You know, I never thought about that angle. Hmm, I guess that means I don't really care one way or the other. I've always fancied the idea of going out in a blaze of glory."

Vito had run out of things to say. How many times could you tell a person they were crazy before they would either get pissed or start to believe you?

"I think I've figured it out, Karen," Vito said, his words barely audible. He knew he must have been losing a lot of blood. He was weak and no longer in pain.

"I'm listening," she said, never turning away from her task of preparing Lizbeth and Gregg for whatever fate she had in store for them.

Vito wasn't sure where he was going with this, or if it would even phase her in the least, but he knew he had to try something, and fast. "Raymond was sharing his little girls with your husband George, wasn't he?"

She didn't say a word.

"But what I don't understand is, if you loved me like you said you did, then why would it bother you if your husband was boinking some fresh, young things."

Still, Karen seemed unfazed.

"Maybe I've got it all wrong. Maybe it was Raymond who pissed you off the most. Maybe you wanted Raymond. Is that it? Were you in love with Kyser?"

Vito nearly messed himself as Karen spun around, grabbed the shotgun and fired a round just above his head. His face burned from where the hot powder and a few stray pellets had peppered him. His cheek stung where the plastic wadding had struck the tender flesh. If nothing else, at least he knew he had grated on a raw nerve. Although he rethought his plan of attack several times, he kept coming back to the fact he had to piss her off. He felt he had nothing to lose. He was certain she planned on killing them all regardless of what he did or said. He needed to knock her off balance somehow. Maybe then he could get lucky and find a way of getting the upper hand in a hopeless situation.

"Did George come home and tell you all about the fun Raymond was having with these girls? Could you smell them on him?"

"Shut up! You are wrong! So wrong. I never wanted Raymond Kyser, never in a million years."

"That's not the way it looks to me. And that's not the way it's going to look to the media either. Blaze of glory my ass, you're going to be portrayed as nothing more than a scorned lover who flew into a fit of jealous rage," his tone was mocking and sarcastic.

"You son of a bitch," she screamed. Like lightning she crossed the room and slammed the butt of the shotgun into his mouth.

Vito's head recoiled and blood erupted from his mangled lips. He was dazed, but struggled to keep his focus. He turned his head just in time to save his front teeth.

"Just some bitch who was pissed off because she wasn't the only one getting dick," his tone had turned hateful.

She grunted something completely incoherent and began storming around the room flinging trays and pans and whatever else she could get her hands on. She spun to face him once more, her eyes wild with unbridled fury.

"Maybe he wasn't even giving you any. Is that what it was? He would fuck all of them, but when it came to you, you weren't even good enough to polish his knob," Vito spat a chunk of bloody phlegm to the floor.

"You God damned worthless piece of shit. How dare you! You take that back," she jammed the shotgun barrel under Lizbeth's chin so hard she split her skin.

Vito watched blood trickle down his sister's chin while contemplating his next move. He had Karen just where he wanted her, pissed off and irrational. But he had to be careful not to make her too irrational or then things would spiral out of his control. As if they hadn't done that already.

"Weren't you good enough for him?" Vito almost choked on his own fear. His mind was entertaining him with visions of his sister's scattered face, and he prayed he wasn't pushing Karen too far.

"You," the word came out with such hatred and vehemence that Vito felt his bladder threaten to loosen. She trained the shotgun at him and jabbed the air with each word she spoke. "You don't even have a fucking clue," thick, white foam beaded up in the corners of her mouth like a rabid dog as she spoke.

Vito saw something move behind Karen's right shoulder but wasn't sure if it was his fear creating something out of nothing. She must have seen his expression change because she gripped the shotgun tightly and readied herself to spin on the intruder.

"Don't Karen, just put the gun down, honey," a soothing voice called out of the darkness.

Vito had heard the voice before, but it was only once or twice, so he couldn't place a face with it.

"Fuck you!"

"Karen, I mean it. You know I won't miss from this distance."

"You don't have the balls. You've never had any balls, at least none Raymond Kyser didn't have the squeeze on," she twitched as she calculated her odds.

"I mean it, honey, I don't want to shoot you. This has gone way too far. I can't let you kill anyone else," the man's voice was choked with tears.

"It went way too far when you killed my little girl, daddy," she spat. Her voice was thick with loathing.

"I didn't kill her, Karen. She killed herself."

"No!" she screamed, still staring into Vito's eyes. He could see her eyes pulsating with anger and knew she was a volcano ready to erupt. "You and that fucking Raymond Kyser killed my baby. Our baby," she looked deeply into Vito's eyes. He saw the tears streaming down her face and it dawned on him what this was all about.

"Honey, I didn't know Raymond was going to do that to her. It was just supposed to be photo shoot, that's all."

"Was that what he told you about me too?"

"No, he never told me about you," his voice was weak and rueful.

"Vito, I'm sorry, I never wanted to kill anyone. You've got to believe me. Say you believe me," she was near sobbing now.

"I believe you, Karen. Now, please, put the gun down. We can sort this all out later. You need help."

"From you! The same kind of help you gave your daughter?" Her face twisted up into an angry swirl once more.

"But how on earth was I supposed to know? I didn't even know we had a daughter, let alone know she was in trouble," Vito argued defensively.

"I wrote you letters, but that bitch didn't let you see them," she glanced over at Lizbeth who was now awake and wide eyed with fear. "She has to pay," Karen said, her voice barely even a whisper.

"Karen, you listen to your father and put down that gun," Blake Stoddard's voice echoed throughout the slaughterhouse.

Karen looked at Vito and he knew this was the end. "Fuck you, daddy," she spun on her heels. The first bullet struck her high in the chest, forcing her backward into Lizbeth's gurney. The second bullet ripped through the soft fleshy spot at the front of her throat. She never even got off a shot. Karen slid off the gurney and onto the floor with nothing more than a gurgled death rattle.

Vito stared at her lifeless body for several minutes before looking up into the haggard face of her father.

"I never meant any of it. I never meant to hurt her."

"How could you give your own granddaughter to that bastard?"

"He promised me," Blake whimpered.

"And what about Karen? What did you do to her?" Vito spat angrily.

"I didn't know it was her. He tricked me. He didn't trust me, I was a cop, so he needed something to hold over me."

"You're as fucking sick as he was."

"I know," he said in a whisper. Blake Stoddard then shoved the barrel of his revolver into his mouth and pulled the trigger.

The last thing Vito remembered was hearing Lucy Davenport's cackling voice resounding throughout the slaughterhouse.

Epilogue

Gregg, Lucy, Amanda, Lizbeth and Vito sipped at their drinks and tried to ignore the ambiance of Gus's. Evy and Freddie Junior were down the street at Vincenzo's Pizza getting a slice while Gregg was secretly hoping that was all the hormone riddled teenager was trying to get. Vito had only been out of the hospital for a few hours and wasn't quite ready for reality yet. And even though Gus's was too loud for conversation, it felt safe, and it was home.

"We found some hard drives in a safety deposit box rented by Blake Stoddard. These files were a detailed electronic journal of Stoddard's relationship with Kyser. According to Blake Stoddard, he and Kyser had first met when Blake was still a rookie patrol officer. He busted Kyser for solicitation of a minor but then decided to give the man a slap on the wrist. The prostitute in question was a twelve-year-old boy. Kyser would have been ruined had that information been released to the public. Stoddard made the collar disappear. Some time later Kyser sent an "anonymous letter" to Stoddard about some inside information on a real estate deal. Kyser had tried to approach him several times before that, but Stoddard had always refused to get into bed with him so to speak. But this time it was different. Karen's mother had fallen gravely ill and the medical bills were piling up against Blake. To make a long story short, Stoddard foolishly took the bait.

Karen's mother died the year after that and Blake took it very hard. He started drinking heavily and Kyser nudged him along the trail of recreational drug use. One thing led to another. The deeper into Kyser's world Stoddard was drawn, the more of it Kyser revealed to him until finally he was participating in

Kyser's underage orgies. At some point or another, Blake sobered up, got his shit together and decided he had finally had enough of Kyser's sick, twisted world. He went to Kyser and threatened to expose him if he didn't quit his obscene partying. Kyser threatened to expose Stoddard's jaded past as well, but Blake didn't care at this point. He had finally eaten enough guilt he was choking on it," Gregg explained.

"I still don't understand how Karen became involved in all of this?" Lizbeth said.

Gregg looked to Vito as if to ask whether or not he should continue.

"She's a big girl," Vito said, wanting to hear the rest of it, even though he was sure he had figured out the gory details for himself.

"Well, according to Stoddard, he went to Kyser's to confront him again. On this particular night, Raymond Kyser was doing one of his infamous calendar shoots. Stoddard can't recall any details of that night, but he did see the pictures. He felt Kyser had somehow drugged him into a euphoric state and got him to join in the orgy. At some point they had kidnapped Karen and brought her to Kyser's warehouse. Blake Stoddard ended up raping his own daughter while Kyser's photographers captured it all for posterity. This put Blake Stoddard so deeply into Kyser's pocket he was never getting out. It wasn't so much the threat of Kyser exposing Blake to the world. It was the threat of his showing the photographs to his only daughter Blake couldn't live with."

"I can't believe he was able to talk Stoddard into letting him have his granddaughter though," Amanda said.

"At this point, he was as far down as a human being can go, I would suspect," Davenport said.

"One thing I don't understand though. Karen said she wrote me letters, and accused you of throwing them away," Vito said to Lizbeth.

"I wouldn't have done that, regardless of how I felt about her."

"I didn't think you would. But who then?"

"Freddie did. He also suspected she was responsible for Gloria's car accident. He couldn't prove it, but he never gave up investigating it. He was about to share his feelings with you once he felt he knew exactly what was going on. I know that's why she killed him. I couldn't tell you what I thought or what I knew, Vito, I couldn't take the chance of losing you too," Lizbeth said with tears of remembrance welling up in her eyes.

Vito stared back at his sister with tears in his eyes, all words escaping him.

"And by the time she started kidnapping the girls, she was too far gone to ever come back. Poor little girl. I hope God can forgive her," Lucy said, wiping a tiny tear away from her own eye.

Evy and Freddie bounded through the smoky bar and plopped down at the table with the adults, putting an end to their sullen conversation. Vito looked at Evy and found it hard to fight back his tears. Even though this chapter of his life was over, another one was just beginning. It would be an investigation that would take all his detective skills. He needed to find out the person his daughter Ashleigh had been, before this nightmare world had so cruelly sunken its deadly talons into her.

www.ingramcontent.com/pod-product-compliance
Lightning Source LLC
Chambersburg PA
CBHW070538260626
47161CB00002B/444